This is a work of fiction. The people, events, locales, and circumstances depicted are fictitious or used fictitiously and are the product of the author's imagination. Any resemblance to any actual events, locales, organizations, or persons, whether living or dead, is entirely coincidental.

Cover Art: Roberto Bovo, Red Frog – Italy

The dragon tasted the corpses of her hatchlings.

The bodies were cool, their internal fires stilled. She moved them aside, finding the carcass of a man beneath them. He lay face-down, arms spread wide. She rolled him over; his face had been smashed in, rendered concave and unrecognizable.

She peered at the man for some time, considering. The damage had been done with a weapon. He must have come with companions, and they had crushed his head to keep her from taking it, showing it to other men, tracking him by his appearance.

"Cursed man," she hissed. She examined the body, turning it this way and that, but he bore nothing that spoke of origin or maker. He looked no different from any other thug who had come into her lair in search of booty; only the torn and broken remains of her young marked him as more remarkable than most.

"I could swallow you whole," she told the dead man, "but you are vermin and unworthy of such an honor." She tossed him into the bone pit, hearing him clatter to the bottom and come to rest in the darkness below.

Dragon Stones

a novel

by James Viscosi

1

T'SIAN SMELLED BLOOD AS SOON as she landed, there on the barren spine of the mountain, where the orange-grey rock crumbled under the ceaseless onslaught of rain and snow.

Pressing herself flat against the stone, the dragon crept along until she came to the black mouth of her lair, concealed by the jumble of boulders she had heaped around it. She flicked her tongue into the opening, tasting the stale air that wafted from the depths of the cavern. The meaty aroma of decay: Nothing unusual about that. The little ones were always hungry, and since they had grown large enough to hunt, they had made a practice of dragging small beasts back to the cave, where they could feed in safety. Something else, though, some alien odor, had woven itself into the customary smells of fire and flesh.

Men had been here.

T'Sian pulled her wings close, molding them to her body, and entered the chimney, crawling down the near-vertical shaft, narrow and well-worn from the scouring of her metal-hard scales, her talons finding their familiar holds in the stone. At the bottom, the tunnel curved sharply, becoming horizontal. Her long body, malleable and supple as a snake, bent with it; she emerged into her lair, slipping through a crack in the wall.

She immediately turned and climbed up to the ceiling, her long, curving claws finding easy purchase in the craggy rock. She scanned the mammoth chamber that formed the main portion of her lair, a natural cavity that she had spent decades excavating, shaping, transforming it from cavern to home.

The darkness held no secrets from her, but where she should have seen the warmth of her hatchlings, she saw nothing. Perhaps they were not here; but that was a false hope, and the dragon knew it. T'Sian tasted the air again.

Men. Their scents were not fresh; they had been and gone some hours earlier, while she had been sunning herself on the rocks to the west. Lured by rumors of dragon hoard, most likely; in their arrogance, men insisted on believing that she had some use for the gilt trappings of their petty civilizations.

She spotted something, a flicker of warmth from the back of the lair, faint as a long-extinguished fire. She let go of the ceiling, twisted in midair to land feet-first on the stone floor. T'Sian moved cautiously toward the heat source, her black tongue flicking in and out, bringing her the strengthening scent of blood. She found the little ones in the back, near the pit where they tossed the bones they did not care to eat.

They had been hacked to pieces.

The dragon tasted the corpses of her hatchlings, tasting men as well. The bodies were cool, their internal fires stilled. They were not the source of the warmth she had seen. She moved them aside, finding the carcass of a man beneath them. He lay face-down, arms spread wide. She rolled him over; his guts spilled out, stringy, stuck to the floor. His face had been smashed in, rendered concave and unrecognizable.

She peered at the man for some time, considering. The disembowelment was the work of dragon claws, but the damage to his head had been done with a weapon. He must have come with companions, and they had crushed his head to keep her from taking it, showing it to other men, tracking him by his appearance.

"Cursed man," she hissed. She reached out with her long and clever tail, extending it forward over her head, snaking it around the man's waist, lifting him up. He was clad in some sort of armor, leather with pieces of metal affixed to it, a feeble imitation of her own scales. She examined the body, turning it this way and that, hoping to identify where he had come from, but he bore nothing that spoke of origin or maker. He looked no different from any other thug who had come into her lair in search of booty; only the torn and broken remains of her young marked him as more remarkable than most.

"I could swallow you whole," she told the dead man, *"but you are vermin and unworthy of such an honor."* She tossed him into the bone pit, hearing him clatter to the bottom and come to rest in the darkness below.

The dragon backed away from the corpses, feeling the heat in her breast where the crystals danced. She raised her head and let the flames fly, illuminating the lair with dancing light. Nictitating membranes slid across her eyes as the flames poured out, preventing the close, intense heat from blinding her temperature-sensitive vision. The stone ceiling, already cracked and soot-stained, took the punishment mutely; fire rippled along its surface, flowed around the stumps of sheared stalactites. She cried out, a hissing wail to accompany the silent inferno, echoing up the chimney and out across the rocky slopes and thinly forested valleys of the mountain range.

At last she closed her throat, choked off the fire. She would put her scalding breath to better use, once she found the men who had invaded her lair. She crept along the floor, up the wall, to the alcove where she stored her crystals. She thrust her head and neck into the niche, and knew at once that what she sought was gone. She should have seen and felt the radiance of the stones, but there was nothing, only the faintest of traces, lingering in the rough rock walls. Her tongue flicked across the dry, empty pocket of stone.

The dust tasted like men.

She drew her head back, shocked. The humans had taken her stones. Why? Had they, in their ignorance, thought the crystals some sort of precious gem?

That was certainly possible; but men were superstitious, unpredictable. She knew how they thought: Always believing that some secret ingredient, some missing element, would cure whatever ailments bedeviled them. Perhaps some alchemist had decided he needed the crystals for a potion to turn lead into gold, or some noblewoman believed that they would keep her youthful. Over the years, she had heard both those excuses, and more, from men she had caught searching for her lair.

T'Sian returned to the bodies of the hatchlings. She hated to do this, but she had wasted a considerable amount of fire venting her rage, and the stones were of no use inside her dead young. Delicately, she lifted one of the carcasses, only to find that the small dragon's chest had been cut open, the leathery sac slashed, the crystals taken. She dropped the corpse and examined the other. It, too, had been plundered of its stones. What she had taken for mere brutality had instead been surgical: The men had slit open her babies and taken the stones from their gizzards.

Now she understood. Men had come here specifically to steal her crystals. There had been no mistake. They had not thought they were taking diamonds or rubies; they had no interest in dragon's horns or scales or whiskers. They had wanted the stones and knew, somehow, where in the body they could be found. These were no mere adventuresome bumpkins; these were knowledgeable, dangerous, murderous villains.

The dragon pivoted, turning back on herself. She crawled to the crack in the wall, climbed up the chimney, emerging onto the windswept summit where the rocks were as cold as the wind. She crept away from the opening to her lair, sweeping her head back and forth, flicking her tongue along the ground. She quickly picked up the scent of the men, following their trail along the ridge until it disappeared in a riot of strange, birdlike odors. Perhaps they had carried chicken carcasses, dragging them around to confuse their scent.

She raised herself up, tasted the air: Rain and pines and distant snow. No trace of the murderers lingered; no trail led off the mountain, showing her where they had climbed. It was as though they had simply vanished from that spot.

The dragon lowered herself again, hugging the rocky spine, considering her next move. She needed more of the red crystals; she could tell, by the chill in her belly, that they would soon be exhausted, leaving the blue ones inert as the rocks that lay scattered on the mountaintop. Obtaining red crystals meant a long flight to the distant volcanoes of Enshenneah, giving the killers ample time to flee; but these were unusually devious villains, and she could not face them without her fire.

The dragon's idly twitching tail dislodged a small boulder, sending it bouncing and clattering off the cliff and into the cold, barren valley below. She glanced at the rolling rock as it vanished into the chill mist; then, her course of action determined, she tore down a few scraggly nearby trees and jammed them into the chimney. That would keep trespassers out until she returned.

Satisfied, T'Sian spread her enormous wings and leaped off the cliff. The vast membranes filled with air; lazy flaps carried her away from the mountaintop. She circled it three times, scanning the crags and crannies for any sign of the murderers.

Nothing. How could men just disappear?

Frustrated, she veered away, flying off to the southwest, toward the distant volcanic islands.

Tolaria had been waiting outside Klem's office for hours, responding to an urgent summons, only to find herself perched on a narrow, uncomfortable bench, staring at the senior oracle's closed door. With nothing else to occupy her, she had begun going over all the other slights she had endured over the three months she had been here.

Three months! She remembered her excitement at being assigned to the Crosswaters, the largest oracular institution outside the college at Flaurent. Situated with Barbareth to the south, Dunshandrin to the east, and Madroval to the north, overlooking the frothing union of the Knopp, Achen, and Red rivers, the Crosswaters saw petitioners from throughout the continent. Even Enshennean traders stopped by from time to time, and merchants brought her news from her homeland, icy Yttribia, beyond the grey waters of Lake Achenar.

Unfortunately, she was not permitted to show off her skills as an oracle to any of these visitors, because—

The door to Klem's office opened, and her sour-faced superior poked his head out into the barren waiting room. If a raisin had been given ears, nose, and mouth and trained to speak, she thought, it would likely look and sound like Klem.

"Tolaria. So sorry to keep you waiting. Please come in."

She entered the man's office, finding nowhere to sit. Klem did not trouble himself with such foolishness as chairs for visitors. The room smelled of food; he had probably kept her waiting so that he could dawdle over his breakfast.

The senior oracle settled into the chair behind his desk and regarded her with small, sunken eyes, his raisin face inscrutable. Was he waiting for her to say something? Had she transgressed again in some way? She would not speak first, she decided. He had summoned her; let him begin the conversation.

She had not been in this room since the day of her arrival, when she had handed him her letter of introduction from the headmistress at Flaurent. Tolaria had not been permitted to read the missive, but she had been given to understand that it named her the most gifted oracle that the headmistress had seen in a generation. Klem had perused the letter, given Tolaria an unfriendly look, and promptly assigned her to dispute mediation.

Finally she could no longer bear the silence, and said: "Sir, may I ask what this is—"

"I've received a request from Lord Dunshandrin," he said.

"Oh?"

"He has requested the immediate dispatch of our best and most accurate oracle. Naturally I thought of you."

"Me, sir?"

"Of course." He pulled a parchment from his desk, unrolled it, looked it over; she recognized it as the letter she had brought from Flaurent. Had he kept it all this time? When she had left his office, fighting back tears, he had been holding the paper near a candle and she assumed he had burned it. "Headmistress Damona sings your praises quite loudly in this document."

"She does?"

"*Tolaria's visions are of a clarity and quality quite extraordinary for one of her youth and inexperience,*" he read, his voice a mocking singsong. "*She exhibits a discipline that would be remarkable in one twice her age.*" Klem fixed his gaze on her face. "*Tolaria has the makings of a superb head oracle.*"

As Klem rolled up the parchment and put it away, Tolaria felt herself growing flush. Little wonder he had treated her with such hostility; he hadn't even found a room for her in the main temple, instead housing her in a ramshackle cottage, once the dwelling of a groundskeeper, on the periphery of the grounds. The banishment hadn't sat well with her at first, but at least it allowed her some privacy, as well as giving her a small plot to tend; she could grow the aromatic herbs she needed for her unused trances, medicinal plants to practice her healing skills, flowers to brighten up her surroundings. The small hut had fallen into disrepair since the groundskeeper's death by drowning, and Tolaria was expected to fix it up; but this proved an unexpected benefit, as working with her hands helped relax her after days of tense mediation.

Now she would lose even the comfort of her routine. The Headmistress's enthusiasm had not done her any favors here, under Klem's petty tyranny.

He shut the drawer with a bang, startling her from her reverie. "You will attend to me while you are in my office," he said severely, the raisin angered.

"My apologies. Sir."

"You are dismissed. Gather your things quickly; a wagon waits for you at the front gate."

"May I ask why Lord Dunshandrin requires an oracle dispatched, rather than coming here to see us, as is custom?"

"When you meet him, perhaps he will tell you."

"Very well." Seething, she turned, started for the door.

"Oh, another thing," Klem said.

She stopped, waited.

"Your servant. She will be needed here in your absence; I am afraid she cannot accompany you."

She pivoted, facing the other oracle again. "So I am to be sent to Dunshandrin alone."

"Of course not. Lord Dunshandrin's emissary will travel with you." He smiled, showing her his teeth; then he looked away and began shuffling papers on his desk. "Enjoy your journey."

"Thank you," she said. "I'm sure I will."

Pyodor Ponn didn't think his newest guests had come to Enshenneah on a holiday.

They had arrived two days earlier, landing in his wife's garden, riding eagles as big as horses, trampling her vegetables with their enormous yellow claws. Ponn had never seen such creatures before, and had no idea how to care for them. Fortunately, the men didn't expect him to; in fact, after moving moved the birds into the stable, they had given explicit instructions that the stalls were not to be approached.

Two days after the eagle-riding strangers had arrived, Ponn's wife came into the kitchen as he was washing the wooden breakfast bowls and said: "Pord tells me the birds are gone."

"Are they?"

"Yes. I checked."

This suited Ponn; he didn't like the sharp looks the creatures had given his smaller children. It reminded him of hawks eyeing prey. "And have their riders gone as well?"

"No."

"Do they know that their mounts left without them?"

"Yes," she said. "I asked them about it, and they just smiled." Then, after a moment: "Who are they, Ponn?"

"I don't know, Plenn," he said. He handed her a bowl, which she dried and placed on the rack. "It's better not to inquire."

"They're asking about the islands."

"They are?"

"Yes." She folded her arms. "They aren't merchants; they have nothing to sell. They aren't traders; they have nothing to barter. What are they doing here?"

"Perhaps they came to buy," he said. "They brought an extra bird, it could be a pack animal. Why are you so curious?"

"I don't like them."

"It is not necessary to like our guests; it suffices to serve them, and keep our judgments to ourselves."

He handed Plenn another bowl; she held it up, studying the interior, as if trying to read the future in the grain of the wood. "I think they are up to unsavory business."

"So are half our other patrons," Ponn said.

She put the bowl in the rack. "They asked about a boat."

He turned to face her. "A boat?"

"Yes."

"They want to *go* to the islands?"

"Yes."

"Don't they know about the dragons?"

"I told them, but they insisted."

Ponn studied his wife's face. "Perhaps you misunderstood which islands interest them?"

"No, Ponn. They want the islands with the volcanoes. They were very specific. Go out and ask them, if you doubt me."

"I don't doubt you," Ponn said, "but perhaps they don't properly comprehend the danger. I'll go and speak to them."

"Yes," Plenn said, taking his place at the wash basin. "Do that. And find out when they will be leaving. There is some trade that we are better off without."

He nodded, then went into the common room. Three of the strangers sat together at a table on the other side of the round dining area. One of their number was missing; perhaps he had gone with the eagles, or was up to some other sort of mischief.

The leader of the group had been eyeing the door to the kitchen; he waved his hand as Ponn entered, summoning him to their table. These guests had made no formal introductions, but Ponn had heard the others refer to their leader as *Gelt* in his absence; when he was present they called him *sir*.

When he reached their table, Gelt said: "Innkeeper, your wife is uncooperative."

"I'm sorry you feel that way," Ponn said. "Allow me to make amends. She said you gentlemen were interested in a boat?"

"Yes, that's right."

"If you would tell me your purpose, perhaps I can recommend a vessel and captain who will meet your need."

"Our need is for a swift and sturdy boat, with a shallow draft, that can carry a goodly cargo."

"What sort of cargo?"

"Furthermore, we need a guide," Gelt said. "Someone who knows the coastal waters and can chart a course through the shoals." The man cocked his head, looking at Ponn like a chameleon observing an insect that had nearly wandered within range of its tongue. "You're an islander, aren't you, innkeeper?"

"I am," Ponn said, liking neither the man's tone nor the direction of the conversation. "But I do not offer my services as a guide, and I do not charter boats."

"You've got one, though, don't you?" Gelt said. "You make a good living running wood and spices from this accursed jungle up to Barbareth, cheating your lords out of their rightful tariffs. Don't you, innkeeper?"

How could these men know that? As he glanced around, wondering if anyone had heard Gelt's statement, Ponn's well-practiced smile felt like a frozen rictus on his face. "I'm afraid you are mistaken," he said. "I'm a simple innkeeper, and my money comes from the steady patronage of good travelers such as yourselves. As I said, I am neither a seaman nor a renter of vessels, so I must suggest you look elsewhere."

"You must?" Gelt said. "Pity."

"I'm sorry I couldn't be of more service. Now, if you'll excuse me, I have work to do." Ponn gave the men a shaky bow, turned, and started back toward the kitchen; but then Gelt rapped his wooden cup several times on the table, the sounds sharp and hollow. Ponn stopped short; the inn fell silent, all the patrons turning to look at the table in the corner.

Gelt said: "Have you seen your youngest lately, innkeeper?"

Ponn steadied himself with one hand on the shoulder of a nearby guest, a regular patron; he did not turn around. "I saw her this morning," he said.

Gelt said: "We saw her this morning as well."

Ponn whirled, was back at their table in a single step. "If you have harmed her, I will—"

"You will give us the use of your boat," Gelt said. "You will go with us to the volcanic islands as our guide. And when we have safely returned and our mounts are ready to leave, you will have your small, pretty daughter back unharmed. If you refuse to serve us, if you work to thwart us, or if you set your friends against us, you will *not* have her back. Am I clear?"

"Don't be a fool," Ponn said. "You cannot go to the islands. The dragons will not tolerate—"

The man raised his hand, palm out, forestalling Ponn's protestations. "Am I *clear*, innkeeper?"

They stared at each other.

"Yes," Ponn said. "You are clear."

"Good. Make your preparations quickly." Gelt drained his cup, put it back on the table with a bang. "We will leave at first light, two days hence."

Adaran clung to the great bird's neck, buried his face in its feathers, and tried to pretend that he was on the ground. The rushing wind and ceaseless beat of its wings continually reminded him that he wasn't; in fact, he and the others were thousands of feet in the air, their lives depending on the ability of these enormous, stupid avians to get them well away from the mountain before the dragon returned.

His mount flew near the end of a train of seven overgrown eagles, all of them yoked together with drooping leather thongs, keeping them in rough formation behind the leader. That bird carried their guide, one of Lord Dunshandrin's men, a grimy, reckless maniac who, Adaran believed, deliberately performed erratic aerial maneuvers to make the rest of them sick.

The bird's feathers were beginning to smell like his own stale sweat. He risked a glance behind him, at the last eagle in the line. It carried the crystals they had taken from the dragon's lair. He didn't know what Dunshandrin wanted them for; people who sat upon thrones rarely shared much information with those they retained to do their dirty work, and hirelings who asked too many questions tended to have bad accidents. He *did* know that Dunshandrin had dispatched another group on a similar mission to Enshenneah, and another to the icy wastes of northern Yttribia; he and Redshen had tried to finagle an assignment to that expedition, thinking to visit their homeland of Madroval along the way, but Dunshandrin had insisted that their skills were needed here.

Looking back didn't seem to make him need to vomit, so he ventured a look downward and discovered that they were nearer to the ground than he'd expected; in fact, they seemed to be descending toward a mountainside meadow, where a few small campfires burned among a knot of tents. Relieved, he relaxed his grip, only to be thrown when the eagle made a rough landing. He tumbled to the ground at its feet and was trampled by the avian bringing up the rear; fortunately it was still flapping its wings and he didn't receive its full weight, although its talons gave him a painful jab in the side.

As he picked himself out of the dirt, one of Dunshandrin's men approached and helped him to his feet. "Are you all right?" the man said, not trying to conceal his amusement.

"I'm fine," Adaran said.

"Are you sure? You look a bit … downtrodden."

Adaran eyed the birds. They fluttered and preened a short distance away as the other riders dismounted in a more or less orderly fashion. "That is no way for a man to travel. Give me a fine horse, and leave the skies to the dragons."

The soldier, evidently disappointed with this response, shrugged and drifted back toward the camp. Adaran noticed that he had lost a dagger in his tumble; it lay on the ground at his feet. He picked it up, hefted it, and aimed it at the soldier's back, then spun it around and sheathed it in his belt.

He turned away, looking to the north, toward the dragon's lair. He could not see her mountain, of course; it was lost in mist and distance, hidden behind other summits. The ridge on which they had landed did not rise above the snow line, but the surrounding peaks did, the dark pines and barren rocks like flies on sugar. The wind from the south felt stiff and chill, and smelled of winter.

Redshen ran up to meet him, flushed and exhilarated, as if she were ready to cut her mount free and fly off into the night with it. "Wasn't that marvelous?" she cried. "I may buy one of those creatures from Lord Dunshandrin! I saw you fall, are you all right?"

"Yes." Then, with a wink: "Just a bit downtrodden." She laughed, the sound like glass bells. Adaran gave silent thanks to the clever soldier who had mocked him. "You enjoyed the flying, then?"

"Oh, yes! Didn't you?"

"I hated every moment of it."

"Well, when I obtain one of those creatures, you can stay on the ground and watch me do tricks in the air," Redshen said. She glanced past him, looking up the slope. "Here comes Dosen."

The two of them rejoined the others as the nominal leader of their expedition—a pudgy, blustery steward from Dunshandrin's castle—approached, his short legs pumping rapidly, his breath forming white clouds around his head. He stopped in front of the pilot. "You were successful?" he said.

"We have the stones."

Dosen's small, red-rimmed eyes scanned the horizon in the direction from which they had approached. "You were not detected?"

"If we had been, would we be here now?" The pilot clapped Dosen on the shoulder. "Don't worry, there will be no dragon coming out of the clouds. It wouldn't eat you, anyway. You're nothing but fat and gristle."

Redshen pinched Adaran's arm and whispered, "Gristle."

"Dragons will eat anything," Jenune said. A warrior from Barbareth, he hadn't impressed Adaran at first; the man wore little armor and used a metal-shod wooden pole as a weapon. Then Adaran had watched him defeat a dozen guards during a practice session at Dunshandrin's castle, and had revised his opinion upward. "Filthy, voracious beasts."

"There's no need to worry." The magician, Orioke, spoke softly, but his voice carried the weight of utter confidence. "The dragon is well south of here, and traveling away from our location. She is unaware of our presence."

"You are sure?"

Orioke fixed his glittering gaze on Dosen. "Of course," he said. "I have no more desire to be eaten or incinerated than you do. I spoke Words throughout our flight to conceal us from her senses, as well as to track her movements. She went southeast. We went west." His eyes narrowed. "I wonder, though, why we stopped here. This is closer to her lair than I would like."

"Yes, yes," Dosen said, running stubby ringed fingers through his thinning hair. "Plans change. All is well, all is well." He signaled a group of henchmen over to relieve the eagles of their burdens.

The five of them moved aside as the grooms worked, separating the eagles from each other, unloading supplies. The wizard watched them, his face pinched and inscrutable. Clearly something troubled him; Adaran wondered what thoughts moved through the man's head.

"A shame that our flight was cut short," Redshen said. "I could have stayed up there for hours!"

"I'm quite happy to be back on the ground," Adaran said.

"I second Adaran," Jenune said. "A man's place is with his two feet on the earth."

"That may be," Redshen said, "but a woman's place is in the sky, where she can look down upon you plodding earthbound men!"

Adaran chuckled, then glanced to the right, where he had noticed furtive movement among the rocks. For a moment he thought Dosen had arranged some sort of ambush, but it was only a group of three young soldiers. They had evidently managed to corner a ground squirrel and were now throwing rocks at the frightened animal. He wasn't sure if they were merely being malicious, or if they hoped to cook it for their supper; if the latter, they would likely go hungry, as their aim appeared quite poor.

"I understood that we would proceed directly back to Dunshandrin's castle," Orioke said. "Dosen, explain why we stopped here instead."

"I told you already," Dosen said, sounding peevish.

"No," Orioke said. "You didn't."

Dosen sighed, as if he were a father tired of repeatedly explaining the same thing. "Rather than overtax the eagles with a long flight back to Lord Dunshandrin's castle, you will rest here and continue your journey in the morning."

"They're birds," Redshen said. "Birds are meant to fly."

"Perhaps you failed to notice, but these are hardly ordinary birds. You would not ride a horse across the continent without stopping to rest, would you?"

"If I had material I urgently needed to transport, I would arrange to have relief horses along the way," Orioke said.

"And so we have," Dosen said. "The crystals will continue on their way with another rider on a fresh eagle."

Adaran said: "And our payment?"

"You will receive your money tomorrow."

"Why not now?"

Dosen folded his arms. "You will have your coin once the crystals are safely underway, and not before."

"What does he want them for, anyway?" Jenune asked.

Dosen looked at the warrior; so did Adaran, surprised that the man had asked that question so directly. He and Redshen had wondered about this too, of course, and had speculated wildly in private, but they knew enough not to voice their curiosity to those who had hired them.

The steward said: "I'm sorry ... What?"

"I asked why Dunshandrin wants the crystals. What use are they to him?"

"I'm sure that if *Lord* Dunshandrin had cared for you to know his business, he would have shared it with you," Dosen said. "Now, if there are no more questions, let us show you to your tents." He looked at each of them in turn; when no one spoke, he snapped his fingers several times, the sound like small branches cracking. The men who had been tormenting the squirrel gave up their pastime and approached, allowing the creature to escape into a nearby bolt-hole. One of the young guards—the same one who had helped Adaran up after the eagle had stepped on him—winked at Redshen, who burst into laughter and turned her face against Adaran's shoulder. Dosen shook his head, turned, and walked away, moving up the ridge toward the large pavilion.

As they followed the guards to their own, considerably smaller, tents, Redshen pulled Adaran's head down to her mouth and whispered: "I'll wager that Dosen keeps the payroll in that big house of his."

He raised an eyebrow and held up eight fingers, the number of guards he had seen so far; Redshen gestured toward the eagles, then fluttered her hand through the air like the wing of a bird. He shook his head slightly and pointed at the ground. She sighed, rolled her eyes, and looked away.

Whatever plan she was cooking up, Adaran knew he hadn't heard the last of it.

2

DURING THE BOAT TRIP UP the river to Dunshandrin's castle, Tolaria had learned more details about the tenuous situation she would have to defuse. Lord Dunshandrin had been struck by a sudden illness, provoking a succession dispute between his twin sons. Their father, with the shortsightedness of those who thought they would live forever, had never officially designated a successor; instead, he had encouraged the boys to fight and speculate over who was firstborn and thus would become the next Lord. Perhaps he had thought this strategy would prove which child was the stronger.

Now, with their father's death imminent, the argument had turned deadly serious; the twins threatened to take up arms against each other and split the realm with civil war. They had become so suspicious of each other that they would neither leave the castle nor accept a written statement from the Crosswaters, even one bearing the official seal of Flaurent. They insisted on hearing, from an oracle's own lips, who the rightful Lord would be.

She learned all this, bit by bit; the emissary parceled out information in tiny morsels, like a pinched miser dispensing one coin a day to the beggars. Fortunately, the man had proven vulnerable to needling, during the hours they spent together in the tiny cabin below the deck; constant rain and a chill, blustery wind from the north ensured that they stayed indoors for nearly the entire trip.

The rain at last abated as they entered the choppy grey waters of tiny Red Lake, so named for the color of the stony hills that surrounded it. Tolaria went to the rail, peering across the whitecaps at Dunshandrin Town. It looked low and ramshackle, hardly the sort of village where a Lord might dwell. Behind it, on a particularly ruddy butte, she made out the lines of a sprawling castle. That would be Lord Dunshandrin's keep, looming over his subjects in an almost volcanic fashion. She looked forward to spending as little time as possible there, and then returning to her cottage at the Crosswaters. She might suffer under Klem's jealous glare, but she had every confidence that she would eventually fulfill the headmistress's expectations.

As they neared the docks, Tolaria found a spot where she could watch without getting in the way of the sailors. She noticed a carriage with Dunshandrin's device painted on the side waiting on one of the wharfs and guessed, correctly, that the ship would tie up to that pier. Once the vessel had been secured, Dunshandrin's man appeared and directed her to the wagon, saying it would take her to the castle; then he took his leave, making an oblique statement about other business that needed his attention.

Feeling vaguely abandoned, Tolaria retrieved her trunk from the cargo hold, struggling it up the ramp, then across the deck, then down the gangplank. As she dragged it to the wagon, the driver turned to regard her without much interest. He watched as she attempted to lift the heavy burden into the wagon, but offered neither assistance nor encouragement. Finally two of the sailors from the ship happened by and helped her.

In a foul mood now, she settled onto the uncomfortable wooden bench in the back of the cart. The driver looked back at her and said, in a tone that implied he had been forced to wait much longer than he should have, "Ready?"

"Yes, thank you."

He slapped the reins and the horse began walking, jerking them forward with a lurch. Leaving the pier, the driver turned right onto the rutted, poorly-tended shoreline road. It had once been paved with cobbles, and some stretches still were; but large sections of the stone had washed away and been replaced with wooden planks, rocks, and gravel, while others consisted of nothing but mud. Lord Dunshandrin must not think very highly of the traders and merchants who came and went from his town, or he would not present them with such a poorly maintained waterfront.

The road improved somewhat as the cart left the area of wharfs and warehouses and seedy taverns, the road climbing from the lakeside and up the bluff. Still, the shops and homes that lined the rough street conveyed a sense that their best days had long since passed, and had been nothing to impress anyway.

She tried to remember what she had learned about Dunshandrin —the realm, not the man; in keeping with local tradition, he had taken the name of his country at the same time he took the throne. The lord was identified with the land, as she recalled, their fortunes entwined. Perhaps that explained the general malaise that seemed to cling to Dunshandrin Town. She wondered if things were similar in the countryside, if the crops had failed this summer, if the fields had withered. Landlocked and agricultural, with little in the way of resources to spend on imported grain, a bad year for Dunshandrin's crops spelled a dismal winter for Dunshandrin's people.

At the top of the hill the road grew rough again; the constant jostling began to give her a headache. She felt quite sure that when Lord Dunshandrin and his sons ventured out of the castle, they did not travel in a charmless buckboard like this one. Still, the carriage drew envious glances from the villagers who scurried out of its path, splashing through the puddles, slipping in the mud. They could scarcely dream of affording even such a simple wagon; the closest they would come to one would be when it nearly ran them down in the street.

At length the cart bore her through a large square, where merchants hawked wares from shabby tents and children frolicked, or perhaps bathed, in the greenish water of a dribbling fountain. After the square the buildings grew sparse and the road began to climb again, crossing a narrow stone bridge over a fast, grey river. Tolaria looked down at the rushing water, foaming and splashing as it cascaded over rocks and debris, feeling its cold mist settle on her skin.

Not far beyond the bridge, they came to the outer wall of Lord Dunshandrin's castle. The road narrowed to the width of a single large carriage, hemmed in on either side by buttresses that extended from the primary stockade. They stopped briefly at the main gate, where a guard questioned the driver as to his purpose. He handed the man a rolled-up parchment, which the soldier did not open; but he clearly understood the wax seal well enough, calling other guards over and showing it to them, making quite a fuss. Finally he returned the scroll to the driver and let the wagon pass into the bailey.

Like the route they had taken through town, the cincture was partially paved with cobbles, forming a broad avenue that led to the main gate of the inner keep. Most of the stones were reddish-brown or orange, but she noticed some variation in hue, perhaps indicating where repairs had been made. To the left of the paved area she saw small, fallow gardens, not much larger than her own plot back at the Crosswaters; these ended at a high wall that looked freshly mortared. Beyond that she could see an odd structure, like a gigantic cage, just peeking around the side of the keep. To the right, a narrow stone path crossed wet, churned earth, leading to the shadowed arcade of a long, low building that flanked the high wall. Storage or stables, she thought, probably both.

The wagon pulled to the right and stopped. A groom emerged from beneath the arches, hurrying through the mud to take the horse's reins. Taking this as her cue, Tolaria climbed down from the buckboard, making sure to step onto the cobbles instead of the mud. She began struggling with her chest again, but a page appeared at her side and said: "A servant will get that for you. Come."

"I can manage," Tolaria said, continuing to tug at her trunk.

"Leave it," the page said. "You must come with me."

Reluctantly, she let go of the chest and followed the boy toward the towering keep. It rose five or six stories above the bailey, ruddy sandstone held together with blackened mortar. A blank wall faced the courtyard at ground level, interspersed with tiny vertical slits for archers' arrows; windows appeared higher up, beyond the reach of invaders, each as tall as a man. These alternated with additional chamfers, such that the defenders of the keep could direct a hail of shafts toward any invader who breached the outer wall. She wondered how many men stood at the ready behind those dark, narrow openings.

Like the outer gate, the entrance to the castle was flanked by protective walls that curled out and around, restricting traffic to two or three men abreast. Guards stood on either side of the entrance, looking bored and alert at the same time; she noticed a further series of slits on either side, staggered from each other so that archers could create a punishing crossfire without inadvertently shooting each other. Tolaria glanced at the ceiling and found it riddled with small holes, like a ground squirrel's warren, for more arrows or spear thrusts or boiling oil.

Did Dunshandrin really have so many enemies? Did anyone?

She had hoped for warmth and dryness, but got little of either inside the keep; the rain had found a path through unpatched leaks and joints, while the clever wind turned the innumerable arrow slits into a chorus of ill-tuned whistles. Within the broad central hall, some servants used strange brooms in an effort to sweep the standing water toward drains near the walls; others followed behind, scattering straw to soak up the moisture that remained.

The page brought her directly to Dunshandrin's chambers, leaving her standing in front of the massive entrance. A guard opened the door for her, but did not accompany her inside or announce her presence as he shut the door behind her.

She had wanted warmth; now she had it. The room was blazingly hot, badly overheated by a fire that roared in a massive hearth to her right. Two high-backed chairs were drawn up to it, facing the flames; a table stood between them, its polished surface marred by old water rings. Dust-ridden tapestries flanked the fireplace, showing faded scenes of battle and the hunt.

She approached the bed, a massive, canopied four-poster, the footboard decorated with ceremonial daggers crossed before a shield. The weaponry was of a piece with an ornate suit of armor displayed in the far left corner; likely Dunshandrin had worn it as a costume while presiding over whatever martial rituals they practiced in this realm.

The lord himself lay beneath layers of fur and fabric, his face flushed, his eyes bright. The flesh of his face was sinking in on itself, tightening on the bones. It looked like fever, she thought; so what fool had decided the room must be hot as an oven, to bake the poor man further?

"Lord Dunshandrin?" The shaggy head did not turn to her, the eyes did not search for her. "My name is Tolaria. I am an oracle from the Crosswaters."

"Our father has deteriorated since we sent for you," a voice said. Tolaria looked up, startled, at the man who had risen from one of the chairs by the fire; a moment later, an identical man stood from the other. The feuding twins, she realized.

"First he was delirious," the second man said.

"Then he began to see things."

"Now he lies there and sees nothing."

"I am Tomari," the first one said.

"And I am Torrant."

Tolaria found herself disconcerted by the way they spoke in short alternating sentences; it felt like being confronted by a man with two heads. She looked at Lord Dunshandrin, then back to his sons. Whatever resemblance there had once been had been erased by the ravages of time and illness. "I assume a physician has seen him?"

"Of course," Tomari said. "Physicians, clerics, brewers of potions, even a madwoman who claimed she could drive out illness with the touch of her hands."

"His sickness defeats them all," Torrant said.

"Now we just wait for him to die."

"Well, you're certainly hastening that day by keeping the room so hot and stuffy," Tolaria said. "If I may suggest—"

"No, you may not," Torrant said. "You did not come here to treat our father. You came to settle our dispute."

Obviously she had overstepped. They had no interest in her opinion of Lord Dunshandrin's condition; perhaps they had brought her to this room merely to demonstrate that his illness was genuine. She felt quite sure that they did not spend all their days at his bedside, whispering words of comfort in his ears. "Yes," she said. "Yes, of course. My apologies. I will need the box from my trunk, so that I can prepare the vapors, and then—"

"Yes, we are familiar with your oracular affectations," Torrant said. "But the nature of your service has changed. We've decided to implement our own method for settling our disagreement."

"You have?"

"Yes," Tomari said. "We have decided to eliminate our quarrel by dividing the kingdom between us."

Tolaria looked from Tomari to Torrant, then at Lord Dunshandrin, lying insensate in his sickbed. Two days in the hold of a boat, sleeping on the floor, fending off unwanted advances, only to be told her services were no longer required. "A sensible decision, and one I recommended to your father's emissary," she said, managing to keep her voice even. "What need have you for an oracle, then?"

"Well," Torrant said, "the basis of our argument remains. Half our current territory is quite insufficient. One of us would inevitably be cheated of his due."

"Half our fields would not produce adequate food; half our mines would not produce adequate gold; half our forests would not produce adequate lumber. We would both be reduced to little better than local nobles, scraping for subsistence."

"I'm sure that my lords underestimate the richness of their holdings," Tolaria said. "Besides, you needn't create entirely separate fiefdoms. You could form a federation, for instance, and share your resources."

Tomari shook his head. "No. We need more land."

"Yes." Tomari nodded. "More land."

The direction of their thought seemed worrisome. "But, my lords, there is no more land to be had."

"On the contrary," Torrant said. "There is plenty of land, and the obvious place to look for it is within Barbareth."

"They have much more territory than we do."

"Certainly they have more than they need."

Tolaria stared at them, not quite comprehending what they were getting at. "I apologize for my ignorance," she said. "Are you proposing to annex Barbareth?"

"Only part of it," Torrant said. "The northeastern quadrant, perhaps, from the river to the bay at Astilan, and west to your own Crosswaters."

She was unfamiliar with the geopolitics of the region, but she did know one thing. "Barbareth is four times the size of Dunshandrin. Why would you want to start a conflict that you can't possibly win?"

Tomari smiled. "Are you speaking as an oracle, or merely as a stupid peasant woman with no knowledge of our capabilities?"

Torrant put a hand on his brother's shoulder. "What Tomari means is that we have certain advantages, advantages of which you are unaware, and that you should consider the limits of your experience before you speak."

"What advantages?"

"I'm sure you don't expect us to tell you all our secrets right away," Torrant said. "In any event, this audience is at an end. You will now be escorted to your quarters; we will call on you soon." He clapped his hands; the door to the chamber opened, revealing the guard who had admitted her.

"My quarters?" Tolaria said. "But ... I cannot stay here; I must return to my duties at the Crosswaters."

"No, that is precisely what you must *not* do," Tomari said. "You will be far better off here, predicting for us."

"We have seen your letter of recommendation from Flaurent; you were criminally underused, mediating disputes among villeins." Torrant glanced at his brother. "Someone should punish Klem for his small-mindedness."

Tomari seemed to find this quite funny, and began to giggle.

"You are taking me prisoner," Tolaria said. She could hardly believe it; convention, enforced by superstition, held oracles immune from such harassment.

"You mustn't think yourself a prisoner," Torrant said. "You are an honored guest."

"Yes," Tomari said. "So honored, in fact, you cannot leave."

Someone shook Adaran awake. He opened his eyes and found a small, slim shadow beside his bed, its hand on his shoulder. "Redshen?" he murmured.

She shushed him, then whispered: "Get dressed."

"Why?"

"We're stealing the payroll, remember?"

Adaran sat up and looked at his partner. She was ready to go, her black cloak cinched tight, hood up over her head. He shook his head. "No," he said. "I remember that we are *not* doing that."

She grinned. "If it were up to you, we would be long since retired, living a dull existence in some drab slum."

Adaran snorted. "It would be a coastal village, and we would lay by the ocean eating figs all day," he said. Then: "You really think Dosen has something worthwhile in his tent?"

"Of course. He's the steward. The steward always has the silver and gold."

"Well, I suppose it can't hurt to look." He got out of bed and dressed, aware that Redshen was watching him appraisingly. They had slept together once, a long time ago, after consuming a great quantity of wine in celebration of a particularly successful job; it had been a fumbling, embarrassing experience, and she had actually fallen asleep during it. Now she was more like a sister than a potential lover; but still, she was only *like* a sister, not really one.

As he slipped into his black cloak, he said: "And after we rob Dosen, how do you propose we escape?"

"Oh," Redshen said, as if discussing a new belt she hoped to purchase, "we'll steal eagles."

Adaran stopped, his cloak unfastened, and stared at her. "We will not."

"Of course we will." She made flapping motions with her arms, then laughed. "We certainly won't get away on foot. Now close your mouth and finish getting dressed."

He tied up his cloak, reached for his black leather gloves. "But we don't know how to fly them."

"*I* do," Redshen said. "I didn't have my face buried in feathers the whole ride; I was watching how our fearless guide controlled his bird. They're not so different from horses. You kick them to start, you pull the reins to stop, you squeeze with your knees to go up and down—"

"I'm starting to think this whole plan is just a pretext for you to steal an eagle," Adaran said.

She grinned at him, but said nothing.

"Fine. We'll steal *one* eagle, then, and you can fly it."

"Of course I will," she said, as if that were the most obvious thing in the world. "You would run us into the mountain, flying around with your eyes closed."

Adaran made a face at her, then pulled on his gloves and slipped into his boots. He pulled up his black hood—his cloak matched Redshen's almost exactly, having been made by the same tailor—and cinched it tight. The two of them looked like versions of the same shadow, one short, one tall. Redshen looked him over. "Ready?" she said. Adaran nodded. She gave him an *everything will be fine* wink, then turned and ducked out of the tent; he followed close behind. But as he emerged into the crisp night air, hands grabbed him from behind, pinning his arms behind his back. He couldn't see who had him. He felt himself lifted off the ground, spun around in a half-circle. There was Redshen, struggling with one of Dosen's men. He had her in a headlock, his other arm around her slim waist.

What was going on? Had someone overheard them plotting to

raid Dosen's tent? Perhaps; but too many men were about, their shapes grey in the wan moonlight, for this to be a response to Redshen's little scheme. They had fanned out among the tents, weapons drawn; and now he could hear a commotion from Jenune's tent, the clash of steel and wood.

Suddenly the wizard's tent exploded in a burst of smoke and noise and white light. Two of Dosen's thugs tumbled away from the blast, rolling along the stone face of the mountain before coming to a stop, twitching and smoldering. Taking advantage of the distraction, Adaran wrenched his shoulders up, dislocating both of them and slipping away from the henchman who held him. The thug cursed and lunged, trying to regain his grip, but Adaran spun away, cartwheeling to the side and delivering a solid kick to the side of his head. The man grunted and went down. Adaran landed in front of Redshen, dagger drawn and ready, but before he could do more than aim the weapon, a shower of hot, sticky liquid sprayed him, spattering his face and neck.

"Redshen!" Adaran cried. Dosen's minion had cut her throat, and now he tossed her aside like a piece of garbage, lunging at Adaran, stabbing with his short, fat sword. He was too slow by far; Adaran easily sidestepped the thrust, grabbing the man's arm and using his own momentum to pull him off balance. He thrust his dagger into the thug's abdomen, slicing through the thin fabric of his shirt, opening up the flesh beneath.

As the wounded guard moaned and clutched at his belly, Adaran raced to Redshen's side. He knew at once that he could do nothing to help her; the gash in her neck was long and ragged, blood spurting out with the weakening pulses of her heart. She looked up at him, eyes unfocused and blinking rapidly; she tried to speak, but the words whistled through her severed windpipe. Her lips told him to run.

He looked to the right. Three more retainers were coming at him from the direction of Jenune's tent. Their weapons were drawn and bloodied, their faces bruised and pummeled. Even caught asleep and unarmed, Jenune must have put up a ferocious struggle. But there was no more use in fighting; he was outnumbered at least five to one, with more killers on the way. He took a last look at Redshen, but she lay still now, her slashed throat steaming in the cool air.

Cursing, Adaran turned and ran for the edge of the ridge, racing along the rugged stone. He could hear Dosen's men break into pursuit behind him but didn't spare a look back, concentrating on his keeping his feet amid the rocks and rubble. If he slipped or fell, they would be on him in a moment.

Something clattered against the stone nearby, bounced away in front of him. A crossbow bolt. He cast a dire glance at the moon, which had chosen this moment to emerge from the dark clouds that had obscured it earlier, and began to zigzag as more arrows came skittering across the rocky spine of the mountain.

He had almost reached the edge now, where the ridge dropped away to the trees below. He needed to find a way down. Off to his right he spotted a cleft in the stone, like a chute leading into the forest. He darted that way and vaulted into it, but it was steeper than he'd expected, its damp floor strewn with loose rocks and years of accumulated dirt, foliage, pine cones. He lost his footing, fell, and started to slide, shooting over the edge of the ridge into open space, falling, the ground rushing up to meet him. He let his legs take the brunt of the landing, bending at the knees to absorb the shock, going into a roll that took him under the trees and out of sight of his pursuers. He dug his feet into the loam, checking his tumble, and came to rest just shy of the trunk of a massive pine.

Adaran stood, brushed himself off, listening to the debris pattering to the ground and the distant voices of the men trying to figure out where he had gone. He doubted they would be able to climb the sheer cliff to reach him, but come the morning they could search for him from the air. He had to think of these pursuers as hawks, not as men. He started down the slope, moving away from the ridge, darting quickly from one tree trunk to another, not stopping until he came to an abyss. This precipice appeared much higher than the last; the ground dropped away into a vast, howling darkness, as if he had run to the edge of the world.

Well, he had known all along that escaping from Dosen's camp would not be a matter of walking down a slope, into a valley, and out of the mountains. He was going to have to climb, with little knowledge of what he'd be climbing into; he had not watched the terrain during their flight from the dragon's lair, and so he had no idea where exactly they had landed. He remembered that Orioke had said they'd flown west. If the wizard was correct, that would have put them deeper into the mountains, perhaps even past the Salt Flats. In the morning he would be able to see into the gulf at his feet, and have a better idea of what he faced.

For now, he moved back under the shelter of the trees, curled up beneath the concealing spread of a thick pine, and drifted off into an uneasy sleep.

Pyodor Ponn gathered Plenn and the remaining five children in the living room of their small apartment at the back of the inn. He had put out some discreet inquiries around the village, but no one had seen Prehn, his youngest, since the previous morning. He let it be known that anyone who happened to find her would be rewarded; if this individual also happened to return her, the reward would be doubled. He held out little hope, though; astride their eagles, Gelt's men could have taken Prehn far beyond the reach of any rescue.

He sat on the floor in the center of the room, the four younger children on his lap or in his arms. Only Pord, the oldest, sat apart, his arms folded, sulking. Ponn knew that the boy wanted to be out with his friends, chasing a ball or swimming in the warm waters of the lagoon; instead, he and his siblings had been stuck indoors for the better part of two days. As long as Gelt remained in the vicinity, the children would not leave the inn. Ponn had failed to protect Prehn, but he would protect her brothers and sisters.

"Tomorrow morning, your father has to go away for a few days," Plenn said. "He has to take some men out to the islands."

Pord perked up. "The islands?"

"Yes, that's right."

"Can I come too?"

"Not this time," Ponn said.

"But you promised I could come next time you went out in the boat. I'm old enough now, I can help sail!"

"This isn't a regular voyage," Ponn said. "We're going to the volcanoes."

"The volcanoes! You mean where the dragons are?"

Ponn realized that he had only piqued the boy's interest further; he should not have mentioned their destination. "There probably won't be any dragons," he said. "They don't come very often anymore."

"I want to see them!"

"Hush," Plenn said. "You can go with your father next time, but this time you must stay home."

"But—"

"No, Pord," Ponn said. "Next time."

Pord settled back, looking even more cross than before.

"The people who are going in the boat with your father are not good men," Plenn said. "They're the ones who rode the big birds. Remember the birds?"

The children made noises of assent, and Pres, the next to youngest girl, said: "The birds are pretty."

"Yes, they are pretty," Plenn said. "But they're dangerous. They eat little children. You must stay away from the birds and the men who ride them."

Pronn, Pres's twin brother, said: "They asked me if I wanted to come see the birds, but I said no."

Plenn stared at the child. "When was this?"

"Yesterday."

Ponn and his wife exchanged a glance. Perhaps that was how they had lured Prehn away, Ponn thought. She loved animals, and would perhaps have accepted such an invitation. He had imagined one of Gelt's thugs simply picking the little girl up and carrying her off; the thought that she might have gone willingly, a trusting smile on her face, made him feel even more guilty.

"It's good you didn't go," Plenn said. "If you had, they might have taken you, the same way they took Prehn. Isn't that right, Ponn?"

"Yes," he said. "Yes, they would have taken you away. They could have taken any one of you."

"Not me." Pord made a fist with his right hand, slammed it into his left palm. "If they tried to take me, I would punch them. I punch hard."

"Me too!" Pronn said. "I'll punch them the next time I see them and make them give Prehn back!"

"You will do nothing of the sort," Ponn said. "You'll stay away from them. You will all stay away from them. In fact, none of you will leave the yard until I return from my journey and your sister is back home."

This injunction raised predictable howls of protest from the smaller children, but Pord merely frowned and remained silent. "You heard your father," Plenn said. "Now, off to sleep. Come on." She shepherded the children back to the room they shared, leaving Ponn alone for a few minutes.

Feeling aimless and ineffectual, he stood and wandered into his bedroom, stretching out on the pallet, staring up at the underside of the thatched roof; then he rolled over onto his stomach, buried his face in the mat, inhaled deeply. They had stuffed the mattress with fresh fern leaves only three days ago, and it was still spongy and fragrant. Prehn had attempted to help, toddling back and forth holding fronds taller than herself, beaming every time one of them had been used.

Plenn came in and pinned down the beaded curtain over the doorway, then slipped out of her sarong and settled onto the mattress next to him. "Ponn," she whispered, "they *will* give Prehn back after you help them, won't they?"

He had wondered that himself. "I don't know. I hope so."

"Who *are* they? Where are they from?"

"I have not been able to find out."

"Gelt has a northern accent. Madroval, I think."

"Yes, but he's a mercenary. Anyone could have hired him. They wear no country's colors, carry no country's emblem."

"What about the birds?"

"No one I've spoken to has ever seen such creatures. Some of the villagers think they must be gods."

Plenn snorted. "They're hardly gods. Devils, perhaps."

"Devils indeed," Ponn said.

3

ADARAN WOKE WITH A START as someone touched him on the shoulder. He rolled away and jumped to his feet, reaching for his daggers; but he swiftly realized that he was alone, and what he had taken for the tap of fingertips was nothing but a small pine cone that had fallen out of the tree under which he'd slept.

Shivering, Adaran tightened his cloak and slumped against the broad tree trunk. He stayed there for a few minutes, gathering his wits, and then slid around it and went to the edge of the cliff. The first traces of dawn had become visible, veils of dim blue light creeping over the mountains to his right. He crouched near the precipice, watching as the scene below slowly became visible.

His position was even worse than he had feared; he appeared to be facing the Salt Flats from the southwest. The flat, arid wasteland stretched to the horizon, rimmed by mountains to the east and west. Even if he managed to find a way down, there would be no villages, no towns, no farms, no trade. He had only been in the region once, many years ago, with a small party coming out of the swampy fens of southern Yttribia. They had passed around the spur of Lake Achenar, then skirted the eastern edge of the wasteland before reaching the sprawling city-state of Achengate. Not much worthwhile came out of the Salt Flats, but everything that did went through Achengate.

The job that had brought him to the Achengate—breaking into the vast salt warehouse and stealing a copy of the seal used for stamping salt crates—had been called off at the last minute when the merchant bankrolling the operation had backed out. The trip had not been an utter waste, though; it had earned him the acquaintance of a clever young burglar named Redshen.

Traveling along the edge of the Salt Flats had been unpleasant, but it would be paradise compared to trudging through the heart of the wasteland. He would find himself wandering among clouds of drifting, stinging powder, fording streams of toxic brine, slogging through noisome thigh-deep slurries of dust and water. He was not equipped to travel through such an environment; but the alternative was to try to cross the mountains and then descend into the wild jungles of northwestern Enshenneah. He'd never been there, although he had heard tales of snakes as big around as a man, ground that looked solid but would suck you in and drown you, plants whose intoxicating fragrance made you lay down and sleep while their roots burrowed into your body.

It seemed his options were to die slowly of thirst in the Salt Flats, of exposure in the mountains, or as a meal in the jungle. Or he could return to Dosen's camp and die quickly, taking some of Dunshandrin's henchmen with him.

Adaran looked up the steep, wooded slope, toward the stony ridge, invisible through the trees. It wasn't necessarily such a bad idea, sneaking back into camp; if he could steal some supplies—a few water-skins, some dried meat, some bread—and ration it properly, he might be able to reach one of the mining operations in the barrens below.

He moved away from the tree, making his way slowly up the slick, loamy slope. He soon reached the edge of the trees, where the spiny ridge broke through the skin of the earth. The umber cliff rose thirty feet or more above his head, weathered and crumbling; fortunate he hadn't been killed, falling blind from such a height. He quickly located the chute he had come down, not far to his left; the ground was disturbed where he had landed. Something gleamed from the earth and brown needles: A lost dagger, the same one he had dropped when he'd tumbled off his eagle yesterday. Evidently the strap that held it in its scabbard was in need of a leather-worker's attention.

He retrieved the weapon and slipped it back into its sheath; then he moved closer to the cliff, eyeing the stone. The gully would be a good spot to climb, offering concealment during the crucial moment when he hauled himself over the edge of the cliff, unless Dosen had realized the same thing and thought to post a guard over it. That was unlikely, Adaran decided; Dosen wouldn't be expecting him to come back. One man against twenty? Only a desperate fool would willingly walk into those odds.

Adaran assessed the rock face, his experienced gaze locating the cracks and crevices where his fingers and toes could find purchase. After fully planning a route, he climbed the wall as quickly as he could given the crumbly slickness of the stone and the need for silence. He soon reached the lip of the chute and scrambled inside, pausing there to listen for sounds of movement from the camp. Nothing. He moved forward, crouching as the crevice grew shallow, stopping at a spot where he could peer out without being seen. The camp looked much as it had yesterday; they had left up the tents where he and the others had slept, where Redshen and Jenune had been murdered. Orioke's tent, of course, had been destroyed. He wondered if the wizard had survived, or if he had immolated himself and taken Dosen's men with him.

The steward's pavilion stood some distance away, flanked by the smaller shelters used by his men. Beyond the tent city, the great birds were tied to iron posts driven into the rock. He noted that most of the eagles were missing; he only saw two of them, one sitting like a hen on a nest, the other idly scratching at an animal carcass, the remains of an earlier meal. Where were the others? Out looking for him? On their way back to Dunshandrin with the dragon stones?

The supply tent stood near the eagles; in order to reach it, he would have to sneak past all the guards, and then past the giant birds.

Fortunately, sneaking was his specialty.

Adaran lifted himself out of the crevice and scurried up the slope toward the camp, his soft leather boots silent against the stone. The avians saw him coming, of course, and watched him with unblinking eyes, but they did not screech or otherwise raise an alarm. Perhaps they remembered him.

Suddenly he realized that what he had taken for the bodies of goats or sheep were not animals at all. He froze, appalled, an unexpected fury coloring his face. Last night's treachery, while odious, was at least comprehensible as an attempt to conceal Dunshandrin's plot, to eliminate hirelings who might speak of it; but what manner of men would use human beings for offal, as if they were of no more consequence than squirrels or rabbits?

Adaran realized that he had taken out two daggers, holding one in each hand. He didn't remember drawing them, and though he felt a strong urge to use them, he forced himself to put them away. The birds did not act out of malice; their handlers had given them meat, and they had eaten it. If he were going to wake the camp, it would be by sinking his blades into Dosen's fat belly, not by attacking a pair of overgrown chickens.

Trembling, he crept the rest of the way to the supply tent, opening the flap and ducking inside. The cache of food and water was smaller than he had expected; perhaps they had taken some of it away on the missing birds. He rummaged through the sacks and crates, taking whatever looked useful or edible and stuffing it into his voluminous pockets.

Pulling aside a blanket, he came across a small woven net, not much bigger than a bird's cage, with a sturdy wooden floor and topped by a thick leather loop. Something lay curled up inside of it. He knelt down for a better look and then paused, shocked again, staring at the occupant: A very small, copper-skinned, black-haired girl, apparently asleep. With the blanket removed, she shivered in the morning chill; she wore only a thin green wrap that looked more appropriate to the tropics than these windblown peaks.

Suddenly, the eagles outside began to squawk loudly. Leaving the girl, Adaran peered outside. One of Dosen's thugs stood nearby, urinating off the edge of the ridge. He turned his head to the screeching birds and shouted, "Be quiet! I'm not feeding you, you stupid birds!"

Adaran drew a throwing knife, weighed it in his hand. He could certainly hit the man from here, but there was no guarantee of a kill, and if he failed the guard would rouse the others. He still didn't know how many henchmen remained in the camp, but he had to assume there were enough to overwhelm him. He reluctantly put the knife away and withdrew into the tent.

The commotion had awakened the child; she clutched at the woven bars of her prison, small fingers curling through the gaps, huge dark eyes staring up at him. "What is your name?" he whispered. "Where are you from?"

No answer, other than whimpers. He eyed the basket, trying to figure out how it opened, but there didn't appear to be a door. Maybe they had put her on the wooden base and then knitted the thing up around her. He took out a dagger, intending to cut through the tough-looking fibers, but the girl took one look at the blade and began to scream, her voice shrill and piercing. How could someone so small be so loud?

"Hush!" he hissed, looking at the entrance to the tent and then back to her. He put the dagger away. "See? All gone."

It didn't help; she kept screaming. Adaran looked at the flap again. Between the birds and the girl, the entire camp must be awake by now; someone would come to investigate. He quickly tossed the blanket back over the net and then moved to the back of the tent, up against the canvas wall, sliding into a dark corner behind a half-empty crate of dried meat. After a moment he grabbed a piece of jerky and stuffed it into his mouth. Tough and salty, but edible. He started to reach for another, then froze as a man came into the tent and said: "Shut up already!"

The child's cries subsided into a muffled whimper. The man's expression softened a little bit; he knelt down and lifted the blanket. "Are you hungry?"

No answer.

"You must be cold. I'll put you by the fire." The soldier picked up the little prison by its leather handle and hauled it out of the supply tent.

Adaran snatched another bit of meat and gobbled it down as well, scarcely bothering to chew it this time. He wondered if the man would return; he didn't know whether or not the girl could talk, or what language she spoke, or if she would tell the soldier that a stranger was in the tent. Finally thirst got the better of him and he crept out of his hiding place in search of water, finding it in a barrel with a tap. He took a drink directly from the spigot, then filled a water skin for the journey out of the mountains.

He heard someone approaching and scrambled behind the water barrel. He stayed motionless in the pocket of darkness, watching as another man entered, rummaged in the food, and left with a handful of bread and some dry cheese.

This was a bad place to hide; people would likely be in and out of here all day long. He was trapped now, though; the camp had come awake, and if he exited through the front of the tent he would certainly be seen. Perhaps he could cut a slit in the back and slip out that way.

But what about the girl? What was she doing here? A little morsel for the eagles perhaps, something to whet their appetite?

He had to be sensible. If he tried to rescue her, he would probably get himself killed. But he couldn't stand to see anyone in a cage; and if Redshen were here, she would want to rescue the child. She had a maternal streak that she was determined to keep hidden. On the other hand, the child didn't appear to be in immediate danger. The soldier hadn't made any move to harm her, other than frightening her by shouting.

He needed time to think, to plan. Rescue the girl, or not? Try to escape by day, or wait until dark and sneak off into the woods?

Leaving the questionable safety of his hiding place behind the water cask, he picked up the girl's blanket and took it to the far back corner of the tent, moving into the gap next to the crate of dried meat. He enshrouded himself with the rough fabric, leaving a gap so he could see the entrance, and then cut an escape route in the tent so that he could slip out in case of emergency.

He took another piece of meat, chewed it slowly, wondering what he should do next, until sleep crept up on him and transformed his worries into disturbing dreams.

Tolaria sat at the window of her room, staring out across the narrow valley at the scrubby slope of the hills opposite her prison. She thought she must be in the northern tower of the keep; the river rushed by almost directly beneath her sill. She could jump from it and land in the water and be swept away, and might have done so, if not for the ornate iron grille that blocked the aperture.

Her fire had run low, but she couldn't add wood; the hearth, too, stood behind a barrier of black wrought iron, and could only be tended from the other side of the wall. No doubt this was to prevent her from removing burning logs and setting the room alight. She supposed she should be thankful that she had a fire at all, that they hadn't locked her in some dank corner of their dungeon like a cutpurse or common thug; they craved her services, and so they maintained the fiction that she was an honored guest instead of a prisoner.

She had begun to wish for both food and warmth when she heard a key in the lock. She looked toward the door but didn't bother to stand as the twins entered, followed by a pair of burly servants. The men carried the trunk that contained her belongings; she hadn't seen it since abandoning it in the wagon when she had first arrived here. How long ago was that? Astonishing how quickly one lost track of time when one's existence was reduced to sleeping and waking in a single chamber, day after day.

"Good morning," one of the twins said. Tomari? He carried a sack; she felt mildly surprised that he had not brought a boy along to bear that burden for him. "I trust you slept well?"

"I have nothing to do here *but* sleep, so I have become quite adept at it," she said. "Have you come to your senses? Are you here to apologize for imprisoning an oracle in violation of all courtesy and convention?"

Torrant laughed and called her saucy, while Tomari looked affronted; the servants exchanged an uncomfortable glance as they set the chest on the floor. The twins felt themselves unbound by the usual codes of conduct and were manifestly unsuperstitious regarding her gift, but perhaps their henchmen could be persuaded that keeping her captive invited retribution from a higher power. She knew what sort of legends about oracles circulated among the uneducated classes.

Torrant said: "We are here to conduct a small test."

"What sort of test?"

He glanced at the two men. "You will wait outside."

The twins watched silently as the men departed, shutting the door behind them; then Tomari removed a length of rope from the sack and advanced on her. He motioned for her to move to a straight-backed chair in the corner. She had examined that seat when she had first been imprisoned here, and hadn't liked the look of it; it sported iron loops fastened to the arms and legs, a leather strap that could go around the midsection, and what appeared to be a restraint for the head. Bolts attached it securely to the floor. "I'm quite comfortable here, thank you," she said.

Tomari grimaced, showing her his teeth; then he grabbed her arm, hauled her to her feet, dragged her across the room, and threw her roughly into the chair. If it were not fastened in place, it would have tipped over and spilled her out onto the stone.

"Gently," Torrant said; he had gone to her seat by the window and closed the shutters against the morning breeze. "Don't damage her."

"She's fine," Tomari said. He bound her feet and arms tightly to the chair, running the rope through the iron rings and tying it off near her feet, then fastening the belt across her stomach, his hands quite deliberately brushing her breasts. He leered up at her. "More than fine."

"This is intolerable!" Tolaria cried. "When word gets back to the Crosswaters, they—"

"There's no one there to receive word," Torrant said. He had opened her trunk—she had left it locked, but they doubtless had people who could open such things—and was now rummaging around inside.

"What?"

"There was a fire and the building was gutted," Torrant said. "Many of the oracles perished. You could well be the sole survivor. Ah, here they are." He removed the box of herbs and the stone mixing bowl, inspecting them as if they were treasures found at the bottom of a river.

"You … you burned the Crosswaters?"

"We didn't say that," Tomari said.

"We said there'd been a fire. Just because someone brings news of a storm doesn't mean he caused it."

"But you *did* burn it, didn't you?"

"Perhaps you'll see the truth during your next vision." Torrant brought the stone bowl over to the chair and placed it in her lap. Now she knew why Tomari had tied her so tightly; she couldn't even wriggle enough to knock it to the floor. "First we put in the herbs, then the powder, then the water. Isn't that right, Tolaria?"

She stared at him, aghast. How could he know that? The mixing of the vapors took place in private chambers, out of sight of petitioners, be they commoners or nobles. "You *never* wanted me to settle your dispute," she said. "Even when you called for an oracle, your intent was to imprison whoever came."

"Have you only just realized that?" Tomari said. Then, to Torrant:

"Perhaps she is not so clever as you thought."

"She is clever," Torrant said, "but she is also naïve."

Tomari laughed. "We will cure her of that."

"You must realize that I can't forecast like this," she said desperately. "These ropes—the chair—everything is wrong."

"Don't worry," Torrant said. "We have every confidence in you." He scooped out some herbs and sprinkled them into the bowl, then handed the box to Tomari and said, "Put this back and fetch the powder."

Tomari returned the herbs to the trunk, poked around a bit, and then said: "There are two jars of powder."

"Red is for wisdom, white for divination," Torrant said. "We'll be mixing the two, so bring both."

"How did you learn all this?" Tolaria said.

Torrant winked at her. "Perhaps I'll tell you some time." Then he stepped aside as Tomari brought the jars, placing them on a table beside the chair. Torrant opened them and began spooning the calx into the bowl, first a pinch of white, then red, then a little more white.

"Please," Tolaria said, "you must not do this."

Torrant raised an eyebrow. "Why not?"

"You're abusing my gift."

"This seems like quite a good use of your gift, actually," Tomari said. "Certainly better than wasting it on some moldy farmer with a question about crop rotation."

"You must let me prepare the mixture," she said. "If you've done it incorrectly, the vapors could harm me. I would be useless to you then."

"Not to worry," Torrant said, smiling in what he probably thought was a reassuring manner. He liked to maintain eye contact; she was not sure if he meant to intimidate her, seduce her, or both. "The powders and herbs are in the correct ratio, more or less. Tomari, the water, if you please?"

"I am not your servant," he said.

"In this matter, you are," Torrant said.

Muttering, Tomari fetched the pitcher from her washbasin, then dumped the entire contents into the bowl. Water sloshed over the side, spilling onto Tolaria's dress; the mixture of powder and herbs fizzed and bubbled, making her knee tingle.

"You fool!" Torrant cried. "That was too much!"

"But you said—"

"You were to use the bottle, not the pitcher!" Torrant pointed at the bed, where her flask lay on its side, unopened. "We must untie her! There will be too much vapor!"

Fumes had begun to billow out of the bowl; Tolaria held her breath, blinked away tears as the miasma stung her eyes.

"There's no time," Tomari said. "We must go before we're affected as well." He seized his brother's arm and dragged him toward the door.

"You had better pray she survives the exposure intact," Torrant said, "or Father will have your head."

They exited, slamming the door behind them.

Tolaria struggled against her bonds, but they held her fast. She couldn't hold her breath any longer and gulped for air, inhaling a draught of the vapor. It made her lightheaded and dizzy; it made her want more. She inhaled again, deeply, then tried to stop herself; but it was already too late, she was slipping away from consciousness, sliding into a strange, shadowed hall where past, present, and future flowed together like the three rivers joining at the Crosswaters. She could still perceive the room around her, but it seemed false and faint, the palimpsest of an old drawing that had been erased and covered with something new.

At length she heard the door open. Footsteps hurried across the room. She heard the shutters bang open, felt a cool draft; then the footsteps retreated and the door slammed shut.

Some time later, the door opened again, then closed. Two men approached. Their movements were strange, slow and jerky, like figures in a sketch book that danced as the pages flipped by. She knew them, she thought. They looked the same as each other. Who were they? What were their names?

One of them said: "Tolaria? It's Torrant." His voice sounded slow and thick, like honey on a cold morning. "Can you hear me, Tolaria?"

"Yes."

The other one said: "Are you all right?"

She said nothing.

"I asked if you were all right."

Still, she said nothing.

"Why does she answer you but not me?"

"Perhaps she dislikes you," Torrant said. "Or perhaps it's because your first question was not explicitly directed at her, and your second question was a statement. Tolaria, who will be the first to return with the stones?"

"The steward, Dosen."

"Tolaria, when will Dosen arrive with the stones?"

"Before the sun reaches its apex, Dosen will have been and gone."

"Gone?" Tomari said. "Why will he be gone?" Pause. "Tolaria, why will Dosen leave again after he arrives?"

"He has unfinished business in the mountains."

"Unfinished business? What sort of—"

Torrant cut his brother off. "That can wait for Dosen's arrival. Tolaria is here to help with larger issues than his slipshod performance."

"Fine," Tomari said. "Let's ask her if we'll win, then."

Torrant rolled his eyes. "She won't answer that, Tomari."

"Why not?"

"I explained this already. She's directly involved in the outcome. They can't accurately forecast events that are tied so closely to themselves."

"Nonsense," Tomari said.

Dropping their voices, the two of them started squabbling; then Tomari turned to her and said, "Tolaria, will we be successful in this war?"

She sat, silent, as the voices in the dark hall of the future swirled around her, contradicting each other, saying things that couldn't possibly all be true. The clamor prevented her from seeing anything clearly, and so she said nothing.

"Well? Answer!"

"She won't answer," Torrant said. "I told you so."

Tomari grunted, then said: "Tolaria, what about the party we sent with Dosen to kill the dragon?"

"What about them?" she said.

"Enough, Tomari," Torrant said. "Dosen's coming back, so he must have dealt with them. There's no need to waste time on trivialities."

"She said there was unfinished business," Tomari said. "Tolaria, did Dosen eliminate all the villeins who accompanied him?"

"No."

Tomari shot his brother a triumphant look, then turned back to Tolaria and said: "Who escaped?"

She said nothing.

Torrant sighed. "Tolaria, which hirelings did Dosen fail to kill?"

"A speaker of Words, and a picker of pockets."

"A speaker of words?" Tomari said. "Everyone speaks words."

"A speaker of *Words*. She means the wizard."

Tomari blanched. "The wizard? That fat fool let the *wizard* escape? What if he comes here?"

"We will deal with him. I'll speak to Qalor."

"You think potions will suffice against the wizard?"

"Unkind. You know that Qalor is responsible for our more unconventional defenses. They will come into play if the wizard attacks."

"What about the other one, then? The picker of pockets?"

"One of the rogues, no doubt."

"I realize that, but which one survived?"

"Does it matter?" Torrant said. "At the moment, an escaped thief is the least of our worries."

Before setting off for the cove where he kept his boat, Ponn stopped by the children's room, pulling back the curtain and peering into the darkness. Not wanting to wake them, he did not venture inside; he merely looked at them, memorizing their sleeping faces.

When his gaze fell on Pord's bed, he frowned; the boy was not there. Pord had made a rudimentary attempt to conceal his absence, wadding up his blanket into the semblance of a body, but the subterfuge was transparent and did not fool Ponn for a moment.

Uneasy, Ponn went to the kitchen, where Plenn was preparing a small sack of food for him to take. "Almost ready," she said. "Do you want hard cheese, or—"

"Pord is not in his bed," Ponn said. "Have you seen him?"

She shook her head. "I heard someone moving about in the common room earlier, but I didn't look. I thought it was you, or a guest."

"Find him, but don't leave the other children alone. Send people out to look for him if you must."

She nodded. "And you?"

"I have to go," he said. "Gelt said to meet him at sunrise. If I don't leave now, I will be late." He hugged her tightly, feeling her cheek wet against his. "None of that," he whispered. "I'll be fine. I'll take them to the islands, and then they will give Prehn back to us."

"You believe that?"

"I must."

"How do we know they haven't already—"

Ponn put his finger on her lips. "I'll bring Prehn back safely," he said. "I promise."

He left then, forgetting to take the sack of food, hurrying out the door so that she would not see the tears in his own eyes. In the darkness before dawn, few people were about; those villagers he did see averted their eyes and didn't greet him, as if acknowledging his presence might cause their own children to disappear.

His route took him by a communal well, where he paused for a drink and then to duck his head in the trough. It was a warm and sticky morning, the air dense and still; the cool liquid refreshed his hot, tired eyes, helped wake him up. He had not slept well last night.

Water coursing from his thick black hair and dripping down his shoulders, Ponn left the well, following a little-used path into the brush that grew along the interior of the village stockade. He followed the wall of tall, dark wood until he came to the notched log; then he began counting the panels as he passed, one, two, three. When he got to fifteen, he stuck his fingers into a recess beneath the stub of a branch, pressed up on a hidden latch, and pulled. The lower section of log pivoted open and he slipped into the jungle beyond the fence.

Once out of the village, he patted the yellow bone handle of his long, curved dagger. He was quite sure that Gelt would confiscate it once he reached the boat—that was why he hadn't brought his good blade—but one simply didn't go into the jungle without one's knife.

The trail to the cove ran straight and flat through the jungle for some distance before turning sharply to the left and climbing the volcanic ridge that surrounded the lagoon. By the time he reached the top, pink traces of dawn had begun to spread from the horizon.

Still no breeze in the air; they might have to use the oars in order to reach their destination. The dragon islands were not visible from here, shrouded as they were by smoke and steam, like a shy girl covering herself in veils.

Beyond the arms of weathered black stone that protected the tiny harbor lay empty ocean, placid this morning, glittering under the rising sun. The oarsmen were going to be spending a long, hot day rowing below decks, Ponn thought. At least he, as the putative navigator, was unlikely to be pressed into that particular service.

Below, Ponn could see Gelt and his sailors—Enshenneans, he thought, though none he recognized—loading *their* supplies onto *his* ship. It looked like they had even tossed some of his own cargo overboard; debris bobbed in the water near his vessel. He bit back on his anger, thinking of Prehn. They held her, and so he had to cooperate.

His gaze traveled up the beach to the caretaker's hut; he paid a man to live out here and keep an eye on his ship and the cove. Two thugs stood outside the door of the cottage, arms folded, obviously on sentry duty. He supposed that meant they hadn't killed poor old Shaumi; or maybe they had, and had put something in his cabin that required guarding. Prehn, perhaps.

Four great eagles, tethered to a wooden post driven into the black sand, paced and strutted, their taloned feet leaving little tick marks on the beach. They stopped their patrolling and stared at him with glossy black eyes as he descended the path and approached the ship. Gelt hailed him as he approached. "Good morning, innkeeper!" he called, waving as if they were long-separated friends.

"Who are these men?" Ponn said, gesturing at the people working on his boat. "They are not from my village."

"No, of course they aren't," Gelt said. "You think I want to sail on a ship full of your friends and cronies?"

"You don't have enough sailors. I sail with a crew of ten. You have half that number."

"You aren't counting me or my companions."

"I thought your skills ran more to kidnapping and larceny."

"You wound me, innkeeper! My men are experienced seamen. I have no more desire to be shipwrecked than you do. Is that a knife I see?"

"Yes. You'll want it, I imagine."

"Clever innkeeper. Yes, I want it."

Ponn drew the weapon and turned it around, offering the handle to Gelt. He made a gesture and one of his lackeys took it, inspecting it as if it were something he might like to buy. As the man carried it away, Ponn called: "I'll have that back at the end of the voyage."

Gelt laughed. "I hope that wasn't a family heirloom." Then, cocking his head: "Do you savages *have* heirlooms?"

Ponn ignored the jibe. "My oldest boy is missing."

"You do have trouble keeping track of your children, don't you? If it makes you feel better, we didn't take him."

"I thought he might have sneaked aboard the boat."

"Nobody's come on board while we've been here," Gelt said. "He probably got tired of living in the jungle and ran away."

"I'd like to go aboard and search for him."

"I'm afraid not," Gelt said. "I can't have you wandering the ship, getting in the way, learning all our secrets."

Ponn took a deep breath, then said: "And my daughter?"

"Impatient innkeeper! You'll have her back when we return safely. No treachery on the high seas from you."

"Is she here? Are you keeping her in Shaumi's hut?"

"Who?"

"The caretaker." Ponn pointed at the guarded hovel.

"Caretaker?" Gelt glanced over his shoulder at the cabin. "Oh, is *that* the old man's function? We thought he was some sort of crazy hermit. He raised quite a fuss when we arrived; I'm afraid we had to get rough with him."

He was grinning as he said it. Ponn imagined Gelt's brutish thugs surrounding Shaumi, knocking the poor man to the ground, kicking and stomping on him, laughing all the while. He shook his head in disgust, walked away, and sat in the shade of the ocean palms as Gelt's hirelings finished preparing the boat. When they started leading the eagles aboard, he stood and found Gelt again. "What are you bringing those creatures for?" he said.

"You're the guide, not the captain," Gelt said. He looked at the sun. "It's time you came aboard and had a look at our maps."

"Have you found any sign of Pord on the ship?"

"Pord? What's a Pord?"

"My son," Ponn said icily.

"Why do all your names sound alike? Pord, Ponn, Prehn."

"It's a family tradition. All our names start with the same letter."

"You savages have traditions? How amusing. What about your wife? Her name's Plenn, isn't it? Did you wed your own sister?"

"She took that name when we married," Ponn said. "Have you found Pord or not?"

Gelt shrugged. "I don't know. All you people look the same to me. If he stowed away, he'll just have to come with us. Perhaps we'll find him and put him to work, eh? Can he sail?"

Ponn, tight-lipped, said nothing.

"Boys do love an adventure," Gelt said. He threw an arm around Ponn and steered him toward the gangplank. "Now come aboard. There are charts to be reviewed."

Gelt guided Ponn onto the ship and directed him to the forecastle, where he found the navigator plotting a course on a hand-drawn map of the nearby waters. Ponn immediately saw that it was badly out of date. "Where did you get this?" he asked.

"Gelt gave it to me."

"Gelt must want to run aground, then. The sea changes quickly here because of the volcanoes. A chart this old is worse than useless." He took the man's charcoal and reshaped the reefs and islands, then began adding new ones.

While he was working, Gelt entered, watched for a while, and then said: "What are you doing?"

"Updating your chart so that you don't wreck my boat."

"You see, this is why I needed you along."

Ponn put down the charcoal and looked at the man. "I don't suppose it occurred to you to hire me instead of coercing me by abducting my daughter."

"You wouldn't have accepted a hire to go to the islands."

"No, but I would have drawn a chart for you. What do you want out there, anyway?"

"You're forgetting your place again. I'm the captain, you're the guide." He gave Ponn a pat on the back. "I know you savages have difficulty learning, but try to remember that, at least." He turned and went back out onto the deck.

Seething, Ponn returned to the chart.

They set sail just as the sun cleared the mountainous ridges surrounding the lagoon. The helmsman guided them through a narrow gap in the barrier reef; they sailed directly out to sea until the water became deep enough to alleviate the danger from unseen, uncharted shoals. Gelt gave an order to swing the bow south and head for the islands. The riggers adjusted the limp sails, the rowers grunted with their oars, the navigator consulted the chart, the wheel squeaked in the helmsman's grip. Ponn went to the prow and watched the hull split the water. To his right, the jungle scrolled by, thinning as the chain of fire mountains came down to the sea, finally replaced altogether by smoking, steaming piles of black rock.

Since Ponn had last taken the boat this way, a new peninsula of lava had grown, like a spiny, smoldering black finger jabbing into the sea. The water around its outermost edge bubbled like broth in a soup pot. Ponn looked over his shoulder at Gelt and the helmsman. "Stay well clear of that!" he shouted, pointing at the formation. "There will be shoals all around!" Gelt nodded; the helmsman guided them farther out in the water.

As they cleared the high promontory, the distant archipelago came into view, the volcanic islands eternally shrouded by a haze of smoke and fog. The seas were very active out there, bubbling and steaming with underwater heat. Ponn shaded his eyes from the sun, looking for dragons in the mist. He didn't see any, but that didn't mean they weren't there; they could be slumbering on a warm stretch of newly-born rock or playing in the hot water of a tidal pool.

It had been years since Ponn had set foot on any of those bleak and barren rocks; only the northernmost few were remotely habitable, with green plants and colorful birds and rich soil in which to grow crops. He'd been raised on one, a tiny pelagic island with a single village at the foot of an extinct volcano. The dragons didn't bother them; the monstrous beasts preferred to flit about the jagged, smoldering active craters, drawn by the heat and smoke and fire. But if they caught a man on one of *their* islands, they would surely make a meal of him.

Gelt appeared at his side. "Your map has worked flawlessly. Keep cooperating like this, innkeeper, and you'll have your daughter back soon."

Ponn didn't bother to reply. He knew better than to trust Gelt's word; and even if he did, the seas out here were treacherous, the weather fickle, the dragons intolerant of trespassers. There was a good chance that none of them would survive this madman's errand.

And if they *did* return, what would Gelt be bringing back with him?

Tolaria awoke with a sour taste like iron in her mouth and a fuzzy, unpleasant tingle in her head; but the mere fact that she had returned to consciousness was an unexpected blessing. After Tomari had botched the preparation of the vapors, her last conscious thought had been that she would never emerge from the ensuing trance with her mind intact. And her mind *was* intact.

Wasn't it?

"My name is Tolaria," she whispered. "I'm an oracle. I was born in Yttribia and taken to Flaurent as a child. I was at the Crosswaters for the last three months, before I came to this forsaken castle." Yes, that all sounded true and accurate; although if she had gone mad, she would surely believe all her delusions to be sterling fact.

She remembered being tied to a chair, but now she was in a bed. The matted straw shifted beneath her as she rolled over and sat up; the blankets fell away from her naked body, but her fire had been replenished and the air against her skin felt pleasantly warm. Who had removed her garments? The twins? She thought of Torrant's leer, Tomari's wandering hands, and wondered what liberties they may have taken while she was unconscious. She reached down, touched her sensitive areas. To her enormous relief, everything remained intact; they had raped her mind, but left her body alone. For now.

Her trunk stood on the floor beside the bed. She knelt in front of it, rummaging through her belongings. They had taken her oracular supplies, toiletries, everything but her clothing. She pulled out a tunic and breeches, suitable for traveling, although it seemed unlikely she would be leaving the castle any time soon.

As she dressed, she tried to recall what the twins had talked about while she'd been entranced. She couldn't remember much after the vapors had begun to fill the room. This was not unusual; oracles often came out of a fugue with no memory of what they had said or heard. The Crosswaters employed a number of scribes whose function was to discreetly record everything that transpired during a session, but she doubted the twins had brought anyone in to write down their nefarious plans.

She heard a gentle rapping at the door as she was pulling on her boots. Not the twins, she thought; they wouldn't bother to knock. She finished adjusting her clothing, stood, and went to the door. "What is it?" she said.

A voice from the other side said: "I heard you moving around. Would you like some food?"

"Yes, please." Tolaria had had nothing to eat since arriving at the castle; at first she had simply refused all the meals that the twins had sent up to her, and then she had spent an unknown length of time lying insensate in bed. Now she was ravenous, and willing to abandon her hunger strike. It hadn't accomplished much anyway.

She stepped back as the lock turned and the door opened. A guard entered, bearing a tray of bread and cubed cheeses, dried fruit and meat, and a clay flagon. He brought it to the table near the window and set it down, watching as she descended on the food with the abandon of a starving beggar, ripping off hunks of bread and mashing them around pieces of cheese, washing the huge mouthfuls down with gulps of water from the flagon.

"I'm sorry the food is a bit stale," he said, apologizing for something that Tolaria hadn't even noticed. "I was told it would be a long time before you woke up, but I was starting to think they had killed you."

"How long was I unconscious?" she said, her words muffled by a mouthful of bread.

"A day and a half." The guard hesitated, glancing at the door. "I've heard that you are an oracle."

"I am."

"Is it true, what they say?"

She stopped eating, looked at him. "I don't know. What do they say?"

"That if you harm or waylay an oracle, you'll go mad."

Tolaria had hoped for this opportunity; the twins were too worldly to influence, but she could play up the possibility of supernatural retribution with this man and let him spread the word among the guards and servants. Eventually, someone might decide the risk was too great and help her escape.

"Well? Is it true?"

She opened her mouth to encourage his fears, and said: "No, it's not true." Then, startled by her own words, she took a drink of sour water from the flagon.

"It's not?"

"No. It is a common superstition, and encouraged by oracles for our own protection, but it has no basis in fact." She turned back to the table and put her hands on either side of her head. Why was she saying these things?

"But everyone has heard stories about highwaymen who rob an oracle and are struck blind, about kings who imprison oracles and lose their minds. Aren't those stories true?"

"No. They are apocryphal at best."

Now he looked confused. "What does that mean?"

"It means they are of doubtful origin, and probably false. The events likely never actually occurred, and if they did, their correlation to the attack on an oracle is merely coincidental."

Why was she telling this man the truth? Why was she answering him at all? She put a piece of jerky in her mouth, chewed it worriedly, hoping he would stop asking questions.

The guard watched her eat for a little while, then said: "How do I know you're not just telling me this because you want us all to go crazy?"

"You don't. But I would rather be set free than remain a prisoner, so why would I lie?"

The guard pondered this, scratching his stubbly beard. At length, he said, "Why would you tell the truth?"

"I don't know," Tolaria said. She had lost her appetite and pushed the tray away from her. "I'm not hungry anymore."

"Keep it. You'll want more later."

She looked up at him. "I would still appreciate it if you'd help me escape."

The man scratched his head, clearly uncomfortable in her presence now. He probably thought she was mad. "I don't know if you're telling the truth or not, but the princes would have my head if I let you go, and that's for certain." He opened the door and went back into the hallway, pausing to add: "If you need anything, just call or knock. There'll be someone out here all the time."

The door shut; the lock clicked.

What had just happened? She had wasted an opportunity to sow uncertainty in the minds of her guards. She'd formed lies in her head, but been unable to speak them. Something in the food, she thought; the twins had drugged her, given her some sort of truth potion.

But that explanation rang false. Much more likely, this was a side effect of the excessive vapors that Tomari, in his ignorance, had inflicted upon her. The fumes had left her mind intact, but stripped away her ability to speak untruths.

If that were the case, she hoped it would wear off soon.

How could one go through life without ever telling a lie?

Gelt's hired men proved to be adequate sailors. They stayed tightly fixed on the course that Ponn and the navigator had plotted, and when he spotted new shoals—by tiny black jags just breaking the surface like a baby's growing teeth, or by the pattern of the swells as they crossed shallow water, or merely by the bubbles that indicated heat below the surface—they quickly obeyed his shouted instructions to avoid the obstacle. And when a breeze finally came up from the west, they quickly unfurled the sails to take advantage of it and give the rowers some relief.

As the ship neared the volcanic archipelago, they adjusted the canvas, slowing their forward momentum. Ponn had warned Gelt that the waters here were shallow and especially treacherous, and it appeared that he had taken the threat seriously.

"Innkeeper!"

Ponn looked over his shoulder at Gelt, who stood nearby, eating some sort of sandwich. "What?"

Gelt jerked his thumb upward. "Into the rigging. If the sea here is as dangerous as you say, I want warnings as soon as you can give them."

With a sigh, Ponn left the prow and climbed the mast, settling into the rudimentary crow's nest. From here, he could see a vast network of black reefs beneath the water, forming a treacherous maze surrounding the islands. The shoals grew and shifted so fast that it was pointless to chart them; any sane mariner gave the region a wide berth.

"This is your last chance to turn back!" Ponn shouted. "Once we're in there, we won't get out again quickly!"

Gelt grinned up at him, waved, and went back to eating his meal and looking at the islands.

Ponn clung to the rigging and scanned the crazy patterns of stone, trying to guide the ship through the labyrinth without dead-ending or running aground. "Port!" he shouted. "Starboard! Hard starboard! Hold fast!" A couple of times they scraped reefs that Ponn didn't see; they were too deep, or obscured by dazzling reflections of the sun. The vessel's shallow draft kept them from being wrecked or running aground, but still, Ponn found it unnerving to imagine sharp, jagged stones clawing at the hull of his boat.

The near misses didn't dampen Gelt's enthusiasm in the slightest. "Keep it up, innkeeper!" he bellowed, after they had just navigated a narrow gap between craggy black heaps of frozen lava. "You're making your daughter proud!"

Then they entered the archipelago, and Ponn's task became more difficult still.

While the volcanoes slumbered, the smaller vents and fumaroles spewed steam constantly, producing drifting banks of acrid fog. Every time they entered such a patch of vapor, the sailors retched and cursed as they breathed the noxious fumes. Conditions were slightly better up in the rigging, because the miasma tended to hang low above the water, but Ponn still found himself coughing and wiping away tears with increasing regularity.

The clouds thickened as they progressed; the air became even hotter and closer, redolent of ash and sulfur, smotheringly humid. They must be very near an active underwater eruption, Ponn though, molten rock seeping out of the earth and boiling the sea above it. It must be terribly hot in the hold; Ponn prayed that Pord wasn't hiding down there.

The sunlight dimmed as smoke enshrouded them. Navigation became impossible. Gelt shouted a command to drop anchor; there was a splash, and a moment later the ship halted, an indication of just how little water supported them. "Innkeeper!" Gelt shouted, coughing. "Get us out of here!"

"I can see no better than you!" Ponn said. "I warned you—"

"You said nothing about these stinking clouds!"

"Are you mad? What did you think you would find when we neared the volcanoes? Until the wind shifts, we are blind!"

A fit of coughing overtook Gelt, preventing him from answering; and then, over the hiss and bubbles, Ponn heard the sound of wings. A massive shadow passed overhead, longer and wider than the ship, heading toward the west; a moment later a tremendous downdraft shook the vessel, nearly knocking Ponn from his perch. He swung around, clinging to the rigging, feet kicking in the air. The smoke thinned momentarily, revealing an open channel running at an angle to the left, passing between high walls of rock into open water. Gelt had stopped them in a volcanic bowl, perhaps the crater of a newly-forming island, the absolute worst spot he could have chosen; if they could make it through the gap and into open water, they might be able to see again. One thing Ponn knew: They could not stay where they were. The pitch would boil out of the planks, the ship would sink, they would all roast.

"What was that thing?" Gelt cried.

"That was a dragon, you fool!" Ponn said. "We have to get out of here before it notices us! If he's at all competent, your navigator has been plotting our route; tell him to retrace it!"

"Turn back?" Gelt said.   "Not when we're so close to our destination!" He began speaking to the helmsman; Ponn couldn't hear his instructions over the lather of the sea, but he knew well enough what the man was doing; despite the presence of the dragon, he was going to push on to the island and doom them all. But it had been flying to the west; it may have been departing the islands rather than arriving.

He could only hope it was so.

Now Ponn heard the clink and rattle of the anchor being raised. The ship began to move again, slowly, angling to the left. Gelt's rowers would be doing this work; how could they perform in such heat? They entered the channel. Stone scraped against the hull. Gelt barked orders, sending men down into the hold to check for leaks, to the sides to pole them away from the walls. Ponn clung to the rigging and waited for them to be wrecked; blinded, there was nothing more he could do.

At last, they emerged into open water. Gelt's target island loomed ahead of them, a hellish landscape of barren rock and smoke; but compared to where they had just come from, it looked like paradise. Two arms of the island curved outward, forming a small, sheltered cove. The oarsmen guided the boat into this unwelcoming harbor, but there was nowhere suitable for a landing; they dropped anchor in the center and set about preparing a large canoe.

Ponn climbed down from the rigging. Gelt ignored him, moving from position to position, issuing instructions. Ponn trailed along behind him, and finally said: "You can't possibly go ashore here."

Gelt did not favor him with a glance. "Of course we can."

Ponn gestured at the unbroken black rock that surrounded the sapphire-blue water. "But there's nowhere to beach a canoe. It's nothing but stone!"

"I'm not worried," Gelt said. "I'm sure you'll manage."

4

Adaran awakened from a nightmare with a stiff back, a dry throat, and no idea where he was. He sat up and looked blearily at his surroundings, remembering that he was hidden in the supply tent at Dosen's camp. The ability to sleep under adverse conditions was an important skill, but this time he had taken an enormous risk; he was not very well hidden, and could easily have been spotted if anyone had hankered for a bit of beef jerky, or if they had decided to break camp. Fortunately, his luck seemed to be holding for now.

He peered at the tent flap. From the light filtering in, he guessed it was late afternoon. Apparently they were going to stay for at least one more day; perhaps they were still out there searching for him, while he dozed right under their noses. That provided a small amount of satisfaction, but didn't make up for the fact that he was still quite likely to perish out here.

He shook his head. That sort of thinking was not going to help him escape. Slipping out of his hiding place, he began looking for something to keep him warm as he trekked out of the mountains; his cloak and tunic would not be sufficient against nights as cold as last. He'd hoped to see furs lying about, but no such luck; the men probably kept such things in their own tents, to insulate themselves from the chill. He picked up the blanket that had covered the girl's cage. Thin, but better than nothing. He folded it as small as he could and stuffed it into one of his many large pockets.

And what about the girl? What had they done with her? He crept to the tent flap and peered out at the camp. Afternoon light slanted from the south, filtering through the tallest pines, stretching out the shadows. The temperature had dropped from earlier in the day, the air nipping at his face, promising another icy night among the dripping pines.

Dosen's men—he counted five of them, gathered around the fire a few dozen yards down the slope—wore warm, if tattered, fur cloaks. The little girl's woven prison sat on the rock near the fire; he could see her inside, a tiny shadow, like a caterpillar inside its cocoon. If they were planning to feed her to the eagles, why would they bother putting her near the fire? What was she doing here?

He withdrew into the tent, contemplating the odds. Five to one? Suicide. Dosen's henchmen were not the most competent fighters in the world, but neither was he. He might dazzle them for a while with his speed and agility, but eventually one of them would score a lucky thrust with a dull sword and it would be over.

Whatever plans they had for the child, her fate was not his concern. He had to escape now, and take advantage of what was left of the light to get some distance down the mountain.

Returning to the back of the tent, he slipped out through the slit he had cut earlier, sliding out onto the weathered, uneven stone.

He froze.

Scarcely ten feet away, a guard crouched at the edge of the ridge, breeches wadded at his feet, straining to relieve himself. No time to duck back into the tent. Adaran drew a throwing knife and flung it as the soldier looked his way. The man opened his mouth to cry out, but the blade struck his throat before he could make a sound; he toppled backward and vanished over the cliff.

Shaken, Adaran pressed himself flat against the tent and waited, listening. Had anyone noticed what had just happened? Had they heard the guard fall? He didn't think so; no one came to investigate, no one called out.

He had just decided it was safe to move again when someone said: "Looks like Dosen's coming back."

Dosen? Coming back? Adaran crept to the edge of the shelter, peered at the henchmen. They were looking off to the northwest. He followed their gaze to a group of dark shapes, hanging low in the sky. Eagles. He counted at least five; he couldn't tell how many of them had riders, but Redshen had speculated that each eagle could hold two men. Dosen might be bringing in ten additional soldiers to help search for Adaran; or he might be coming to break down the camp and carry everything back to Dunshandrin.

Adaran looked toward the fire again. The men had moved away from it, gawking at the sky, leaving the little girl more or less unattended.

Now.

He dashed out from behind the tent, loping silently along the stones. He snatched up the net by its leather handle, pivoted, and fled to the edge of the steep, rocky, jagged slope on the western side of the ridge. He could see the body of the man he had just killed, wedged into a fissure where a great boulder had begun to shear away from the mountain. Too bad he didn't have time to retrieve his knife.

The little girl had begun to whimper; crying was probably imminent. There was no time for subtlety, or even to pick a likely route down the slope. Instead he flung the net over his shoulder, leapt off the edge, and started running. He bounded from rock to rock, maintaining a precarious balance on the steeply angled mountainside. He reached the tree line and plunged into the wall of pines, heedless of the slapping branches and jabbing needles; then he slowed down and cut to the right, moving at an angle through the forest. This direction led deeper into the mountains, but the cover seemed thicker, and Dosen would likely expect him to head in the opposite direction.

The girl, who had been fairly quiet until now, suddenly began screaming and beating on his shoulder with her little fists. He stopped, panting, and held her up in front of his face. She lay in the bottom of the sack, curled up as if she were in a hammock; but she was glaring at him with big, dark, suspicious eyes, as if she expected him to throw her off a cliff. "I won't hurt you," he said. "I rescued you from those men. They're bad men."

She snuffled, then wiped her nose with the back of her hand, but she didn't say anything or give any sign that she understood. What language did she speak?

"I'm Adaran," he said, tapping himself on the chest. Then he pointed at her. "Do you have a name?"

Silence.

"If I let you out of there, do you promise not to run off?"

She just looked at him. He rubbed the back of his head. That was a stupid question; of course she would run off. Then she would get lost in the mountains and freeze to death, if she didn't get eaten by some wild animal first. Perhaps she would have been better off if he'd left her for Dosen to carry off.

Well, too late to worry about that.

"I have to leave you in there a little while longer," he said, "but I'll try not to bounce you around so much anymore."

No answer, of course. He put her net over his shoulder again and resumed walking, moving at a less frantic pace than before.

Some time later, as the light began to fail, Adaran started looking for a relatively safe place to spend the night. He chose a tree that looked suitably sturdy, hooked his arm through the leather strap of the girl's sack and slid it up to his shoulder, and started to climb. Having the extra weight on his back unbalanced him somewhat, but he still managed to get a good distance off the ground and find a bough to wedge himself into. He positioned the woven cage in front of himself, then covered them both with the blanket.

It looked like his ability to sleep in bad situations would be coming in handy once again.

In addition to Pyodor Ponn, the canoe carried Gelt and two of his henchmen, Tolsus and Horm; it also carried a number of large, heavy-looking sacks. Ponn eyed the sacks, wondering if Gelt believed in tales of dragon hoard, gold and jewels stolen from fallen empires throughout the ages. Did he think to carry off gilded candlesticks and silver mirrors?

The mercenaries and their leader settled into the canoe, watching Ponn as the sailors lowered the small craft into the water; evidently he was expected to do all the work. He picked up an oar and proffered it to Gelt, who sat nearest him. "The person in front has to row, too, or we'll just go in circles."

Gelt took the oar and passed it forward to Tolsus, who passed it to Horm. He accepted it with bad grace and clumsily dipped it into the water. Obviously the man had no skill in paddling, but all he had to do was provide momentum; Ponn would steer from the back.

Tolsus tested the water with a finger, then stuck his hand in the lagoon. "Feels like a hot bath," he said.

"When have *you* ever had a hot bath?" Horm said.

"Your mother gave me one last week."

Horm glared over his shoulder, then slapped the oar into the water, splashing steaming water over the three of them. "That's enough," Gelt snapped.

"But he—"

"I said that's enough. Anyway, I've seen your mother, and I wouldn't let her bathe me unless she had a bag over her head."

Horm harrumphed. He turned away and resumed paddling, more forcefully now, so they made faster progress across the sour, steaming water of the lagoon. While Gelt scanned the rocks, no doubt looking for a place to beach the canoe, Ponn glanced back at his ship. Under the direction of Gelt's third henchman, the Enshennean sailors were bringing up the birds from below. The creatures looked decidedly unhappy; their feathers were damp and ruffled, their beaks open, their breathing rapid. They darted glances this way and that as the men led them to the railings and tied them up. Perhaps they smelled the dragons, and wanted to get away from the island; if so, they had more sense than their masters.

Suddenly Gelt pointed at something and said: "There."

Ponn followed the line of the man's finger and spotted a small creek that spilled over the twisted jags of rock, emptying into the lagoon. The rill had created a narrow crevice in the black stone. Ponn turned them toward it; when they reached the gap, he told Horm to stop paddling, a command that was instantly obeyed. Ponn guided them into the opening, like a ship entering a berth. Stone scraped against the sides of the canoe as they pulled it into the shallows, coming to rest at the base of the small waterfall.

Gelt eyed the cliff where the water came down, and said: "Looks like we'll have to do some climbing." He gave Ponn a meaningful look.

Ponn sighed and got out of the canoe, examining the rough black stone. He had spent his childhood scaling rock like this in his bare feet; it was easier to climb without shoes, when your soles and toes could feel the lay of the rock, but it had been a long time since he had done so and the callouses that used to protect his skin had long since softened and disappeared. He paced up and down, the water hot around his calves, looking for the best place to attack the wall. He selected a spot where the rocks were not so jagged, the handholds relatively plentiful; the climb proved brief and easy, and soon he was at the top, waiting for the others to follow the route he had chosen.

As Gelt and his men grunted and strained their way up the short cliff, Ponn wandered away from the edge, looking at the landscape. It had been many years since he had been on one of these islands, and while their details constantly changed, their entirety always stayed the same. Twisted stone in ebony and crystal; wisps of steam rising from cracks and hot spots; pockets of young, fragile-looking vegetation. He lifted his gaze to the cone itself, across the upward-sloping lava plain. The stream no doubt flowed from it, forced out of the depths by heat and pressure. The volcano was not all that impressive, neither particularly tall nor particularly steep, but it was broad and shrouded in whitish-grey vapor. He scrutinized the slope, searching for any trace of the dragon that had passed by earlier, but saw no activity. Perhaps he had been right, and the creature was departing the region.

"Innkeeper!"

Ponn turned. Gelt had reached the lip of the lava plain, stretching out a bloodied hand. "Help me up," he said.

Ponn grasped the man's wrist and hauled him to the top. "The damned stone cut through my glove," he said, looking Ponn up and down, evidently inspecting him for cuts or abrasions. "I see *you're* not hurt."

"Perhaps the island knows its own," Ponn said.

"I think it's just that you savages have thick skin."

Tolsus arrived next, uninjured, but Horm was bleeding from both hands and his knee, where the stone had torn a hole in his breeches. He rinsed his injuries in the warm water of the stream, cursing Ponn, the island, and his companions as he did so. Meanwhile, Gelt sidled up to Ponn. "We will follow the stream to the mountain," he said. "The ground will likely be cooler along it. Does that sound like a good idea, innkeeper?"

"It's no worse than many other ideas I've heard this day."

"Lead on, then."

They walked slowly alongside the creek. The vapor from it grew thicker as they progressed; finally they came to its source, a split in the lava rock, as Ponn had suspected. The water bubbled furiously through the opening, accompanied by malodorous fumes, like rotting eggs left too long in the sun.

"Makes me want to take a piss," Tolsus said, eyeing the burbling fountain. He dropped his trousers and did just that, urinating a thin stream onto the rocks. As he did so, a minor tremor shook the earth, rumbling down from the cone and across the island. "What was that?" Tolsus said, wide-eyed.

"Just the voice of the mountain," Ponn said.

"Is it going to erupt?"

"Who can say? Perhaps it is angry at you for defiling it."

"Don't listen to the savage and his superstitions," Gelt said. "The island can no more be angry than a rock or a tree."

The ground shook again. No mistaking it; this island was alive beneath their feet.

Sounding a shade less cocksure, Gelt said: "Finish up, and no more stops until we get what we came for. Innkeeper, we're going north. That way."

Tolsus quickly tied up his pants and they started walking again, Ponn out in front, watching for crevices and patches of uncertain ground. The terrain grew rougher as the land sloped upward, the heat of the earth penetrating the thick soles of his sandals.

The route Gelt had chosen led them to the foot of a near-vertical wall of jagged rock at least three times as tall as Ponn. It tumbled over itself like a cataract locked in stone. Ponn looked at Gelt, and saw that the man was removing a length of thick rope from his backpack. Strips of leather had been woven into it, making it stronger and more resistant to cuts and fraying, but also heavier.

"What's that for?" Ponn said.

"You." Gelt handed it to him. "Tie it off when you get to the top, and toss it down to us."

Ponn looked at the rope, then at Gelt, then at the obstacle that rose before them. "You knew this cliff was here," he said.

"Of course I knew. Do I seem like the sort who would be caught unprepared?"

"And the lagoon? The stream?"

"Those too."

"You've been here before."

"No. I had a man fly out and do reconnaissance."

"Why did you need me, then? Why take my ship? Why take my

daughter? Why not just fly on your accursed birds, and leave me out of it?"

"You ask too many questions, innkeeper," Gelt said. "I thought men in your trade were supposed to be discreet. Now, climb."

Resigned, Ponn draped the rope around his neck and eyed the precipice. The stones were somewhat weathered, not so jagged as those by the stream; but the wall was much higher, a tumble more costly. He moved back and forth, trying to find the most hospitable spot; finally Gelt said: "Get on with it."

Ponn glanced at him. "Do you want to reach the top, or do you want to fall and dash your brains out? If you say you want to fall, this will be much easier."

"That sort of attitude will not get your daughter back."

No, he supposed it wouldn't. Chastened, Ponn removed his sandals and tucked them into his garment, then selected the most promising spot and started to climb. He worked his way up the crag, hoping there would not be another tremor; he silently thanked the mountain when he reached the top safely. Stepping away from the edge, he eyed the tilted, cracked shelf on which he now stood. It seemed stable enough, but not as wide as he would have liked; the cone loomed overhead, seeming much larger now.

There were plenty of rugged stone fingers to which he could tie the rope. He selected a sturdy-looking one, making a knot that would tighten under load, and then tossed the rope down to the others. As they started to climb, one by one, he moved closer to the volcano, hoping for a bit of shade; even he was starting to suffer from the heat, the humidity, the sulfurous air. He found a small overhang and settled beneath it, waiting. The mountain thrummed constantly here, a low vibration that shivered through his body, as if he were filled with swarming bees.

At last, Gelt appeared at the top of the cliff, puffing and grunting. He hauled himself over the edge, rolled onto his back, and lay there for a few minutes; then he turned over and joined Ponn in the shade. "Almost there, innkeeper," he said. "You are doing well."

Ponn couldn't resist asking. "Almost where?"

Gelt grinned at him, then went to help Horm, whose climbing was hampered by his injured hand. Soon Tolsus joined them as well. After a brief rest, the three men moved along the ledge to the west, circling the cone.   Ponn followed behind, his guidance no longer required.

Eventually they reached a hundred-foot cliff, a sheer drop to the frothing, gnashing sea. Had they come all this way only to reach a dead end? But once again Gelt knew the terrain; an even narrower shelf continued from here, angling sharply up to the right. It led to a hole in the mountain, a narrow vent that had once spewed magma into the ocean below, gobs of molten rock that had solidified in the water like dumplings in stew.

Gelt turned to Ponn. "Wait here," he said.

Ponn watched the three men pick their way up the narrow ledge and vanish into the lava tube. Wait here, the man said? If Gelt thought that he might have otherwise decided to follow them into the mountain, he was quite mistaken.

He turned, gazing out across the eastern sea, mostly open ocean, the cerulean water punctuated by black crags lurking just above the surface, ambush predators waiting to rip the bottoms out of ships. To the south, he could see a few of the other islands, smoldering silhouettes through the haze of smoke and steam. The setting sun stained the vapors a golden orange. Dusk already? Had they spent so long making their way across the island? Back at the inn, Plenn would be serving dinner to their guests, the children carrying trays and bowls and flagons of sweet wine. Perhaps Pord was there, back from wherever he had gone, sullen, but helping just the same. Pord was a good boy, if headstrong; all of his children were good, and he hated to be deprived of any of them.

A beating of wings and rush of air drew him from his reverie. His first thought was of a dragon and he flung himself back against the stone, searching the sky for a great shadow; but instead he saw Gelt's four eagles, holding themselves motionless just off the ledge. They were tethered together in a square formation, a large, hooked mesh strung between them, one bird at each corner, as if they were going to be trawling for fish later. Each eagle bore a saddle, but only one carried a rider. "Have they gone into the mountain?" he shouted.

Ponn nodded. What was this all about?

"How long ago?"

"Not long!"

The man cast a worried glance at the sinking sun. "They must hurry!" he cried. "We can't land here, and hovering tires the birds out!"

"Well there's nothing *I* can do about it," Ponn said. "You'll just have to wait." But even as he spoke, Gelt emerged from the tunnel, followed by the others, carrying bulging sacks over their shoulders. They made their way unsteadily down the ledge, stopping at the edge of the shelf in front of the hovering eagles. The rider brought his formation in low and close, maneuvering the net within reach. The men transferred their burdens to the webbing, using the hooks to secure the load. Then Gelt climbed into it himself, crawling across the ropes and clambering into an open saddle. Tolsus followed, then Horm. Ponn took a step forward, but the eagles rose and retreated out of his reach. "I apologize, innkeeper," Gelt called, "We don't want to overburden the eagles with unnecessary weight. We've a long flight ahead of us!"

Ponn stared at him.

"Come now. Don't look at me like that. I'm leaving you a perfectly seaworthy ship to sail home in."

"But my daughter—"

"We'll keep her safe," Gelt said. "If she grows up to look like her mother, she'll never want for company!" Gelt laughed and waved a farewell as the birds wheeled back and banked away to the north. Ponn ran around to the front of the shelf, where the rope dangled down the cliff. In the waning light he could still see his ship, but the deck was clear of men; the vessel appeared to be deserted. Where had the other sailors gone? He could hardly sail it all by himself.

The canoe. Perhaps he could get back to shore in it, or at least reach one of the inhabited islands. But not tonight; it was too near dark, he probably could not reach the lagoon before nightfall. Stumbling blindly across the lava field, he would likely fall and split his skull open; he would have to wait until morning to begin that arduous trek.

By then, Gelt—and his daughter—would be far, far away.

Tolaria wondered if it was possible to actually die of boredom.

Her prison contained nothing to amuse her; no paper for sketching or writing, no books to read, no plants to tend, no instruments to play. Instead, she engaged in her new favorite pastime: Sitting on her bed, watching darkness gather outside her window, envisioning the princes dead in a dozen different ways. Then, because it was more diverting, she began ordering the manners of their death alphabetically.

She had reached *hanging*, picturing the two of them dangling by thick, creaking ropes from the twisted limbs of a barren tree, when the door opened and one of the victims of her imagination came in. It was the first time she'd seen them apart, and she found it oddly disconcerting, as if half a person had entered the room.

"Good evening, Tolaria," he said. "How are you feeling?"

"Bored."

"Understandable. I'm sorry we haven't come to entertain you in the last few days, but we have been quite busy, and you needed time to rest." He stepped away from the door. "How are you feeling? Have you recovered from your exposure to the vapors?"

He was getting at something, she thought; what had he heard? "Yes," she said. "I feel fine."

"Really? I understand you've been unusually … truthful."

"I am not by nature a liar," she said. "Would you mind telling me who you are?"

"Of course; forgive my lack of manners. You don't know us well enough yet to tell us apart. I am Torrant."

She'd suspected as much. "So tell me, Torrant. How did you come to know so much about the ways of oracles? The herbs, the powders, the vapors?"

Torrant smiled. "Perhaps I'll tell you someday."

"Why not tell me now?"

He seemed to consider this, and then said: "Indeed, why not?" He went to the chair in which they had bound her and sat down in it, tracing one of the iron loops with his finger. "When I was ten years old, I started falling into trances. At first my father called in his physicians, thinking that I had some variation of the twitching disease, but their potions and concoctions did nothing to help me. So he brought me to the Crosswaters, where they concluded that my spells were predictive in nature, that I could well become an oracle. That was unheard of, of course—a noble becoming an oracle!—but my father sent me to Flaurent in the Salt Flats to develop my talent, if such it was. I spent three years there, stranded in the wasteland, shaking salt dust out of my clothes and writing letters asking to come home. But I also learned everything I could about your rituals and powers. By the time the Headmaster decided that whatever ability I'd had as a child was lost in puberty and sent me on my way, I was quite conversant with your secrets."

"But when you left, did they not give you a draught to make you forget everything you'd learned?"

"They did," he said. "But Qalor, Father's alchemist, devised a remedy. He's quite clever; you'll meet him soon."

"Will I? When I'm released from this prison, perhaps?"

"Prison? You wound me. Is this not a finer accommodation than your hovel at the Crosswaters?"

"It's certainly more sumptuous, but the bars and locked door do give one pause."

Torrant chuckled. "You won't be confined to this room forever. In time, you may even enjoy the run of the castle. But for now you must stay here." He stood. "If you'll excuse me; much as I enjoy your lovely presence, there are decisions to be made, and my brother cannot be trusted to make them on his own." He strode out of the room, pausing at the door to give her a smile and a bow before locking her in again.

She gave a strangled shriek, picked up a pillow, and threw it at the closed door, then turned and went to the window, clutching at the ornate bars. She was so tired of this room, of this castle, of the twins and their machinations!

"Arrogant pup."

Tolaria gasped and whirled, seeing a man in a hooded red cloak standing in the corner near the door. He knelt and picked up the pillow she had thrown, held it in his hands, examining it. "I could have struck him down where he sat."

"Who ... who are you?"

"How unconscionably rude of me." The man tossed the pillow onto the bed, then slipped off his hood, revealing a narrow face, hollow cheeks, gleaming eyes. He sported a scruffy growth of beard; it looked out of place there, as if it had wandered over from someone else's chin and couldn't find its way back. "Most call me Orioke."

"A speaker of Words," she murmured.

"Why do you say that?"

Why had she? It had just come from her lips, unbidden, like an unexpected sneeze. "I don't know."

The man took a step forward. "Have you heard my name?"

"I don't think so."

"Well, I have heard yours. You are Tolaria, an oracle from the Crosswaters. You are an *honored guest*; that is to say, a prisoner."

"Yes. What do you want with me? Why are you here?"

"I haven't decided yet." He studied her, idly scratching at his stubble. "Lord Dunshandrin hired me, along with several others, to remove some stones from a dragon's lair. We chose a time when the large dragon was away, slew its hatchlings, and made off with our prize. We returned in triumph to camp; but that night, Dunshandrin's men attempted to murder us in our sleep. I escaped and stayed hidden until the next day, then returned here along with Dunshandrin's booty."

"They brought you back after trying to kill you?"

The wizard smiled. "Dunshandrin's men didn't know I had accompanied them. They still don't. I have been going about the castle, uncovering what I can of their plans."

"Their *plans* are to start a war," she said.

"Yes, I know."

"It's madness. Barbareth will crush them, and hundreds or thousands will die for no reason."

"Is that what you predicted for them?"

"I don't remember what they asked or how I answered, but for some reason, they think they might win such a conflict."

"Indeed, they do think that. And I have learned some of the reasons for their confidence. One of them, fair lady, is you."

She watched as he went to the window and looked through the iron grillwork at the night beyond. Did he intend to harm her? If she screamed, her room would quickly fill up with guards; but she had the unsettling impression that this man was not concerned with being discovered.

"If I were to kill you," he said, "that would disrupt their plans, wouldn't it?" He spoke without looking at her; for some reason, this frightened her more than it would have had he said it while gazing into her eyes.

"Yes. I don't know how badly." Then: "Are you going to?"

After a long moment, he said: "I don't think so."

"Will you help me to escape?"

"No."

"Then why have you come?" Tolaria thought for a moment, considered everything the man had told her, what he had been doing, what he had learned; and suddenly she understood. "You are going to join forces with them."

He looked at her, not answering, half his mouth turned up in a smirk. Evidently she had pleased him.

"Are you mad? They tried to have you killed!"

"If I approach them as an ally in their larger cause, I am no longer a hireling to be disposed of. Instead, I am a supporter who deserves to be rewarded."

"They won't reward you. They'll murder you."

"They tried that once; I doubt they'll make that mistake a second time. Not once I have … persuaded them." He walked to the door, turned, and bowed to her, the gesture a clear mockery of Torrant's mannerism. "If all oracles were as fair as you, Tolaria, I would have stayed longer at Flaurent."

"You were at Flaurent?"

But he only smiled, and leaned toward the door, covering his mouth, speaking words she could not hear. A moment later his body shimmered and faded, became nothing more than an outline, a haze, like heat rising from a fire; then he moved from where he had been and she could not find him again.

The door opened and a guard entered. "Yes?" he said.

"What?"

"You called."

"No," Tolaria said. Should she tell him about her visitor? She opened her mouth, then shut it again, almost as if someone had reached out with unseen fingers and pushed her jaw closed.

"You did," he said. "I heard you."

Tolaria shook her head.

"But—"

She heard herself say: "I need nothing. Everything is fine. Please leave me alone."

She couldn't tell if the man was confused, or angry, or both. "All right, then." He backed out of the room and shut the door, locking it behind himself.

Tolaria sat down on the edge of her bed. Had she completely lost her mind? She picked up her pillow. "There was a wizard in my room," she told it, "but now he's gone."

Silence.

"Has *everyone* been at Flaurent?"

But the pillow, uncooperative as it was, refused to answer.

5

T'SIAN PLUNGED FROM THE LOWEST layer of clouds, lines of vapor trailing along behind her. The ocean lay far below, glimmering in the last shreds of daylight that trickled over the horizon. She could see the islands off to the southeast, smoldering blotches of crimson against the cooler waters.

She banked to the left and began descending. In the many years since her last flight to the archipelago, the islands would have changed, reshaped themselves; but the crystals would still be there, as always, pushed to the surface by heat and pressure. They could be found within any of the volcanoes, but the largest and most accessible formation grew within the hollow mountain of the easternmost island. As she neared it, she noticed that a lagoon had developed where two arms of the lava flow had extended into the sea, forming a small, sheltered harbor. A human ship lay moored there, leaning on its side; the tide had gone out, stranding the vessel in water too shallow to support it.

Astonished, She veered in that direction, landing on the rough stone that surrounded the cove. She peered at the vessel, finding no sign of activity, no movement on the deck, no warm bodies hiding from her gaze. She splashed out into the warm water and sniffed around the ship. It was redolent of birds, the same type of scents that she had encountered at her lair.

How very interesting.

T'Sian dug her talons into the hull and tore it open, breaking it apart. Bodies fell out, men, dead of cut throats and stab wounds; but there were no birds. She continued to dismantle the ship, ripping out interior walls, lifting up sections and shaking their contents out into the water. Before long, the lagoon was awash in drifting wreckage and floating corpses; she found none alive to tell her what the ship was doing here or why it smelled the way it did.

She spied a small, thin craft drawn up on the rocks near a waterfall. She made her way to it, tasted the little canoe, the nearby stones.

Men. Perhaps there were still some alive on the island for her to interrogate; they had not yet returned to claim their tiny boat. She pierced it with two of her talons in order to sink it; then, deciding that the damage would be too easily repaired, she picked it up and ground it to kindling.

That done, she followed the scents the men had left behind as they climbed the low wall, then stayed alongside the stream as they moved into the interior of the island. Four of them, she thought, three similar to each other, one different. She slunk along the same path, continually tasting the air to make sure that she didn't lose the trail, finally coming to a near-vertical wall of rock. A rope dangled down the palisade, indicating that the men had climbed up to the cone.

No doubt remained: They had come here seeking the stones that grew in the volcano, as if the ones they had so cruelly cut from her hatchlings had not been enough.

She spread her wings and lifted herself into the air, landing on the edge of the crater. She circled it slowly, scanning the darkness for the men. Eventually she found one, a single body, nearly invisible against the surrounding heat of the rock. He was curled up, apparently asleep; she did not think he was dead.

Could this single human have killed all those others? She didn't know much about men, but she doubted it; there must be others somewhere. Perhaps this one had somehow escaped their attention.

He would not escape hers.

Ponn hurried along a jungle path, running at top speed toward his village, paying no attention to dangling vines, protruding roots, moss-slicked rocks. He reached the main gate of the stockade, found it closed; but with a great push, it swung inward, then fell off its pivot with an echoing crash.

He ran through the opening. The town was quiet, deserted. Houses which had been in good repair when he had left lay in ruins, thatched roofs torn away, interiors open to the sun and rain. He raced to his inn; miraculously, it stood undamaged, exactly as he remembered it. He went inside. No guests, no fire, no family. Ponn crossed the common room, entered the apartment. The children's room was bare, just walls and floor, bedding and toys gone. He moved on to his own room, which still contained its accustomed furnishings. A shape lay in the bed, covered by a blanket. Plenn? He went to the bed, knelt on the edge, pulled back the covers.

"Clever innkeeper," Gelt said, stabbing Ponn in the heart with his own bone-handled knife.

Gasping, clutching at his chest, Ponn awoke, not in the village but on the island, under the volcano, shivering with a chill. He had rolled out of the niche where he had been sleeping, perhaps while thrashing in the grip of his nightmare, and now lay beneath the cloudy sky.

Horrid, horrid dream, suggesting that Gelt had returned to the village and further harmed his family. It could not be true. Gelt was done with him; he had taken what he wanted. He had no reason to visit any more malice upon Plenn and the other children. None but his own malicious amusement, anyway.

Suddenly, Ponn heard something from the slope above him, faint scraping noises, like something large and hard moving over the rocks. A landslide? He scrambled back toward the shelter of the overhang, only to be blocked by a thick, scaly tail that descended in front of him like a giant snake. He cried out as a massive claw closed over him, knocking him down. Long, knobby fingers curled around his body, sword-like talons digging into the stone, sealing him in a warm, living cage. His greatest fear had been realized; a dragon had discovered him.

A sibilant voice said: *"Do not struggle, or I will crush you. Do you understand?"*

"Yes."

"Then understand as well that if you fail to answer to my satisfaction, I will crush you," the dragon said. *"Did you arrive here on the boat that was in the lagoon?"*

"Yes."

"You did not come alone?"

"No."

"Where are all the others?"

"They left," he said.   "They went into the mountain, and when they came out, they flew away."

The enormous fingers tightened around him.   "*You lie.   Men cannot fly.*"

"They rode giant eagles as if they were horses! I swear it!"

For what seemed a very long time, the dragon said nothing. Ponn closed closed his eyes, waiting to be crushed as a scoundrel and a prevaricator, because men did not ride upon the backs of birds. But the claw did not come down on him, the fingers did not squeeze him to jelly; and finally the beast said: "*So that is the answer.   They* ride *the birds.   But tell me, man: Why did they bring a boat, if they flew away in the sky?*"

"I don't know," Ponn said. "I think the birds couldn't land on the lava, or it was too far for them to come and go back again carrying whatever it is they took."

"*And why did your companions leave you behind?*"

"They weren't my companions! They only wanted my ship, and once I got them here, I was no longer of any use and they abandoned me."

The dragon made a snorting sound. "*Consider yourself fortunate, then. When I found it, everyone aboard this ship of yours had been killed.*"

Oh, no. "Everyone?"

"*I found none alive.*"

"Tell me—was there a boy on board? A young boy. He would have resembled me, but—"

"*I did not look that closely*," the dragon said. "*They were dead men, of no interest to me.*"   The huge claw suddenly pulled away, but it was replaced a moment later by the dragon's face, huge and terrible. Its interlocking scales glimmered in the moonlight like a series of small, black mirrors; its eyes, deep and smoky, glowed like glass orbs full of molten stone. Its snout was blunt and broad, not unlike that of the water lizards that frequented the coastal waters near Ponn's village, though on the dragon it looked capable of swallowing a man whole. A scarlet beard of fleshy tentacles surrounded the jaws, whiskery, faintly luminous, each as thick as his finger. They wriggled and shook when the creature spoke. "*So tell me, man, before you die: What reward did these men offer to persuade you to bring them to our islands?*"

"Reward?" Despite his predicament, he had to give a bitter laugh.

"They offered no reward, for they knew I would not bring them here for any price. Instead, they took my daughter, and told me they would kill her if I failed to help them. I did as they said, and instead of returning my little girl, they left me here to die."

The dragon said nothing; it just looked at him. Ponn waited to be eaten or incinerated or disemboweled, but instead of killing him, the creature pulled back, its reptilian visage unreadable. Then it scuttled up the side of the volcano, vanishing into the darkness above.

Where was it going? Had it decided to spare him? Ponn moved away from the slope, peering at the sky, looking for some sign of the dragon. Nothing.

Now that his immediate peril was over, Ponn had a moment to consider what the beast had told him about the sailors. All murdered? That went some way toward explaining why Gelt had sailed with a skeleton crew; he had surely been planning from the start to slaughter them, and would not have wanted to risk their overpowering his henchmen. He crept to the edge of the cliff, staring in the direction of the lagoon, though of course he could see nothing; the gathering clouds had blotted out the moon and stars like a blanket drawn over the islands.

What about Pord? Had he been on the ship? Had they found him and killed him as well? He contemplated this, and decided it was unlikely that the boy had stowed away. From what he had seen back at the cove, Gelt's men had been working on the boat for several days, creating space in the hold for the eagles and whatever else they had brought with them. They would have caught Pord if he'd tried to sneak onto the ship.

And if they'd caught him? What then? Wouldn't Gelt have killed him, disposed of the body, and cheerfully lied about it in response to Ponn's inquiry?

But no. If they had killed Pord, they would have told him about it before abandoning him here. It had amused Gelt to leave Ponn alive, stranded on the island, knowing that they still had his daughter; how much more amusing, then, to also leave him with the knowledge that his boy bobbed in the waves or lay on the beach, food for crabs?

Suddenly Ponn felt a hand on his shoulder. With a surprised yelp, he lost his balance and nearly fell off the cliff; but a powerful grip closed around his wrist and pulled him back from the precipice, spinning him around, putting him face to face with a woman. She had a mane of hair that looked black in the moonlight, and eyes that seemed to flicker in the darkness. Her mouth was broad, her chin and lips protruding slightly; he got the impression that if she opened her jaws wide enough, she could bite off his head. A shimmering garment clung to her body like a tightly fitted layer of iridescent scales, glittering in what feeble moonlight penetrated the clouds.

Was this the dragon? He had heard that they could assume human form, but had always believed this to be one of many myths about the creatures. Before he could ask, she said: "They like to strike against young ones." Her voice, softly menacing, retained some of the sibilance it had evidenced in her serpentine form. "They butchered my hatchlings. Your daughter was probably dead before you even knew she was gone."

He refused to accept it. "No."

"Believe what you must." The dragon released her grip; he pulled his hand away, rubbing his wrist. He would have a bruise. "So tell me. Who were they? How many? Where did they come from? Where did they go?"

"There were four in the main group," Ponn said. "Their leader was a man named Gelt. I don't know where they came from, they didn't say and they wore no colors that I recognized. But they flew to the north."

"That means nothing. If the range of their eagles is as limited as you believe, they would *have* to fly to the north."

"Yes," Ponn said. "Yes, you're right, of course."

"My name is T'Sian," she said. "What are you called?"

"Pyodor Ponn."

"Well, Pyodor Ponn, will you remember this Gelt and his men if you see them again?"

He nodded; then, thinking she might not understand the gesture, said, "Yes, I would."

"Would you like to be revenged on him for what he has done to you, to your child?"

"Of course."

"Good." Her smoldering eyes were bright, her broad mouth smiling; at least, it looked like a smile, but then, so did the jaws of the great reptiles that prowled the tidal salt marshes. "You will come with me, then."

"Come ... with you?"

"Yes."

"But—"

She raised a forefinger, and he remembered that a short while earlier, that one digit had been as thick as his arm. "No arguments."

"Yes. I mean no. No arguments." Ponn ran a hand through his hair. "May we stop at my home and tell my family that I am all right?"

The dragon looked at him for a while, and then said: "No. Gelt believed you would never get off this island, or he would have killed you. He thinks you will die here. I want him to continue to think that."

"I will swear my family to silence. They will tell no one."

"Gelt may have spies in the area. You could be seen."

Obviously, further argument was pointless. "As you wish," Ponn said. "When will we leave, then?"

"In the morning," she said. "I have business here, and then I must rest. I have had a long journey. You will remain in this spot; do not try to escape."

"Where would I escape to?"

The dragon's mouth broke into a broad and disconcerting grin, unmistakable, this time. "Nowhere," she said.

Adaran awoke as the first rays of the sun filtered through the pine needles that surrounded him. He felt grimy and sticky; his muscles ached as a result of his uncomfortable position, wedged into the crook of the bough. He lifted the blanket and checked the girl. She was asleep, but stirred and whimpered as the cold air touched her skin.

He slipped his arm through the strap of her prison and climbed out of the tree. Going down was easier than going up; soon they were back on the ground among the gnarled, shallow roots. He set the net down gently, then crouched in front of it. The girl, fully awake now, gave him a baleful look. "I'm going to cut you free," he told her. "Don't scream, and don't run off, all right?"

She stared at him, saying nothing, giving him no idea if she understood or not; but he could hardly leave her in there until they found civilization. He took out a dagger and pantomimed cutting something with it, hoping she realized he didn't mean her; then he started sawing at the fibers of the net. It proved a good deal tougher than he expected, but he finally sliced through one of them, then another; and then the entire thing unraveled and fell to pieces.

The girl immediately jumped to her feet and ran around behind the tree in which they'd spent the night. He started to give chase, but then he realized that she was relieving herself. That sounded like a good idea; he went to a different tree and did the same.

When he returned, the girl was back, standing over the sad little pile of rope that had been her prison. She looked at him, made a face, and stomped all over the net, then picked it up and threw it. The bundle only flew a few feet, but this seemed to satisfy her; she turned her back on it and folded her arms, hugging herself.

"Are you cold?" Adaran said.

She nodded.

So, she *did* understand him, but had elected not to respond until he set her free. He supposed that was reasonable; until now, he had probably seemed like just another kidnapper.

"I can make something to keep you warm." He took his dagger and sliced a square of cloth from the blanket; a pair of cross-cuts created an opening for her head. He handed it to her and she slipped it on, wearing it like a small, thin poncho. It wasn't much, but it would help. "Is that better?"

She nodded.

"Good. Now, listen. We're lost in the mountains. I'm going to try to find our way out, but there are animals up here that would eat a little girl, and the men who put you in that cage are going to be searching for us. You must stay near me so that nothing bad happens to you. All right?"

She nodded again; for all he knew she just nodded at everything. Perhaps it would be better if he actually held onto her. He approached, intending to take her hand, but instead she darted around behind him. He turned around and she scurried to his back side again, giggling; apparently this was some sort of game. He pivoted, but was too slow, and only saw one of the girl's feet as she disappeared again.

Not only was this a waste of time; it was also vaguely embarrassing.

A professional thief and burglar, unable to catch a small child? What would Redshen say?   Nothing, of course; she would be too busy rolling on the ground in a fit of laughter.

Suddenly the girl grabbed his cloak and started to pull; in seconds she had climbed to his shoulders, where she plopped down, legs dangling down his chest, arms around his neck.

"So you'll be riding up there, then," Adaran said.

She giggled and kicked her feet. Well, at least she didn't appear likely to run off. He dipped into his supply of stolen rations and found a few pieces of jerky; he handed one up to his passenger, took one for himself, and put the rest back in his pocket. Chewing the food, he started walking, moving in the opposite direction from the way they had been running the night before.

The girl pulled on his ear and then pointed at the pocket where he had put the food. He took out another small piece. "Don't eat too much," he said. "This has to last a while." He handed it to her and she gobbled it down, then pointed at his pocket again. Had Dosen's men even bothered to feed her? He reached into a different pocket, pulled out a piece of bread, and gave that to her instead. She took it eagerly, dropping crumbs down the back of his neck as she chewed.

They continued along the slope, moving steadily downward, though he wasn't certain where this route would lead. Probably to another cliff. The ground began to grow rockier, the trees thinner; they seemed to be approaching a clearing. He slowed, moving from tree to tree, wary of detection from the air.

Suddenly he heard a screech, the cry of a very large bird. One of Dunshandrin's eagles. He froze, trying to figure out where the sound had come from. Ahead? Behind? He couldn't tell; the mountains created confusing echoes, the trees blocked his view of the sky. He stayed motionless until, with much fluttering of wings, one of the avians landed in the clearing that Adaran had been approaching. They had been tracking him much more closely than he had suspected. He flattened himself against a tree, scarcely remembering to breath. Had he been spotted? Would other avians be landing, their riders fanning out into the woods to hunt him down?

"Stupid bird." That was Dosen's voice. Adaran peered around the trunk and watched as the man dismounted clumsily and began inspecting his mount; evidently it was not performing to his satisfaction. "What's the matter with you?"

Adaran slowly, silently, reached up and lifted the girl off his shoulders. He placed her on the ground and put his finger to his lips. "Shh," he whispered.

She nodded, as usual. Hoping she would be quiet, Adaran drew a throwing knife and moved closer to the edge of the clearing, beginning a slow, silent circuit. Dosen, meanwhile, had given up inspecting the bird and was now pissing on the cracked stump of an ancient tree. He continued to mutter complaints about his mount, the forsaken nature of the mountains, his general lot in life. Adaran felt little sympathy for the man; as far as he was concerned, anyone not being hunted through the wilderness by a gang of eagle-riding killers was faring better than himself.

When Adaran had reached a point where he had a clear shot, he stepped out of the trees. Dosen still hadn't noticed him, so he stole across the clearing, drawing closer but staying well out of sword reach. The eagle watched him with those gleaming eyes, tracking his movements but making no sounds.

He said: "Dosen."

The steward looked at him; his eyes widened in shock.

Adaran threw the knife. It flashed across the clearing and sank into Dosen's breast, burying itself to the hilt. Dosen looked down at the jiggling handle, then at Adaran; then he toppled over in an unmoving heap.

Adaran closed the remaining distance between them. Nudging the man with his foot, he said: "Surprise does make a difference, doesn't it, Dosen?"

No response, of course; Dosen wore light leather armor, little better than parchment against Adaran's sharpened blade. He knelt and retrieved the knife, wiped it on Dosen's clothes, returned it to its sheath. As he stood, he saw that the girl had entered the clearing and was toddling toward him. He motioned for her to stay back from the eagle, fearing it would snatch her up as a morsel; she gave it a wide berth, coming to stand beside him. If the sight of a dead body disturbed her, she gave no sign. "Stay here," he told her, drawing a line in front of her; the gesture was obviously futile, given that she had ignored all his earlier instructions, but he could at least pretend to be in control of the situation.

He went to the great bird, examining its reins and harness, which looked similar to the bridle of a horse. The one he had ridden had not been so equipped; it had merely followed the others, attached by a tether. He moved on to the broad saddle that rested between the creature's wings. A series of straps ran down the side to hold the rider's legs in place; side pouches held crossbow bolts and poorly-balanced throwing knives, as well as a small amount of food and water. A mysterious tube made of wood drew his attention; it had curved, polished glass at each end, one side large, the other small. Adaran picked it up and looked through the large end; it made the cliff wall appear to be miles away. He lowered the device and made sure that the mountain hadn't actually moved, then dropped the thing on the ground. Whatever it was, its ability to make things look farther away than they really were did not seem useful. Another odd device was affixed to the front of the saddle; it was a small glass dome partially filled with liquid. Inside, some sort of needle floated on a bit of wood, pointing off to the right. Perhaps it was trying to tell him they should go that way.

The girl appeared at his side, reaching up to try to pet the eagle's feathers. She had, of course, disregarded his injunction to stay put. He picked her up and placed her on the saddle. The straps didn't come close to holding her short legs, and he would be too busy trying to fly the creature to maintain a solid grip on her. He lifted her down again, then cleared a space in one of the saddlebags. "What do you think?" he said, picking her up and showing it to her. "Can you fit in there?"

She gave him a withering look.

"Sorry," he said, "I can't think of anything better." He lowered her into the saddlebag, then closed the flap and buckled it into place. A moment later her head pushed through the gap between the side and the cover, followed by her arm. He took her little hand and pushed it back inside. "We're going to fly away. You have to stay in there." He made a flapping motion with his hands and then pointed at the sky. "Fly. Away from the mountains." He pointed at the bag. "Stay in there."

She rolled her eyes; but at least she had stopped squirming. Adaran put his foot in the lowest strap of the saddle and climbed into position. He figured out how to buckle himself in, then took hold of the reins. Much as he had hated flying, it was their best chance of getting out of the wilderness alive.

First, though, he had to get them into the air. He tried to remember what Redshen had told him, what she had observed, but he'd never expected to have to use the information himself and hadn't paid particularly close attention. He gathered up the reins and gave them a tug; the bird made faint clicking noises deep in its throat, but it didn't move. He pulled again and the thing stood up, screeching a little, sounding petulant.

"Fly away," Adaran said. He gave the reins a little slap. "Fly away, stupid bird."

It squawked, but it didn't do anything.

"Fly away!" he said. He yanked the reins hard. Annoyed, the eagle shook its entire body; Adaran squeezed his legs reflexively, afraid that he would fall off. The bird spread its wings and started running along the clearing toward the edge of the cliff; at the precipice it launched itself into the air, first dropping sharply, then catching the wind and leveling out, leaving Adaran's stomach somewhere far behind as they soared away from the cliff, sweeping over the trees far below, rising high above the ridge.

Adaran thought he might throw up.

From the saddlebag, he could hear the little girl laughing.

Pyodor Ponn awoke to the rumble of thunder; before he even sat up, the sky let loose with a blast of wind and rain that threatened to blow him off the narrow ledge. He hauled himself to his feet, bracing himself against the rough stone wall, moving south along the edge of the volcano, hoping to put it between himself and the storm; but the wind seemed to follow where he went, buffeting him first from one direction, then another, the intensity increasing rapidly.

This was shaping up to be a hurricane rather than some mere cloudburst; he needed to find real shelter, something better than a nook beneath a ledge. The only thing he could think of was the lava tube, whence the dragon had forbidden him. He edged along the narrow path, both hands gripping the jagged stone, resisting the force of the gale. By the time he reached the tunnel and ducked into it, his arms and legs ached. He collapsed on the floor just inside the entrance, exhausted, catching his breath. At length he sat up and took stock of his surroundings. It wasn't as dark in here as he had expected; a faint orange glow emanated from the depths of the lava tube, illuminating the jagged, scratchy walls with deep, weird shadows. Was it magma?

A blast of wind blew up the tunnel, spattering Ponn with rain. He moved deeper into the mountain, noticing odd veins of crystal running through the walls, none thicker than his thumb; these proved to be the source of the luminescence, lit from within by the color of a sunset. He traced one with his finger, and found it warm to the touch. His skin tingled lightly at the point of contact.

Intrigued, he continued farther into the tunnel. The veins of crystal thickened; the air grew dense, a metallic tang riddling the pervasive stink of sulfur. Before long he emerged into a huge, open chamber, a gigantic bubble beneath the crust of the mountain. A jagged hole in the curving wall showed the dark, wild clouds, admitted driving rain that hissed and fizzled against the hot stones, filling the room with thin steam. The reddish-orange crystal that illuminated the tunnel proved ubiquitous here, growing in spiny clumps and many-faceted spires. A large formation jutted out of the wall just to his right; glittering shards littered the floor around it. Ponn saw a metal pick embedded in it, the shaft broken off just below the head. Dragons certainly had no need for such tools, so this must belong to Gelt; but what could he have wanted with the glowing crystals?

Suddenly a massive shadow came at him, bearing down on him like a ship on a swimmer. Ponn bolted for the tunnel, but a rush of brilliant orange flame cut him off, the heat driving him back toward the crystals.

From somewhere in the mist, the dragon said: *"What are you doing here, man?"*

"I was trying to escape the storm."

"You do not belong in here. This place is for the dragons." He heard her scales sliding across the stone floor as she approached, stopping only a few yards away from him, her hot breath washing over him with a smell like molten metal. *"I should kill you for intruding."*

Ponn opened his mouth, but found he had nothing to say and closed it again.

T'Sian tilted her head to the side, looking past him now. Her tail flicked out of the fog and touched the broken shaft of the pick. "*See what they did, man? They took the crystals.*"

"Yes."

"*Tell me why your kind would seek our stones.*"

"I don't know."

The slender tip of her tail curled around the shaft and deftly plucked it free of the formation. She lowered it down in front of him; after a moment he realized that she wanted him to take it, and so he did. "*Look at the tool, man,*" she said. "*Does it bear any symbols that you recognize?*"

"No," he said, examining it in the ruddy glow. "There's no craftsman's mark, if that's what you mean." Then, impetuously: "You asked my name, before, and I gave it to you. Why do you not use it?"

"*Because I do not remember it.*"

"My name is Pyodor Ponn. It's not difficult."

"*The names of men are of little importance to me,*" the dragon said, "e*xcept for this Gelt, who has earned my revenge.*" Her massive head retreated into the steam, sending whorls of vapor swirling around in front of Ponn. Her voice echoed from the mist. "*You may stay here, and shelter from the storm. Be thankful I am the only dragon present at this time; others would not be so merciful.*"

His knees suddenly turned to water and he collapsed where he had stood, shivering despite the warmth of the chamber.

Outside, the storm howled like a pack of lost and lonely wolves.

6

As they spiraled up and away from the mountainside, Adaran breathed through his clenched teeth and managed to keep his gorge down. The eagle kept climbing, climbing, climbing, leaving the earth far below; Adaran finally realized that he was still squeezing with his knees and, remembering now what Redshen had told him, eased up on the pressure. The bird leveled off, its broad wings stroking through the air, circling above the ridge.

He took a moment to get his bearings. Below and to the west, he could see Dosen's camp; details were difficult to make out from this distance, but it appeared that they were dismantling the tents, packing up supplies, getting ready to depart. They would most likely mount their eagles and head due east for the flight back to Dunshandrin.

The wise thing, then, would be for him to take his own mount in a different direction; but to the west and south, massive summits towered over the lower peaks where Dosen had set up his base. Given Dosen's apparently involuntary landing in the clearing, it seemed unlikely that the beast would take them safely over the mountains to Enshenneah. He could head southeast, though, skirting the peaks, then turn north at the central arm of the Oronj Mountains, making for the lakeside city of Achengate. He had contacts there; they could help him get rid of the eagle without attracting too much attention. Then he would find an orphanage or cloister to take the child, and make his way across Lake Achenar, to Madroval, and lie low until Dunshandrin forgot about him.

He tugged the left side of the reins and guided the eagle toward the

93

Salt Flats.   As it wheeled in the icy air, he glanced down at the saddlebag, making sure the girl had not fallen out.   The flap was closed, but the bulge showed him she was still inside.   She had probably withdrawn to escape the chill.   Shivering, Adaran wished he could do the same, just crawl into a nice, warm pocket and sleep for a few days.

Ha.   No chance of that.   He spotted dark shapes skimming the treetops, heading this way, two from the direction of the camp and another from the southeast, the direction he had intended to flee. The missing avians.   He had to assume they had spotted him and were coming to intercept him.

Adaran pulled on the reins and his mount stopped; they hung motionless, hovering, the only sound the whistle of the wind and the occasional beat of the creature's wings.   He hastily patted himself down, trying to remember what weaponry remained at his disposal. A throwing knife and two stabbing daggers, not balanced for hurling. The eagle carried a crossbow and a score of quarrels, but he had never used one and didn't know if he could even load the thing, let alone hit a moving target; and Dosen's putative hurling blades were about as aerodynamic as tent stakes, and nearly as sharp.   Certainly he wouldn't be able to take down all three enemy riders before being shot himself.

The only option was to run and, if possible, hide.   On the ground he would have melted into the shadows; but where could he find concealment here, in mid-air?   He looked left, looked right.   He supposed he could make for the mountains, try to duck into a valley, but then he would effectively be trapped.   They would see where he had gone, and patrol the area until they found him.

Then he looked up.

A layer of thick, low clouds roiled overhead.   They would not be able to see him in there; he would be as blind as they, of course, but given the circumstances theirs would be the greater handicap.   He squeezed with his legs and the eagle began to beat its powerful wings, climbing toward the leaden underbelly of the sky.   It looked sturdy as any ceiling made of lath and plaster, stretching in every direction like a lid over the world.   Far to the southeast, the clouds thickened into an ominous dark sludge; Adaran realized that he was entering the leading edge of what looked like a powerful storm.   He would have to keep that in mind, and get them on the ground and under shelter before the bad weather struck.

They entered the lower layer of clouds; chill vapor closed around them, leaching the warmth from his body like a dense winter fog. He reduced the pressure from his legs and the eagle stopped climbing, leaving them momentarily motionless, hanging in the frigid mist.

Now what?

Well, they couldn't stay here; the other riders must have seen where they went into the clouds, and they would be heading for that spot. He gave the beast a little kick and it began flying. Moisture accumulated in the pockets of the saddle, in the great bird's feathers, in the creases of Adaran's cloak; it dripped from his hair, tracing wet tracks down his face. They passed through bands of fine, icy rain that seemed to be falling up instead of down. The frigid air stung Adaran's exposed hands. He looked down at the saddlebag again; the girl remained tucked inside, protected from the worst of the cold.

Eventually, Adaran decided they had gone far enough; his teeth had begun to chatter, his entire body shook from the cold and the damp. He tried to figure out how to tell the eagle to descend. Squeezing with his knees had made it climb, so he tried applying pressure from his ankles instead. It worked; the creature was only too happy to head for the ground, folding its wings and plunging headlong toward the earth like a hawk diving for a rabbit. Adaran frantically jerked up on the reins and the thing slowed its heart-stopping descent.

They emerged from the clouds over the vast, stinging wasteland that was the Salt Flats. It looked like they had been heading roughly north instead of southeast. He searched the sky for Dosen's men, but saw nothing; perhaps they had chased him into the clouds and were still up there, or maybe they had given up and returned to the camp. How badly did they want to capture him?

While scanning the horizon, he spotted what looked like a fortified settlement to the east. It was the only visible hint of civilization, so he turned them that way. The eagle appeared to have a different agenda, however, taking them lower and lower despite Adaran's efforts to get it to fly higher. It was looking for a place to land, he thought.

"No," Adaran said, pulling on the reins, squeezing with his knees.

"No, don't land! Stupid bird!" The eagle ignored him and they touched down roughly, kicking up a large cloud of salt dust. The creature hopped a few paces and then stopped, settling down onto its legs like a watchful hen upon its nest.

Adaran unbuckled himself and tried to dismount, but fell off instead, landing on his back in the dirt. He got up, brushed himself off, and fumbled the saddlebag open, finding himself facing a baleful look from his young passenger. "Don't give me that," he said as he lifted her out. "At least we're not in the mountains anymore."

The wind gusted suddenly, engulfing them in a whorl of stinging dust; it died down as quickly as it had started, but the thickening clouds promised more to come. He took the bird's reins and tugged at them, but the creature resisted; he had to dig in and begin walking backwards in order to pull it to its feet. It made an unhappy noise in its throat. "It's your own fault," he said. "You're the one who wanted to land." This earned him another look from the child, this one saying that he clearly was out of his mind.

Well, maybe so.

But at least he had gotten away.

The day after Tolaria's first visit from the sorcerer, he returned, this time accompanying Torrant and Tomari. The twins entered first, with Orioke walking behind. He still wore the same threadbare cloak, though his scruffy beard had been trimmed, his hair groomed and coiffed. He remained near the door, looking smug and inscrutable, as the princes approached her.

"Good evening, Tolaria," one of them said.

"You are looking lovely as always," the other added. That would be Torrant, courtly and charming, hoping to seduce her. She might play along, try to find an opportunity to escape, if only she had the ability to tell lies; but a compulsion to always answer questions truthfully seemed to fatally compromise one's feminine wiles.

Orioke yawned and inspected his fingernails, looking bored with such pleasantries. Something occurred to her then and she said: "You two *are* aware that there is someone else in the room with us?"

The twins exchanged a glance, looked toward Orioke, then turned back to her. "Yes, of course," Torrant said. "We brought him with us." He took her hand, squeezed her wrist, felt her forehead with his fingers. "Are you feeling all right?"

"I'm perfectly healthy," she said, pulling away from him.

"Good," Tomari said. "We do want you to be content."

"*Content?* I said nothing about being content. If that is your desire, release me. Then I will be content."

"We cannot do that. You are too important to our plan."

"Your mad scheming could hardly be called a plan."

Tomari stiffened; she might have gone too far this time, goading him into actually striking her, but Torrant caught his brother's shoulder and restrained him. "Really, Tolaria, you must mind your tongue," he said. "We are not accustomed to being spoken to by our subjects in such a manner."

"I am not your subject."

"No," Orioke said. "You are a weapon." He moved up between the princes, sliding between them like a bookmark between the pages. "It is time you were used to your full potential."

"I wasn't aware that I had fallen short in that regard."

He smiled inscrutably, like a child with a secret. "The princes are concerned with happenings in the Oronj Mountains. They would like to know if the footpad has been recaptured yet."

"Do you expect me to spout fortunes on command, like a parlor amusement? You are asking for clairvoyance, not prophecy, and in any event I can't answer without my potions." She jerked her thumb at the twins. "They know that as well as you do."

"*Do* we know that?"

"Of course we do. Without the vapors, I am no more capable of farseeing than you are."

"So the masters of Flaurent would have us believe," Orioke said. "But what if I told you I could invoke your innate abilities without need of weeds and powders? What would you say then?"

"I would say you were as mad as your employers."

Torrant stifled a chuckle.

"Ah. But I am *not* mad, my sweet. Observe." He raised his hands over his head in a dramatic sweep, throwing his cloak up; it settled slowly over his outstretched arms, like black wings. He began muttering, his voice low and quick, the words unintelligible.

She became aware of a buzzing noise around her, like an approaching swarm of bees; but if the others heard it they gave no sign. It grew louder and louder until it became deafening, shutting out all other sound. Then, suddenly, it stopped, leaving her in a zone of utter silence, surrounded by the faded shadows of events long past, the pallid outlines of things yet to be. She felt her legs sag and she would have fallen to the floor, but Torrant caught her and lowered her onto the bed. "You'd better not have harmed her, wizard," he said.

"Harmed her?" Orioke said. "I am saddened that you have so little confidence in me. Tolaria, have I harmed you?"

"No."

"There, you see? You know she must answer truthfully. Now, ask her what you will."

A moment passed, or a century; in her present state, it was all the same to her. Then Tomari said: "Tolaria, has the man Adaran been captured yet?"

She saw an image, a tall, thin, weary man carrying a small brown girl on his shoulders, dragging a large, reluctant bird by taut leather reins. "No."

"Where is he?"

She did not answer.

"Tolaria, where is Adaran now?" Torrant asked.

She felt a stinging wind blow through the room, tasted salt dust on her lips; she saw a small settlement, high walls that helped to block the clouds of dust, deep deep wells to draw water from far below the cracked, parched, barren land. This place she knew well. "In the Salt Flats," she said, "near to Flaurent."

"Flaurent?" Torrant said. "How did he make it that far?"

"Perhaps he stole one of the eagles you entrusted to Dosen," Orioke said. "He *is* an accomplished thief, after all."

"Ask her, ask her," Tomari said.

"Tolaria, how did Adaran reach Flaurent?"

"He has not reached it yet."

"Tolaria, how did he get near to Flaurent?"

"He rode a giant bird."

"Where did he get the bird, Tolaria?"

"He slew the well-fed man and took his mount."

"Well-fed man? That can only be Dosen," Torrant said. "The fool got himself killed and let the thief escape."

"I told you we should have sent Gelt to the mountains."

"That would have been difficult, as Gelt was busy in Enshenneah at the time, and has not returned even yet."

"Are my lieges done bickering?" Orioke said. "If so, I would break Tolaria's trance. Maintaining it is a bit … draining, for both of us."

"You will maintain her trance as long as necessary," Tomari snapped. "You arrogated this power over her, and we expect you to use it as we see fit."

"Of course, my lord," Orioke said. "But do you not have all the information you need? You know Adaran's location; you may send a delegation to Flaurent and negotiate for him to be remanded to your custody."

Tomari snorted. "A delegation? Negotiate? Why not just send a few armed men to take him?"

"I doubt you would want to spare the necessary force."

"It is a school, not a fortress."

"Wrong," Torrant said. "It *is* a fortress, guarded by creatures of the Salt Flats, strong and tireless, able to travel like dust along the wind."

"You speak of the withered ones," Orioke said. "But there is another guardian, a powerful spirit named Deliban, which dwells beneath and has power over the earth."

"I have no knowledge of such an entity," Torrant said.

"I would not expect you to. It is bound to the service of the college and spends all its time underground, digging ever deeper wells, shoring up the ramparts, bringing salt to the surface for shipment to Achengate. The headmistress would only bring Deliban to bear in a time of dire threat."

After a moment, Tomari said: "We must have this creature!"

"It is bound to Flaurent, as I mentioned."

"What is bound may be broken," Tomari said. "You are a wizard. Can your magic not claim power over Deliban?"

"I can try, my lord, but the binding to Flaurent is very old." Then: "Actually, that may work in our favor, if the spell has been allowed to weaken; and we do have access to a crucial piece of information. Tolaria, what is Deliban's one, true name, the name that was used to bind it to Flaurent?"

And, because she could not stop herself, she told him.

* * *

Some time later, Tolaria opened her eyes to find Tomari and Torrant sitting silently at the foot of her bed, watching her. The wizard was no longer present, as far as she could tell.

"Look, Torrant," Tomari said. "She is awake."

She sat up, her head throbbing painfully, the way it used to when she was a novice, new to Flaurent and unaccustomed to the effects of the vapors.

"Yes, I'm awake," she said. "I wish I weren't."

"Do you still think Orioke mad?" Torrant said.

"I don't know if he's mad or not. He was not lying about his power." She leaned forward, massaging her temples with her fingertips.

"You seem to be in some pain. Did the wizard hurt you?"

"I have a headache, probably as a side effect of the way he evoked my trance. It will pass."

"Perhaps we can make you feel better." Torrant moved around behind her, began to massage her shoulders. She loathed him, but he knew what he was doing; his clever fingers expertly kneaded her muscles. She closed her eyes and allowed herself to enjoy it, just a little. "I think we should move you out of the tower," he said, one of his hands moving to the base of her neck, the other to the small of her back. "You should be closer to us. All this climbing up and down the stairs has grown tiresome."

"Yes," Tomari said, as he removed her slippers and began rubbing her feet. He took less care than his brother did. "Most tiresome."

"We are not so odious as you think." Torrant's hand ventured lower. "You may come to enjoy our company."

It was time to end this. She pulled her feet out of Tomari's grip, stood and moved away from the bed. Torrant had somehow managed to work her shirt loose; she hastily rearranged it, covering herself.

Tomari stood as well, his face flushed, his hands formed into fists. Through his tunic, she could see his arousal, fading as she watched. "You are a fool. Any woman should be pleased to receive our attentions." He whirled and stormed out of the room.

Torrant merely looked at her, his expression amused. "You have left him frustrated again. No doubt I will find some hetaera in his chambers tomorrow morning."

"The ladies of your court may let you and your brother take such liberties, but I am not one them."

"You will be," he said.

The storm lashed the island for hours, lasting until morning before moving off to the west, leaving behind clear skies and the impending dawn. Through the gaping hole in the mountain, Ponn could see the first streaks of the rising sun seeping through the purplish remnants of night. The storm would likely be departing his village soon; it would have begun lashing the shore long before the rain had stopped here. He hoped the roof of his inn had held against the wind, that his family had stayed warm and safe and dry.

"*Man.*"

He looked across the cavern as T'Sian slipped off the bulging dome of rock that she had used as bedding for the night. Wisps of steam rose from tiny cracks in the stone; if he were to cross the cavern and touch it with his bare hand, his flesh would no doubt burn and blister. "*It is time to go.*"

"I told you," he said. "My name is Pyodor Ponn, or simply Ponn. My name is not *man.*"

She moved across the whorled obsidian floor toward him; her scales on the stone sounded like a group of soldiers dragging their fallen comrades on their shields. "*Very well, Pyodor Ponn. But it is still time to go.*"

He eyed her serpentine form. "Should I climb on your back?"

"*I will carry you. I am not a horse to be ridden.*"

She reached out with an iron-shod forelimb; her talon closed around his body, each finger as thick as his arm. Now he knew how the mouse felt when the hawk snatched it. She gripped him so tightly that he cried out, feeling the breath being crushed out of his body. "Too hard!" he gasped.

The dragon loosened her grip. "*You creatures are so fragile,*" she said. "*Is that better?*"

"Yes. Thank you."

Moving easily on her three free legs, the dragon walked to the hole in the mountainside, climbed to the edge, and then leapt outward. For a dizzying moment they hung in the air; then they plunged toward the jumbled lava plain far below. T'Sian's wings snapped open as the black rock rushed to meet them. The thin, tough membranes caught the wind, billowing like the canvas of a great ship. She leveled off and they streaked across the island, scant yards above the rock; then she banked to the right, following the curve of the mountain, bringing them over the sea. In a tight, dizzying circle, they were over land again, rising on the warm air of the volcano, climbing into the lightening sky.

Ponn could see the lagoon far below, clogged by a mass of splintered wood and ghost-white canvas, rising and falling with the swells. T'Sian had destroyed his ship, and claimed to have have found none alive on board; if Pord had stowed away on the vessel, his body would be down there among the boards, bobbing lifeless and battered.

Then the cove vanished from his sight as they turned to the north. The sea receded beneath his dangling feet, waves becoming foamy streaks, then disappearing into a rippled sheet of grey-green water. He found himself clutching at the warm, pebbly scales of the dragon's fingers, fear of falling leading the rodent to grip the raptor. The wind pilfered the warmth from his body though his still-damp clothing; soon he was shivering with the chill. He drew up his legs, trying to make himself smaller, to increase contact with the dragon's body.

They stopped climbing once they reached the lower level of clouds, turning toward the northeast. He felt a surge of momentum, like a strong gust of wind in the sails, with every beat of the dragon's great wings. In the distance, moving over the low mountains that separated eastern Enshenneah from Barbareth, he saw the dark, swirling edge of the storm that had buffeted the island. The dragon kept well clear of it, staying parallel to the coast. Ponn could see high surf pummeling the black sand beaches near his home, the waves little more than soft white lines of foam from this height; and then the beaches gradually gave way to rocky shores, which grew into the craggy toes of the mist-shrouded Oronj Mountains, the high peaks lost in haze and storm and distance.

Suddenly their forward motion stopped, as abruptly as if they'd smashed into a wall. He felt the downdraft from her wings; each thrust felt sufficient to knock over a row of small, poorly-built houses. She extended her long neck, lifted her claw, the two motions bringing her head down to within a few feet of Ponn's. "*Man!*" she said. "*I see one of your cities along the coast ahead. What is it called?*"

He peered into the distance, but couldn't perceive the city; as far as he could tell the coastline went on forever, miles and miles of cliffs and rockfalls gradually blurring into the green plains of Barbareth. "It must be Dyvversant," he answered, shouting to be heard over the wind. "That's the only large city in this region. Do you see a harbor?"

She turned to look; the glowing orbs of her eyes narrowed. "*Yes. A large one. Would the men who brought you to the island have stopped there?*"

"Very likely. Outside Enshenneah, it would be the nearest town of any size where they could rest and resupply."

"*Then we will stop there as well.*"

She lowered him again, pulled in her wings, and fell into a terrifying dive; as before, she leveled out, converting the downward momentum into forward speed. Before long, Ponn could make out the city she had seen, little more than a brown smear on the verdant coastal plain of southern Barbareth. It was certainly Dyvversant; he had never seen it from above before, but he recognized the contours of the bay, the shape of the tor that loomed over it to the west.

As they approached, the dragon began descending toward the winding canyons south of the city, where runoff from the mountains had carved a labyrinth of channels great and small. Ponn could see the entire network of gullies and ravines; many were dry this late in the season, but some still contained ribbons of cold, grey water. They landed in one of the dry ones, a broad, shallow ravine with a sandy floor overgrown by clumps of tall grass and grey weeds. T'Sian beat her wings rapidly as they touched down, kicking up an enormous cloud of dust. She released Ponn roughly, as if she were casting dice; he stumbled away, trying to avoid being stepped on.

T'Sian said: "*Wait here.*" She moved up the canyon, around a bend, out of sight. Ponn, relieved to be back on the ground and having no intention of disobeying another of the dragon's orders, found a large, smooth rock and sat. Before long, she returned, walking upon human legs. Her scales, reduced to the form of a clinging garment, glittered in the sunlight; her mane of tawny hair spilled over her shoulders and reached well down her back. She looked like a striking, voluptuous woman, for the most part, but she was hardly inconspicuous. She came up to him him and said, "We will walk from here."

He nodded, open-mouthed, trying to formulate a question.

"Do you mean to speak, or merely to stare?"

"I apologize," he said. "The change in your appearance confounds me."

"It is meant to."

"Tell me, what are your plans once we reach Dyvversant?"

"Plans?"

"I mean, what are we to do? Do you intend to walk into the nearest building and demand information?"

"Yes."

"Oh." Of course the dragon would prefer a direct approach. "The thing is, quite a bit of black market shipping comes and goes through this town. If you start asking questions in the wrong places, you are likely to end up with your throat cut."

"You mean I will be murdered?" T'Sian smiled. "Unlikely."

"Perhaps you need not fear, but I am not so mighty, and have no desire to be killed in an alley. In any event, approaching people too directly won't get you any information, even if you aren't worried about your own safety."

"If I terrify them enough, they will talk."

"They will talk, yes, but you cannot rely on what they say."

"What do you mean?"

"A frightened man will tell you whatever he thinks you want to hear in order to save his own life. He will speak whatever lies are necessary to make you go away."

"I see." She cocked her head. "Then what lies did *you* speak, Pyodor Ponn, there on the island? Do you really have a kidnapped daughter? A missing son? Do you have any children at all? Perhaps you killed all those other men yourself."

He had opened himself up to this, hadn't he? "Everything I said was the truth."

"So you would name other men liars, but exempt yourself?"

"I had no need to lie, but had it been necessary, I would have said north was south and day was night."

"How do I know you are not lying now? Perhaps I should kill you as a scoundrel, and proceed on my own."

He hardly liked the direction this conversation was taking. "Whether you believe me or not, you need my help. I'm well known in Dyvversant; I can gather information without drawing attention."

"Lies," she said mildly, inspecting her fingernails.

Had she already made up her mind? "Kill me, then, and be done with it," he said.

She looked at him, and for a moment he thought she would do it, would jam those long, sharp fingers into him and pull him apart; but then she shrugged and said: "For now, you may continue to live. I must have some guide to help me move among you men. But if you prove to be useless, or treacherous, or a liar, then I will find another. Do you understand?"

"Perfectly."

"Good. Then let us proceed."

"Wait. We'll need a story to explain who you are and why we're together. And I need something to eat; I'm starving."

"A story?"

"Just something to tell the people who know me. They will wonder why I am traveling with you."

"The people here really do know you?"

"Some."

"I do not want them to tell Gelt that you are alive."

Ponn found himself worrying about how she might enforce that. "My associates here are unlikely to spread information to the likes of Gelt. Or to anyone else, for that matter."

T'Sian eyed him with her unblinking gaze; at length she said: "Are you some sort of criminal, Pyodor Ponn?"

"No, of course not," Ponn said. "But I do some … trading in goods, without the proper paperwork."

She raised a red eyebrow. "A smuggler? You had best not deal in animal parts, man. I've killed more than one fool who came to my lair seeking dragon horns as a cure for impotence or scales to be sewn into armor."

"Wood," he said, alarmed. "I only deal in wood and spices. No animals or animal parts."

"More lies?"

"Truth. I swear it."

She glared at him for a little while, and then said: "Very well.

Every moment we delay, Gelt gets farther away. We will tell people that you and I are lovers, and—"

"We can't say that!"

"Why not?"

"Word will get back to my wife."

T'Sian made a dismissive noise. "You can explain later."

"You would have me tell her that it was all just a story concocted by a dragon so that she could get revenge on the men who killed her hatchlings?"

"Yes."

"Would *you* believe such a tale?"

"Of course I would," she said.

Adaran cinched his cloak tighter around his body, trying to keep out the constantly blowing fine-grained grit. It insinuated itself through the seams of his clothing, up his sleeves, down his collar, settling on his skin to itch and burn, its sting revealing the location of every scratch and wound he had sustained during their escape from the mountains.

The girl, in her light garment and ill-fitting poncho, must be suffering even more than he was; she had climbed down from his shoulders some time ago, and now stayed near him, using his body to shelter herself from the worst of the wind. Its intensity increased as the storm moved over the mountains to the southeast. If they didn't reach the walled city soon, they would be caught in the open, suffering the full force of the cyclone without protection from the sand and dust.

And if they *did* reach the city? What then? The Salt Flats held little to sustain any sort of genuine civilization. Existence here centered around the extraction, transportation, and sale of salt. Each mining operation was a petty kingdom; he had heard of full-blown wars between rival camps, of raiding parties and marauding bandits who waylaid merchants as they traveled in flatboats along the alkaline streams. What would the miners make of a man suddenly appearing at their gates with a child and a giant bird in tow?

He realized suddenly that his feet were wet; they had begun to cross a shallow rill, one of many that lay like drab ribbons on the surface of the salt flats. The water, originating in the fresh, clean snowpack of the surrounding mountains, became undrinkable as it flowed across the poisonous waste; he'd heard that a single draught could kill a man.

The girl knelt down, scooping up water in her cupped hands; Adaran dropped the eagle's reins and grabbed her wrists, spilling the liquid from her palms. "No," he said. "You can't drink this. Poison." She looked at him, her brow knitted in irritation. Perhaps she didn't understand what *poison* was. He pointed at the water, then clutched his throat and made a gagging noise. She seemed to comprehend that, at least; she looked at her hands, then quickly wiped them off on her poncho. Then she cried out and pointed with a chubby finger; the eagle had its beak submerged in the toxic water, drinking its fill of deadly liquid. "No!" he shouted. "Stupid bird! Stop!" The eagle blinked at him, water dripping from its mouth; it made a croaking sound and went back to drinking.

Adaran grabbed the reins and pulled the creature away from the creek; it came reluctantly, its feet dragging through the dust, squawking and fluttering its wings in annoyance. For a moment he thought it might attack them, but then it made a hiccuping sound and sat down in the dust. It blinked and chattered, evidently in some discomfort.

"Stupid bird," Adaran said. "You didn't feel well to begin with, and now look what you've done."

The girl rolled her eyes. "Bird can't talk," she said.

Suddenly a particularly fierce gust of wind staggered Adaran, nearly knocking him over. The child shrieked and hid her face; the eagle buried its head under its wing as its feathers blew and ruffled. It pulled in its legs and settled down into a hunched ball of feathers.

The squall abated, then intensified again. There was no more time; they would have to find what shelter they could. Adaran took the girl's hand and led her up against the eagle, forcing the creature's left wing away from its body, creating a space for the child and himself. The hollow was cramped, and smelled like a hen house, and soon became stiflingly hot; but at least it provided some protection from the storm. They didn't have to fear being flayed and choked by blowing sand.

Instead, they just had to worry about being buried alive.

* * *

The morning after the twins had attempted to seduce her, three servants and two guards came to move Tolaria from her prison in the tower. She protested, not caring to be any closer to the royal suite; but her wishes in the matter were, of course, ignored. Dunshandrin's sons were the masters here.

Escorted by the guards, followed by the servants who carried her meager possessions, Tolaria descended from the tower and walked through the dim, deserted corridors of the regal wing. Threadbare tapestries and faded artwork adorned the walls; drab sculptures reposed in dusty alcoves. The scene put her in mind of the subterranean storage halls of the Crosswaters, where they kept old furniture, statuary, and other disused items. This castle had obviously seen better, livelier days.

They passed by the door to Lord Dunshandrin's chamber, where she had met the twins; she wondered if they had bothered to make any further provisions for their father's care. She doubted it. The sooner he died, the sooner they would have a kingdom to divide. Now that she thought about it, she was mildly surprised that one of them hadn't murdered him by now and blamed it on the other. "May I look in on his lordship?" she asked; but the guard in front of her merely shook his head and kept walking.

They stopped in front of an ornate door just around the corner from Dunshandrin's room. The lintel was decorated with a relief of flowering vines, the door with sheaves of wheat and loaves of bread. Fertility symbols? Perhaps this had once been the Lady Dunshandrin's room; assuming that there *was* a Lady Dunshandrin, that the twins hadn't been gotten upon some scullery maid or courtesan.

The exterior of the door had been fitted with a newly-added bar to keep her in; she may have been moved out of the tower, but she was still a captive. The guard slipped the bar and gave the door a push. It swung inward without a creak, revealing a chamber twice as large as her previous prison. Light flooded through enormous glass windows along the wall opposite the door. In addition to a massive, ornately wrought bed, the room boasted enough seating for an entire retinue; she could choose to sit in a different gaudy, overstuffed chair every day for a week.

She noted heavy doors in either wall, and wondered what they led to. Were there additional rooms in her suite? She asked about them, and learned to her dismay that Torrant's chambers were on the left, Tomari's on the right. Either prince could come or go as he pleased.

The servants set her trunk down near the bed, and then withdrew. The door closed; she heard the bar slide home. Locked in again. She hesitated, then tried the door to Torrant's room. The gilt knob turned, but the door would not move. Barred or blocked from the other side. She saw no way to lock it from here. Nor could she pile furniture in front of it; it opened the other way, into the prince's room.

Feeling ill at ease, she went to the windows. The middle pane proved to be a large glass door, giving access to a wide balcony. She tried to open it, but it was chained from the outside and would not give more than a few inches. She put her palms flat against the pane and stared out at the countryside that was denied her. She could see down the hill to ramshackle Dunshandrin Town, and beyond that, the glistening waters of the small lake. A single road emerged from the northern edge of the village, crossing the river over a narrow stone bridge and then meandering up the hillside before disappearing from view behind the castle wall. She couldn't see the courtyard or the gate by which she had entered, but she had a better idea of her position within the castle, and which direction to go if she got the chance to slip away.

The yellow sun glowed bright in fair skies; but off in the distance, beyond the rolling hills and scrubby forest, dark clouds promised wind and rain in the near future. She recalled all the activity she had observed when she had arrived here just after a storm: Servants sweeping water, scraping up mud, spreading straw. They would close the doors and shutters against the storm, but after it passed they would open every aperture while they aired out the castle. A good time to escape, perhaps, if she could find a way out of this room.

She turned away, and gasped as a straw-haired slip of a girl approached. "Who are you?" Tolaria said.

"My name is Wyst."

"Why are you here?"

"I have been assigned to be your servant."

"My servant? Why do I need a servant?"

"To attend your needs."

"My only *need* is to get out of here."

The girl flushed a bit, bit her lower lip, glanced to her right, said nothing. After a moment Tolaria turned her head to see what she was looking at: Torrant, standing in the entrance to his suite, watching her with an amused expression. She hadn't heard his door open, which worried her; he could slink in during the night, stand at the foot of her bed as she slept.

"I hope you're not already trying to subvert poor Wyst into helping you escape, Tolaria," he said.

"Escape? And forgo your lavish hospitality? Why would I do such a thing?"

"I've no idea." Torrant smiled, looked at Wyst. "If you did, though, we would have to punish your attendant most severely."

The girl blanched; if she grew any paler, Tolaria thought, she was liable to disappear. "I'm sure Wyst will do her utmost to prevent my slipping away."

"I certainly hope so, for her sake. And in time, you will stop harboring such thoughts. You may even grow to like it here."

"Perhaps so," Tolaria said. "And at the same time, flowers will start to grow out of my ears and my hair will turn purple."

He laughed then, and said: "You're such a pessimist."

Tolaria sank into a chair near the window, staring at the azure sky, feeling the sun warm on her face. "Are you here to make small talk, or do you want something from me?"

"Do you dislike small talk?"

"It depends on the subject, and the speaker."

"The subject? Let us speak of Flaurent, then. Would that interest you?"

"Flaurent? What of it?"

"We have dispatched a party to deal with our escaped thief. The wizard has gone with them; we expect him to bring back something special."

"Oh? A crate of free salt, perhaps?"

"You *are* in a mood, aren't you? Fortunately Tomari is not here to be goaded. Tell me, Tolaria, do you remember anything of what you told us when you were under Orioke's influence?"

"No. Oracles usually don't remember what they say when they make predictions. Or," she added, "when they are being abused by wizards."

"You gave us the true name of some sort of elemental that resides at the school, working underground, manipulating earth and stone. Orioke is quite confident that, armed with this information, he can bind it to our service."

"Just think of all the mud huts you can raise."

"I'm more interested in what we may be able to knock down." He dragged over another chair and sat beside Tolaria; Wyst, evidently grateful to have been forgotten, melted away, returning to a distant corner and settling onto a pallet. "You were at Flaurent for many years; did you ever hear of this creature before?"

"No."

"Nor did I. Yet the wizard knew of it."

She shrugged. "Wizards know things."

"This one knows too much."

"He's your servant now," Tolaria said. "Have him give you a full accounting of everything he's ever learned."

"If only I could," Torrant said. "If only I could."

7

PONN AND T'SIAN ENTERED DYVVERSANT from the southeast, following an old trade route that came out of the Oronj Mountains. The season was late for crossing through the pass; they encountered only a single plodding caravan heading out of the city. He couldn't remember the last time he had arrived via the overland route. Why take the treacherous path through the mountains, when the sea was so much faster?

T'Sian drew interested glances from the drivers. Ponn, watching surreptitiously, spotted no one he knew among those on horseback; but some acquaintance or business partner of his could be riding in one of the enclosed wagons, peering languidly out from heavy purple curtains, eyes widening as Ponn went by in the company of this strange, striking woman.

At the outskirts of the city, Ponn took T'Sian's wrist and pulled her to the side of the road. Her skin, which looked soft and fair, felt hot and unyielding as sunbaked rock; it was like grasping a marionette made of newly-fired clay. She looked at the hand that held her, then at him; understanding the unspoken message, he released her and said: "Is it possible for you to assume a less ... impressive appearance?"

She stared at him, eyes smoldering. "What do you mean?"

"You are very ... memorable. If you wish to go unnoticed, then you might want to look more ordinary."

"I wish for *you* to go unnoticed," she said. "If my appearance distracts others from you, so much the better."

"I have friends here, connections. No matter what you look like, they will know me. They will want to see me, discuss business, buy me drinks." Then, pointedly: "They will ask me about you."

Her reptilian tongue flicked out and across her lips. "And what will you tell them, Pyodor Ponn? Will you tell them I am a dragon who stole you away from your home? Will you tell them I could burn their city to the ground if the whim took me?"

He didn't like the gleam in her eye when she said that. She would, he thought, be more than happy to carry out that threat. "No, of course not," he said.

"Perhaps you should. Perhaps they would be frightened and give you information."

"More likely they would think I had lost my wits."

"It does not matter to me if your associates think you are mad." She turned her back on him, looking at the outskirts of Dyvversant instead. "Now, Pyodor Ponn, where are we going?"

"To an inn."

"What is it called?"

"Nowhere Special."

She glanced over her shoulder. "If it is nowhere special, why are we going there?"

"That's its name."

She raised an eyebrow.

"It's something of a joke. Someone asks where you're staying, and you say *Nowhere Special*. Someone asks where you've been, and you say *Nowhere Special*. Someone—"

"Enough. Let us go. When we arrive, you will describe Gelt and his men and find out if they have been seen."

"As you wish," he said. "We can stay there for a few days while I make inquiries." He would also leave a message to be smuggled back to Plenn, but there was no reason for T'Sian to know that.

They started walking again, proceeding into the city. Unlike Astilan, the capital city far to the northeast, Dyvversant lacked an outer wall; it merely began, first with farms and granaries, then neighborhoods of small houses and shops; as one approached the downtown, the architecture became dense, buildings abutting each other, narrow dark alleyways between them. As Ponn had expected, T'Sian drew some attention.   Usually when he came to Dyvversant, he was the one who attracted the casual eye; despite its proximity to

Enshenneah, few of Ponn's countrymen wandered the streets of this city; those who did come tended to be sailors, arriving at and staying close to the harbor. Now, however, he was a mere curiosity compared to the giantess by his side.

After a passing group of young rakes assaulted her with catcalls, T'Sian glowered down at Ponn. "People are staring at me," she said, her tone suggesting this was somehow his fault.

"I told you they would."

"Those men whistled at me."

"They must have found you attractive." He supposed they were probably intoxicated; otherwise they would have noticed that despite her voluptuous shape and form-fitting garment, T'Sian was no ordinary woman, and certainly not someone to be idly propositioned. "Perhaps you would like to assume a less striking form once we reach the inn?"

"No. How much farther is it to this nowhere place?"

Ponn paused, looking around. They had entered a square, with a small grassy area separated from the surrounding streets by low split-rail fencing. The barrier did not look particularly functional; it served more as a warning not to enter the knoll than an actual impediment. Within the fenced area, a wooden gallows stood, along with stocks, a post with chains, and other devices of punishment. These held no prisoners at the moment, but the pile of burst and rotting fruits and vegetables in the sandy area beneath the stocks indicated that someone had been there recently.

"I think we need to take that road," Ponn said, indicating a wide dirt track to the right. It descended at a fair angle, lined with shops, taverns, boarding houses; in the distance he could see the ocean, glittering in the afternoon sun. A faded, hand-lettered sign at the corner said *Harbor*, with an arrow pointing toward the sea.

"You *think*? You said you knew this city, Pyodor Ponn."

"I do, but I don't normally come this way on foot."

"Are we lost?"

"No, we're not lost. This is Execution Square."

"Execution Square?"

"It's a place where criminals are put to death by hanging. They also imprison people here for minor crimes, make them stand for public humiliation, that sort of thing."

"Men come to watch other men be killed and tormented?"

"Some do, yes."

"Do you?"

"No."

She eyed the gallows, the stocks. "A dragon would never stand for this sort of treatment."

"Well, dragons don't live in cities, do they? Humans have a society, with rules; dragons have lairs."

She looked at him. "Dragons have rules as well."

"Do they?"

"The first rule is to stay away from another dragon's lair."

"That doesn't surprise me," Ponn said. "I'm quite sure the inn is this way. Come."

As she followed him toward the harbor road, she said: "The second rule is to kill any men who intrude upon your lair, or in the caves where the crystals grow."

"Well, you've broken that one, then," Ponn said. Then: "Unless you plan to kill me later?"

"Because you are assisting me," she said, "I see no reason to kill you at the moment."

Ponn wasn't sure how to take that, and fell silent; T'Sian, meanwhile, named a few more rules—one a quota of men that a dragon must eat each year, another governing how deep a dragon's hoard of gold and treasure must be—and he began to think she was making them up just to have sport with him.

The road brought them into a neighborhood that Ponn recognized. He began looking for a shortcut he knew, an alley that led to the wharf, bypassing several blocks where the road meandered like an old river. At night the alley could be dangerous, but in daylight it should be fine; and if there were any ruffians who thought to make a scene, T'Sian could certainly deal with them.

He soon spotted the street, and led her into the narrow, crooked avenue, stepping over a drunkard who lay sleeping just inside the opening. The dragon looked down at the derelict with what Ponn took to be distaste, but she made no comment. The passage wound through the spaces behind and between the buildings; it suffered from poor sanitation and worse drainage, so that they were forced to slog through muddy puddles strewn with unsavory refuse.

"Worse than a troll's warren," T'Sian muttered. Ponn wondered what she might know of trolls or their warrens, but elected not to inquire. Soon they emerged from the alley onto a shoddily cobbled street overlooking the shallow harbor. A few small merchant craft floated in the water; another sat in dry dock, undergoing repairs. It looked similar to Ponn's own boat, but if he wanted his vessel salvaged, he would have to carry it to the shipwright in a sack. That thought led him to thoughts of Pord; had his son had been hiding somewhere on board during the voyage to the volcanoes? Had he been there when Gelt's men had murdered all the sailors, when T'Sian had destroyed the ship? No way to know, now; not until he got back home, and found the boy at the inn, waiting for him. Or not.

"This place stinks of dead fish and unwashed men," T'Sian said, bringing him out of his reverie.

Did all dragons complain so much? "Well, it *is* a wharf, so there are plenty of both."

She grunted. "Are we near to this inn of yours?"

"Not far now." He led her along the tilted road, past gaudily painted bars and taverns and flophouses vying for attention from merchants and seamen. This late in the season, trade was not brisk; some of the smaller houses had already closed, and those that remained open were quiet. The lack of activity in the neighborhood reflected the dearth of ships in the harbor. They had rounded the bend of autumn, and winter was in sight up the road, threatening more storms like the one that had lashed the islands.

He stopped at the front step of the inn. Unlike the other buildings in the vicinity, it displayed no garish colors, no sign above the door, no lettering on the front shutters; after all, this was nowhere special.

Eyeing the building, T'Sian said: "This is it?"

"Yes."

"Now I see where the name comes from."

Was that a joke? "I am part owner of this inn," Ponn said. "Please don't destroy it."

"It hardly looks worth the trouble."

This fell far short of a promise, but it was probably the best he could hope for. "Also, try not do anything overtly inhuman." The dragon pulled back her lips into a grimace and flicked her serpentine tongue across her immense teeth. "Yes, exactly," he said. "Don't do anything like that." Ponn opened the door and they went into the common room. He had expected to find it quiet, but in fact it proved completely deserted. The tables all stood vacant, the chairs pushed in, like flowers closed up for the night. Where were the local rowdies? Where were the sailors between voyages?

"Your inn does a brisk business," T'Sian said. "You must be quite wealthy."

He turned to retort, but couldn't think of anything to say; being the target of sarcasm from a dragon left him flummoxed. As they moved into the room, the door to the kitchen opened and the bartender emerged. The man glanced their way and said: "The inn is closed." Then he took another look. "Pyodor Ponn?"

"Yes." Ponn crossed to the bar. "Timmeon, what's going on? Why is the inn closed?"

"Didn't you get my message?"

"Message? What message?"

"The message I sent."

"*When* did you send it?"

"Yesterday."

Ponn sighed.   "Timmeon, I could not possibly have gotten a message that you just sent yesterday."

"Then why are you here?"

"Never mind that," Ponn said, glancing at T'Sian. She stood near the door, arms folded, watching in anticipation, as if she expected Ponn to reach behind the bar and pull Gelt out. "Just tell me what's going on."

Timmeon leaned forward, reduced his voice to a whisper. "They know, Ponn."

"*Who* knows *what*, Timmeon?"

"The tax men. They know about the … the special trading. They came with soldiers. They took all the books, both sets, and they arrested Parillon, and they made everyone who was staying here leave."

"The tax men? You mean the King's tax men, from Astilan?"

"Yes. And the mayor was with them too."

"*Apperand* was with them?"

"Yes," Timmeon said. "You should have seen him, Ponn! Acting surprised, *tut-tut* this and *shocking* that and *cheating the King of his due*." He banged a big fist on the bar. "After all the meals he ate with you and Parillon."

"He's just trying to save his own skin, now that we've been found out," Ponn said. Then, to T'Sian: "We must go."

"Why?"

"Because I just walked quite obliviously through the center of town, and it's quite likely that by now the mayor knows I'm here and where I can be found. If we stay here, we'll be arrested and taken away in chains."

She curled her hands into fists. Ponn could only imagine what it might feel like to be struck by one of those rock-hard mallets. "If they try to chain *me*, they will regret it."

"No fireworks," Ponn said. "You promised."

"I made you no promises, and I said nothing about not harming foolish men who lay hands on me."

"I know, but you can't just—" He broke off as the front door opened and four soldiers, wearing the colors of King Varmot, entered the inn. Too late to flee now. He had been foolish to stand here debating with the dragon; they should have left immediately upon hearing Timmeon's news, or at least gone into the second hidden cellar, the one Apperand didn't know about. But very likely they were watching the inn and had seen him enter; they would know he was inside, and would have searched until they found him.

He watched as the soldiers spread out, forming a wall of blue and black to block the exit. With their long-handled, largely ceremonial bills held vertically in their left hands, they resembled an oddly-painted, dangerous-looking fence. If it came down to a fight, he knew, they would drop the pole arms and draw their sharp, curving swords. What would such a blade do against the dragon's scales?

The guard on the left looked Ponn over, then said: "You are the one called Pyodor Ponn? Co-owner of this inn, partner of the smuggler Parillon?"

"No, no," Ponn said. "I am merely a traveler, looking for a place to spend the night."

"A traveler, you say? How did you arrive here, then?"

Nearly everyone who came to Dyvversant arrived by ship, but if they had been shadowing him through the town they knew he had been on foot. "We walked."

"From where?"

"Enshenneah."

"Over the mountains? Just the two of you, alone, with no packs or supplies?"

"We were with a group," he said, "but we had a falling out. We stopped here and the others continued north."

The soldiers exchanged glances, then made way for Apperand to enter. "This is Pyodor Ponn, all right," the mayor said, standing behind the soldiers as if they were his personal bodyguards. "We may add lying to the King's men to his list of crimes; he tries to mislead you with this tale." He glanced at T'Sian, who stood watching the soldiers with detached interest, the way a sated snake might watch a group of mice in a field. "And who is this? Another of your conspirators?"

"No," the dragon said. "I am his lover."

"What?" Timmeon cried. "Ponn! You should be ashamed!"

Marvelous. "She's not my—"

The soldier who had spoken earlier banged the handle of his weapon loudly on the wooden floor. "Enough," he said. "The woman is not named in the warrant and we have no interest in her at this time. But you—" He tipped the bill forward so that the spear-tip pointed at Ponn's heart. "You will come with us."

It seemed to Adaran as if the storm would never end; the howling wind rose and fell like a cry of mourning, every lull followed by a renewed fury. The girl stayed huddled up against him as they were slowly covered by sand and grit, trembling with the chill, or with fear, or both. He moved her around to the other side, nestling her against the eagle's prickly feathers. Leaning up against the beast himself, he closed his eyes and waited for it to be over.

Some time later, he awoke to someone tugging on his left arm. He grumbled and looked around, but found it too dark to see. They must be completely buried now; no wonder the air tasted sour and stale.

The girl tugged on him again. "I'm awake," he said, his voice dry as old firewood. He shifted position, felt grit trickle down his neck. He couldn't hear the wind any longer; had the storm ended? He pushed up on the bird's wing, feeling resistance, as if a weight were pressing down against it.   Dust cascaded into their space, making both of them cough.

Definitely buried. He would have to dig. He moved forward and began to claw at the powder. Salt found its way into every crevice of his skin, stinging each nick and cut; it coated the inside of his throat, making him retch and spit. Before long, though, he had opened a hole to the outside, letting in fresher air and the breaking light of dawn. The storm had blown all night, creating a dune up against the great, immobile bird; fortunately they had been in the lee of the wind.

He reached back toward the girl. "Take my hand," he said. She did; he hauled her forward and pushed her out of the hole. She rolled down the slope and out of sight. He crawled after her, worming and twisting, finally pulling free. He tried to stand, but lost his footing on the shifting dust and fell on his backside in a plume of dust that made his eyes burn and water.

"Don't move."

A muffled voice, young, not yet deepened from a boy's tones to a man's. Something gleamed near his face. He blinked away his salt-induced tears and realized he was looking at the point of a spear, ready to strike, held by an apparition swaddled in grey cloth. Nearby, a similar figure held the struggling, squirming girl. A few hundred yards away, the walled city rose from the dust, with dunes piled high against the side that had taken the brunt of the winds. He hadn't realized they were so close to safety.

The figure in front of him said, "You wouldn't have made it."

"What?"

"If you had kept going once the wind picked up, you wouldn't have made it. You would have gotten turned around in the dust, gone the wrong way, and died in the storm." He coughed, raising the back of his left hand to his mouth, even though it was swathed in fabric. The spear never wavered. "In any event, we didn't expect to find you alive."

"We were lucky to shelter when we did, then."

"Yes. You were." The tone held faint menace; Adaran wished he could see the boy's face better, read his expression. He wasn't sure yet if they were being rescued, or if something else was taking place.

The guard pointed at the mound behind Adaran. "Where did you get that … creature?"

"What, the bird?" He glanced over his shoulder. The eagle's back was visible through the top of the dune, a few sad feathers bent by the weight of salt and dust, fluttering in the gentle breeze. He looked back at his questioner. "I stole it."

"And the girl? Did you steal her, too?"

"I suppose you could say that."

"I just did. Who was the victim of all this larceny?"

After a moment, Adaran said: "Some men who were trying to kill us."

"That's rather vague. Who were they and why were they trying to kill you?"

This line of questioning was straying into uncomfortable territory; if these marauders found out Lord Dunshandrin was after him, they might decide to sell him back in hopes of a reward. "I'll tell you everything," he said, "but first, if you please, the girl and I are hungry and thirsty. We ran out of food and water some time ago." A lie, but unless they wanted to dig in the sand, the men would not find their provisions.

"Did you, now? What makes you think I'm inclined to give you either? What makes you think I won't just spit you where you stand, rob you, and leave you for the beetles?"

After a moment, Adaran said: "I'm sure you and your companion are good and kind men who would not waylay poor travelers."

The figure regarded him for a moment, then burst out laughing. He lowered his spear and thrust the blade into the powdery earth near Adaran's side, then reached up and unwrapped the cloth from around his face. The first thing Adaran saw was an unruly cascade of raven curls; the second was a porcelain face, flushed and sweaty from the scarf. Seeing him goggle, the woman laughed again, then said: "As you can see, you are quite wrong about my being a good and kind *man*."

"Yes," Adaran said.

She gestured at her companion, who released the girl; in a flash she was at Adaran's side, clinging to his dusty cloak. The enrobed woman observed this with a sardonic smile. "For a stolen trinket, your little friend seems quite attached to you."

"She was being kept bound in a net when I rescued her."

"Oh, now it was a *rescue*." The woman tossed him a water skin, which he handed to the child; she began drinking greedily. "What an interesting story this will be for the headmistress."

"Headmistress?"

"Yes. Of Flaurent." Then, in response to his blank look: "The oracular college and retreat? Surely you've heard of it."

"You're an oracle?"

"Hardly," she said. "My duty is to ensure that the oracles are not bothered by the likes of you landing giant birds in their midst." She pulled her weapon out of the ground and pointed with it toward the gates of the city. "You'll come with me. You can relate your tale to the headmistress. If it suits her, she may arrange your transportation out of the Salt Flats."

She turned and began walking toward the walled city; Adaran followed, pausing to allow the little girl to swarm up his cloak and plant herself on his shoulders again. The other guard fell in behind them.

"Do you have a name?" Adaran said to the woman's back.

"Yes. Do you?"

She was a chary one. "I'm Adaran."

"And the girl?"

"I don't know her name. She doesn't talk much."

"I am called Diasa," the woman said.

Adaran nodded, then glanced behind him at the other guard, who had remained silent. "And what's his—"

"He doesn't have one."

Adaran eyed the silent figure. If it objected to Diasa's statement, it gave no sign. His gaze strayed to the weapon it carried; it clutched the shaft with gnarled, withered fingers, reminding Adaran of the beef jerky on which he had been subsisting for the last few days. Disconcerted, he turned away, examining Flaurent instead. It looked more like a fortress than a college; the walls seemed to be solid stone, with no evidence of joints or masonry. Robed figures, similar to the one behind them, were already at work clearing mounded sand from the walls; it seemed like a futile, endless job, and probably was.

When they reached the gates, Diasa raised a hand and gave some sort of signal. The broad stone door groaned ponderously inward, revealing green grass, trees, flowers.   Adaran stood there for a moment, agog; Diasa glanced back at him, a smirk on her face. "Our wells are deep, and our irrigation system is remarkable."

"I suppose it must be."

Another black-robed sentry approached, similar in form to the silent apparition who had brought up the rear of their little procession. "Your weapons," Diasa said. "You'll get them back when you leave."

He had wondered when they would get to this point. "I won't use them, I promise."

She snorted.

Adaran sighed and started handing over his daggers, one at a time, handle-first. Diasa took each one and passed it to the robed figure, who collected them in a sturdy pouch. By the time he gave her his last throwing knife, the sack contained quite an assortment of gleaming weapons.

"That's the last of them, is it?"

"Yes."

"You're a heavily armed little man, aren't you?" Diasa said. "What have you been up to besides stealing birds and children?"

"I suppose I shall tell the headmistress that."

Diasa grunted, then nodded at the swaddled henchman at the back of the line. Adaran found himself the subject of an intrusive pat-down as the creature searched for hidden weapons. It came away with one last blade, a small, thin dagger that he'd had down his boot. "Forgot about that one," Adaran said, untruthfully, as the guard took it away. Diasa raised an eyebrow, but said nothing.

The gate creaked shut behind them; Adaran, meanwhile, watched his arsenal disappear into a small building set into the thick walls, next to the gate. "I will get those back, you said?"

"If it pleases the headmistress. Come." They proceeded along a broad central avenue of crushed stone held together with some rubbery black substance of a sort that Adaran had never seen before. Flower beds lined the street, although most of the blooms had faded, leaving only foliage. Buildings poked from the trees here and there, made of the same sort of stone as the walls, and equally lacking any sign of masonry. A thin layer of dust covered everything: Residue from the storm, or perhaps just the natural state of things in this arid region.

The interior of Flaurent was smaller than he had expected; the scale of the walls gave it the illusion of great size, but he judged it only occupied a few acres. The college was obviously meant to mimic an oasis in this wasteland, which would of necessity limit the size that could be sustained.

"So this is a school?" Adaran said.

"Among other things."

"I don't see any students."

"There are never very many," she said. "But look carefully. They are here."

He peered around, and spotted a few figures moving along paths through the trees; but they wore hooded robes and he couldn't be sure if they were people or more of Diasa's unconventional henchmen. Then they passed a small, grassy amphitheater, where a man in a faded blue cloak lectured to a small group of similarly clothed people who sat on the grass before him. The speaker fell silent as they passed. He and the students watched them go by; then the lecture began again, only to halt almost immediately, subsiding into murmurs and pointing fingers. Adaran heard running footsteps approach. He whirled, fingers reaching for weapons that he no longer carried, clutching at empty scabbards as a wizened little man came to a breathless stop just in front of him. Pointing up at Adaran, he cried: "I've seen this one! I've seen him coming!"

Diasa moved next to Adaran, regarding this new arrival with amusement and a small degree of curiosity. "Have you, now, Wert?" she said.

"I have! I've dreamed of him!" Then he dropped his voice and added, conspiratorially, with a sly look to either side: "He has enemies."

Diasa shot Adaran a glance. "Yes, I expect he does."

"They are powerful. They seek him from the sky."

"Yes? What else?"

Wert raised his hands up high; his dirty sleeves slid down, piling up at his shoulders, revealing pale, smudged, bone-thin arms. "They will turn the earth against us! They will rain fire upon the plains!"

"They do sound fearsome," Diasa said. "Is that all?"

The little man blinked at her a few times and lowered his arms.

He looked somewhat bewildered. His sleeves stayed bunched up for a moment, then unrolled to his wrists. "Yes, that's all."

"You've finished?"

"Yes."

"Run along, then."

Wert turned and toddled away, heading for the lecture that Adaran had noticed earlier. The students hastily got to their feet and retreated, following the instructor toward a low, ivy-covered building that extended from the outer wall.

"That was Wert," Diasa said. "Wert the Wart, the students call him."

Adaran stared at the little man as he hurried after the retreating students. He was much too slow; by the time he got to the building the door was securely closed and, apparently, bolted against him. Turning back to Diasa, he said: "Is Wert an oracle?"

"Not exactly. He inhaled too deeply of the vapors a long time ago and has been raving mad ever since. He always makes wild predictions, and they never come true."

"Never?"

"Well, hardly ever."

"But what he said about enemies from the sky ... people *are* searching for us, and they will be riding eagles like the one I stole. How would he know that?"

"How? Because we spotted you leading that creature across the flats, and word spread quickly. It takes little enough imagination to realize what a giant, saddled bird is for."

"You saw us? Why didn't you help us?"

"We were making ready for the storm. Perhaps if I had taken note of the child I would have made a different decision, but I was not prepared to risk losing men in a rescue attempt."

"You call those ... *things* men?"

She fixed him with a glare that was every bit as sharp as the point of her spear. "You are at the very bottom of my list of concerns. First come the students, then the staff, then the Withered Ones, then the physical structures of the college. You rate somewhere below the flower beds." She turned away. "Now, come along. We're almost there."

Adaran, seething, was not inclined to follow Diasa any further, but the guard who had been shadowing them—a Withered One, he supposed—prodded him with the butt end of his pole-axe, encouraging him to move. They soon turned left onto a side path that led to a squat building made of orange rock. A chiseled sign above the door said *Headmistress*. Diasa stood on the front step, holding the door open. Adaran entered, finding himself in a small, square chamber. Stone benches lined three of the walls; the fourth, opposite the entrance, was punctured by a pair of doors.

Diasa entered and shut the door, leaving the guard outside. "Sit," she said. "I'll be back shortly." She vanished through the door on the right, leaving them alone in the waiting room. Adaran reached up, lifted the girl from his shoulders, and set her down onto one of the stone benches. She sat there swinging her feet, looking around with interest, although there was not much to see in this dim and tiny space. Slit-like windows painted lines of illumination on the floor, creating an effect uncomfortably like a prison cell. Probably it was meant to intimidate those who waited for an audience with this so-called headmistress.

He went to the door on the left, gave it a jiggle. Locked. He moved to the door Diasa had gone through, cupping his hand over his ear and listening at it carefully. He heard nothing, so he tried the knob. Unlocked. He debated opening it, going exploring, but thought better of it and went to sit next to the girl instead. "Are you ready to tell me your name?"

After a moment, she said, "Prehn."

"That's your name? Prehn?"

She nodded.

"How old are you?" She smiled, shrugged, continued kicking her feet in the air; perhaps she didn't know the answer. "Where are you from?"

The girl rolled her eyes, as if this were the stupidest question she had ever heard. "Home."

"Well, yes, but where is that?"

She shrugged.

"All right. My name is Adaran. Can you say that?"

"No."

"Do you know why those men kidnapped you?"

She shook her head and then started whistling tunelessly.

Evidently, all he was going to get out of her was her name. He pitied anyone who tried to interrogate this child.

Before long, Diasa reentered the waiting room through the door on the left; just as well he hadn't tried to sneak out through that one. "The headmistress will see you now."

They followed her down a short hallway, generously appointed with woven rugs and hanging plants that overflowed their baskets, tumbling in green disorder to the floor. Tiny, rectangular windows gave a limited view of the grounds outside; through them, Adaran caught a glimpse of a small, blue-clad figure furtively moving through the trees, apparently shadowing their own movements. He pointed this out to Diasa, who merely shook her head.

At the end of the corridor, they came to a closed wooden door. A tall, empty bin stood beside it. Diasa opened the door and ushered them into a chamber scarcely larger than the waiting room, though better lit. A broad desk made of stone took up most of the available space; papers, scrolls, and even a few books cluttered its surface. Adaran eyed the tomes, thick and hand-bound. He knew how valuable such items could be, having stolen more than one, and was surprised to find them treated like common objects.

The woman who sat behind the desk was busily rolling up parchments, tying the bundles off with bits of string. She looked about the same age as Adaran's mother, the old whore, with a face dry and creased as old leather, white hair streaked with black falling loosely past her shoulders. Without looking up from her labors, she said: "Well, have them sit."

"Working on it," Diasa said. She had removed a stack of scrolls from a chair, and her arms were quite full. "This office would be less cluttered if you didn't leave your things everywhere."

The headmistress looked at Diasa's burden as if she'd never seen such things before, then said: "Put those in the hallway. They need to go back to the library."

"Well, they won't get there sitting on your furniture," Diasa muttered as she dumped them into the bin outside the door.

"I heard that," the headmistress said.

"As you were meant to." Diasa maneuvered Adaran into the chair that she had cleared; Prehn climbed into his lap. Then Diasa shut the office door and went to stand behind the desk, arms folded, looking down at him with half-lidded eyes. He supposed this was meant to intimidate him.

The headmistress finished collating her papers and dropped them on the floor next to her desk, then leaned back and examined Adaran as if he were an interesting sort of rodent that had appeared unexpectedly in her kitchen. Adaran shifted uncomfortably, waiting for her to speak, but she didn't; finally he said: "We could use something to eat."

The Headmistress blinked a few times, then looked at Diasa. "Go and fetch Wert. You'll find him lurking outside. I would ask him a few questions."

Diasa nodded and departed through a narrow side door wedged between two shelves overflowing with papers and knickknacks. The headmistress watched her go, then returned her gaze to Adaran, templed her fingers, and said: "Diasa tells me you stole a giant bird."

"Yes, I did."

"Some of the students have seen such creatures."

"Flying around the college, you mean?"

"No. In visions. They appear to figure in some sort of event that's about to happen. Unfortunately we are not at all certain what that event is."

"Can't you just look into the future and see?"

"It's not a matter of turning a book a few pages ahead and reading what's written," she said. "Where do they come from?"

"What, the eagles?"

"Of course."

"They belong to Lord Dunshandrin."

"And where does he get them?"

"I don't know."

"How did you happen to steal one?"

"That's a long story."

"I have the time to hear it."

And so Adaran launched into a highly edited version of what had happened in the mountains, from stealing the dragon's crystals to the double-cross that had killed Redshen and the others. He played up his heroism in rescuing Prehn, played down his killing of Dosen, and ended with their blind flight through the clouds and unexpected landing not far from the college. Throughout his tale, Prehn sat in his lap, staring at the headmistress with the sort of unreserved fascination usually reserved for storytellers and grandmothers. Perhaps she was the oldest woman the child had ever seen.

When he finished, the headmistress said: "Interesting."

Her tone made him wonder if she knew the details he had left out. "Interesting? That's all you have to say?"

"At the moment. I do wonder, though, why Dunshandrin would go through all the effort and expense of sending you to get the dragon's stones."

"I can't say. He didn't tell us."

"Unfortunate."

"He could just want them for a potion. Or perhaps he's making himself a new crown."

"No. He is up to something grave, and we don't know what it is." The headmistress leaned forward to look down at Prehn. "You've been very quiet, child. Where are *you* from? Why did they have you prisoner?"

Prehn squeaked and buried her face in Adaran's dusty cloak. After a moment, he said: "She's a bit shy."

"So I see." The headmistress leaned back in her chair. "She's clearly Enshennean. With that skin, that hair, she could be nothing else." She looked at him. "This is a long, long way from Enshenneah."

"I don't know what you're getting at," Adaran said. "I didn't kidnap her, if that's what you're suggesting; I've never even been to Enshenneah."

"Nothing there but jungles and savages and insects." She shuddered. "So many insects."

The narrow door opened and Diasa entered, dragging Wert by the collar of his robe. The little man's feet scrabbled against the floor in a futile effort to escape. Holding him with one hand, Diasa swept a huge heap of papers aside, revealing another chair. She tossed Wert into it, then stood there glaring at him. He tried to stand up twice; she pushed him down both times.

"Wert!" the headmistress said sharply.

The old man stopped squirming. "Yes, Damona?"

"Wert, I've told you, you must call me *Headmistress* like everyone else."

"Yes, Damona."

She sighed, then said: "Wert, what did you see happening when you spoke to this man today?"

"I've never seen him before. May I go now?"

"Wert, you accosted him on the avenue not one hour ago."

"Oh." Wert inspected Adaran again. "That was him?"

"Yes," the headmistress said. "That was him."

Wert nodded slowly, and made a clucking sound with his tongue. The headmistress watched with steadily compressing lips as he leaned back in the chair, looked up at Diasa, and said: "You're pretty. Your mother looked like you once."

Diasa and the headmistress both flushed red.

"This seems pointless," Adaran said. "Why can't you just ask one of the other oracles?"

"I told you, whatever is coming, we cannot see it clearly. But Wert came up to you and made a very specific prediction. It may help us to understand, if only he can be persuaded to tell us what he saw."

"But Diasa said he was always wrong."

"*Nearly* always," Diasa murmured.

Adaran eyed Wert, who sat there goggling at them, a tiny bubble of foam on his bottom lip.   "What makes you think he even remembers any—"

"Beware," Wert said suddenly, his voice deep and resonant, nothing like the wheedling tone he had used before. Was this the way he had sounded before he'd gone mad? "Earth and fire unite. Future and past are interchanged.   The shadow of the two-headed beast falls over us all."

He paused, shivering all over, as if suffering a seizure. The room remained utterly quiet except for the faint rattling of the chair in which he sat; when his convulsions stopped, as suddenly as they'd begun, the silence seemed a physical presence. "The scales go out of balance," Wert cried. "Stone burns! The ground flows like water! Fire falls like rain!" He turned, looking directly at Adaran. "The river. Remember!"

Then the old man slumped in his chair; his head fell forward and he shuddered once more, just for a moment. When he looked up again, it was with his former pop-eyed look of bewilderment.

The headmistress said: "Wert?"

The old man farted loudly, then said, "Damona, I'm hungry."

She would not kill the soldiers right away, T'Sian decided, even though she certainly could. Slaughtering the four armed men, while satisfying, would not bring her any closer to those who had slain her hatchlings. She noticed the one called Pyodor Ponn glancing at her nervously as the soldiers took him into custody. He was probably afraid she would spit fire at them and burn down his inn, or turn into a dragon and swallow them all whole. He did not know her capabilities; his fear and ignorance would help to ensure that he continued to do as he was told.

The soldiers put shackles around Ponn's wrists, black iron cuffs linked together to keep him from moving his hands freely. He had said he would be led away in chains; this must be what he had meant. "Where are you taking him?" T'Sian asked. "Will you put him in your punishment area, with the fence and the wooden things inside?"

"Not that it's any business of yours," Apperand said, "but he will be dispatched directly to Astilan."

"What?" Ponn said.

"Oh, yes, Ponn. A special prison wagon has already been prepared for Parillon; you will join him on his journey. King Varmot is most eager to meet the men who have cheated him of duties and taxes for so many years."

"I see," Ponn said. "Then will you be coming as well, Apperand? Is Varmot not interested in what taxes *you* may owe him?"

The mayor laughed tightly. "You would do well to follow Parillon's example, Enshennean, and avoid making claims you cannot substantiate." He snapped his fingers at the soldiers. "Take him away."

The other men exchanged a look that T'Sian recognized as contempt; they obviously did not like being ordered around by this little man. Still, they surrounded Ponn; one attached a longer length of chain to the manacles that bound him, so that they could lead him like a beast on a leash.

This changed the situation; T'Sian had not understood that they were going to send Ponn off to their human king in some faraway palace. She needed his help to navigate this strange human world, and he was the only person she knew of who had seen Gelt and his associates. Apperand held the door open as the soldiers marched Ponn toward it; T'Sian watched, not intervening, as they took him out of the building. A cart waited outside, surrounded by more armed men. Ponn climbed into the back, a guard on either side. He faced straight ahead, his jaw clenched, the muscles of his neck tight.

She approached Apperand. "I will accompany you."

"I hardly think so," the mayor said, "unless it be in irons."

"I would prefer not to be separated from Ponn."

"Arrange your own transportation, then. The prison wagon does not carry freight."

His tone insulted her; she raised a hand and he shrank back, frightened. A coward, like most men. She thought better of striking him, running the hand through her hair instead. Apperand turned and departed quickly, slamming the door behind him. A moment later she heard the wagon's wheels clattering on the cobblestones as it drove away.

She turned to the one called Timmeon. He was larger than Ponn and probably more physically powerful, but he was also manifestly less intelligent; and he had never seen Gelt. Or had he? "Have you seen any men recently who rode on large birds?" she said.

The man looked confused. "Birds?"

"Yes. Feathered creatures, with wings."

"I know what birds are," Timmeon said. "I've never seen one big enough for a man to ride on, though." Pause. "Do they have big birds where you come from?"

"No."

"Oh. Where *do* you come from?"

"The mountains."

"How did you meet Ponn? Did he go to the mountains?"

"No."

Evidently deciding to change the subject, Timmeon said: "Are you going to stay here tonight? All the rooms are open, I could get one ready for you. No charge, you being Ponn's ... friend and all."

"I do not need a room," T'Sian said. "I will be traveling to Astilan with Pyodor Ponn."

"But the mayor said—"

"The mayor said to arrange my own transportation." She smiled at Timmeon, showing him her teeth. "I will be doing exactly as he suggested."

8

After sending Diasa to take Wert back to his home, or wherever he lived, the headmistress sat for a long time, elbows on her desk, chin resting on her interlaced fingers, staring at Adaran with a fixed gaze that he found disconcerting. At length, though, he realized that she wasn't really seeing him; her eyes were unfocused, her mind elsewhere. He had begun to think she had suffered some sort of stroke or brain seizure, when suddenly she shook her head and blinked for the first time in many minutes.

"Are you all right?" he asked.

She coughed into her closed fist. "Yes," she said, when the fit subsided. "I'm getting old, I'm afraid, and unexpected visions sometimes take me."

"You mean you see the future, just like that?"

She nodded. "Our young oracles, the students and the inexperienced, use a mixture of herbs and powdered stones to create vapors that allow them to open their minds and exercise their gifts. After a lifetime of exposure to those vapors, I find that my mind is sometimes open when I wish it to be closed."

"What did you see? Anything interesting?"

She looked at him sadly. "You do not understand. You are a common ruffian; you think knowledge comes, unbidden and fully formed, with tags and labels to explain its meaning."

This remark was uncomfortably close to the truth, and it annoyed him to hear it. "Yes, very well; but what did you see?"

The old woman sighed, then said: "I saw a piece of blue stone in a huge glass tank. It breathed like a thing alive, and grew before my eyes. The tank shattered and the stone flowed out, as a glacier in the mountains; it spread across the land and covered everything like ice." She cocked her head. "Does that have any meaning to you?"

"Some of the stones we took from the dragon's lair were blue, but they didn't grow and they certainly didn't breathe."

"Dunshandrin is getting up to some mischief with these crystals," the headmistress said. "I must send a messenger to the Crosswaters, and tell Klem to be wary."

"Who's Klem?"

"The head oracle, and my agent out in the world."

"Shouldn't you warn the other kingdoms as well? Madroval, Barbareth, Yttribia? Enshenneah?"

"Warn them of what? These kings and tyrants are already suspicious of each other. They do not need vague warnings from me to increase their paranoia."

"But obviously the blue crystal is Dunshandrin spreading his territory," Adaran said. "Isn't it?"

The headmistress shook her head. "A common ruffian," she said again. "Things are rarely so literal as that."

The narrow side door opened, revealing Diasa; she looked grim, and did not enter. "Something has happened to Wert," she said. "He started hitting himself in the head and wailing, and then he collapsed." She paused, and added: "I think he may be dying."

The headmistress rose. "Where is he?" she said.

"The Withered Ones carried him to the infirmary."

"I will go and see him. Take our guest and his charge to the hall, find him an empty room." To Adaran, she said: "A flatboat is going downriver tomorrow. It will take you to Achengate, and from there you can go where you will."

Diasa stood aside as the headmistress departed through the side door, then entered the room and glared down at Adaran. "On your feet," she said.

He lifted Prehn onto his shoulders, then stood. "You needn't speak to me like an enemy," he said.

"Are you not? Twice now, Wert has named you as inviting our destruction."

"I have no intention of—"

"*Your* intentions are not of concern," she said. "I'm worried about those who will come here seeking you."

"But you said Wert was always wrong."

She grimaced. "Almost always. Just follow me, and for your own sake, pray nothing happens."

They left the building the way they'd entered, down the short hallway, through the foyer, out into the parklike environs. The sky had taken on a dusty bluish hue as the sun crept from one set of mountains to the other. Diasa led Adaran back to the hard-surfaced path, then up a narrow gravel walkway that ran between beds of fern and foliage. It ended at a small, long, squat building, where it turned into a narrow patio. About a dozen doors alternated with tiny windows; candles flickered behind some of them. It looked not unlike a stable, but for humans instead of horses. "This is where the students stay?" he asked.

"Yes. Students, honored guests, visiting dignitaries." She gave him a sidelong glance. "Interlopers. All reside here."

"Charming," he said. "It reminds me of a prison."

"Well, as the headmistress likes to say, we all do see things through the prism of our experiences."

By the time Adaran realized he'd been insulted, Diasa had already ushered him to an unoccupied room. Producing a truly prodigious keyring from somewhere inside her garment, she unlocked the door and opened it, revealing a barren stone chamber. It really did resemble a jail cell; a narrow cot stood against the wall on the left with a chamberpot nearby, while a counter made of projecting stone ran along the back wall. An old mat, woven of what looked like river reeds, lay in the center of the floor, worn smooth and fraying at the edges.

Diasa nudged Adaran and Prehn into the alcove. "I'll come back for you tomorrow, when the boat leaves," she said, "and someone will be along shortly with food and drink."

"Wait—" Adaran said; but before he could get another word out she had shut the door and he heard the click of a key in the lock. Setting Prehn down on the cot, he went to the window, standing on his toes so he could see out. Through the dusty glass, he saw Diasa striding away.

"I've escaped from worse prisons than this before," he told her retreating back, "and I'll do so again."

Behind him, he heard the little girl giggling.

Tolaria sat in her usual spot by the tall windows, watching the shadows lengthen as the sun neared the horizon, turning the sky to crimson gold, burnishing the distant grass to bronze. The remains of dinner, half-eaten as usual, sat on the table beside her. Too much food and a lack of appetite meant that she never finished a meal. It would not go to waste, though; Wyst would eat what was left. Tolaria's leftovers seemed to be the girl's only source of food, and so she was careful to leave more than just fat and gristle and crusts of bread. Poor Wyst; everyone treated her as if she didn't exist, and she often acted as if she believed it herself.

She looked over as the door to Torrant's chambers opened and the prince entered. He came and went as he pleased, as if Tolaria's room were his own; she almost preferred Tomari's quick temper to Torrant's casual over-familiarity.

"Good evening, Tolaria," he said. "I am here to invite you to a demonstration in the north garden."

"A demonstration of what?"

He smiled. "It's a surprise."

She looked away. "I'm afraid I must decline," she said. "I am comfortable here in my chair, and as you can see I have not finished my supper."

"Ah," Torrant said. "When I called it an invitation, I was merely being diplomatic. Your presence is required."

Of course it was. She sighed, stood, and followed him out the door. He led her through the quiet halls of the castle, accompanied by a pair of guards who kept a discreet distance and, even farther back, Wyst; the girl slunk along behind, like a dog that knew it was somewhere it didn't belong.

They soon left the better-lit parts of the castle, passing into cold and gloomy corridors that smelled like dust and forgotten furniture. Candelabra had been placed at intervals on stands that clearly didn't belong there, providing dim, flickery illumination; darkness pooled in the spots where the incessant drafts had blown out the flames.

"Where are you taking me?" Tolaria said. "I hope you don't intend to give me this entire wing of the keep; I should hate to have to keep it clean."

"The north garden sees little use these days," Torrant said. "It will do nicely for what Qalor intends to show us."

"Oh, I finally meet your mysterious alchemist tonight?"

"Indeed. You will see strange sights this evening, him not least among them."

They came to the head of a narrow flight of stairs, curving down and to the right, following the castle wall. Turning to their retinue, Torrant said: "You will wait here." The guards nodded and took up positions on either side of the opening; Wyst, lurking some distance back, skulked and glimmered like a ghost.

Torrant took Tolaria's arm and they descended the steps. A door at the bottom stood propped open by some rubble. They went out into a small courtyard that faced the mountains. A number of braziers had been erected around the perimeter of the area, lending it a ruddy illumination, filling the air with a greasy tang. A towering platform stood in the center of an overgrown flowerbed, the mishmash of boards and planks haphazardly nailed together, as if by a child in a hurry. Steam or some other vapor drifted from within the structure. In front of it, a number of large, flat stones had been laid, crushing the weeds.

A few soldiers stood here, along with Tomari, who stood with a man she hadn't seen before. Torrant brought her to them. Tomari gazed at her coldly, then looked away; evidently he still hadn't forgiven her for rebuffing their advances. The other man, an older fellow wearing thick, soft-looking violet robes trimmed with faded gold stitching, stood half a head taller than either prince. He looked down at her imperiously.

"You must be Qalor," she said.

Tomari made a choking noise and brought his hand to his lips, covering a grin.

"Hardly," the man said.

"Tolaria, this is our father, Lord Dunshandrin." Torrant nudged her and, in a whisper, added: "You might wish to bow."

Lord Dunshandrin? Aside from a superficial resemblance, this man looked nothing like the frail, sickly creature she had seen on her first day in the castle. "I most certainly would bow, were I being presented to Lord Dunshandrin as he sat in his chair in his great hall," she said after a moment. "However, under the present circumstances, I will instead look him in the eye and praise his miraculous recovery."

Dunshandrin glared down at her, then looked at Tomari. "I see that you were not exaggerating about this one," he said.

"No."

"Your sickness was a ruse," Tolaria said, "to lure me here. You wanted a pet oracle. How did you fake the signs of illness so well?"

"The signs are not faked," Dunshandrin said.

"We found a man who looks somewhat like father, and exposed him to fever victims in the almshouse until he took ill," Torrant said.

"We have a most excellent physician endeavoring to keep the poor soul alive," Tomari added.

"I don't understand," Tolaria said. "You have me here now. Why keep up the charade?"

"I think you will find that I am making a gradual recovery," Lord Dunshandrin said. "Soon I will be well enough to appear at my court. By the time Barbareth sues for peace, I will be quite recovered enough to parley with its King."

"Enough about such matters." Torrant eyed the ramshackle tower. "We are here for a demonstration. Where is Qalor?"

"He is still making ready," Tomari said. "Apparently, if he botches this, we could all be killed."

"A hefty responsibility," Torrant said.

Dunshandrin grunted and then, in a strong voice, called: "Qalor! We are tired of waiting out here in the cold! Show us what your new device can do!"

Tolaria saw movement between the loose boards of the tower; then a large man emerged and shambled over to the royal group. Although he towered over Dunshandrin and his sons, he had a unhealthy air about him; he was nearly bald, with hair growing in tuft-like patches, and his grimy face was pocked with small lesions that glistened in the firelight. He wore a long apron that may once have been white, but was now stained in a variety of bilious colors and exudates. He carried a small, thick-looking leather sack, holding it away from himself at the end of a pole, as if he didn't want it to touch his body. Qalor gently set the sack down in the grass. "Lieges," he said, sounding out of breath. "My lady."

"Qalor, this is Tolaria," Torrant said.

"Ah yes," Qalor said. He wiped his right hand on the filthy apron, then extended it to her. "The oracle. A pleasure."

"All mine, I'm sure," Tolaria said, shrinking from the proffered hand. The alchemist's teeth were dark and rotting, and his mouth stank of infection.

"Never mind the girl," Dunshandrin said. "Show us your device, and prove that we have not been chasing shadows."

"Of course, my liege." Picking up the sack again, he raised it for them to see. "This is a smaller example of what the eagles will carry into battle." He squinted at it. "Much smaller. It contains a box with two chambers, each holding a powdered form of one type of crystal. A third chamber holds a chemical of my own devising that will act as a catalyst upon the powders. I used minute amounts; more than a little would be dangerous for my lieges and their distinguished guest."

Tolaria supposed that meant her.

"Yes, yes," Dunshandrin said, impatient. "You've explained your design to us before. Now show us how it works."

Qalor nodded and returned to the tower. Tolaria watched the apparatus wobble back and forth, apparently as he climbed a ladder or stair within; one of the boards fell off, then another, and she began to worry that the entire structure would collapse and crush them. Eventually, though, Qalor emerged onto a platform, twenty feet above where they stood. He brought his sack to the very edge and held it out in the empty space above the flagstones. "Observe, now, what happens when I release the device!"

He let go of the pole.

The bag fell.

Tolaria gasped and shielded her eyes as a burst of smoke and flame erupted from the point of impact, momentarily lighting up the night. A fireball rose into the air, curled in on itself, and disappeared, becoming a cloud of black vapor that drifted slowly away. Where the sack had landed, the rock was cracked and blackened. Some of the boards of the tower had ignited. Qalor had evidently been prepared for this, however; attendants rushed over with buckets of water and doused the flames.

"As you can see," Qalor called, "even a tiny device is quite destructive."

"Indeed," Dunshandrin murmured.

The alchemist turned and disappeared into the platform, which once again began to shiver as he climbed back down. He soon reemerged from the opening in the side, and came back to where they stood. "Of course, the eagles will carry much larger devices," he said. "Their destructive power will be an order of magnitude greater."

This was the second time Qalor had mentioned eagles; Tolaria wondered what he meant by it. Did he have a flock of trained raptors ready to fly over Barbareth, dropping explosive packages? How much weight could such a bird carry?

"Even a small squadron will be able to destroy a city and burn out large sections of enemy forces," Tomari said eagerly. "A larger force could devastate an entire region!"

"Need we go so far?" Torrant said. "We don't want to rule a wasteland. The threat of destruction may serve us as well as destruction itself."

"Would it?" Lord Dunshandrin said. "I wonder. The threat will be dismissed if our ability to carry it out has not been demonstrated."

"What do you have in mind, Father?" Tomari said.

"Astilan." Lord Dunshandrin looked at Qalor, standing some distance away, like a creature that had dragged itself out of the grave and was contemplating whether or not to attack. "How soon can the eagles be made ready?"

"A new generation is almost fully grown," the alchemist said. "Their strength and endurance continues to increase, so they will no longer need to stop and rest so often, and they will not tire so quickly."

"But how soon can we put them into play?"

Qalor scratched his chin, thinking; he inadvertently dislodged one of his scabs. Pale fluid began to leak from the wound, but he did not seem to notice. "The grooms have been training them to the saddle since they were small, my lord, so once they are of a size they will be ready for your riders. I would say that it is now only a matter of days."

"And the crystals? They will be ready as well?"

"They are growing in the solution I prepared; no further expeditions will be required."

"Very good," Dunshandrin said. "You have done well."

Qalor made several rapid, shallow bows. "Thank you, my Lord," he said. "Thank you."

Dunshandrin turned to Tolaria. "So, young oracle, what do you think of our plans?"

"I think you're mad," she said. "The lot of you."

The blow caught her off guard; one moment Dunshandrin was glaring at her, and the next she lay on the ground at his feet, looking up at him, her cheek burning and her head ringing.

"My sons may tolerate such talk from you," he said. "I will not. When you speak to me it will be with the respect I am due."

Her mouth tasted like blood. "The respect you are due as a man who fakes illness in order to lure and imprison an oracle?" she said. "Or the respect you are due as a man who would invade another kingdom for no reason other than avarice? Or perhaps the respect you are due as a man who strikes a woman half his size? Please, my lord, tell me which type of respect you feel you most deserve, and I will show it to you."

He stared down at her, and for a moment she thought he might kick her or haul her to her feet in order to knock her down again; but then he began to laugh. "I will either kill this wench, or marry her off to one of my sons," he announced. "We shall see which!"

She almost said she would rather be die than be wed to either of the princes, but held her tongue; she had a suspicion that if she asked Dunshandrin to kill her, he might oblige.

There had been a delay in getting the prison wagon ready, a broken axle or some such problem; and so Pyodor Ponn spent a cold, uncomfortable night locked in the stocks at Execution Square, under the steely gaze of a town sentry. By the time the fifth person hit him with rotten vegetables—a number more had thrown, but missed—he was beginning to wish T'Sian would, indeed, assume her dragon form and burn the city to the ground. But she had apparently abandoned him; she didn't come to the square, not even to taunt him or ask him absurd questions about human punishments.

Early in the morning, before the sun had risen over the mountains, a black carriage pulled up alongside the wooden fence. Two guards rode on the front bench, one serving as the driver, the other as a lookout; two more sat on top of the boxlike compartment that housed the prisoners. The sentry released Ponn from the stocks and hustled him along to the wagon, loading him into the windowless chamber in the back. Parillon was already inside, chained by his ankle to an iron ring in the floor. One of the king's men secured Ponn in a similar fashion, then shut and bolted the door, leaving them in utter darkness.

"Hello, Ponn," Parillon said.

"Hello, Parillon." The wagon lurched into motion, swaying and creaking along the rough streets. "I notice they didn't put *you* in the stocks."

"I bribed Apperand to let me spend the night at home. Don't be upset, Ponn. I didn't know they had you, or I would've bought you a night of bed rest as well, before our journey."

"He would have taken your money and put me in the stocks anyway," Ponn said. "I angered him by suggesting that he was involved in our business."

"As, of course, he was. Miserable cur. Well, you may be pleased to know that his residence burned during the night."

"It did? With Apperand inside?"

"So I'm told. I didn't have the pleasure of seeing it myself." Parillon was silent a moment, then said: "What are you doing here, anyway? You should be in Enshenneah."

"I'm not here voluntarily, believe me," Ponn said.

"They sent men to Enshenneah to get you?"

"Not exactly."

"Well, you're being very mysterious, aren't you?"

"If I told you how I came to be here, you would never believe it."

"Really? You must give me the whole tale, then. Perhaps it will help pass the time until we reach our destination."

So Ponn recounted his adventures of the last several days, starting from the beginning: The men and their eagles; Prehn's disappearance, followed by Pord's; the voyage to the dragon islands, his abandonment, encountering T'Sian. Parillon mostly listened, asking few questions, though he did express surprise that the dragon could assume human form. "It seems a strange thing, doesn't it, that such a creature would be able to pass as a woman?"

"Believe me," Ponn said, "unless you were half-blind or the light was very poor, she couldn't." He continued his story, ending with his being locked in the back of the wagon. "But you were there for that part."

"Yes," Parillon said. "I remember it like it was only a few hours ago. But what will this dragon of yours do now, Ponn? You said she was insistent on your company. Perhaps she will come after you, and rescue us from this predicament."

"I don't imagine I made myself so useful that she cannot continue on without me," Ponn said.

They traveled on in relative silence for some time after Ponn finished his story, speaking only occasionally; Parillon would curse the driver every time the wagon hit an especially large bump, and complained loudly about having to relieve himself. If the guards heard any of this, they ignored it. Neither of them mentioned the likely fate that awaited them in Astilan; but Ponn knew that Parillon must be thinking of it, even as he was. Smugglers earned the death penalty in Varmot's kingdom.

Suddenly the wagon jerked to a halt. Ponn slid forward along the floor before being brought up short by his leg irons. "By the bells on my mother's toes!" Parillon cried. "Have you never driven a wagon before? Open your eyes, you blind fool!"

Silence.

Then the carriage began to shake; Ponn could hear the horses whinnying in terror, the guards shouting. Something smashed into the cart, nearly tipping it over. It rocked back and forth, sending Ponn tumbling first to the left, then to the right, then back to the left again. The cuff bit painfully into his ankle each time the chain brought him up short.

At last the wagon stabilized; for a few seconds, all was still. Then Parillon said: "That was no log in the road. What's happening?"

"I don't know," Ponn said.

Suddenly wood groaned and splintered, but in the darkness he couldn't see what was making the noise. A moment later, Ponn felt a wrenching sensation similar to what he'd experienced when T'Sian had snatched him off the ground at the volcano. She must have swooped down on the wagon and slaughtered or driven off the guards, and now she was carrying the entire thing away.

In a tiny voice, Parillon said: "Ponn?"

"It's the dragon," he said.

"You mean that absurd story was *true*?"

"Of course it was true. Did you think I was lying?"

"I thought you were making it up to entertain me!"

Their flight continued for some time, and then they dropped sharply; for a few dizzying seconds Ponn had a sensation of weightlessness, as if he were floating on the end of the chain that attached him to the floor. They hit the ground with jarring force. The wagon broke open, revealing the dusky sky above, and the dragon's face as she tore the top off the carriage and peered inside like an inspector examining the contents of a suspect crate. She smelled of smoke and metal; her eyes flickered like distant bonfires. Her long tongue snaked out and danced across Ponn's body, dry and rubbery; then it did the same to Parillon, causing him to cry out in fear.

She continued tearing apart the prison compartment, until there was little left of the wagon but floor and wheels. Then she reached out and touched their chains with her talons. Hooking two of her claws into the links, she snapped them with no more effort than a man would expend to break a twig.

"*Well, men,*" she said, "*You are free again.*" Then she thrust her head into the older man's face. "*You are the one called Parillon?*"

"Yes," he said, his voice breaking like a boy's.

"*I am searching for some men. Pyodor Ponn, describe the one called Gelt.*"

"Brown hair, curly. Brown eyes. Short beard streaked with white. Tall and broad. Walks with a swagger. He has a scar on his right cheek, long and narrow, from his ear to his chin."

"*Sufficient.*" The dragon's head swiveled back to Parillon. "*Have you seen this man?*"

Parillon said: "Yes, I … I believe I have."

"You have?" Ponn said, startled.

"*Where?*" T'Sian demanded.

"He dined at the inn the day before I was arrested. He was with Apperand. Apperand declined to introduce us, but the gentleman did make a point of inquiring how business was."

"Gelt knew about our operation," Ponn said. "He must have turned us in."

"*Apperand* knew about our operation," Parillon said. "He profited from it. Why would he turn us over to King Varmot on Gelt's information?"

"Perhaps Gelt is an agent of this King Varmot."

That possibility had not occurred to Ponn. "What would Varmot want with the crystals Gelt took from the island?"

"What would any man want with them?" T'Sian said. *"I do not know; but I will find out, and I will have my revenge."* She turned her head and breathed a blast of fire that momentarily lit up the night. *"Where is Astilan?"* she said, turning back to them, smoke accompanying the words.

"Northeast," Parillon said, sounding very much as if he would prefer to be back in the prison wagon, bumping along toward his execution. "It's on the coast, not far south of Dunshandrin's border."

"We will go there. We will find this Varmot, and make him tell us what he knows." T'Sian leaned forward, reached out with her two front talons. Parillon cried out and shied away, but the dragon snatched him up in her right claw, and took Ponn in her left. With a rush of wings they took to the air, leaving the wrecked wagon far below.

Over the sound of the wind, Ponn could hear Parillon screaming.

Adaran lay on his back on the cot, Prehn curled up next to him, and stared at the orange stone ceiling. Their stomachs were full of bland food that had been brought to them on a wooden tray; any thoughts he'd entertained of trying to escape during the delivery had faded when he saw that the meal had been brought by one of those strange withered creatures and three of its friends. He suspected Diasa had posted several of them to watch the door of his room and make sure he stayed where she had put him. Not knowing their capabilities, he was disinclined to challenge them.

What a crashingly dull end to an eventful day.

Adaran glanced over at the sleeping child. What was he going to do with her? He was hardly qualified to raise the girl himself, nor was anyone he knew. The circles in which he moved were hardly parental. If Redshen were still alive, she may have decided to retire from her thieving ways and taken on the challenge; but Redshen was gone.

Perhaps he could leave her here, with the oracles; but what would her fate be then? A life of scullery work, perhaps? The Headmistress appeared to harbor a low opinion of Enshenneah and its inhabitants, but surely Prehn would be better off at Flaurent than living on the dagger's edge of criminality.

He heard a faint rumble, like thunder. Another storm? Adaran got up and went to the tiny, square window. Dust coated the outer surface of the glass, making it like trying to peer through sand; all he could tell was that it was dark outside. Dusk had arrived while he'd been lying there napping and contemplating the ceiling.

Something was rattling.

He turned and saw that the pitcher and basin on the wall counter, brought earlier by one of the Withered Ones, had begun moving, slowly turning and traveling across the stone as if being toyed with by an unseen hand. He went to the counter and put his hand on the pitcher, stopping its motion. He could feel it thrumming beneath his fingers.

Earthquake?

He went to the door. Locked. He bent over and peered into the keyhole. It looked old, and went straight through to the other side, where a piece of leather covered the opening to help keep dust out of the inner workings. He doubted that this was effective.

They had taken his weapons, but not his tools, which were secreted throughout his clothing in hidden slots and pockets. For this lock, he would need one of the larger picks. He reached into his trousers, down to a slit in the inner seam along his right thigh, and pulled out a thin, flexible piece of metal. During a pat-down such as the one he'd received earlier, the presence of the tool would be concealed by the stitching. Only someone very thorough, very sensitive, and very well trained would have noticed it; the Withered One had been thorough and well trained, but its stiff fingers apparently were not very sensitive.

He stuck the tool into the lock, jiggered it a bit, and was soon rewarded by the sound of the latch coming undone. He carefully withdrew the pick and returned it to its hiding place.

The great thief escapes again, he thought.

He woke the little girl, who seemed unfazed by the trembling of the earth. Perhaps it happened all the time where she came from. He crept outside into the night, a yawning Prehn toddling along beside him. Stars sparkled in the cloudless sky; the blowing, drifting salt was still tonight, waiting for the next storm to come. He didn't think the rumble had been thunder. They moved away from the building. He could feel the ground humming beneath his feet; the vibrations seemed to be getting stronger. Was he the only one who found it disconcerting?

Suddenly a shadow appeared in front of them: One of Diasa's silent, hooded guards. The sentinel barred their path, holding its long weapon horizontally like a barricade, though it made no move to engage them. "Return to room," it said, its voice a thin, raspy whisper, like sand sliding across rock.

He hadn't expected the creature to speak, and it took him a moment to find his voice. "The ground is shaking," he said.

"Only servant of the college, working under the earth," it said. "Nothing to fear."

"Working under the earth?"

"Digging mines and wells."

"I don't understand," Adaran said. "Why would that make the ground shake?"

"Maybe mine collapse. No danger." It pointed its weapon in the direction of the dormitory. "Return to—"

Suddenly a flare from the sky lit up the night, as if someone had thrown a torch to reignite the sun. The Withered One hissed and covered its eyes with a black-robed arm; Adaran found himself temporarily blinded, the sudden change in illumination physically painful.

This could only be an attack. Dunshandrin's men, come looking for him with magic. He remembered passing a copse of stunted trees on his way to the dormitory; it would be to his right, and ahead. He broke into a run, listening to the ground, moving in the direction where he thought he could find cover.

By the time his vision cleared, he was already there.

Damona said: "What do you think of our guest?"

"I think he's trouble. Would you like some more water?"

"Please."

Diasa filled the headmistress's cup and put the pitcher back in the center of the table, between the bowl of steamed vegetables and the platter of meat. She didn't know what sort of meat it was, exactly; in the Salt Flats, one quickly learned not to ask what one was eating, because the answer seldom pleased. At least it was tender and well-seasoned; but that only made its origin even more suspect.

"What sort of trouble do you expect?"

"Dunshandrin's people are looking for him. They may come here and try to take him."

Damona shook her head. "They will know better. Flaurent stands above the machinations of lords and kings."

"You give Dunshandrin too much credit. You heard that story about the dragon's crystals. He's clearly gone mad, wasting his resources on such foolishness, not to mention risking the ire of a dragon."

"He must think he has something quite significant to gain, to take such a chance."

"I can't imagine what."

"Power. What else does such a man want?"

"Women? Gold? Territory?" Diasa shrugged. "A few chips of shiny glass won't help him with any such thing."

Damona sighed and waved a hand dismissively. "You have a quick tongue, Diasa, but you can only see that which is in front of you, that which you can touch."

"You see enough things that aren't there," Diasa said. "I certainly don't need to. Give me something I can stick with a sword and I'm happy."

Damona leaned back and regarded her with half-lidded eyes. "Sometimes I wonder if you are really my daughter."

Diasa snorted. "Only a daughter would put up with you."

Suddenly Damona's eyes widened; a moment later the room lit up, as if a white sun had risen outside the building. Diasa jumped to her feet, whirled. The small windows of the dining room, opened to admit the night breeze, had become squares of brilliant illumination. It almost hurt her eyes to look at them.

"What is this?" Damona whispered.

Diasa went to the window and peered out, squinting. The surrounding landscape was lit up, the colors grey and washed out; she could tell from the shadows that the light came from above, somewhere nearly directly overhead the college.

She knew what this was, even if her mother didn't.

This was an attack.

Suddenly a great voice boomed: *"We want the one called Adaran!*

Surrender him, or face destruction!"

Diasa turned to the headmistress. "I told you so."

Damona had already risen from her chair. "This is not the way one comes to Flaurent to claim a fugitive," she murmured.

"Evidently it is, if you are Lord Dunshandrin."

"No. It is not. Go, Diasa. Summon the Withered Ones. Adaran will not be taken from us by threat of force."

"Mother, he is not worth it."

"The precedent cannot be set!" Damona cried. "Flaurent is and must remain a refuge!"

"A refuge." Diasa snatched up her belt and scabbard from the back of the chair where she had hung it. "He doesn't belong here. We should just hand him over and be done."

"That is not for you to decide, child. Go!"

Diasa left the headmistress's quarters. Outside, night had become day, the grounds harshly lit by the brilliance flaring from above. She could scarcely look up, and if she did, she could see nothing; this, of course, was the intent.

The Withered Ones had already begun gathering outside, attempting to respond to the threat. They seemed seriously affected by the glare, stumbling along as if finding their way by hearing rather than by sight. Sunlight didn't affect them in such a way, but this was not sunlight; perhaps it interfered with whatever sense served as their vision. She knew they didn't see as she did, because their eyes were shriveled things, raisins in their puckered faces.

Only a true sorcerer could generate a display such as this; Dunshandrin had sent a wizard to claim Adaran. Diasa didn't think much of wizards in general, considering most of them cheats and fakers, purveyors of tricks and sleights of hand; but the fact that this one could light up the entire college and blind her guards suggested that he might be formidable.

She strode across the grounds to the dormitory where she had left Adaran and the girl. The students had assembled on the patio, babbling amongst themselves, shading their eyes and trying to look into the sky. Diasa was somewhat surprised that they weren't mixing their potions and powders in an attempt to identify the intruders. "Get back to your rooms," she told them. "It's not safe out here."

"Are we being attacked?" one of them said.

"Not yet. Go on, get inside." She directed the Withered Ones to encourage the students to take cover, then went to Adaran's door, only to find it ajar. She opened it and looked inside, but the room was empty, the occupants gone. She'd assumed he had the wherewithal to pick a lock, and had posted a guard outside; but the guard had been blinded, and Adaran had escaped. He could be anywhere in the college by now, or even outside it, if he had managed to find his way through a gate or over the wall.

She slammed the door in frustration and turned. A figure approached, weapon in hand. Not one of her guards; they carried pole arms, and this one had a sword. She drew her own blade. The man stopped advancing and stood there looking at her. Now that he was closer, she saw that he wore something over his eyes, smoked goggles, protecting him from the blinding light. "Who are you?" she said. "What do you want?"

"My name is Gelt," he said. "I've been following you."

"Why?"

"Because you seemed like a woman who knew where she was going. Is Adaran in here?"

"He was, but it seems he has escaped."

"Really. Where do you suppose he's gotten to?"

"I've no idea," Diasa said. "Why doesn't your pet magician just conjure him up?"

"Pet magician? What makes you think I'm not making this light all by myself?"

"If you were, you wouldn't need to shield your eyes."

He grinned. "Clever girl."

"I'm not a girl," Diasa said. "I'm a woman, and more than a match for the likes of you."

"We'll have to test that theory." Gelt pointed his sword at her heart, then hesitated, cocking his head as if listening to something only he could hear. He lowered his blade. "But not tonight. Orioke has found the thief's hiding place."

"Thief? What did he steal?"

Gelt didn't answer; instead, he turned and ran toward the fish pond, which was surrounded by a heavy growth of trees. Diasa watched him go. Damona's instructions had been very clear: She was not to let Dunshandrin's men take Adaran by threat of force.

Diasa still didn't see why they should risk the safety of the college over an obvious scoundrel, but as the headmistress had said, the decision was hers, not Diasa's.

She sighed, signaled the Withered Ones to follow, and went after Gelt.

Following several hours of flying along the dark shoreline of Barbareth, Astilan came into view, a compact collection of square buildings hugging a bluff that overlooked a harbor. T'Sian had told Ponn to alert her when they approached the city, and so he did, shouting to be heard over the wind. She gave a little burst of flame from her nostrils and altered course, starting to descend toward the city.

He looked at Parillon. The other man hung limply in the dragon's talon, as he had for some time; Ponn was concerned that T'Sian may have injured him, either when she had wrecked the trailer or when she'd snatched him up.

She circled low over the city a few times, giving Ponn a view such as he had never thought to experience. In the torchlight of the main streets, he saw a few people going about whatever business—begging, illness, adultery, murder—took them from their homes at this hour. Furtive shapes stood in doorways and in the mouths of alleys, waiting to ply their questionable trades on customers or victims. A night patrol passed by beneath them, four soldiers and a youth with a lantern; the denizens of the night scattered at their approach, retreating deeper into the shadows, where the flickering light could not reach. They passed by the king's castle, the compact fortress a smaller version of the walled city that surrounded it, like a shell within a shell. It stood on a small rise, helping to lift its towers high above the surrounding buildings. Standing at those parapets, an observer could probably see the entire town, from wall to wall.

What must T'Sian see, with her undoubtedly superior vision? Did anyone down there feel the dragon's gaze upon them, and look up into the night sky with a fleeting shiver?

After surveying the city, T'Sian flew to the north and landed in the rolling hills, in a sandy area that had not been cultivated for crops or livestock. She beat her great wings rapidly, settling down on her hind legs, then leaning forward to release Ponn and Parillon. Ponn quickly went to his friend, who lay on his side in the grass. The other man's skin was cold and clammy, his breathing rapid and shallow. Gently, he rolled Parillon onto his back; his eyes were wide, staring at nothing.

"Parillon?" Ponn said. "Can you hear me?"

No answer.

Ponn didn't like this at all. He was not very familiar with Astilan, but there had to be a healer there, and Parillon needed one. He looked for the dragon but she had gone, most likely slunk off to change into her human form. Turning back to Parillon, he whispered: "Don't worry. We will find someone in the city who can help you."

Parillon's lips moved as if he were trying to speak, but Ponn heard no words. Where was T'Sian? After what seemed a very long time, she approached from the west, coming around an eroded bluff. She stopped a few feet away, looking down at Ponn and Parillon. "Get up," she said. "We must go into the city and learn if Gelt and his men are agents of this King Varmot. If they are, we will punish him."

"First Parillon needs a healer. I think you hurt him."

She cocked her head. "But I was careful."

"Not careful enough. The way you grabbed us and just took off, the shock alone could have killed him."

She crouched down beside Parillon, looking at him as if he were an unusual and interesting sort of insect. "You men can be killed merely by being surprised?"

"Sometimes. We are not so durable as dragons."

T'Sian, evidently fascinated by this topic, said: "How else can I kill you?"

Ponn thought a moment. "Are you asking me because you want to avoid hurting people accidentally," he said, "or because you want to be able to kill us in a wider variety of ways?"

"I have been killing humans quite effectively for years without your assistance," she said. "I am merely curious. You would be well advised to tell me how *not* to kill you, so that you do not come to harm through misadventure, like your friend."

"Another time, perhaps," Ponn said. "Right now we must tend to Parillon. He must be kept warm. If I gather wood, will you ignite it for us?"

She shrugged.

"You *can* start a fire without creating an inferno?"

"Of course I can," she said. "I am not the lightning. Gather wood, if you can find any, and I will burn it."

She made a good point; the plains of Barbareth boasted little in the way of forest, and by the moonlight he could see that this wasn't a very good spot to find anything more than kindling. There were no trees, only tall grass, weeds, and the occasional shrub. He walked some distance from Parillon and T'Sian, up a low, sandy rise, then circled around to the north and east and back down again. From the terrain—scattered large stones with debris gathered beneath them, sand, ridges with eroded edges—he concluded that T'Sian had landed in a dry flood plain. He picked through some of the detritus, but it consisted mostly of the same vegetation he saw around him, bent into odd shapes by the force of old torrents.

He returned to the others empty-handed. T'Sian looked at him for a moment, then said: "I thought you were going to gather wood."

"There is no wood."

"Why not just carry him into town? I can lift him easily."

"No, you mustn't do that. Moving him may cause further injury."

"Oh." T'Sian looked down at Parillon, then back at Ponn. "I already picked him up once, to see how unwieldy it would be to carry him while I am in this form."

"What?" Ponn cried. "I told you he needed a healer!"

"You never said not to move him."

"But ..." Ponn trailed off. Argument was pointless; the dragon would merely say, with utter truthfulness, that she'd had no idea that moving an injured man could hurt him, and then make some comment on the infirmity of humans. He shook his head and hurried to Parillon's side. He didn't appear to be breathing. Ponn checked Parillon's wrist and then his throat, feeling for the heartbeat, but there was none; he held his fingers beneath the man's nose and felt no exhalation. Looking into Parillon's wide, staring eyes was like peering through the windows of an empty house.

He glanced at T'Sian, who was watching his efforts with close attention. "I think you killed him."

"Does that mean we have no need for a healer now?"

"There's no point. You cannot heal a dead man." He reached out and shut Parillon's eyes. "Good night, my friend."

"Why did you do that?"

"Do what?"

"Close his eyes."

"Tradition. Respect."

"That shows respect?"

"Yes," Ponn said. "Respect for the dead."

"Why do the dead care whether their eyes are open or not?" T'Sian said. Then, after a moment: "You just do not like having a dead man watch you."

Exasperated, Ponn stood. "Why do you bother to ask me so many questions, if you are already so wise?"

"To find out what lies you men tell yourselves."

"And what lies do *you* tell, T'Sian?   Did you kill Parillon intentionally while I was looking for wood, to relieve yourself of an inconvenience?"

"Of course not. I wanted his assistance." Her eyes glittered in the moonlight. "And if I did choose to kill him, why would I bother to lie about it?"

The explanation rang true; her fury was directed toward Gelt and the others she believed had harmed her hatchlings. She had no real reason to have injured Parillon deliberately. "All right," he said. "I believe you."

"Imagine my relief."   She nudged Parillon with her foot; Ponn noted with some astonishment that her rear talons had molded themselves into the form of greenish-black shoes. Amazing. "This one will attract dogs or other scavengers if we do not dispose of the body."

A disturbing thought. "Yes, I suppose he will."

"I will take care it." She looked at him with those faintly luminous eyes. "Turn aside, if you do not wish to see."

"No. I'll watch."

"Very well. But you must move away." She waited until he had backed off some distance, then turned to Parillon's body. Her chest swelled, as if she were drawing a deep, deep breath; then she opened her mouth in what looked like a yawn. A stream of orange fire flashed out, engulfing the corpse and the surrounding grass, consuming them in an instant. Still breathing fire, she moved in a circle, creating a sort of fiery whirlwind that somehow contained the blaze she had created. When she was finished, the fire had burned itself out, leaving a large circle of ash and blackened sand.

T'Sian looked at Ponn. "Was that a suitable disposition of your friend's body?" she asked, little wisps of smoke escaping from her mouth as she spoke.

"It will do," Ponn said.

From the cover of the trees, Adaran assessed the situation. First off, the voice; even though it was dressed up with thunder, he recognized it. Adaran had suspected all along that Orioke had escaped Dosen's treachery; but what was he doing here, now, demanding Adaran's surrender? Had the attack on the wizard's tent been staged? He didn't think so. Orioke must have found his way back to Dunshandrin and come to some new arrangement with the lord and the princes. Now they had sent him out as their agent, to deal with Dosen's failure.

Adaran doubted that Orioke had the power to level the college's sturdy structures, but the headmistress and Diasa would not know that. Faced with this display, Adaran thought, they would certainly hand him over to spare themselves the risk of destruction. He would have to escape from these walls, before—

Suddenly the light changed, intensified, and he found himself standing in a glaring column of it, scarcely filtered by the foliage overhead. Orioke was illuminating him for all to see. He bolted, running toward the central avenue where he had walked with Diasa earlier in the day. The spotlight moved with him, blinding him; he crashed into someone and they both went down in a tangle of limbs. He rolled away and sprang to his feet, but couldn't see who he had knocked down, or where the he was, or even what direction he was now facing. "Who's there?" he cried.

A voice, dark and scratchy like the surface of a well-worn bar, said: "You knocked down an old woman. She looks angry."

"Barbarian!" That voice belonged, unquestionably, to the headmistress. "This is not how you come to Flaurent to claim a fugitive!"

Suddenly the harsh column of light around Adaran faded, and the original glare returned; what had seemed intolerably bright before was now a welcome relief. The headmistress was getting to her feet, adjusting her besmirched robes; a man with a sword stood nearby, watching this with a smile, as if he found them both to be amusing clowns. Adaran realized he had met this fellow before, in Dunshandrin's castle, when they had first been dispatched on their errand. "Gelt?" he said.

"The very same."

"You're supposed to be in Enshenneah."

"My job there is long since finished. I've a new task now."

Realization dawned. "*You* took the little girl."

Gelt laughed. "Here I am, come to kill you, and *that* is your concern? But you are correct. One of my men delivered her to Dosen for safekeeping. I hear he succeeded in that no better than he did in dealing with you lot."

Diasa was coming, running toward them with a group of guards at her back. They seemed to have adapted to the light, or perhaps they found its reduced intensity less troubling. Gelt appeared not to have noticed them yet.

"Dosen was unsuccessful in many things," Adaran said.

"Yes, well, perhaps Dunshandrin will thank you for ridding him of one of his less competent servants. I warned them not to entrust Dosen with that operation, but they were damned impatient." He pointed his sword at Adaran. "Where would you like it? I've nothing against you, so I am willing to make this quick."

"Why kill me?" Adaran said. "I'm no threat."

"Because they told me to."

"Can we make a deal?"

Gelt cackled. "What have you got to barter with? A crone and an Enshennean toddler?"

Diasa and her soldiers were closing, a hundred yards away, maybe less. Gelt glanced their way, turned to meet them. Suddenly the ground began to shake, throwing Gelt and the headmistress off balance; Adaran managed to keep his footing, adjusting to the heaving earth. A chasm opened in front of Gelt, spreading, widening, dirt and sand falling down into darkness. Diasa skidded to a halt just shy of the edge, then urged her creatures back as the lips began to crumble. More than one of them was lost, vanishing silently into the crevice.

Then something emerged from the abyss, a column made of shifting earth and stone, bearing a lopsided figure that a child might have assembled of rocks and mud.

"Deliban!" the headmistress cried. "I did not summon you!"

The golem raised its arms and spread them wide; a roar filled the night as the crevice spread east and west, splitting the college in two. Smaller cracks appeared, branching off from the large one. Trees toppled over; water gushed from broken pipes; grey fingers of dust scratched at the air. The ground itself swelled beneath Adaran, bulging, pushing him upward. Now he did fall, toppling over backwards, but talons clamped onto his shoulders, cutting through his clothing and digging into his flesh. Moments later he felt the earth fall away as beating wings lifted him into the sky. He reached up and felt the scaly legs of a great bird.

"Hello again, Adaran," Orioke called from his saddle on the beast's back. "I've come to take you back to Dunshandrin's castle. The journey will go by faster if you sleep through it, don't you agree?" The wizard muttered a few Words in a nonsensical tongue; Adaran found himself growing weary, even though the pain in his shoulders was fresh and raw, and his feet were kicking over empty space, and the air was full of screams as the creature called Deliban tore Flaurent to pieces.

Moments later, Adaran was fast asleep.

9

PONN AWOKE NEXT TO THE blotch of scorched earth that marked Parillon's pyre. The heavy, greasy stink of burning flesh hung in the air like a lingering spirit. He stood and moved away from the spot where his friend had died, but the smell followed him; the smoke of the burning had touched him, contaminated him, clinging to his clothes and skin. He needed to wash it off.

He followed the downward slope of the ground to a creek that flowed through the area. He had heard its quiet waters last night while searching for wood, but hadn't actually come upon it. The stream was narrow and shallow, but would have to do. He tested the water with his toe. Frigid. Was this really necessary? He lifted up his tunic and sniffed it. Yes, it stank. He'd had guests who smelled worse, but even so, he didn't want to go around carrying the odor of Parillon's cremation with him.

Ponn stripped off his clothes and climbed down the bank into the rill. His skin puckered into gooseflesh and he felt his balls creep up his thighs. He quickly splashed water over his body, wiping himself down as best he could; then he dragged his garments in and repeatedly submerged them, wringing them dry each time. Lacking soap, he could do no better.

Naked, he climbed out of the stream and spread his clothes on the tall, spiky grass, hoping they would dry quickly. From behind him, T'Sian's voice said: "What were you doing down there?" He whirled, startled, then remembered that he had no clothes on and tried to cover himself.

T'Sian smirked in a very human-like manner. "Do not trouble

yourself with modesty on my account," she said. "Your body holds no charms for me."

"Likewise, I'm sure," Ponn said. Then: "If you must know, I was trying to wash. The stink of last night's fire was upon me."

"Stink?"

"From when you burned Parillon."

She came up close and flicked out her long, serpentine tongue, tickling his throat and collarbone. Its touch was light, soft, and quite warm. "I still taste smoke," she said.

Ponn backed off, uncomfortable with the contact, and picked up his clothes. They were still wet, but he began to put them on just the same. "I washed as best I could. I have no perfume to mask the odor."

"It is not unpleasant."

"To you, perhaps," he said. "Men don't like to go around smelling of burned flesh."

"What do I smell like?"

"What?"

She stepped up close to him. "I burned your friend. I stood at the edge of the flames. Tell me what I smell like."

"All right. If I must." He leaned into her, their bodies touching; it was like embracing a clay statue still hot from the kiln. After his dip in the icy water of the stream, though, he welcomed the warmth. He sniffed her shoulder; she smelled of smoke and ashes, of hot iron, of molten rock. Ponn doubted this odor could be washed away by the water. He stepped back. "You smell like fire and volcanoes," he said. "You smell like destruction."

T'Sian appeared to consider this; then she said: "Good."

Of course she would be pleased to hear something like that. "Some may wonder why a … person of your appearance smells like a blacksmith fresh from the forge."

"Let them wonder."

"Yes, of course. And if any should dare to ask, a sharp glare will silence them."

She raised a red eyebrow at that. "When it comes to odors, you men have little enough right to complain. That inn of yours reeked of sweat and vomit, and I am quite sure more than one patron relieved himself in the corner."

"True enough, but in a certain kind of establishment, from a certain kind of customer, that is only to be expected." This led him to another thought. "As we have no money, our options for lodging are going to be limited. We may have to work in exchange for a room, and that room will probably smell worse than the inn at Dyvversant."

"We have money."

Startled, he said: "We do?"

"The men driving your wagon carried a trunk full of coins. I took it."

"Did they?" He rubbed his chin. "It must have been tax revenue. How much?"

"I have not counted it," she said. "The trunk is too heavy for a single man to carry. I buried it before I changed, not far from where we landed."

"Well, that improves our prospects. We should take enough for rooms, food, and a few bribes, and leave the rest buried for now."

"Fine," she said. "And when we have finished our business, you can have what is left."

"You don't want it for your hoard?"

"I have no hoard." She shook her head. "You men and your fairy tales about dragon loot."

She turned and began walking up the slope, back toward where they had spent the night, where she had burned Parillon, where she had buried the money. Ponn had to hurry to catch up with her. "So you don't sleep on a mound of treasure, then?"

"No," she said. "I sleep on a mound of the bones of foolish men who came looking for a mound of treasure."

Ponn stopped, picturing the dragon curled up on such a macabre bed; but then he heard her making a strange noise, a cross between a hiss and a series of hiccups.

After a moment, he realized she was laughing at him.

An unfamiliar voice said: "Wake up, little man."

Adaran heard the command, but he couldn't quite open his eyes. He would much rather stay where he was, asleep, than awaken and learn what sort of predicament he was in. Besides, he was having the grandest dream about little Redshen.

"Wake up," the voice said again. "Wake up!"

"You cannot rouse him until I release the spell." This was Orioke's voice. Adaran stirred a bit at the sound; here was a speaker to whom he was required to listen.

"Release the spell, then. Or did you bring me down here to stare at a sleeping thief?"

Orioke laughed and spoke a few Words.

Awakening at once, Adaran found himself chained to a wall, wrists and ankles manacled, the stone hard and cold against his back. He blinked a few times, clearing a film that had formed over his eyes while he slept, allowing him to see the cell that held him. It was almost the same size as the room he'd been given at Flaurent, but it was damp where the other had been bone-dry, cold rather than warm, musty, loud. Moisture seeped down the walls, collecting in small puddles on the floor; he could hear water rushing nearby, a steady, dull roar, like rapids or a waterfall. The walls thrummed with the vibration.

Adaran finally focused on the men in the room. He recognized two of them, Gelt and Orioke, but had never before seen the third. He would have remembered such a scabrous creature, with skin marred by oozing sores and hair growing in small, odd tufts, as if he had numerous tiny brushes glued to his skull. Orioke and the misshapen fellow stood directly in front of him; Gelt leaned against the wall near the far corner, holding up a torch to provide some light.

The pustulate man said: "He looks disoriented."

"It's the spell," Orioke said. "Have you never awakened from a deep sleep and wondered where you were?"

"I don't have deep sleeps."

"This is all a very interesting demonstration of how you put a man to sleep and wake him up again," Gelt said, "but remind me why you brought him back, instead of just killing him?"

"I have my reasons," Orioke said.

Gelt said: "I can only imagine what they might be."

"I hope there's no disloyalty brewing here," the other man said. "I will have no part of it."

"Your fealty does you credit, Qalor, and will, I'm sure, be richly rewarded," Orioke said. Gelt coughed, then snorted as if he'd choked on something. "In any event, you needn't worry. Does this pathetic fool strike you as a threat?"

"Perhaps you've forgotten that he evaded an entire camp full of guards, killing a number of them in the process, then slew Dosen and escaped on a stolen eagle."

"No, indeed, I have not, but he will not escape this time." Orioke put his hand on Qalor's shoulder. "Enough lingering in the dungeon! The cold and damp is not good for our lungs. We three can retire to your chambers, Qalor, and discuss matters of importance to us all."

Qalor sighed. "Very well."

Orioke smiled and steered Qalor toward the door. They departed through it; Gelt followed, shutting the door behind him. Adaran heard a bar being thrown and a bolt turned as they locked him in.

As the lantern light receded, it became quite dark in the cell; the only illumination came from a flickering torch somewhere outside, flowing wanly through a narrow, barred opening in the door. Adaran jogged the manacles at his wrist, listening to the noise that the chains made. They sounded thick and sturdy, lacking the dull scratch of rust or the tinkle of shoddy manufacture. The irons at his ankles seemed just as strong.

He tested the amount of play in the chains that held his wrists. Not as much as he would have liked. He shook the manacles again, wondering if he could get his hands free. He judged that the left manacle was the looser, and so started on that one first. He pulled his hand as far into it as it would go, then slowly rotated it, searching for the angle where the cuff was widest; he had yet to encounter one that was perfectly round. He soon found the most promising position, and set about making his hand as uniformly straight as possible, to eliminate the curves and bulges that kept the manacle from sliding off. That meant doing something with his thumb. He worked it in and out, left and right, trying to dislocate the bone from its socket. In, out. Left, right.

Abruptly, it popped.

Agony shot up Adaran's arm, as if he'd put his fingers on an anvil as the smith struck a blow. Clenching his teeth, he slowly began to draw his hand out of the confining band of metal. The sharp edge of the cuff peeled off layers of skin as if it were a potato bound for the pot; the manacle was above his shoulder, so the blood that could have lubricated his effort was wasted, flowing down his arm to drip from his elbow. The pain became too great and he had to stop, sweating from hurt and tension, holding steady for a little while before starting to pull again.

At last, his hand popped free of the manacle. He slammed it against his chest, popping the thumb back into position. He looked at it for a few seconds, then wriggled all his digits. Everything still worked, though the flesh was scraped and raw and bleeding.

He patted himself down, feeling for his hidden pockets, looking for a tool. Nothing. He realized that he wasn't dressed in his own clothing anymore, but instead wore prison rags like a common criminal. He would have to do the same thing to right hand that he had done to his left.

Well, if the price of escape was a little pain and a little lost skin, he would pay it gladly.

Tolaria stood at her tall windows, in her usual spot, and looked out at the placid surface of the lake, far below, past the town. Dawn had stolen across it, lending the warmth of its ruddy colors to the steel-grey water. The forested hilltops to the north and east were afire with light as the sun climbed over them. The town itself looked quiet, thin trails of smoke rising into the sky from hearths and chimneys, pushed off across the plains by a gentle wind. Dunshandrin hardly seemed like a nation that was mobilizing for war; but then again, the people in that village didn't know that war was imminent, did they?

Tolaria started as someone draped a blanket over her shoulders: Wyst, creeping up, silent as the sun moving through the sky. "It's a chill morning, my lady," she said. "You'll take sick."

"I'm quite warm enough, thank you," Tolaria said. "I did manage to survive for a number of years without anyone to bring me furs and slippers whenever I shivered."

Wyst mumbled some sort of apology and fled back to her corner. The oracle shook her head. She shouldn't take her frustrations out on the girl; Wyst was a simple creature, doing as she was told, and terrified of punishment. She must think Tolaria a horribly ungrateful mistress.

Tolaria turned away from the window and padded back to her bed. She sank onto its softness and contemplated the vision that had jolted her from sleep and sent her to stare out into the darkness as it lightened into day. She had dreamed of Flaurent, where she'd been taught to control her gifts. The walled oasis in the Salt Flats had been her home for many years; she'd learned letters there, lost her virginity, gained her vision.

In her dream, she had returned to the college, gliding up the grey river on a flat-bottomed boat with no pilot; but she had not found the school intact. Its walls lay in ruin and rubble, its buildings crumbled and half-buried in dust and salt. The waters of its broken fountains had flowed in short, dark dribbles before vanishing into the thirsty earth. Stepping off the boat, she had wandered through the devastated college, seeing in the ruins the traces of places she had once known. She called and called for her teachers and her friends, but her voice merely echoed off the dead walls and blew away in the wind. Eventually, she found a single body: The headmistress, buried up to her neck in sand and rubble, her face blistered and peeling from the relentless sun and the stinging clouds of salt. Tolaria had stood, looking down at the dead woman, and suddenly the dry eyes had opened and the silenced mouth had spoken to her, using a language she had never heard before. She began to grow dizzy and it seemed as if the words were in the air, flying around her like angry insects, cutting her with their sharp sounds, stinging her with their pointed meanings; despite this, she had no idea what the headmistress was trying to convey.

Tolaria knew they had sent Orioke to Flaurent; she feared that this nightmare was something more than the workings of her ignorant imagination.

Suddenly the door to Torrant's room banged open, rousing her from her thoughts. The prince stood in the open doorway, wearing his purple nightshirt and a matching pair of soft slippers, ornamented to the point of absurdity with gold thread and tassels. "Good morning, Tolaria," he said. "I heard you moving about. Why are you up so early?"

"I couldn't sleep."

"Ah, yes. Sleep can be elusive when great events are underway." He stepped into the room, stretched, yawned, and scratched himself, making it painfully obvious that he wore no undergarments beneath the nightshirt. "If you would care to come into my chambers, perhaps we could while away the morning in pursuit of something other than rest."

"No, thank you," Tolaria said. "I believe I will stay here and count the cracks in the ceiling again. I think some new ones may have formed since yesterday."

Torrant chuckled. "As you wish. Of course, I will be back again tomorrow to make the same proposal." Then his face grew serious and he added: "Eventually it will *not* be a request." He withdrew, shutting the door behind him.

Tolaria threw one of her pillows at the closed portal, but missed, instead striking the porcelain bowl and pitcher that stood on a table beside it. The impact knocked them off the table and they fell to the floor, shattering. Water darkened the stone. Wyst gave a little shriek and scurried over. "Oh, look what's happened," she said, picking up the pieces. "Your basin fell off the table."

"It didn't *fall*," Tolaria said, coming over to help Wyst collect the fragments. "I knocked it off."

"Stay away, my lady! You may cut your feet."

"Perhaps Torrant will come back and cut *his* feet," she said, with malicious hope.

"Oh, no, the prince mustn't do that!" Wyst exclaimed. She continued picking up shards, down to the most minuscule slivers of white, collecting them on the table. "There, now we needn't worry about the prince's poor feet. You stay where you are, my lady. There may be more pieces across the floor. I'll fetch a broom and a new basin."

Wyst crossed the room, reached into the neckline of her shift, and pulled out a key. Using it, she unlocked the door and exited into the hallway, closing the door behind her. Tolaria sat on the bed, staring at the door, too astonished to move. Wyst had a key! Why hadn't she noticed that before? Well, the simple reason was that Wyst had never left her side before. She had seen the string around the girl's neck, and had assumed it carried some worthless trinket. But a key ... now *that* was something interesting.

Tolaria went to the door and tried the knob. Wyst had locked it again, of course. But that was actually a good thing; she would hear the key turning before the door opened, giving her a chance to react. She quickly moved about the room, seeking something to use as a weapon. Not the chairs; they were huge and ornate, far too heavy for her to lift. She could scarcely manage to drag them. The basin and pitcher were smashed, the pieces too small to be of any use. A candlestick? Three stood on the mantel, silver and solid-looking, gifts from Torrant not long after they'd moved her to this room. To help lighten her mood, he'd said, trying to make a little joke. She grabbed one, hefted it, swung it a couple of times. She could manage this. Clutching the candelabrum, she hurried back to the door, flattened herself against the wall beside it, and waited.

And waited.

And waited.

She began to wonder if Wyst were really coming back. How long did it take to get a basin and a pitcher? Where did they keep them, in the kitchen? Where *was* the kitchen, anyway? Had the girl found something better to do? Perhaps she had stolen away to meet a boyfriend? No, Tolaria couldn't believe that. Wyst was far too cowed to neglect her duty in such a fashion. If she had not returned yet, it was because something or someone had prevented her.

She heard a low voice, nothing like Wyst's, mumbling in the hallway just outside her door. She raised the candlestick just as the lock unfastened and the door opened, then brought it down hard on her visitor's head. It connected with a solid *thump*; the man crumpled to the floor like a heap of unwashed laundry. She quickly dragged him inside, shut the door, and rolled him over. Orioke. Why would *he* be sneaking into her chambers? Had he met Wyst in the castle halls and interfered with her? Well, no matter. The wizard had decided to join forces with her captors instead of rescuing her; now he would help her unwittingly, by lending her his garments. She quickly stripped him of his hooded cloak and the robe beneath, leaving him naked except for his underclothes. He turned out to be a pallid, scrawny, thin-limbed creature, not much larger than she was; if she'd found him in the gutter, she would have taken him for a pathetic wastrel rather than a dangerous magician.

She trussed his wrists and ankles with cords from the draperies around the window, gagged him with a pillowcase, and shoved him as far as she could under the bed. Then she donned his clothes; they smelled of sweat and dust and salt, reminding her of Flaurent. She went to the door, opened it a crack, and looked around. The hallway was quiet, deserted; it was very early, and few denizens of the castle would be awake. Her door was not guarded. Perhaps the twins thought it unnecessary to have her watched so closely now that she was in the royal wing, or perhaps Orioke had sent the sentry away.

Tolaria pulled the hood of her stolen robe over her head and slipped out of the room.

She soon found herself hopelessly lost in the castle corridors. She had no idea where any of these hallways went or where an exit might be, and didn't dare speak to the guards or servants she met for fear of being asked a question. As she had hoped, they took her for the wizard and made no attempt to engage her, instead pretending to look elsewhere as she passed; Orioke had obviously made himself well-loved during his time in the castle.

She wandered a while, following breezes that felt like they came from outside in hopes of finding an exit; but the castle was so drafty that this was fruitless. Draughts came through chinks in the wall, ill-fitting shutters, arrow slits, gaps beneath barred doors. Tolaria began to grow anxious. Wyst may have returned, found her gone, and raised the alarm; even now there could be men scouring the castle in search of an impostor dressed in wizardly garb.

She decided to try something different, turning into any corridor she found that was larger than the one she was in. This seemed to work better; she soon found herself in a hall that she thought she recognized. Hadn't she come through here the day she'd arrived? The stone floor was covered with dried mud, tracked in by people entering from the rain-soaked courtyard. The mud grew thicker to her right, so she went that way, eventually coming to a large door, half-open, letting the light of early morning trickle in. Guards stood on either side, looking sleepy and bored.

To hesitate would be to invite scrutiny. She marched right past them, unchallenged, into the courtyard. She had made it out of the keep, but the outer wall of the castle still stood between her and freedom. The large gate remained closed against those who would intrude in the night; no tradesmen or villagers came or went at this hour. She would have to speak to the guards to be let out through the postern, and without the ability to tell lies, she would have difficulty talking her way past them. She hesitated, and then headed for the stable instead, staying close to the castle wall. The men stationed at the outer gate watched her, but said nothing and issued no challenge.

Entering the darkened horse barn, she relaxed a little. She was out of the open now; perhaps she could find a place to hide until the outer gate opened and traffic began to flow. By then, though, they would no doubt be looking for her; perhaps she could waylay a groom, steal his ragged garments, and escape in the guise of a boy.

She made a quick circuit of the stalls, peering through the slats at the spaces within. Most were empty, and many of the ones that were occupied contained horses that seemed old and thin, not likely to survive a hard day's ride. Certainly she found nothing suitable for a rapid flight across the plains with Dunshandrin's men in pursuit. At the far end of the stable she came upon a large sliding door, held shut by a hasp and padlock. She could see daylight around the edges.

Might this be a way out?

She jiggled the lock, but it felt very sturdy. She doubted she could break it even with leverage, and the noise of such an attempt would bring guards to investigate. She let it fall and it clanked against the door, provoking a chorus of squawks and screeches from the other side. Startled, Tolaria pressed her ear against the crack and listened. Birds, definitely birds, but they sounded oddly loud and throaty. She thought of Qalor's talk about eagles. Was this where he kept them? She put her eye to the gap and squinted through it. She saw large shadows moving, much bigger than any bird she had ever seen, but could make out no details.

Suddenly Tolaria became aware of voices approaching from the direction of the entrance. She looked around for a place to hide, spotted a stack of baled grass teetering against the wall to her right, and darted behind it. Through gaps in the bundles she could see two young men coming toward the rear of the stable. One was loudly describing a chambermaid who had evidently pleasured him the night before. "Her tits were this big!" he said, mimicking breasts with his hands; if he were telling the truth, which Tolaria doubted, the unfortunate woman probably couldn't stand without assistance.

The other youth said, "Have you seen the wench the twins put in the Queen's old room?"

"No, but I heard about her. They say she's an oracle."

"Oracle!" The second groom snorted. "Oracles are old crones. I saw her the day she came in, she's a whore if there ever was one."

"She never comes out of the royal wing."

"Of course not, she's busy servicing the twins. I'd like to get a piece of her, let me tell you!"

"The princes would have your balls."

"They wouldn't know what to do with balls, since they've got none of their own."

The boys laughed, then opened a nearby stall. One stood back, holding the door, while the other coaxed out an aged horse that had been quartered inside. They led it toward the sliding door, its hooves falling silently on the soft earthen floor. One of the grooms produced a shiny black key and undid the padlock, then opened the hasp. Grasping the iron handle, he slid the door to the side. The bird noises got much louder; now Tolaria could hear great wings fluttering as well.

The groom strained to hold the door open as his companion led the horse inside, then ducked through himself; the door began to close on its own, rolling along a track in the floor. She hurried over and caught it just before it shut. Its momentum pulled her off balance, but she braced herself against the wall and managed to stop it, then dragged it open enough to slip inside. She found herself in a short hallway that ended in another sliding door, this one made of metal bars. It had already closed, but didn't appear to have a lock on it. She approached it slowly, staring through the bars at the open space beyond.

It *was* an aviary; but where other kings might keep exotic, brightly colored birds from distant lands, Dunshandrin had a flock of monstrous hawks and eagles ranging from the size of a large dog to bigger than a horse. They hopped and fluttered around an enormous cage made of interlocking wooden beams, forming a dome that rose above high walls of bricks and mortar. The area looked like it had once been part of the courtyard, and she guessed it had only recently been converted to its present use; the wood looked fresh, not yet weathered by winter storms or bleached by summer sun. Within the confines of the bars, the ground had become a morass of churned mud and chalky white droppings, littered with the picked-over carcasses of animals.

The two young men led the quaking horse toward the center of the aviary. The birds swarmed around them, screeching and carrying on. A blade flashed in one groom's hand; Tolaria turned away, feeling sick. She fled back to the panel, wrenched it open, and stumbled into the darkness of the stable. The door banged shut behind her, stifling the sounds of the chattering eagles, the screaming horse.

She heard the iron gate crash closed beyond the door, and hurried back to her hiding place just as the grooms re-entered the stable. The one with the knife still held it out, the horse's blood dark on the gleaming surface. He came over to the pile of hay, scant feet from where Tolaria crouched in the darkness, and wiped the blade clean on the dry grass; the other, who had earlier been boasting about his prowess with a serving girl, now seemed pale and shaken, and very, very young. "I liked it better when we were taking care of horses, not killing them," he said, no trace of bravado left in his voice.

"Do what you're told." The groom checked his knife, then sheathed it. "Otherwise they'll be feeding *us* to those things."

Silent now, the two of them locked the sliding door and left the stable. Tolaria stayed hidden for some time, until she was sure they were gone; then she crept out from behind the bales and moved to the door of the stable. She saw activity in the courtyard now; the postern stood open, townsfolk arriving to spend their day working in the castle. The large gates remained closed, but would likely open soon, to admit carts and wagons and traders on horseback. When that happened, the stable would no longer be a good place to hide.

She adjusted her hood, then walked purposefully to the postern. She kept her pace even, unhurried, trying not to look like a person fleeing the castle. The guards paid little heed; if her escape had been discovered, word had not yet reached the perimeter. She passed into the shadow of the wall, through the opening, out the other side; and then she was standing outside of her prison, on the downward slope of the hill, with the road curving away toward the town below. She started down the road, moving at a brisk pace, maintaining a balance between prudent speed and obvious flight. She crossed the stone bridge without incident, eventually reaching the outskirts of town, where the rock and scrub gave way to low, drab buildings and cobbled roads.

Now what?

The fastest way out of town would likely be by boat, which meant she would need to go to the lake. She had no idea how she would buy passage; she carried no money, and could hardly sell her skills as a shipman. She could imagine, though, what other sort of services a woman might be asked to barter in exchange for a berth on a vessel.

Well, she would worry about that when the time came. For now, she needed to concentrate on reaching the docks. When last she had traveled the city, it had been as a passenger in a carriage; she had not paid a great deal of attention to the route, never expecting to have to retrace it on foot, under the threat of pursuit. All she knew was that the lake would be downhill. She began walking along the main road, a continuation of the track that led up to the castle. This part of town consisted mainly of mean one-story houses, with splotchy, muddy yards overhung with stunted trees. The spaces between homes in most cases lay fallow, but she passed several community gardens that supported meager crops of autumn vegetables. In one, a harvest was going on, old bent-backed women collecting squash about the breadth of large tomatoes. Tolaria knew the variety, having grown it herself in the past, but she would have dismissed specimens of this size as hardly worth picking. If she'd needed any further proof of the poverty of the soil here, there it was.

At length she entered a town square, where the cobbles gave way to flagstones surrounding a dry fountain. She recognized this area; it had been the one time in her trip from the docks that the carriage had not jounced unpleasantly. If she remembered correctly, the carriage had entered from the street to her left. She headed for that avenue, moving through the throng of pedestrians and shoppers, ignoring the cries of the hawkers who sold fabric, food, and other sundries in a makeshift bazaar. She felt a hand fumbling in her pockets; as she carried nothing of value, she pretended not to notice the attempted theft. If she confronted the cutpurse, she would only draw attention to herself.

She exited the square, moving quickly down the road toward the lake. It descended at a sharp angle, as she had recalled. This neighborhood was less residential, more business. She passed a clanging smithy that smelled of fire and iron, a stable, an inn, a bakery, none looking particularly prosperous. The street curved off to the right, then back to the left, bringing the lake into view, the muddy waters glimmering crimson in the early light. She could see the docks below; several boats were tied up, their holds in various stages of emptying or filling. She quickened her pace, hurrying along to the waterfront, then moving up and down the wharf eyeing the vessels, trying to figure out which were preparing for departure, and of those, which was closest to being ready.

"Would you be inspecting cargo, sir?"

Startled, she whirled. A short, portly, and rather dirty man stood nearby. He looked as if he had swum through the muddy water to shore, crawled through the muck, and then shimmied up the pilings to gain access to the pier. "No," she said.

At the sound of her voice, one of his eyebrows went up. "You're a woman?"

"Yes."

"You don't look like a whore. What is a woman who is not a whore doing here at the docks, alone, looking so hungrily at the ships?"

"I'm hoping to find passage out of Dunshandrin."

"If it's passage you want, I may have room on my vessel," he said. "Though some say having a woman aboard is bad luck, I haven't much truck with such superstitions. Where would you be headed?"

"The Crosswaters."

"Ah, yes, the oracles," he said. "We're sailing to Achengate with food and equipment for my Lord Dunshandrin's salt mines. We will be passing by the Crosswaters." He eyed her. "How much would you be able to pay?"

"Nothing."

"Nothing? Why not?"

"I have no money."

"No money? You won't have much success booking passage if the first thing you say is that you have no money. What do you think the oracles would say if you asked for a prediction, then told them you could make no offering?"

"If one's need were great, a true oracle would advise and predict anyway."

"And you think that's what they will do for you?"

"No. I think they're all dead, except for me." His eyes widened at that; she needed to end this conversation before it strayed further into dangerous territory. "Can you find room for me on your boat? I must get away from here."

After a moment, he said: "Who *are* you, my lady?"

"My name is Tolaria."

"And you claim to be an oracle, unless I misunderstand you." He reached up, rubbed the back of his neck. "Why would an oracle have need of *my* poor old boat?"

"Dunshandrin has been holding me prisoner in his castle."

"What! Holding an oracle prisoner? I've never heard of such a thing!" He gave her a narrow, appraising look. "Are you having me on?"

"No."

"And why should I believe that?"

"Because of what Dunshandrin has done to me, I am compelled to answer all questions truthfully; even if I wanted to lie to you, I could not."

His eyes narrowed. "You're saying you cannot lie?"

"Yes."

"Well, that *is* quite a story." The man studied her, sucking on his lower lip. "What was your first impression of me, then?"

"That you were small and dirty and probably a ruffian."

He grimaced. "That was brutally said."

"I mean no offense. I cannot control my answers."

In the distance, a horn blast shattered the morning quiet; she looked around nervously as a second horn sounded, this one much closer. The merchant raised his gaze to the castle. "The alarums," he murmured. "You say you have escaped just this morning?"

"Yes," she said. "*Please.* They will be coming for me."

"Perhaps we can exchange services, then," he said. "I will take you aboard, and you will advise me on a few matters. Is that agreeable?"

"Yes, but I have no herbs or powders," she said. "I am unlikely to be able to enter a trance without them."

"You seem determined to scuttle your chances of getting passage on my boat, or any other. Come. We can work out the particulars later."

As he led her along the dock toward his laden vessel, she said: "I may be able to scrape some materials together at the Crosswaters," she said, "depending on how badly damaged it is. Is it prediction that you want?"

He shook his head. "Information."

"About what?"

"My oldest son," he said. "I've never been sure he's really mine.

He's just a lad, but he's this tall!" He stretched to his tiptoes and raised his arms as far as they would go.

"Have you considered asking the boy's mother?"

"She died of fever when he was a toddler."

"And this is worth bringing me on your ship?"

"Yes. I have a … a growth, you see. On my neck." He rubbed the back of his head. "The doctors say they can do nothing for it. I would know, before I die, if I will be leaving my business to blood kin."

Tolaria frowned. She didn't much like this request, but it was unlikely that she would find anyone who would give her passage without demanding some other service, one she would find even less appealing; and she had already told the little man far too much about her business. "Very well," she said.

"I will show you to a room below deck where you can wait until we depart. There will be an inspection before we leave; you will want to be out of sight during that, I think."

She nodded.

"My name is Talbrett. What did you say yours was?"

"Tolaria."

"Well, Tolaria, let us hope you are wrong, and that we find the Crosswaters sound and intact, eh?"

"We won't," she said.

10

As Adaran had expected, the manacle around his right wrist proved much harder to remove than the one around his left. By the time he finally got free of it, his right hand was scraped raw, dripping blood freely to the floor. Dim shapes scurried about his feet; he had the most appalling idea that they were licking his blood off the dirty stones.

Ignoring the rats or mice or whatever they were, he went to work on the irons that held his ankles. Without tools, this would be even more difficult than freeing his hands; he could not do much to alter the shape of his feet or the width of his ankles. Instead he felt around in the dark, in the vain hope that he might locate something carelessly left in the cell—a bit of wire, perhaps, or a fragment of bone, or even, if he were very lucky, one of his missing lock-picks. He found nothing but moldy straw and filth.

Suddenly the door banged open, revealing the twisted fellow who had accompanied Orioke earlier. He stood there and gawked for a moment at what Adaran was doing, then came in and shut the cell door behind him. "Well, well," he said. "Look at you. Half free already."

Adaran sighed and sat on the cold, wet floor. "If it weren't for these leg irons, I would have been gone by now."

"Perhaps. Orioke said that you were liable to escape, and so here I am to check on you." Qalor crouched down, just out of reach of a lunge, and examined Adaran's injured hands. "Tsk. Look at what you've done." He indicated a fresh, bloody bandage on his shoulder, and another on his upper arm. "As you can see, I am also willing to mutilate myself for my work."

"Your ... work?"

"Alchemy. I was not always like this, you know. The chemicals, the potions, the fumes. They take a toll."

"Surely it's not an alchemist's job to check on prisoners."

"Of course not. But discretion is important and my quarters are nearby, so Orioke gave the responsibility to me."

"You take orders from Orioke?"

"No, no. He made a suggestion, and I agreed to it." Then: "I don't suppose you've seen the wizard since we were all here together earlier?"

After a moment, Adaran said: "Might I have a drink?"

"That's your price for answering, eh? A drink?"

"Yes."

"Very well." Qalor stood, raised up his torch, and exited the cell, not bothering to shut the door. He soon returned, carrying a leaky wooden bucket in which dark liquid sloshed. The alchemist put the bucket on the floor and, using his foot, slid it over in front of Adaran. He put his face into it and slurped greedily. The water was fresh and cold, as if served directly from the river; Adaran drained it as far as he could, until his lips no longer reached the surface. Then he picked it up and poured what was left over his head, rinsing away some of the sweat and grime that crusted his face. He contemplated hurling the empty bucket at Qalor, but decided against it. Unless he got very lucky, the best he could hope for was to injure the man, which would surely invite reprisal. Instead he set it down and pushed it away; as if having read his thoughts, Qalor snatched it and moved it out of reach.

"Well?" the alchemist said.

"What?"

"The wizard. Has he been here?"

"No."

Qalor grunted. "He seems to have gone missing. I thought perhaps he may have visited you again."

"No one's visited me except the rats."

"Rats?"

"Big as horses," Adaran said. "They fled when you brought the torch in."

Qalor stared at him. "Rats," he murmured, "big as horses."

Adaran suffered a sudden vision of Dunshandrin's soldiers charging into battle, mounted on gigantic rodents.

The alchemist pointed a gnarled finger at him and seemed about to speak; but then he apparently changed his mind, picked up the bucket, and left the cell instead, this time shutting and barring the door. His footsteps and the light of his torch retreated up the hallway, then faded.

Qalor hadn't even bothered to manacle his wrists again. Perhaps he believed that Adaran couldn't possibly work his feet free; or maybe he had become distracted by the idea of growing gargantuan rats. Adaran went back to work on his leg irons and found, to his great surprise, that they had come unlocked on their own; all he needed to do was slip the pins and they opened, setting him free. He quickly scrambled away, lest they should change their minds and snap shut again; then he picked one up and examined it. There didn't appear to be anything wrong with it. He checked the dangling manacles, and found that they, too, were now unlocked and easily opened. He looked at them mournfully, then at his scraped up hands, and sighed.

No wonder Orioke had been so sure that he would escape.

He heard a sound from the cell door, a faint sliding noise that he recognized as the bolt opening; but he saw no one outside his cell. Still, he went and to the door and gave it a push. It creaked outward, showing him a short, empty hallway leading off to the right, opening into a larger chamber that appeared deserted.

This was such an obvious setup that Adaran almost felt insulted. The wizard had to be behind this; he had either come down here invisibly and spoken some magic words to free him, or else he had cast a spell earlier with a delayed effect. But what possible reason could Orioke have for bringing him back here, imprisoning him, and then setting him free? It was not for Adaran's own benefit, he was sure of that much; but did he really want to stay in the dungeon until someone learned of his presence and finished the execution that Dosen had botched?

He crept into the dim corridor. It had been carved out of the bedrock, the surrounding stone forming an impenetrable wall; there would be no chiseling away at the mortar in this prison. Only the ceiling was man-made, damp bricks formed into an arched roof, supported by buttresses running into the floor. His cell was near the end of the tunnel, which sloped downward to the left before ending at a blank wall. In the other direction, it opened onto a large room, probably a guard station.

Adaran slunk along the tunnel, passing a number of other cells, all unoccupied; apparently he was the only prisoner at the moment. This could mean that Dunshandrin was unusually liberal, or that he preferred to have people killed rather than jailed. Adaran was fairly certain he knew which.

He paused in the shadows at the mouth of the tunnel, flattening himself against the wall as he peered out at the room beyond. A single lantern, the flame turned low, provided dim illumination. He saw a central table where men would take their meals, a hand-operated pump with the spout still dripping, a partially screened latrine, and another screen with two cots behind it. The table was bare, the cots unmade; he could smell the latrine, but the odor did not seem particularly fresh. Perhaps the dungeon was left unguarded when there were no prisoners; and Qalor had implied that Adaran's presence in the castle was a secret, hadn't he? In any event it seemed that there was no one here to stop him. He stole across the guardroom to the stairs that ascended from the far left corner. They rose into darkness. He took them carefully; the stone was slick, he still felt a bit lightheaded, and a misstep would mean a nasty tumble. Eventually he reached a landing, where another lantern hung from a hook and provided just enough light to see a door in the wall to his right; the stairs continued upward.

He tried the door and found it unlocked. Pushing it open, he peered into a small, odoriferous room lit by dim, globed lanterns. A mass of clay pipes hung from the ceiling, running into another room off to the right; liquid dripped from the joints in the pipes, collecting in noisome puddles on the floor, leading him to deduce that this was some sort of sewage disposal system. The setup looked frightfully clever, but a cesspool was of little interest at the moment. Besides, he had a feeling that the way out was up the stairs. He closed the door and continued climbing, eventually emerging into a castle corridor, blundering out right in front of a pair of guards. They were engaged in a heated discussion about a missing prisoner—a woman, from the sound of it, and an important one—and they didn't look his way as he slipped by.

This corridor led him to another, well-traveled by castle denizens going about their business. They walked back and forth, paying no attention to the ratty, bloodied apparition in their midst; it began to occur to Adaran that something beyond his inarguable ability to melt into the shadows was at work here. He fell into step behind a chambermaid as she hurried along on some errand or other, and started whistling. This elicited no response. He began to sing, loudly and off-key.

Nothing. It was as if he wasn't even there.

Suddenly he stopped. They had just passed a corridor to his right that looked particularly inviting; he felt sure that the way out was in that direction.

Abandoning the maid, Adaran pivoted on his heel and hurried into the royal wing of the castle.

Talbrett guided Tolaria up the gangplank and steered her to the left, toward a stairway that led below. Most of the crew was busy securing supplies and making ready for departure, but she did draw a few odd looks; she pulled Orioke's hood closer and looked at the deck, trying to cover her face. "Don't be afraid," Talbrett said, not turning. "Even if Dunshandrin's soldiers question them, my men won't say they saw you."

"How can you be sure?"

He looked back at her. "Because they're my men."

They descended the steps into the interior of the boat. The stairwell was close, dim, and narrow; the air smelled of damp and mildew. They entered a corridor that was little wider than the stairs, and even darker; a single skylight, crusted with grime, let in little daylight. She saw three pocket doors to the left, and several hammocks hanging from the hull to the right. The hallway ended in another set of steps that led down into the hold.

Talbrett took her to the last door on the left and slid it to the left, revealing a space inside that would scarcely have held the trunk she'd brought with her to Dunshandrin's castle. Inside she saw a hammock with a tiny chest beneath it, a single porthole to the outside, and little else.

"I apologize for the cramped quarters," Talbrett said. "Not what an oracle is accustomed to, I'm sure."

"Lately I've been accustomed to being imprisoned." Tolaria stepped into the room, turned in a little circle. There was room to do that, barely, if she kept her feet close together. "This will do perfectly well. Thank you."

Talbrett nodded. "Good. Now, I expect the inspectors will be along soon, as we plan to sail within the hour. Stay in here until we're underway."

"All right."

The merchant stepped back and closed the door, leaving her alone in the tiny cabin. The door had a bolt on this side and she turned it, feeling a strange joy in being able to do so, to control who would come and go from her quarters, even if those quarters were the size of an oxcart. She went to the small porthole. Like the other glass surfaces she had seen, this one was filthy, streaked with dried river water and dirt and bird droppings, but she could still make out the pier and the lower third of the gangplank. As she watched, a squat figure disembarked from the vessel, stepping off onto the pier. That would be Talbrett, she thought, waiting for the inspector.

She stayed at the window and watched; eventually, two men dressed in Dunshandrin's livery came down the pier, stopped at the gangplank, and talked a moment with Talbrett. These must be the inspectors. The stubby merchant greeted them warmly, clapping their shoulders, shaking their hands; then he guided them up the gangplank, exactly as he had guided her.

He seemed much friendlier with these men than she had expected. Why wouldn't he merely tell them that he had a missing prisoner aboard, collect whatever reward was offered, and go about his business? Had she been foolish to get aboard his ship? Should she sneak off right now, jump into the lake, try to swim away?

She checked the door to her cabin again. It was still bolted, as she had left it; the lock had not magically come undone. She put her hand on the bolt, hesitated, took her hand off again. If trusting Talbrett had been a mistake, then so be it; it was too late to run now.

Tolaria heard the stairs creaking outside her cabin as someone descended into the narrow hallway. She stayed where she was, right behind the door, afraid to move lest they should hear through the parchment-thin walls. The floor groaned as footsteps approached her cabin. She clutched the door handle, ready to resist if someone tried to open it; but they passed on by, heading toward the hold to her left. She imagined Dunshandrin's men peering at the cargo, one of them perhaps holding up a lantern to illuminate it. Would they go down and pick through the crates and bags to ensure that Talbrett had packed no contraband? If they found any, would they search the entire ship? Did they know about her, the missing prisoner?

She put her ear to the side wall of her room, listening as the men moved about the hold. She heard them rapping on crates, opening boxes. After a few minutes of this, the footsteps returned to the hallway. A voice right outside her door said: "Everything appears to be in order here."

"Naturally," Talbrett said. "I'm always careful with what comes aboard my ship, you know."

"Indeed you are," the other man said. Then, in a lower voice: "You heard the horns, of course."

"Of course."

"That means an escaped prisoner."

"Ah," Talbrett said. "That's why you brought a companion?"

"Yes. He'll be questioning your men. We've had no description, though, and no explanation of the crime committed, so we are not sure what we're looking for. Have you seen any suspicious characters lurking around the docks?"

"Most of those who lurk around the docks are suspicious," Talbrett said with a chuckle. "But I've seen nothing out of the ordinary. You are welcome to search the ship if you feel the need."

"Hardly. Even if I wanted to, my Lord Dunshandrin has just taken two-thirds of my men for some campaign in the south. We'll scarcely be able to perform our regular inspections, let alone turning every vessel upside-down."

"Well, I appreciate your concern for getting me on my way in a timely fashion," Talbrett said. Tolaria heard faint metallic clinking, and pictured coins falling into an outstretched hand.

"Would that all merchants were as circumspect as yourself."

The footsteps moved away from her door, toward the stairs to the deck. Talbrett's voice, farther away now, said: "But if they were, how would you justify your salary?"

The inspector laughed. "My salary, as you well know, scarcely buys bread for my family."

Talbrett's reply was inaudible; they had gone back above. Relieved, Tolaria shucked Orioke's cloak, throwing it into the corner. She sat on the edge of the hammock, listening to the ropes creak as it swayed slightly beneath her. True to his word, Talbrett had not betrayed her; and despite his ship's ramshackle appearance, he was apparently known to the inspectors as a reputable merchant. But even then, the man might have searched Talbrett's ship, had Dunshandrin not stirred his resentment through low pay and calling up so many of his colleagues as part of his scheme to invade Barbareth. So in a roundabout way, Dunshandrin had helped his own prisoner to escape.

She doubted that he would appreciate the irony.

Ponn and T'Sian had walked from the wash where they'd spent the night, following a dusty path that ran alongside the region of valleys and ravines. Little more than a donkey trail, lined with saw grass and thistle and burst milkweed, it eventually joined with a much larger road that led to the gates of the city. They stood open wide, letting through traffic that consisted largely of farmers' carts bearing the fruits of a late-season harvest.

They stopped inside the gates, in a wide dirt area that apparently served as a temporary market. Many of the wagons that entered pulled off to the side and stopped, the drivers opening them to display their crops. Bored-looking guards oversaw the activity. Ponn noticed T'Sian eyeing them; he moved away from the area, hoping she would follow before taking some sort of action against them. She had already concluded that Varmot must be her enemy, and might decide to try to throttle information out of those who served him. To his relief, she came with him, moving farther into the town, but she continued to cast dark glances at the guards until they were out of sight.

"So who do you know in *this* town, Pyodor Ponn?"

"No one. I rarely come farther north than Dyvversant."

"Why?"

"I'm too conspicuous. Dyvversant is full of Enshenneans, but Astilan is lily-white. When business needs to be done here, Parillon handles it. Handled, I mean."

"Who did Parillon know here, then?"

"I cannot say. His contacts here were his own. I am a stranger to this city."

"Then it does not matter where we stay." She pointed at a nearby inn. "We will go there."

As T'Sian marched off to the place she had chosen, Ponn eyed the surroundings. In his haste to get her away from the market, he had led her into an area of low, dirty houses, ramshackle buildings, shabby parlors. T'Sian's destination looked like a flophouse, the sort of place he would never patronize were he traveling alone; the money that he carried in his pockets would probably be sufficient for a year's lodging there, if not to buy the place outright. It would also be sufficient to get his throat cut if anyone realized just how much currency he had on him. He hurried after T'Sian, suddenly conscious of the sound that the coins made as they clinked in his pockets. He thrust his hands into them, muffling the sound.

By the time Ponn reached the front step, the dragon had already gone inside. He paused a moment to look at the faded sign, which depicted a gaudily-dressed man carrying a sack over his shoulder. It bulged open at the top, revealing a number of ugly little monsters with pointed ears, black eyes, and sharp teeth. The name of the inn, painted beneath the picture, was *The Man with a Sack of Sorrows*.

Yes, Ponn thought, that was him; except that he didn't even have a sack in which to carry his sorrows. He carried them in his arms, where they could scratch and bite.

He proceeded inside, and found T'Sian waiting for him near the door. She had already attracted the attention of the breakfasting patrons, who were favoring her with oblique glances as Ponn entered. They turned their gazes away as he moved to stand beside her; having a companion made her less vulnerable, less a target for mischief. They could not know, of course, what would happen if they accosted her; the sack-bound troubles of the man on the sign would be rich rewards in comparison to what they would reap.

"What now, Pyodor Ponn?" the dragon said.

"We eat." Having had little food in the last several days, Ponn knew he was in no state to judge; but still, the room smelled marvelous: Frying bacon, sausage, eggs, pancakes, strong coffee. He wondered what T'Sian smelled. She would probably complain that the place reeked of body odor and stale drink.

"You may eat. I have no need; I fed last night."

He didn't ask what T'Sian had fed on, certain that he didn't want to know. Instead he guided her to a table near the hearth and sat. She remained standing for a moment, then settled onto a sturdy chair, gingerly, as if afraid it might collapse beneath her. He wondered how much she weighed. "Perhaps we should get you a hooded cloak so you can conceal yourself a bit," Ponn said. "Everyone is staring at you."

She leaned forward and said, softly, "They would stare even more if I assumed my true form and began leveling this city block by block."

"Yes, I suppose they would."

"Why do you fret so?" T'Sian said, reclining once more. "Do you suppose these villeins will scurry off to your King Varmot and tell him a strange woman is sitting by the fire?"

"He's not *my* king. And I doubt the people who come here are likely to scurry off and tell Varmot anything." He smiled. "More likely they would scurry away from him, back into the shadows where they hide."

"Then stop worrying."

"I've done nothing but worry these past few days." He held his hands out toward the fireplace. "I should get some heavier clothes myself. What I have on is too thin for these northern chills. Perhaps we can do that after I eat?"

She grunted in what he took to be consent, then said: "How will they know what to bring you?"

"Someone will come to the table and ask."

T'Sian made a great show of looking around the room. Aside from the other diners, the room was deserted; no serving staff circulated among the columns of dark wood, no host monitored the needs of the guests. Turning back to Ponn, she said: "I am not convinced that you really know how these places operate."

"At my own inn, we are more attentive than this. I suppose we'll have to call for service."

"Very well." She turned her head and bellowed: "Service!" Her voice approached the level of a roar; Ponn was quite sure she had rattled the shutters. The other patrons now stared quite openly, but dropped their gazes when T'Sian gave them her toothy smile. When she turned it on Ponn, he understood why; it was an unhinged sort of grin, as one might see on a madwoman or a pit-fiend in the night.

A side door opened and a thin, white-haired woman peered out, spotted them, withdrew. A moment later a younger woman emerged and came to their table. "What will you have?" she said, looking bored and sounding irritated.

"Food," Ponn said. "Whatever you have ready in the kitchen. And a room for the night." She gave him a price, one no doubt double what they charged regular patrons. He paid her with a fraction of the coins he carried, and tipped her generously, resulting in a noticeable improvement in her demeanor. On her way back to the kitchen, she visited the other tables and collected more money, joking with the patrons. After she returned to the kitchen, the other breakfasters began to disperse, some leaving the inn, others going up the stairs to the rooms on the floor above.

As the room slowly emptied, T'Sian said: "So, Pyodor Ponn, tell me about this so-called king. Why would he send men to the islands? What would he want with my crystals?"

"We still don't know for sure that Gelt works for Varmot."

"Why would he betray you to the tax collectors otherwise?"

"I don't know," Ponn said. "Perhaps it amused him. I think there's a reward, too, for turning in smugglers and tax cheats."

"A reward? You think he did it for money?"

"He *is* a mercenary."

The kitchen door opened again and the wench came out, carrying a tray with Ponn's meal. She brought it over and set it down on the table. Ponn slipped her another coin, which she put into a pouch at her waist. "If you need anything else, just ask," she said, her tone of voice leaving Ponn little doubt that she did not just mean food and drink.

After the woman had gone, Ponn poked at his meal with his knife, inspecting the sausage, the ham, the eggs. The meat was left over from earlier, he decided, judging by the way the fat had congealed around it and the slightly tough texture, and the bread was not at all fresh. Well, he had asked for whatever they had ready, and he was hungry enough to eat anything they put in front of him.

"What are you doing?" T'Sian said.

"Checking the food."

"Why? Do you think they would poison you?"

"No, I'm just making sure it's cooked through."

"Oh." She showed him that grin again. "If *that* is your concern, I could make certain of it for you."

"Cooked," he said. "Not incinerated." He cut off a piece of sausage, speared it with the knife, tucked it into his mouth. "Anyway, it's fine."

T'Sian watched him eat for a little while, then pointed at his plate and said, "What is that?"

"Sausage," he said, pointing at it with his knife. "That's meat in a casing. And this is ham, which is pig. Eggs. Bread. Potatoes."

"May I try it?"

Surprised, Ponn said: "Yes, of course." He cut off a bit of sausage and held it out to her; she carelessly plucked it off his knife and put it into her mouth. She didn't appear to chew, but merely swallowed. "I didn't know you could eat human food. While you look like that, I mean."

"I can," she said. "I hardly make a practice of it."

"How do you like it?"

"It lacks a certain freshness."

"Freshness?"

"Freshly killed meat seared in my own flames," she said. "That is what I eat. This food of yours is stale and long dead."

"That's the way we like it," he said. "We don't want our food to be squirming while we eat it." Then, because she seemed to be feeling talkative, he asked: "So how many dragons are there, all together?"

"What makes you think I know?" she said. "Do you know how many humans there are, all together?"

"No, but there are so many more of my kind than there are of yours." He took a sip of water. "Where I come from, there are tales that the islands used to swarm with dragons. On a clear day, they say, you could see the great beasts wheeling in the sky like flocks of sea birds. But that was long ago, and the dragons do not come in such numbers anymore. I thought you might know why."

"It is true that when I go to the islands, there are fewer dragons than there once were. Often I am the only one there. The same is true when I go to the north, to replenish the blue stones." She frowned. "I thought perhaps the others had found some other source of crystals."

"The north?"

T'Sian regarded him for a moment, then said, "I will tell you a secret, man. We require two different kinds of crystals to make our fire: Red ones, which come from the islands near your home, and blue ones, which are found in the ice sheets far beyond the great lake."

"The great lake?" He thought a moment. "You mean Lake Achenar? You're talking about going north of Yttribia, then?"

"Yes, I believe that is the name of the human country."

"I imagine you dislike the cold."

"Yes. That is why I hoard the blue crystals as much as I can." Her eyes narrowed; she scraped curls of wood off the tabletop with an iron-hard nail. "But my supply was stolen. I must ration my fire until I get them back from Gelt."

"Gelt couldn't have raided your lair," Ponn said. "He was busy making me take him to the islands. There must have been a second team working in the mountains."

She inclined her head slightly. "We will find that out when we catch him and make him tell us what he knows."

"Have you considered going to the north now, to get more of the blue crystals, so that you don't run out of fire at an inopportune moment?"

"It is too far. Besides, you would never survive the trip. You are already complaining about being cold; there, you would freeze to death."

"You would expect *me* to accompany you?"

"What else would I do? Leave you here?"

"Must I go everywhere with you?" He set down his knife, having reduced the meal to a fond memory. "You *do* intend to let me go home eventually, don't you?"

"Once we have finished our business with Gelt and his master, you may go where you like." She eyed his empty plate. "Are you ready to start looking for him?"

"First, warmer clothes," he said. "Then we can ask questions. But we have to be discreet."

"I know," she said. "You don't want to get your throat cut."

"Exactly," he said.

Nursing a wicked headache and a dull throb from the vicinity of her ribs, Diasa surveyed the wreckage that remained of the college. She had set up her headquarters outside the collapsed walls of Damona's house, and had climbed atop the mound of rubble in order to have a look around. There wasn't much to see; Deliban had shaken Flaurent to rubble. Only the library remained intact, more or less, but it looked rather lopsided and there was no telling when it, too, might collapse. She had forbidden any of the remaining students, instructors, and guards from entering, lest it should come crashing down on their heads.

There were few human dead; the college never had many students, and with winter approaching, most of those who had come on retreat had returned to their homes in more hospitable regions. Those who remained, though, had fared poorly. Of ten students, three instructors, and three guests, nine had perished beneath the rubble. They had only found three corpses; these had been buried in shallow graves, the sites marked with crude headstones. Salt and dust and dryness would preserve them, withering the flesh, blackening the skin; in time, shriveled hands might erupt from the sand, the body might dig itself free, leaving behind an empty hollow in the gritty soil. She did not know what would happen to the other bodies, those interred beneath the ruins; if they stirred, they would find no way out of their tombs. This land had a strange effect on its dead.

The Withered Ones had suffered serious losses as well. She had only been able to account for four of them; the rest were missing, lost in the crevasses or under the crumbling walls.

And Diasa had lost her mother.

She'd seen it herself: After the wizard on the eagle took Adaran away, the ground rose up around Damona, closing about her, tightening, squeezing the life out of her like a giant fist; then she had vanished beneath the churned earth, swallowed up like a swimmer going under the water. Digging in the spot where she disappeared had yielded nothing.

Well, there wasn't much point in staying perched on top of the rubble, observing the destruction like some eager carrion bird. Flaurent was obliterated; the headmistress and most of the staff and students were dead; Orioke had turned Deliban against the college and then taken it away. Without Deliban, the wells would dry up, and there would be no more salt coming to the surface to be sold to merchants. Even if Diasa had the ambition to rebuild, there was no way to do so.

She carefully climbed down from the wreckage. Ilfiss, the only surviving instructor, waited for her, his hand on the shoulder of the girl Adaran had brought with him. "Look what I found wandering around in the rubble," he said.

Diasa crouched down in front of the small Enshennean, trying to remember the child's name; she wasn't sure she had ever known it, and if she had, she'd forgotten. "Hello," she said. "Do you remember me? I'm Diasa."

The child nodded slowly, then said: "Adwan?"

Looking for the rogue, the one who had brought all this destruction down upon them. She should have left him to die in the wastes. "Adaran isn't here," Diasa said. "He's been taken away."

"Away?"

"Yes. He's gone."

The girl looked confused and upset. Diasa couldn't think of what to do next, so she ruffled the child's soft, dark hair, then stood. "Have you found any more survivors?"

"Just one," Ilfiss said. "Wert."

"Wert? I thought he was dying even before the wizard came."

Ilfiss shrugged. "I can't explain it, but he seems to be fully recovered. He's wandering around now, looking at everything and shaking his head."

"Really?"

"Yes. He appears to find the destruction upsetting."

"That seems unusually lucid for Wert. Perhaps he's shaking his head at some imaginary conversation with himself. Has he spoken to anyone?"

"Not that I know of. I believe he's down at the jetty if you'd like to see him."

Diasa sighed. "Why not? He predicted this; maybe he'll have more information to dole out." She took the little girl's hand and the three of them walked in silence from the rubble of Damona's residence, crunching across ground strewn with broken chunks of stone, blowing dust, mounded earth. It seemed wrong, somehow, that the headmistress and the students and the staff should have perished, but poor, deranged Wert had survived.

They passed through the remnant of the gates. The great doors would never close again; one hung at a crazy angle, while the other had fallen off and now lay on its side, forming a bridge across a narrow, shallow chasm. Diasa had instructed the Withered Ones to secure it with ropes and pitons, stabilizing it so that it didn't slip into the crevasse.

A chill wind blew from the mountains to the west, sending dust-devils dancing across the desolate plains. Many of the survivors had gathered here; those with the necessary skills helped to patch a damaged flatboat, while others stood about as if still dazed from the disaster. She spotted Wert, out at the very edge of the jetty, his hair all wild in the wind. He stared off to the northeast. Diasa handed the girl off to Ilfiss and approached the old madman alone. She stopped beside him, next to the grey, sluggish river, its surface dull with floating grit. If he noticed her, he gave no sign, not a twitch or a glance.

"Wert," she said.

No response.

She took a step closer. "Wert!" she said.

This time he looked around as if being buzzed by a fly; then he glanced at her and said: "Oh. Hello, Diasa."

"What are you doing out here?"

He turned back to the northeast. Diasa had no idea what he was looking at; there was nothing in that direction but miles and miles of nothing. "She has escaped."

Nonplussed, she said: "Who?"

No answer.

"Wert, *who* has escaped?"

"It may not make a difference, though. It may be too late," he said. "And they will find her again, unless we intervene."

"What are you talking about?"

He gave her a canny glance, and said: "You'll see."

Diasa sighed. There wasn't much use talking to Wert under most circumstances, and none at all when he started babbling like this. She left him to his vigil and went to check on the progress of the boat. Repairs were nearly complete; it bobbed in the water, sheltered from the river's meager current by the curving arm of the jetty. Some of the others had begun piling supplies nearby, preparing to load them into the broad, shallow compartment that passed for the hold. A tarp, stretched tight between four poles, served as a cover for this area; a similar one would be their shelter from the sun or, if the weather took a very unusual turn for this time of year, the rain.

Leaving them to their task, she returned to the college. She made her way through the wreckage, skirting the chasms that had swallowed so many. Nothing had changed since the last time she had done this; no new survivors had emerged, no buildings had knit themselves back together. By the time she had completed her circuit of the college, the four remaining Withered Ones had gathered near the front gate. One of them raised a black-cloaked arm, pointed at the river, and said: "It floats."

"Yes. We'll be leaving soon, I think. You won't be coming?"

They shook their heads. "We stay." When they spoke in unison, it sounded like a gentle storm blowing sand against the walls. "We guard."

"There's not much left here that's worth guarding."

"We guard."

"As you wish," Diasa said. "Guard what you will."

She passed among them, heading for the jetty, but stopped when she felt a hand on her shoulder. Even through her cloak, the grip felt hard, inhuman, like being clutched by a powerful skeleton. She glanced over her shoulder at the shriveled fingers, her gaze moving up its arm to the sunken face, the sightless eyes. "We will meet again, Diasa," the creature said.

Even the Withered Ones were oracles now. It released her, and then the creatures turned and shuffled toward their ruined guardhouse. She had never heard her name pass their lips before; she found it deeply unsettling. Shaken, Diasa watched as they vanished one by one into the shadows.

Ilfiss was waiting for her on the jetty; the others had already gone aboard, claiming their spots beneath the canvas. The little girl stood at the front of the boat, leaning over the flat prow, peering into the water. "Are we ready to depart?" Diasa asked.

"Yes. We've loaded what supplies we salvaged, and I've got

volunteers to help pole."

"Good. If we leave now, we should reach the nearest mining camp before dusk. They will sell us supplies."

"They won't try to press us into service?"

"After all the years we've traded with them? They'd better not." She picked up a pole that lay on the jetty. It was slightly thicker than the shaft of her spear: Another item lost in the wreckage. The poles were only to guide the vessel, to keep it from running aground in the shallow, shifting rivers; normally a boat such as this carried a crew of eight to man the poles, as well as a navigator, a captain, and several spotters to walk the decks and watch for unexpected obstacles. They had only eight all together, not including Wert and the Enshennean, both of whom were essentially just baggage.

Ilfiss said: "What are you doing?"

"I'm going to help pole."

"Diasa. You were nearly crushed trying to rescue people from the dormitory. You need to rest."

She glared at him.

He sighed. "Get aboard, then. I'm sure the world will thrill to your courage as you make your injuries worse."

She joined the others, taking up a poler's position near the back. Ilfiss handed out the remaining poles, then untied the barge from its mooring, tossed the rope onto the deck, and jumped in.

Diasa and the others on her side prodded the jetty with their poles, pushing the ship out into the current. The effort sent pain shooting up her ribs; she gasped and dropped the pole, which fell into the water. Ilfiss retrieved it and handed it to one of the students, then said: "Perhaps you would prefer to act as a spotter, and watch for obstacles?"

"Yes," Diasa said. "I think I would."

As dusk approached, Ponn and T'Sian returned to The Man with a Sack of Sorrows. The only productive thing they had accomplished was getting Ponn a warmer garment; the rest of the day had been spent wandering the city, asking fruitless questions, slipping coins to questionable characters in exchange for equally questionable information. The dragon, increasingly frustrated, had begun to move from bribery to threats, prompting Ponn to call off their search for the day.   She capitulated with bad grace, complaining about the perfidiousness of men, convinced that they were all liars.

"We don't even know that Gelt came to Astilan," Ponn reminded her as they approached the inn.   "That was never more than an assumption."

"Where else would he go?"

Ponn shrugged. "It depends who he works for."

"He works for Varmot," T'Sian said.   Then: "Talking to these street people is futile. We must go to the castle and confront him."

"Confront the king?"

"Yes."

"In your true form?"

"Of course. Showing up at his gate in *this* guise will hardly impress him." She looked at the sky. "This would be a good time to attack."

"But it's getting dark."

"Yes, and you men cannot see in the dark. I can."

"There are many innocent people in the castle," Ponn said. "Women, children, men who had nothing to do with Gelt. If you destroy it, you will hurt them."

"I do not intend to destroy it," she said. "Not right away. First I will damage it a little, to make him come out." Suddenly she stopped walking.   The inn stood nearby; he smelled dinner cooking, heard voices talking, laughing.

"T'Sian?"

She paid him no attention, looking off to the northwest, peering into the darkness.   He looked in that direction, but saw nothing except the gloom of approaching night as it settled over the city's walls.

She said: "Can you see them?"

"What?"

"Things in the sky, coming this way."

"Where? I don't see anything."

"There," she said, pointing a long, crimson-tipped finger at the distant horizon. He spotted them then, in the fading twilight, dark shapes silhouetted against the clouds, little more than specks.

"What are they?"

"Giant eagles, far away," she said, "like the ones you described to me when we first met."

"No. So many? It can't be. It's a trick of the light. They must be smaller birds, flying nearby."

"Believe what I tell you. They *are* eagles, Pyodor Ponn, and they carry men on their backs. Varmot's minions are returning from some other depredation."

Ponn watched them coming closer. T'Sian was right, he realized; they *were* eagles, they *did* bear riders. They carried objects as well, sacks or parcels, clutched in their talons. Loot? It was difficult to tell. He moved into the street, away from the dragon, hoping for a clearer view. Instead he spotted another group, as large as the first, approaching from the southeast.

Two groups, converging on the city from two directions.

An attack from two sides.

He turned back to the dragon. "T'Sian, they aren't coming to bring Varmot treasures! They …" He trailed off.

She was gone.

11

Night.

On the outskirts of town, where the inn stood, Astilan was lost under the blanket of darkness, with only the house-lights to show that men lived here. Deeper in the city, torches and lamps burned along the streets, illuminating the roads and alleys for those whose business extended into the hours of night, or who didn't venture out until the sun had gone down.

As her great wings pulled her higher into the sky, T'Sian could see the whole city beneath her, larger than any settlement of men had a right to be, spreading across the plains like a burgeoning growth. She spiraled higher, above the level of the approaching eagles. As she rose, she spotted a second group, coming from a different direction.

Pyodor Ponn had only spoken of four eagles, but here were two groups of riders, flying in formation, numbering in the dozens. The men astride the birds wore different uniforms than the prison-wagon guards she had killed the night before. A ruse? Ponn said Gelt had worn no colors, carried no device. Rather than attack immediately, she decided to wait, to see what these men would do.

The group from the north arrived first, fanning out as they crossed the river. The eagles clutched cargo in their talons; the packages glowed like embers, not with heat exactly, but with energy, power, like a wildfire contained and waiting to explode in a consuming fury.

Dragon stones. *Her* stones, and more.

She pulled herself higher, rising well above the level where the eagles flew. They came in low, a few hundred feet above the ground. She wondered if anyone in the city had seen them, if an alarm would be raised. She doubted it. The beating of their wings made no sound, and the darkness concealed their approach; only her exceptional vision had enabled her to see them. If she had not pointed them out to Ponn, he would have gone in ignorance of them.

The darkness concealed her as well; they would not know she was in the air with them. She aimed herself northwest, toward the nearer group, gliding high above their heads. Looking down upon them, she saw that they had split into angled rows like migrating birds.

Once she had cleared the ranks of the attackers, she banked around and approached them from behind. She could incinerate them now, but instead she waited, wondering where they would go. Below them was a part of the city she and Ponn had not visited that day, a neighborhood of large homes and broad avenues surrounding the castle of King Varmot, gated and walled off from the rest of the town.

Suddenly all the eagles released their radiant burdens and then banked sharply upward, climbing away from the city. T'Sian watched the glowing bundles fall, mystified. Why would these men go to all the trouble of stealing her crystals, only to drop them in the streets of Astilan? It made no sense.

Then the first of the packages hit the ground, and roaring explosions tore the night to shreds. Smoke and fire belched into the sky, heaving the air against her. She had to struggle to maintain control against the force of the shockwaves. She saw rings of heat and force rippling through the city, leveling buildings, setting them ablaze.

T'Sian pulled up and away from the blasts, afterimages lingering in her vision, fading just in time for her to see the second wave of eagles drop their own packages in another neighborhood to the south. Where the devices landed, Astilan bloomed like a fiery rose. Structures fell to splinters, stones cracked, trees burned.

These men had taken her crystals and transformed them into weapons; they had wanted to make themselves into dragons, and they had succeeded.

Suddenly an eagle swooped up in front of her and stopped, its wings thrumming as it hovered in the turbulent air. Two men rode on its back, one pulling on the reins, the other strapped in behind him. The driver was clearly terrified, but the one behind stared at her with an expression of intense concentration. His lips moved quickly, as if he were whispering rapid instructions to his companion.

She didn't know who they might be; nor did she care. She reared back and spat fire at them, sending a stream of brilliant flame scorching across the night to incinerate them where they hovered in insolent challenge. But the fire broke harmlessly over the men and the bird, curving around them as if they were encased in an invisible, fireproof sphere, leaving them untouched. The driver cringed at the dancing flames, but the one who whispered continued to stare through them, his gaze fixed on her; and then she knew which of them was her true foe, and which was but a fool.

She closed her mouth and the flow of fire stopped. The men and their mount held steady. In the distance, more explosions threw earth and debris into the air, sent smoke billowing skyward in curling clouds. They had begun to bomb other parts of the city, farther from the castle. The night had become full of screams, and for a moment she thought of Pyodor Ponn, wondering if he was safe.

The whispering man suddenly spoke. "Why is a *dragon* defending Astilan?" he said, his voice unnaturally loud and clear, as if he had amplified it somehow. "Surely you are not one of Varmot's minions?"

"*I am no one's minion*," T'Sian said. "*Tell me who sent you and I will spare your life.*"

The man laughed at her. He *laughed*. Incensed, she sent another torrent of flame against them, to no more effect than before. But then she felt something reach down her throat, some force, gripping like a hand; it caught hold of the fire and drew it out of her like a brightly-colored ribbon. She clamped her mouth shut, but even so, the flames kept coming, streaming between her teeth, out her nose.

What manner of man could do such things?

As the last of her fire flickered out and the hand released its hold, she turned and dove toward the city, down into the fiery, ruined streets, crashing into the midst of an inferno. She could feel the cold hollow in her breast where the crystals had been, empty now, nothing but ashes in there. This man, with his words, had drained her dry.

Suddenly the ground erupted beneath her, earth and stone swallowing her feet and the lower part of her legs. Astonished, she spread her wings and tried to take flight, but the bonds held her fast. The flames nearest her sputtered and died, covered over by a creeping tide of dirt; the men on the eagle descended in front of her, hovering near the ground.

"Hold the dragon tight, Deliban," the whispering man said.

Something emerged from the ground in front of her, rising from the earth and stones as if it were part of them. It took a vaguely human shape, perhaps mimicking the form of the one who must be its master, but it made no response.

"Kill the beast and be done!" the driver said.

"*Kill* her? Oh, no. We will bring her back with us. The princes will appreciate such a gift, don't you think? A dragon of their very own? Perhaps it will make up for the loss of the oracle."

"Are you mad?" the driver cried. "Bring a *dragon* back to Dunshandrin? How will you control it?"

"That is not your concern. Take us closer."

"I will not!"

"You will do as you're told."

As the reluctant pilot guided his mount closer, T'Sian lashed out with her tail, which had remained free of the earthen bonds that held her down. It wasn't long enough to reach the humans, but the strange earth-creature was within striking distance; she swept it into the air, sending it flying at the eagle like a thrown boulder. The bird screeched as the creature smashed into it, knocking it out of the sky. The earthen bonds around her loosened and she broke free, pivoting in the narrow space to run in the other direction, away from the men and the earth monster. She veered to the right, down a side street barely wide enough to contain her even with wings fully folded. Burning structures scraped her on both sides, scratching against her metal-hard scales. Hoping that the powerful man would not be able to find her in the smoke and fire, she began the transformation into her human guise. She was not fleeing, not admitting defeat; she was merely assuming a camouflage, so that she would have time to think, to devise a plan.

When her change was nearly complete and her senses restored, she began to hear the man's voice from the sky. She could not see him through the smoke, but thought he must be nearby. "Dragon?" he called. "Where are you, dragon?"

T'Sian had hoped the man had been killed when she knocked his eagle out of the air, but evidently he had survived and found himself a new mount. She peered into the sky but the heat of the inferno polluted the night, kept her from seeing the inconsequential warmth of the man or his giant bird.

"I have realized who you must be, dragon," the man continued; and after a moment she realized that she had begun moving in his direction, walking up the alley toward the wide street. She stopped herself, grabbing onto a burning post, resisting his entreaty. What manner of man was this, who could lure her with the sound of his voice?

"You must be the dragon from the mountains, whose hatchlings we killed to take their stones," he said. "Had we known you were so easily defeated, we might not have waited for you to be gone before we attacked."

So this was one of the men she had been seeking! He would pay for what he had done to her babies! She opened her mouth to name him a butcher and a coward, then checked her rage and remained silent. That was what he wanted; he was trying to find her, to goad her into revealing herself. She was unprepared to face this man right now. She needed to talk to Pyodor Ponn, to find out what he knew of men who used words to bend the world to their will.

And she needed to get out of the street, before he spotted her from his aerial vantage point. She pushed her way into one of the burning buildings to her left. Fire surrounded her, warm and welcoming; but then the floor groaned as she moved across it, and suddenly it split open beneath her, plunging her into a dank cavity beneath the structure. Burning debris came down after her, and then the entire place collapsed in a roar of smoke and timbers, burying her in the heat and the darkness.

Ponn had spotted T'Sian moving toward the gates of Astilan. He'd run after her, calling for her to stop, but she didn't even turn to look at him and he soon lost track of her in the shadows. Figuring she must be going out of the city to transform into her dragon shape, he gave up following and hurried back to the inn. Gazes turned to him as he entered, then turned away again. Some here had seen him earlier and knew him as the strange woman's companion; to others he would merely be a foreigner, and of little interest.

The older woman who that morning had peered out at them from the kitchen now stood behind the bar, filling tankards and bantering with obvious regulars; over the course of the day he had learned that her name was Jalla, and that she was the owner of the Sack of Sorrows. He hurried through the room and up the stairs to the hallway, where a shuttered window opened onto the roof of the dining area. He opened it and climbed out, peering off to the northwest, but was unable to see anything now that the last of the daylight had failed. Nor could he see the dragon; he assumed she had taken to the sky to engage the eagles, but she was just as invisible as they were.

Suddenly a series of explosions rocked inner Astilan. The eruption of light turned Varmot's castle into a silhouette, flat and black against the flashes. A sound like a huge crash of thunder threatened to deafen him; moments later a wave of force, like a great hot wind, knocked him off his feet and sent him sprawling upon the thatched roof of the inn. The rumble died away in his ears as he scrambled across the dry, prickly grasses toward the window. He hauled himself back into the hallway, then turned, blinking away the angry purple flashes that marred his vision. The interior of Astilan was aflame in a half-dozen places, throwing orange light into the sky. Had T'Sian made good on her threat to burn the town? What else but a dragon or a volcano could have generated so much fiery destruction so quickly?

He raced back downstairs. The common room had already emptied of patrons and servers, leaving only Jalla, struggling to haul a massive strongbox out from behind the bar. Ponn went to her side. "Leave that," he said. "The city is under attack!"

"This is all the money I have in the world," she said, "and I'm not leaving it here to be looted!"

"Let me help you, then," he said, reaching to pick up the chest by one of the handles.

"No! It's mine!"

"I'm not trying to rob you, you foolish woman!"

"Leave off!" She swatted his hands away.

"Fine," Ponn said. "Burn for your coins, then, and see how much good they do you in the spirit world." Abandoning her, he went out into the street. The sound of a nearby blast still echoed among the buildings. People ran back and forth against a backdrop of flame and smoke; hot embers wafted through the air like a torpid swarm of fat, luminous beetles. One landed on his shoulder; he smacked it out with his hand, leaving a black smudge on his new cloak.

Another explosion erupted from the direction of the southern gate. He covered his ears as the roar rumbled over him, the ground shivered beneath his feet. Not T'Sian's doing; her breath destroyed silently, no louder than a whisper. The men on their eagles must be responsible for this chaos.

Seeing no good way through the inferno, he returned to the inn. Jalla had apparently given up on taking all her money; the chest stood open and she was stuffing handfuls of coins into her apron. She did not look up as he entered.

"There's no way out," Ponn said. "The fire is everywhere. Do you have a large oven, as for baking bread?"

She did look up then, staring at him. "You want bread?"

"No, I don't want bread! Listen to me. I know how you plainsmen do your baking. Do you have a brick oven or not?"

"Yes. In the back."

"Show me."

Looking perplexed, Jalla closed and locked the strongbox, then led him into a tiny office behind the bar. The coins in her bulging pockets clinked and jingled as she walked. A poorly-fitting wooden door let them out into a long, narrow yard behind the inn. The yard was littered with refuse: Old bedding, tablecloths, a mound of rotting vegetables. The oven stood at the far end, a weathered, dome-shaped heap of bricks and mortar with an iron door, thick walls, and a tiny ventilation hole at its peak. It was smaller than he had hoped, little larger than a child's tree-house, and he began to wonder if this idea he had formed was a very foolish one. But the thick walls of the oven kept in the heat, so it stood to reason they would keep it out as well.

He could see flames over the walls surrounding the yard. The fire was burning closer, racing along thatched rooftops, consuming spindly structures like so much deadwood. He hurried to the oven, felt the iron door. Cool to the touch, as he had hoped. He opened the door, revealing a black opening large enough to crawl through on hands and knees. "In here," he said.

Jalla looked aghast. "You're trying to cook me alive!"

Exasperated, Ponn said: "I had your bread this morning, and it was not fresh; you did not use this oven today. Perhaps you will be extremely lucky and the fire will spare your inn; if not, perhaps you will merely be *very* lucky, and the walls of your oven will prevent us both from being burned to death."

She gaped at him, as if he had sprouted a forked tongue like the dragon's. Well, it was her choice to follow him or not. He crawled through the low, narrow opening like a bee into a hive. The interior of the oven was dark as a moonless night on the ocean, except for a sliver of light that came through the vent-hole at the top; the walls felt slightly warm from its last use, whenever that was, and exuded the odor of bread and yeast.

He heard a huffing and scratching as Jalla entered. She pulled the iron door shut behind her, sat huddled on the brick floor, and said, miserably: "We'll bake for sure."

She was probably right, but there was no reason to make her still more panicky by agreeing with her. "Move to the center," he said. "It will be hottest near the sides."

Jalla glanced at the walls as if they might grow hands, seize her, and hold her tight while the fire roasted her. She slid away from them, joining him in the spot of illumination beneath the vent-hole. He wondered if they should stop it up, but maybe it would help the heat escape.

Suddenly Jalla drew a breath and said: "Your companion—what about her? Is she out there in the fire?"

"If she is," Ponn said, "then she is probably enjoying herself immensely."

After he had wandered into what was clearly the royal wing of the castle, Adaran found himself exhausted and had started searching for somewhere to hide and rest. He'd found a small alcove, tucked away behind a tapestry, and chose it as his bolt-hole. He had to share it with the draped statue of a woman, but that was all right; she was very quiet, and her face reminded him a bit of Redshen's. He spent a moment looking at her, and then he curled up in the narrow space behind her pedestal and fell asleep. He woke with a start some time after nightfall, wondering where he was. After a moment he remembered the dungeon, slipping away, sneaking through the hallways. He vaguely recalled that no one in the castle had been able to see him or hear him; or had that just been a dream, fulfillment of a thief's greatest wish?

He crawled around the statue, lifted the edge of the tapestry, and peered out into the dim, deserted corridor. Runners and throws covered the floor, lest a royal foot should touch cold stone; golden sconces, mostly unlit, glimmered with inlaid gems; tile mosaics showed images of of battle, governance, harvests, the hunt. Decorative and ceremonial armor and weapons hung at intervals, swords and shields and daggers, attractively styled but useless for real combat.

Almost directly opposite his hiding place stood a door, set into an elaborately carved frame that continued the themes of the nearby mosaics; the portal itself depicted a throne, above which a glowing crown hovered, throwing what he supposed were rays of light, as if it were the sun itself.

For no reason Adaran could think of, he went to the door and tried the knob. Locked. He stepped back, eyeing the door. An ornate buckler hung on the wall nearby. He went to it, felt around behind it. A lockpick rested in the bottom, held in a lip of metal that curved under the back of the shield. He took the lockpick, examined it. Not one of his, but he knew how to use it well enough. He inserted the tool into the keyhole and worked it for a few seconds, and was rewarded with a click as the bolt opened. He slipped inside, shut the door, and locked it behind him.

The chamber was hot and dry and smelled of illness and impending death. He turned, scanning the room. A large bed against the left wall supported the small, twisted shape of a man descending into the depths of terminal illness. Adaran crept over and inspected the patient. No one he had ever seen before. He had expected to find Lord Dunshandrin behind such an opulent door, but this was not him.

High windows in the wall behind the bed were mostly obscured by thick velvet drapes, but in the sliver of space between them he could see the darkness outside. A way out, perhaps, depending on what might be found on the other side. Adaran started to move toward them, then noticed the ornamental daggers in crossed sheaths that decorated the footboard of the bed. After a brief hesitation he took one out, hefted it, tested the blade. The edges were dull, but the point looked like it had been sharpened recently. He stood there a moment, then went to the wall on his right, which was hung with tapestries from corner to corner. He paused in front of one that showed an illuminated golden gate leading into a garden, or perhaps into heaven. He moved it aside and discovered a door behind it. This one was locked as well, but it quickly yielded to the lockpick. He opened it and went into the chamber beyond. Although smaller than the room he had just left, this one was more sumptuously appointed; its rich wall hangings, gilded weapons, and massive four-poster bed made the sickroom seem shabby in comparison.

The shaggy-headed form of the real Lord Dunshandrin lay asleep in the bed. Adaran remembered him sitting high on his throne, greeting them all, promising them rich rewards for bringing back the crystals from the dragon's lair. He thought of the blood spurting from Redshen's cut throat.

Rich rewards, indeed.

He fingered the hilt of the ornamental dagger. The blade would not cut bread, but he could still plant it in the old man's heart. He crept to the bedside, dagger at the ready, then hesitated. Murder a man in his sleep? Was that how low he'd sunk? But he couldn't deny the urge to pin Dunshandrin to his mattress; his hand shook with the effort of controlling it.

"Wake up," he said.

Dunshandrin's head lolled to the side and his eyes opened. Glazed with sleep, they regarded Adaran without recognition.

"Do you even remember me? I did the job you hired me to do, and then you tried to have me killed, out there in the mountains."

No response. Perhaps Dunshandrin believed this intruder to be nothing more than an unwelcome dream. He yawned and stretched, his hands sliding up beneath the pillow beneath his head.

"Now I stand before you with a dagger in my hand," Adaran said. "Have you nothing to say for yourself?"

Lord Dunshandrin's mouth opened slightly, as if he meant to whisper something for only Adaran to hear; but then he cried, in a booming voice: "Guards! Where are my guards?" At the same time he pulled a tiny one-handed crossbow, cocked and loaded, from beneath his pillow.

Adaran leapt at Dunshandrin and buried the ceremonial dagger between his ribs just as the man fired his weapon. The bolt whizzed by Adaran's ear and clattered off a shield that hung on the wall.

Panting, Adaran stood back from the bed. The gilt pommel of the dagger glittered on Lord Dunshandrin's breast like a gaudy bauble worn as decoration. He looked around, trying to remember why he had come here, what had led him to this chamber. What had he gained by killing Dunshandrin rather than slipping off into the night?

He opened the door and went back into the sickroom, then crept to the door that led into the corridor. He put his ear to the crack, heard running footsteps. Dunshandrin's dying cry had been heard. He had little doubt that the guards would be able to see him now. He hoped they wouldn't have a key and would have to break the door down instead.

His mind leapt back to the windows. He didn't know what was out there, a balcony or a ledge or a sheer drop to the ground, but that seemed a quibble when a horde of armed men were about to bash their way into the chamber. He went to the window on the right, opened it, climbed up onto the sill. He saw a terrace beyond, quite a large one, arrayed with tables and chairs, fountains, trees in great pots. Obviously this was some sort of royal retreat. He jumped down to it, landing lightly beside a flower-box.

To his right the castle curved inward and away, forming the back wall of the terrace. A glass door immediately beside him appeared to lead into Dunshandrin's chamber. Pale moonlight glimmered off other doors, probably leading to other royal bedrooms. Guards might come charging through any one of them, at any moment.

This didn't seem like a very good place to be, either.

He scurried to the edge, where a waist-high balustrade prevented a drunken fall to the courtyard below. He vaulted it and dropped to the ground, landing on flexed knees, going into a roll, coming out of it at a run. The wall of the keep loomed nearby. He didn't know what was on the other side—freedom, more guards, another wall— but he knew what was on *this* side, and he needed to escape from it.

He leapt onto the wall, dug his fingers into its tiny cracks and irregularities, and started climbing.

Ponn awoke to the smell of ashes. He hadn't expected to fall asleep, but obviously exhaustion had gotten the better of him; or perhaps he had passed out from the heat. He sat up too quickly and his head threatened to detach itself from his body and drift away. He waited until the feeling passed, then rolled onto his hands and knees, crept to the wall, and followed it until he found the iron door. The metal felt warm but not hot, so he pushed it open and crawled out into the yard.

A fine layer of ash covered the ground, blackening Ponn's skin. He stood and stretched, shivering now as the chill night air drew warmth from his sweat; then he took stock of his surroundings. The wooden fence that surrounded the small yard was charred in spots, but mostly intact. He noticed a gate with a latch nearby, something he hadn't spotted in his earlier haste. A small fire smoldered in the pile of refuse at the far end of the garden. The walls of the Sack of Sorrows itself still stood, but its thatched roof and wooden doors and shutters had burned away, like a face that had been stripped of hair and ears and eyelids. The air stank of smoke, with an undercurrent of burnt flesh and something sharp and strange that he had never smelled before, even in the exhalation of a fumarole.

"My inn!"

He had forgotten about Jalla, who had weathered the fire with him. He went to the oven and helped her to her feet, but then she pulled away from him, leaning against the blackened brick dome. "Gone," she moaned. "Everything is gone."

"At least you still have your life," he said; but she only glared at him, as if that were of little comfort. Foolish woman. Leaving her, Ponn went to the gate, turned the latch, and stepped out into an alley. He walked along it to the main avenue where he and T'Sian had separated. He heard a voice shouting somewhere in the distance, but couldn't make out the words. He wandered farther down the street, eyeing the destruction. A large number of buildings in the neighborhood had been damaged or destroyed; some still burned, belching black smoke into the orange-black sky. He saw a few charred shapes, human-sized, lying in the street; he did not inspect them too closely, preferring instead to look at other survivors, like himself, dazed but alive. Few of them spoke, although most gave him wordless greetings.

"You there! Foreigner!"

He turned, startled. Three men on horseback approached, looking like phantoms wrapped in smoke and darkness; a small man hurried along on foot, trying to keep up with the trotting steeds. The riders wore the livery of King Varmot, and the lead horseman carried an unsheathed sword that looked broad enough to fell a tree. He pointed the blade at Ponn and said: "What is your name?"

"They … they call me Pyodor Ponn, my lord."

"All survivors are to gather in King's Square!" the footman cried. "Spread the word!"

"Wait!" Ponn said. "Where is King's Square?" But the soldiers had already spurred their horses onward, scanning the buildings as they passed, ignoring his questions. The crier hurried after them, shouting out the same instructions over and over.

Ponn had no idea where King's Square was, although he supposed it must be near the castle; and he was not at all sure it was a good idea to assemble so many people in a single place. If the eagles attacked again, they could kill hundreds of people with a single strike. He returned to Jalla's small yard. She was no longer near the oven; he found her by the back door of her inn, peering into the dark interior. She glanced at him as he approached. "I am ruined," she said. "Everything is gone."

He looked in through a window. It had once given onto the kitchen, but the walls had fallen and he could see all the way to the other side of the building. The floor of the second story had burned and collapsed into the common room, creating a pile of debris that had buried the bar, the dining area, the storeroom. Smoke hung in the enclosed space like the burnt memory of better times.

"My husband and I built this place," Jalla said. "We ran it together for twenty years."

"I'm sorry. When did your husband pass away?"

She glared at him. "He didn't. The red-nosed bastard ran off with the barmaid two years ago."

"Oh." Ponn considered this for a moment, then decided it would be best to change the subject. "Did you hear the crier? We are summoned to King's Square."

This appeared to shock her. "You and me? Why?"

"Not just the two of us. All survivors. By order of the King."

"The King is all right?" Her pale face took on an eager expression, like a lost child spotting its mother. "He's going to do something?"

Ponn didn't know what Jalla thought Varmot might do about all the destroyed buildings, but it seemed that she needed to believe he had some plan. "I would think so. After all, he *is* the King, and the King has to take care of this kind of situation, doesn't he?"

"Yes. Yes he does." She brushed herself off, then shook her long white hair; ashes flew out, drifting slowly to the ground. She attempted to smooth it back, winding the wispy strands into something resembling a bun. Ponn wondered if she thought she was going to be presented to the King personally.

"All right," she said. "I'm ready."

"Fine," Ponn said. "Lead the way."

T'Sian awoke to warmth and the comforting smell of smoke, and for a moment imagined she might be back in her own lair, with her hatchlings piled up against against her. Opening her eyes, though, she could see nothing; darkness surrounded her, stained red by heat. She felt something heavy across her legs, pinning her down. She squirmed a bit but gained no freedom of movement. She did not think that she was injured, but she was very definitely trapped.

The dragon reached out, felt the wreckage that surrounded her. Splintered wood, rough stone, chalky plaster. It seemed she had smashed through a large beam, which had broken in two and formed a pocket in the rubble. She wondered if the debris would have crushed her if it had fallen on her directly. What a sad fate that would have been!

What to do now? Could she burn herself out? She opened her mouth, then remembered that the powerful man had stolen her flame away, leaving her bereft even of the merest flicker. She struggled again, pushed with her arms, but the rubble refused to shift.

Perhaps if she changed into her true shape, she could push the debris away, dislodge it and break free; but she did not know how deeply she was buried or how much weight was upon her. What would happen if she tried to transform to her full size, and the wreckage on top of her did not move? Would she die?

It was too risky. If she killed herself trying to escape, there would be no one to avenge her babies. She bellowed in fury and frustration, the cry of rage muted and muffled by the detritus that surrounded her.

T'Sian fell silent. She lay there a moment, steeling herself for what she had to do next. Surely it was something no dragon had ever done before.

She shouted, "Help!"

IF TALBRETT'S MEN WONDERED WHO this woman in their midst was, they showed admirable discretion and did not ask. Instead they went about their business with a brisk efficiency, leaving Tolaria to sit beneath the shelter of the cabin's overhang and watch the rocky, scrubby hills scroll past. She kept checking the sky, mindful of the giant eagles she had seen in Dunshandrin's castle; but either they could not spare any to search for her or they did not know where to look, because she saw no signs of pursuit. In the distance, circling above the city, she saw some of the great birds; but they were soon lost beyond the horizon, and did not appear again.

When dusk came, she went below, intending to return to her closet-like room. As she passed Talbrett's cabin she saw a light burning under his door and heard low voices from inside. She hesitated, then knocked. The murmuring stopped and Talbrett said: "Who is it?"

"Tolaria."

"Come in, come in."

She opened the door and found the merchant seated at a tiny fold-down table with one of the sailors, papers spread across the surface between them. Talbrett's room was scarcely larger than her own; with the table open and the two men sitting at it, there was no room for her to actually enter.

"Hello, Tolaria," Talbrett said. "This is Rennald, my first mate. You're sleeping in his cabin, so forgive him if he behaves in an unbecoming and surly manner."

Rennald snorted. "I would hardly call it a cabin," he said. "It is a rather large closet at best." Then, to Tolaria: "With such poor accommodations, it's a wonder Talbrett has any crew at all."

"You see what I mean," Talbrett said. Then, when Tolaria didn't laugh or smile: "Is something troubling you?"

"Have we left Dunshandrin yet?"

"No. We'll cross into Barbareth during the night. But we are in largely unsettled territory, Tolaria. You needn't worry about being spotted from the riverbank, if that's your concern."

"There are other ways for Dunshandrin to search for me. His alchemist has grown giant birds that his men ride upon, and he employs a wizard who likely knows spells of location."

"Well, as far as spells of location go, I once paid a local witch to inscribe wards on the ship to prevent that sort of thing. I can't say for sure that they work, but no one has ever found anything on board that I didn't want them to. And if these giant birds exist, Tolaria, surely they have better things to do than look for an escaped girl?"

As Talbrett finished speaking, Tolaria felt a strange faintness overtake her, a vision, unbidden, brought on by Talbrett's question. She clutched at the door jamb, missed it, and fell to the floor of the hallway as Rennald lunged to catch her.

When she came to herself again, she was no longer on the boat, but rather in a city. It was night, and she was alone, standing in a wide dark street. Lamps lined the cobbled avenue, casting fitful illumination that didn't reach to where she stood in the center of the road. She looked at the sky and knew that something was coming, flying in under cover of darkness, unseen and unheard.

She wanted flee, but could not lift her feet. She looked at the ground and saw that it had risen up around her ankles like a tide, locking her in place. The earth itself was in motion, ripples passing through it, radiating from where she stood. She was slowly sinking into it, up to her shins now, as something pulled her inexorably into the street.

Suddenly light and smoke and flame and sound splintered the evening stillness. Great eagles soared overhead, dropping packages that exploded when they struck, shattering buildings, setting fires, blowing holes in the street, not unlike Qalor's demonstration. But these were not tiny devices like the one he had used to impress his masters; these had been built for true destruction.

The bombardment ended abruptly, as dawn broke over the city.

The eagles had gone. Fires burned all around her. Grimy survivors, dazed and frightened, shuffled past, paying Tolaria no attention. She had sunk past her waist, but no one tried to help her.

Suddenly something came rolling through the crowd, weaving between the legs of the citizens. It went around and around her in tightening circles, spinning like a twirled coin, finally coming to rest upside-down in the dirt in front of her. A crown, tarnished and battered. She leaned forward and tried to pick it up, but she couldn't quite reach it. She grunted and stretched, tracing little furrows in the dirt, until at last her fingertips just brushed the gilt surface of the diadem.

Tolaria opened her eyes, sat up with a gasp. She lay on the cot in Talbrett's cabin. The table was folded up and Rennald was gone, but Talbrett sat in the same chair he had been in before, watching her by the light of a single dim lantern. Seeing her awake, he said: "Are you all right?"

"A vision," she said, sounding like a frog that had been wandering in the desert. "Did I speak?"

"Nothing that made sense to me," he said. "Something about fire, and a crown. What did you see?"

"I don't remember. Wait … I do, a little. There was a city. I was in a street, in a city."

After a moment, Talbrett said: "Ah. A city. Which one?"

"Nowhere I've ever been," she said. "It probably wasn't even a real city, just an … an imago."

"An imago?"

"Something that my mind invented for the purpose of the vision. Something not real." She raised her hands to her head. "I haven't been quite right since the princes made me breathe too much vapor. I think I may be losing my mind."

"You seem perfectly sane to me."

"But if I lose control of my visions, if they start to arise unbidden …" She trailed off, thinking of the warnings she had received while at Flaurent, and of mad little Wert, who spent his days wandering the campus spouting prophecies and nonsense in equal measure, unable to tell what was real and what was fiction.

"You just need time to recover from what they've done to you, that's all," Talbrett said.

"I wish I could believe that," she said. Then, noticing him wince and touch the back of his neck: "Are *you* all right?"

"The pain is bad this evening," he said, not looking up. "It feels like sharp rocks inside my head."

"Have you been to a healer?"

"A healer? Yes, I've been to healers. They've rubbed shredded leaves on the back of my head, so that I smell like an herb garden. They've made me drink potions that would make a dog howl. They've put one hand on my growth and the other in my pocket." Talbrett snorted. "Don't speak to me of healers."

"I've some little experience with healing," Tolaria said. "Perhaps I could—"

"Thank you, Tolaria," Talbrett said, "but my time is nearly over. No charm or drug will change that."

"It saddens me to see you dying. You seem a good man, and there are few enough of those."

Talbrett smiled faintly. "You have not seen me at my worst. The prospect of impending death can be a powerful influence."

"Yes," Tolaria said, "but it is not always a good one."

Jalla led Ponn through the devastated streets of Astilan. It was easy to see where the destructive devices had fallen: There would be a crater in the earth, or a building that had been splintered and blown outward into the street. Nearby structures would be lopsided, partially demolished by the force of the blast; those beyond the inner ring of destruction would be gutted by fire, or not, depending on their susceptibility to burning and the vagaries of the wind. Some neighborhoods were almost untouched by the attack, but as they neared Varmot's castle and King's Square, it became obvious that the attackers had concentrated on this part of the city. The castle stood in ruins, largely reduced to jumbled black stone and smoldering timbers. A row of battered soldiers stood before the wreckage as if daring looters to break through their ranks to get inside; no one took up the challenge.

A number of people had already gathered in the square, their voices a quiet babble as they waited for the king. Ponn and Jalla moved off to one side, where there was some open space, and waited with the others. Ponn continually scanned the sky for some sign of the dragon, or of a renewed attack, but neither materialized from out of the darkness. At length, a single, sad trumpet played a fanfare, announcing the arrival of the king; but it was not Varmot who came to greet the crowd, which had now fallen silent.

"Who's that?" Ponn whispered, as a boy who scarcely looked old enough to grow whiskers climbed up on a dais made of rubble, holding his arms wide as if to encompass the entire crowd.

"That is Prince Laquin," Jalla said. "But why is he wearing his father's crown?"

Ponn thought the answer fairly obvious, but said nothing, figuring it was better for Jalla to hear from her new king what had become of the old. "People of Astilan!" Laquin cried, his voice reedy with youth. "Tonight, we have been the victims of a most cowardly attack!" A murmur swept the crowd; perhaps they had expected Laquin to announce that Varmot would be along momentarily. Ponn glanced at Jalla; she stared, open-mouthed, at the boy as he continued. "My father, the great King Varmot, lies buried in his castle, murdered as foully as by an assassin in the night! His mantle has fallen to me, and I swear this: My father, and all of your dead and wounded, shall be avenged!"

Brave words, Ponn thought; but Astilan would be in disarray for days if not weeks, and he doubted that the enemy would give Laquin the time he needed to organize a defense against them. And indeed, what sort of defense could there be from men who hurled fire from the night sky, laying waste to entire neighborhoods?

The boy-king asked the survivors gathered there to speak of what they'd witnessed, to give him some clue as to the nature of their attackers. There was a period of quiet murmuring as the people summoned the courage to speak; then someone near the front of the crowd cried: "It was a dragon! I saw it with my own eyes!"

"I saw a dragon too!"

"A huge, scaly beast! Its head was bigger than a horse and it was spitting fire!"

"It wasn't the dragon!" Ponn shouted. "It was men, riding giant eagles! They dropped things that exploded and burned!"

This provoked more chatter, as some in the crowd affirmed that they, too, had caught glimpses of men astride monstrous birds, only to be shouted down by others who had seen the dragon. It began to seem as if they would split into two groups, one blaming the dragon, the other blaming men, until Laquin's heralds silenced the crowd with a series of trumpet blasts. "Friends," Laquin said, "tell me: Who is our enemy? Is it men who ride upon birds, or a dragon, or both?"

"I saw a dragon!"

"Men on birds!"

"Both, both!"

"No!" Ponn shouted. "The dragon fought the men!"

Laquin oriented on him, motioning for silence. The babble of the crowd gradually died down.   "Tell me this, friend who knows so much: If the dragon fought these men, where is it now?"

"I … don't know," Ponn said. "She hasn't come back yet."

"*She?*" Laquin picked up the implication immediately. "You speak as if you know this beast."

"We were traveling together," Ponn said after a moment.

Laquin said: "This creature was your companion?"

"It's not as simple as that, but … yes, she was."

A gasp rose from the crowd. The king nodded to a few of the guards, who began clearing a path through the throng, heading toward Ponn. Meanwhile, Jalla goggled at him. "That woman you were with," she whispered. "She was a *dragon?*"

"Yes."

"You brought a dragon into my inn? Are you mad?"

"She didn't do you any harm, did she?" he said, irritated. Then the guards arrived, separating Ponn and Jalla from the rest of the crowd, bearing them to the foot of Varmot's ruined castle. Laquin perched on the edge of the blistered stonework, as if he had climbed up there on a lark and was now enjoying the view. When they arrived he jumped off the wall and stood nearby, eyeing first Ponn, then Jalla, then Ponn again. Up close, surrounded by a ring of heavily armed guards, it became somewhat easier to look at this teenager and see a king.

Laquin walked a circle around them, inspecting them from every side. Ponn stood motionless, waiting to be addressed; and at length, Laquin said: "You're Enshennean."

Ponn thought that must have become obvious some time ago. "Yes, sire."

"What is your name?"

"Pyodor Ponn."

"So tell me, Pyodor Ponn ... how came you to be in the company of a dragon?"

And so Ponn found himself explaining his entire situation to the boy-king, telling him about his daughter's kidnapping, his voyage to the archipelago, his abandonment on the island, his rescue by T'Sian. He strategically omitted his arrest by agents of Laquin's father. The boy listened, evidently fascinated, and when Ponn had finished he clapped his hands and cried, "What an amazing story! How much of it is true, I wonder?"

"All of it, sire."

"And how much have you left out?"

Ponn, startled by the question and the boy's canny gaze, said: "I'm sure, sire, that any bit of my adventure that escaped the retelling is a detail without significance."

Laquin seemed amused by this response. "Yes, no doubt." He gestured to the guards. "Bring him inside. The woman, too."

Jalla choked back an alarmed squeak; nervous now, Ponn said: "I hope I have not offended my lord king through a lack of courtly manners."

"Lack of courtly manners?" Laquin laughed, though his eyes remained grave. "On the contrary, you would do very well at court. Very well indeed. No, I would talk with you and the innkeeper at length about your friend the dragon." He jumped back onto the wall, balancing precariously on the edge, looking down at Ponn with bright blue eyes. All the humor was gone from his face. "This morning I was mainly concerned with which serving girls were prettiest. Now I have a kingdom to run and, evidently, an invasion to repel. If you truly know a dragon, then you, my Enshennean friend, have just become the most interesting man in the city."

From the top of the castle wall, Adaran saw a high drop to a narrow ledge, and beyond that, a rushing river. But the alternative was to return to the courtyard and undoubtedly be caught by Dunshandrin's guards. He tensed, then jumped. For a giddy moment he seemed to fly out into the darkness; then he began to curve downward, falling. He cleared the ledge, but the cliff below struck him a glancing blow, sending him into a spin just before he plunged into the current.

He twisted his body as he entered the icy water, hoping to avoid a damaging encounter with the river bed should it be rocky and shallow; but it turned out to be deeper than it looked and his concern swiftly turned from breaking a limb to drowning. By the time he reached the surface, gasping for air and shivering with the cold, the current had already swept him some distance downstream, toward the bridge that led into town. A lot of debris had piled up against the supports, and being slammed into them was unlikely to prove pleasant. Adaran began to swim hard, reaching the far shore before coming to the span. He hauled himself up among the broken rocks and tiny, gnarled trees that lined the bank, hoping to find cover in the largely nonexistent nooks and shadows.

His assassination of Lord Dunshandrin would provoke a swift response from the castle. There would be patrols out on foot and horseback, possibly even on eagles, by first light; and even now, in the darkness, soldiers would come out with torches and scour the area around the castle.

What kind of fool was he, to have killed Lord Dunshandrin instead of quietly escaping? Why hadn't he just stolen a few jewel-encrusted weapons and slunk away? For that matter, how had he even managed to penetrate the royal wing of the castle? The corridors had been well lit by torches; he hadn't confined himself to the shadows or crept along behind wall hangings. He had brazenly walked along the hallways, and unless he had become completely deranged, he recalled that at one point, he had even started singing. And yet, no one had been able to see him or hear him. There must have been a glamour on him, masking him from those he passed. And who would have woven such a spell around him?

Orioke, of course.

It was the only explanation. Orioke had brought him back from Flaurent and laid some sort of geis on him to make him kill Lord Dunshandrin. To ensure he succeeded, the mage had given him the ability to pass unnoticed through the halls of the castle. Once he had carried out the mission, the spells were broken; his free will was restored, and the guards could see him again.

Why would Orioke agree to work for Dunshandrin, and then contrive to kill him? Revenge? Or did he have some other plot brewing in his tricky head?

Well, at this point, the reason why was moot. The deed was done, and now Adaran needed to find a spot where he could hide from the inevitable search. But along the rocky slopes surrounding Dunshandrin's castle, there was little in the way of vegetation, no bushes to shelter in, no thickets, no meadows, no caverns. And even if there were, Dunshandrin's castellan would already know all the hiding places within half a mile of the castle, unless he was completely incompetent. To further complicate matters, dawn was already on its way, the sky lightening with the approaching sun; it was too late to get down the hill without being seen. He cast a glance back at the castle. Sentries stood along the parapet that he had only recently darted across, scanning the countryside, looking for him. They would scarcely fail to notice a man fleeing across this barren, rocky slope. His only option was to stay where he was, and find what cover he could among the boulders and bracken.

Feeling ill-used and exhausted, Adaran crawled slowly up the bank, looking for somewhere to hide.

Laquin's men brought Ponn and Jalla to an interior chamber of the castle, in a wing that had remained more or less intact despite the destruction that had been visited upon the structure. Along the way they passed a number of spots where workers were shoring up the walls and hallways with wooden stanchions in an effort, probably futile, to keep the entire place from collapsing around them. Ponn wished them all good luck, but thought the more sensible thing would be to abandon the building. Perhaps Laquin had remained in his father's devastated castle in order to boost the morale of his people; they were frightened now, but Ponn could imagine their despondence if the king were to be turned out into the street.

Ponn and Jalla were deposited in an anteroom adjacent to what had once been a great hall. Through an archway choked with debris, Ponn could see the twisted columns of the next room, fallen now, shattered like crushed reeds. The ceiling had come down with them, burying whatever had been in there beneath layers of rock and timber.

A voice said: "That was the throne room."

Ponn turned; a scroll-laden man had entered, his arms so full of papers and parchments that Ponn couldn't see his face except for tired, rheumy eyes and a shock of white hair above them. "It is likely that my lord King's father is still in there, beneath the rubble, along with half his court and a number of his commanders."

Ponn wasn't sure how to respond to this. "I am sorry for your kingdom's misfortune," he said.

"Yes," the man said after a moment. "Misfortune."

A boy entered the room from a narrow, dark opening on the right. Ponn wasn't sure it was really a door; it looked more like a hole torn in the wall by the partial collapse of the throne room. It took him a second to recognize Laquin. Jalla was first to realize who it was, rushing over and falling to her knees in front of him. "Please, sire, I didn't know anything about the dragon!" she cried. "Do not punish me, I beg of you!"

Laquin waved her to silence. "You speak the truth, I'm sure," he said. "I want you here to help ensure that Pyodor Ponn does as well."

"Is there to be punishment, then?" Ponn asked.

"I seek information," Laquin said, "not a scapegoat."

"You know, I have a son not much younger than you."

Laquin looked at Ponn oddly, then grinned in a most unkingly manner. "Everyone does," he said. "I've been told some variation of that by Lebbeck there, two other advisers, the captain of the night watch, and now you."

"My son doesn't conduct himself the way you do."

"I've been practicing to be king for sixteen years," Laquin said. Then, looking very young, if just for a moment: "I never expected my practice to end so suddenly, or under such circumstances."

"My condolences on the loss of your father."

Laquin nodded, all kingly business once more. "Enough about that," he said. "Tell me what you know of these eagle-riders."

"I'm afraid I know nothing more than what I already told you. They came to Enshenneah seeking crystals from the volcano, and succeeded. T'Sian—the dragon—told me that they took crystals from her lair as well, and slaughtered her hatchlings in the process. But as to who commands them or where they come from, I cannot say."

"Then let me tell you," Laquin said. "They struck out of the north and east. That's Dunshandrin's realm. Unless someone has been growing enormous birds without his knowledge, I would say he has just tipped his hand."

"Why would Dunshandrin attack you?"

"Rumor has it that he has fallen ill, and the twins are now in control." Laquin frowned. "I've met them. Even as children they were off-balance, always coming to blows over trivia. They have always argued over who was born first and would inherit their father's mantle—which, I will concede, is not trivia. Perhaps they've decided that the best way to settle their argument is to expand their kingdom to the southwest."

"They'll be coming on foot next," the scroll-laden man said.

The king rolled his eyes, exactly the way Pord would the third time Ponn told him to do his chores. "Yes, Lebbeck, I know that. That's why I have sent scouts to the river to watch for a crossing." Then, to Ponn: "We expect them to strike soon, before we have a chance to rebuild our defenses, although if the twins are directing this attack they may do something erratic. There is something about this situation that troubles me, though."

"The dragon?" Ponn said.

"Yes. A dragon should have easily demolished their eagles in the air. So why did it fail? And where is it now?"

"I haven't seen her since the raid began."

"I am concerned that they captured the beast," Laquin said. "If they did, I daresay that they'll be using it against us somehow."

"You needn't worry about that," Ponn said. "T'Sian detests the eagle-riders. She would never join them."

"Men who are clever enough to grow giant birds and create weapons that can destroy buildings are certainly clever enough to coerce a dragon's assistance," Laquin said. "And if it is dead, we must know how they killed it. They may have additional resources of which we are not aware."

"I don't know what happened to her," Ponn said. "After she flew off to fight Dunshandrin's men, Jalla and I hid in her oven until the fire went by."

Laquin raised an eyebrow. "That was risky."

"It's a good, solid oven," Jalla said. She sounded a bit sulky; Ponn wondered if she was jealous of the attention he was receiving from her king. "Very thick walls. We were safer there than we would have been anywhere else." Ponn almost expected her to claim the idea as her own, but she said nothing else.

"Indeed. Well, here is what we must do. We must find the dragon, if it is still in the city. You two will help Lebbeck organize groups of searchers."

"Me?" Jalla said. "Why me?"

Laquin glanced at her. "Because you know what the dragon looks like in its human guise, of course."

"But I—"

The king raised a royal eyebrow. "Because I said so."

After a moment Jalla said: "Yes, sire, of course."

"Good," Laquin said. "That's settled, then. I'll leave you to make arrangements with Lebbeck." He indicated the man with the scrolls. "He's the acting castellan. Formerly he was an assistant castellan, but there have been many promotions this day. I am told he is the most organized man in the kingdom; I cannot speak to that, except to say that all my birthday parties have gone off successfully." Laquin bowed and departed.

Lebbeck gave them each a starchy look, then tossed his scrolls and parchments to the floor. He pawed through them until finding the one he wanted, which he unrolled, pinning the edges with weights that he took out of his pockets. "This is a map of the city," he said. "We will divide it into sections and search for this dragon of yours."

"But the city is so big," Jalla said. "How will we ever search the whole thing?"

"On foot," Lebbeck said, "and as fast as we can."

13

Diasa stood on the dock at Achengate and looked out over the scalloped surface of Lake Achenar. Saltier than the sea, the vast reservoir of brine lent a sharp tang to the air; anything that remained in the water for any length of time became encrusted with a white, powdery rime. In the distance, across Achenar's narrow arm to her left, she could see the salt fens of eastern Yttribia, grey and drab as the underside of a boot. In a month or two it would be buried under snow and the world would be happier for it.

She noticed a shimmering from the corner of her eye and thought she saw dark figures silhouetted against the dawn; but when she turned it was only Ilfiss and Wert, approaching from farther up the wharf. She turned away again, looking out over the still waters, watching the birds as they wheeled and cried overhead. Ilfiss stopped beside her; Wert had gotten distracted by a crablike creature that had, to its regret, somehow gained the platform and was now trying to scuttle away from him, waving its claws in the air in a futile threat.

"I spoke to the harbor-master. There's a merchant ship coming, one of the last of the season," Ilfiss said. "It should arrive tomorrow. They'll unload and then we'll be able to book passage south to Barbareth, or across the lake to Madroval."

"What about a caravan?"

He shook his head. "There are no more caravans. Winter is too near, no one wants to risk crossing the mountains. At least, not for what we're able to pay."

Diasa grunted. Flaurent had had a sizable treasury, but it had vanished down one of the crevasses that Deliban had created. The only money they had now was what the survivors had carried, and what had been recovered from the pockets of the dead.

Ilfiss said: "The ship is Dunshandrian."

She felt her spine stiffen, and put her hand on the hilt of her sword. "A royal vessel?"

"No. Merchant, as I said. But its cargo is intended for Dunshandrin's mines."

Wert appeared next to them. He had captured the crustacean and was holding the creature in front of him; its spiny legs wiggled in the air as it struggled to escape. "It waves its claws, but it cannot reach me," he said, staring at it.

"Yes, Wert, that's fascinating," Diasa said. Then, to Ilfiss: "I will not set foot on one of Dunshandrin's ships except to scuttle it and send its miserable crew to the bottom."

"Of course you won't. But this is a *merchant* vessel. It does not belong to Dunshandrin. It belongs to a *merchant*."

"A merchant from Dunshandrin."

"You speak of the *Pride*," Wert said.

Ilfiss and Diasa both looked down at the little man. "Yes," Ilfiss said. "Were you listening when I talked to the harbor-master?"

"You must meet the *Pride* when it arrives, Diasa," Wert said, looking at her with the fervid intensity of an eight-year-old describing a monster lurking beneath his bed. The crab, forgotten, had managed to latch onto one of his fingers and was squeezing it without mercy.

Diasa said: "Why?"

"You'll see."

"That isn't good enough anymore, Wert!" she snapped. "If you have seen something, tell me what it is!"

Wert turned away. "I cannot," he said, shaking the crab loose and tossing it into the water. It landed with a splash and disappeared beneath the surface. Diasa balled her hands into fists, resisting the urge to pick him up by his scruffy robes and throw him in after it.

"Leave him be," Ilfiss said. "Shouting won't make him tell you anything more than he already has."

"He's told me nothing. Unless Dunshandrin himself will be disembarking from this vessel, so that I can kill him, I fail to see why I would want to meet it." She aimed her foot at Wert, then turned and kicked a piling instead.

"When was the last time you slept, Diasa?" Ilfiss said.

"I'm fine."

"You are not fine. In fact, you are beginning to look nearly as mad as Wert. Go back to the inn and rest. You will feel better afterwards, I promise."

"You oracles," Diasa said. "Always trying to predict the future."

Laquin had decreed that all able civilians who were not suited for combat would assist in the search for T'Sian. This included the old men, the lame, the women, and the children from among the survivors who had gathered in King's Square. They were split into divisions, given a description of T'Sian and whatever equipment could be scrounged to help them search, and dispatched into the city.

Ponn's group spent the next several hours prodding into open spaces with poles, shifting debris with improvised levers, extinguishing small fires. Occasionally one of the searchers would rescue a loved one or a stranger, and everyone rejoiced; at other times they found bodies, which they laid out in the street for the black wagons that prowled the darkened avenues. These less-happy occasions became more frequent as the night ground on toward morning. Finally, as dawn stole across the ruins, Ponn sank onto an inviting pile of rubble and said: "This is hopeless. We'll never find her."

Lebbeck, who had assigned himself to Ponn's group, gave him a canny glance and motioned for the others to continue on. He waited until they were out of earshot, then said: "There will be no such talk in front of the common folk. They are already on the verge of despair and do not need to hear tidings of hopelessness from you, the dragon's good friend. Do you understand me, Enshennean?"

He was right, of course. "Yes. I'm sorry. It's fatigue that makes me speak this way, I'm sure. I just need to rest."

"Rest? You must be joking. Look at me. I'm an old man, and I'm not ready to stop yet."

"Just a few moments, please," Ponn said. "I haven't slept properly in days."

"There's no time for sleep! Our scouts say Dunshandrin's soldiers are gathering beyond the river at the bottom of the bluff. We have the high ground and will defend it, but the ranks of our soldiers have been thinned by this cowardly attack, and the men we plucked from the crowd are hardly replacements for battle-tested fighters. No, we must find your friend the dragon before Dunshandrin's footmen strike."

"What if you attack them while they're still organizing?"

"Our position is the only advantage we have. Until reinforcements arrive from the interior, we've no choice but to maintain a defensive posture. But these are matters for the prince—I mean the king—and his commanders to fathom. Our simple task is to find the dragon and persuade her to assist us."

The castellan stretched out a gnarled hand. Ponn took it, and found himself hauled to his feet by the man's surprising strength. They rejoined the others and resumed their slow trek through the wreckage, until at last they came to the end of their assigned section of the city. They had found no survivors for some time, and had turned up no trace of the dragon. Lebbeck himself looked haggard now, worn out by the night's fruitless searching. He dispersed the searchers, telling them to find what shelter they could, and then guided Ponn through streets thick with mourning, back toward Laquin's shattered castle.

"I apologize for my earlier behavior," Ponn said.

"There is no need. We did good work tonight; we rescued a number of citizens, and the king's greater purpose was served."

"Greater purpose? But we didn't find the dragon."

"My lord king never thought that we would," Lebbeck said. "Though I had hoped …" He trailed off, then shook his head. "No, this was a way to keep the people busy, to prevent a panic. You saw how many had joined our group by the time we finished. Some of them will go and join other search parties. Others will help put out fires. Even the most exhausted will go to sleep knowing that they did what they could to help their fellow citizens, and will feel less helpless for it."

"Laquin thought of all that on his own?" Ponn said.

Lebbeck shrugged. "More or less."

"But he's just a boy."

"No he isn't," Lebbeck said. "He's a king."

That morning, the *Pride* passed through the Crosswaters, a churning mass of currents and foam where the three rivers came together. The

Red flowed from Dunshandrin and the Santill flowed from western Barbareth, spilling into and diluting the Dead River that came from salty Lake Achenar. Talbrett and his men had to put all their attention into steering the small ship into the Dead River, which would take them through the swamps of Madroval and then into the lake. Left to her own devices, Tolaria stood at the rail of the vessel and tried to see the oracular compound where she had lived. It stood in the western vertex of the cross, on a promontory that rose from the boggy headland. This bluff was the first of the stunted nubs that formed the foothills of the Oronj Mountains.

At first she thought she must be looking in the wrong place; but then she spotted the ruins of the temple where the oracles greeted supplicants and granted visions. She could see that the roof was gone; around the windows, the white walls showed black smudges, like bruises around battered eyes. Many of the trees had died, either burned up in the fire or killed by the heat, their remaining leaves brown and dry. It looked like some of the outbuildings still stood, but from the river she couldn't tell which they were or what condition they might be in.

"Tolaria!" Talbrett was hurrying over to her, evidently concerned about something. "The currents are very bad today, because the rivers are swollen from the storms. We will need to drop you upriver rather than fighting them to land at the Crosswaters."

She glanced at him, then at the ruins of her home. "It really is destroyed, Talbrett," she said. "The twins were telling the truth."

"You told me it had been destroyed. Did you not believe it?"

"I did. But I had hoped …" She trailed off.

"You hoped you were wrong, that they were lying to you."

"Yes."

After a moment, Talbrett said: "Do you still want to return there?"

"There's nothing to return to." She turned her back on the scene. "I will accompany you to Achengate, if I may, and find my own passage to Flaurent."

"Flaurent? You want to go back to the college?"

"Someone must tell them what happened here. Others may have brought them news of the fire, but only you and I know what truly caused it. Only …"

He cocked his head as if wondering what she would say next; but she had not paused to complete her thought this time. Rather, she had begun to feel lightheaded, the way she had below deck, in Talbrett's cabin, when she had suffered a vision and collapsed.

As she slumped to the deck, the last thing she saw was the merchant, lunging forward to catch her. At the same time, her consciousness seemed to splinter, like a painting on glass that had fallen and shattered.

She was on the ship, lying on her side on the cold, wet deck.

And she lay on the muddy ground behind a heap of rocks, covered in broken bits of bracken, half-asleep and trembling with cold.

And she was stretched out on a fluffy bed in a ruined castle, sleeping away days of exhaustion.

And she was pinned beneath the wreckage of a building, battered, humiliated, dreaming of soaring through the open air.

And she was curled up on a cot that was too short for her, caught up in a dream of leading robe-clad Withered Ones in a battle against a living earthquake.

What was this? Were these other minds that she touched? They surrounded her, their awareness mingling with hers; it was a sort of vision, she supposed, but one she had never known before. Did they sense her as well? Or was she merely an observer here, seeing but unseen, hearing but unheard? She spoke, not knowing if her mouth formed the words, or if it was merely in her mind. Who were these people?

As soon as she thought of the question, she knew the answer; she knew all their names, even her own, and spoke them one by one. "Tolaria. Adaran. Ponn. T'Sian. Diasa."

"Who's there?" That was the one called Adaran, who lay in the mud and stones. "Am I dreaming of Diasa?"

"I would certainly hope not," Diasa said.

"T'Sian?" This was the one called Ponn, who slept in the borrowed, regal bed. "I'm in Varmot's castle. Where are you? Are you still in Astilan?"

"I am buried," T'Sian said, her voice a roar in Tolaria's mind; there was something different about her, setting her apart from the others. "Help me, Ponn!"

"This is such an odd dream," Adaran said.

"I don't think it is a dream," Tolaria said. "It is a vision. I am an oracle, and you are all in my vision."

"You're an odd sort of oracle, having visions such as this," Diasa said. "You're Tolaria? Wert mentioned you not long ago. He said you had escaped."

"I have," she said. "I was being held prisoner in Dunshandrin's castle, but no longer. I escaped on a ship."

"Is it called the *Pride*?" Diasa asked.

"Yes. How did you know?"

"So that explains it," Diasa said, apparently to herself.

"Diasa, where's Prehn?" Adaran said. "Is she all right?"

"The little girl? She's here with me in Achengate."

"Prehn?" Ponn cried. "You have Prehn? My daughter?"

"Well, she's *someone's* daughter," Diasa said.

"You must watch over her and keep her safe!" Ponn said. "Will you do that? Will you bring her safely back to me?"

"I don't see myself traveling to Astilan in the near future," Diasa said, "but I will keep her safe, yes."

"Prehn is your daughter?" Adaran said. "I rescued her from Dunshandrin's men in the mountains. I think they were going to feed her to the eagles, or maybe sell her."

"Dunshandrin!" Ponn said the name as if he were spitting it onto the street. "He is behind all this, T'Sian. Not Varmot."

"I do not understand," T'Sian said. "If we are all so widely separated, how can we communicate?"

"It seems to be my doing," Tolaria said. "I don't know how I brought our minds together or how long it will last, but we must take advantage of the situation while it lasts. There must be a purpose to it."

"What purpose might that be?" Diasa said. "To congratulate each other on how ill-used we all are?"

"No," T'Sian said. "I think the oracle means we must work together to defeat this Dunshandrin and his henchmen. You all will help me to avenge my hatchlings."

For a moment, everyone was silent.

Then Diasa said: "Your *hatchlings*?"

"You needn't worry about getting revenge on Dunshandrin," Adaran said. "I already killed him. Oh. Oh, no. I think I've been
—"

Then pain flared through Tolaria, pain in her hands, her feet. She heard a snapping sound in her ears, the sound of crossbows firing. Adaran's consciousness spun away from her and she opened her eyes. She lay in her hammock in her tiny room, swaying as the boat rocked in the current. The merchant sat nearby, on a stool he must have brought in with him.

"This is beginning to become habitual," Talbrett said.

"T'Sian? Adaran?"

Ponn fell silent, realizing that the others were gone and he was awake, a royally soft mattress beneath him, thick blankets covering him from the morning chill. He rubbed his forehead with the back of his hand. Had that all been a dream? Could there really be an oracle hundreds of miles away who had found him in his sleep and sought to bring him allies? Was Prehn really alive, and safe? Was T'Sian really buried somewhere in the city? What had happened to wake him up?

He climbed out of bed, shivering. He had tried to light a fire before retiring, but the chimney was evidently blocked; smoke had begun to fill the chamber, forcing him to douse the flames and open the shutters. The room still stank. He didn't know if this was because of his misadventure with the hearth, the pall over the city, or both.

Ponn dressed, then slipped on the warm cloak that he'd bought the day before. A guard was posted outside his room; Ponn asked the man to take him to the king. A number of delays ensued as the king was located, his permission sought, his more pressing business concluded. Eventually, Ponn was ushered into the same small chamber where they'd met after the attack on the city. Laquin was waiting for him on a throne that hadn't been there the night before. It looked old and battered and appeared to have been recently repaired; Laquin sat in it sideways, with his legs dangling over one of the padded arms and his back against the other.

"Good morning, sire," Ponn said. "I wondered if—"

"This kingship business is incredibly tedious," Laquin said. "You would think that with an enemy army bearing down on us, I would be planning grand strategies and bold maneuvers, wouldn't you?" Pause. "Well, wouldn't you?"

Ponn, who had thought the question rhetorical, said: "I would suppose so, sire."

"You would suppose wrong," Laquin said. "My *captains* are planning grand strategies and bold maneuvers. I am busy looking over petitions, claims, and counterclaims resulting from this destruction Dunshandrin has visited on us. The captains occasionally ask me for my opinion, but I think they ignore it." He shrugged, as if resigned to the fate of irrelevance. "What was it you wanted to discuss with me?"

"I had a dream," Ponn said.

"Oh, no," Laquin said. "Visions and prophecies?"

"There was a woman named Tolaria. She claimed to be—"

"An oracle." Laquin cocked his head at Ponn. "Tolaria is a new oracle at the Crosswaters. We were notified of her appointment by dispatch several months ago."

Ponn said: "I'm surprised you would remember that."

"I was in training to be king someday," Laquin said. "I was sent to the Crosswaters to meet the new oracle." He looked momentarily wistful. "She was very pretty."

"Was she a gifted seer?"

"So we were told, although the oracle in charge of the facility seemed to think her abilities overrated and assigned her to mediation work. What was she doing in your dream?"

"I don't know. There were other people there, too. T'Sian the dragon, a woman from Flaurent named Diasa, and a man named Adaran who claimed to have assassinated Dunshandrin."

Laquin raised an eyebrow. "Really? That's interesting, if it's true. What else did he say?"

"He said he had saved my daughter from Dunshandrin's men. I told you how she had been kidnapped."

"Yes." Laquin scratched his head. "Busy fellow. Is there any chance he can assassinate the princes for us as well?"

"I don't think so," Ponn said. "Something happened to him just as I awoke. He ... may be dead."

"Pity. Well, Pyodor Ponn, I must say that I don't know what to make of this dream of yours. You had never met nor heard of Tolaria before this?"

"Never. Happenings at the Crosswaters are not conveyed to simple innkeepers in Enshenneah."

"And that is all you are, eh?" Laquin chuckled, then grew serious again. "My father employed an interpreter of dreams and visions, though I've no idea if she survived the attack. I haven't seen her, so I expect she did not." He eyed Ponn. "What do *you* think, simple innkeeper?"

"I don't know," he said. "If Tolaria is a real person, there's no reason to believe that the others were not also real. Perhaps Adaran really did kill Dunshandrin, or thinks he did. Perhaps my daughter and the dragon live."

Laquin nodded. "It sounds to me as though Tolaria may still be doing mediation," he said, "but of a different sort. I hope that is the case, and you are correct."

"So do I," Ponn said.

Diasa sat up as the vestiges of her dream fell away, the hum of crossbows echoing in her ears. At least two of them, she thought, discharged at close range. If the dream was real, and they had been shooting to kill, there could be little doubt but that Adaran was dead. Pity it hadn't happened a week earlier.

She looked around the tiny garret room. Yellow light streamed in through the windows, which were set into dormers that poked out through the slate roof of the inn. Diasa sighed and rolled out of bed. Her clothes lay on the floor where she'd dropped them. She tugged on her leather gaiters, then slipped her tunic over her head and cinched it around her waist. She went to the window, opened it, poked her head out, and looked toward the lake. She had slept longer than she'd intended; the sun had begun to climb toward afternoon, sparkling on the surface of grey Lake Achenar. She must have been very tired indeed.

The door opened. She turned and saw Wert, standing in the hallway, looking at her. "So?" he said. "Did she reach you?"

"You knew." Diasa waggled her finger at him. "You knew she was going to find us all."

The old man grinned broadly.

"You've hardly ever been right about anything before," Diasa said. "Why do you know so much now?"

Wert tapped the side of his head. "Overdose," he said.

"I know you overdosed," Diasa said. "Everyone knows that. What's it got to do with anything?"

"Not me, her. The princes overdosed Tolaria. I can see inside her head now. I can help her."

"You can see inside her head."

He nodded.

"Because they fed her too much vapors."

He nodded again.

"And can she see inside yours?"

He appeared to consider this. "I suppose so. Don't know why she'd want to."

"Well, that makes two of us." Diasa sat down on the bed. "Tolaria's coming here. She's on that boat you told me about."

"Yes."

"When will she arrive?"

Wert closed his eyes. Then he opened them again, and looked at Diasa without seeing her at all. "The river is widens," he intoned, his voice flat as the wastelands they had left behind. "Coming into the lake. Open water ahead. The wind is with us and we're making good time. Talbrett says we'll be in Achengate around sundown. I wonder if he's all right. I'm worried about him. He's started to drag his left foot when he walks. The growths go deeper than he knows."

Diasa stared at him, shocked at the ease with which he had slipped into Tolaria's mind—if he was really doing it, of course, and not merely indulging some fantasy. "Wert," she said.

"I will tell the headmistress that Dunshandrin destroyed the Crosswaters. She will find a way to punish him for—"

"Wert!"

He blinked several times, then his eyes refocused and he looked at Diasa. "What?"

"Get out of her head," she said. "I don't want you doing that unless you have a reason."

"Why do I need a reason?"

"Because you're violating her."

"Every oracle is violated in one way or another."

"Well, there's no need for you to add to it."

"You don't understand what it's like." He seemed to be pouting. "The voices. The visions."

"You're right. I didn't inherit any of my mother's talent, and I'm not sorry about it."

"Perhaps you inherited a bit of your father's," Wert said.

She looked sharply at him then. "What are you talking about, Wert?"

The little man said nothing.

"Do you know who my father was?"

Still he said nothing.

"If you know, you had better tell me," she said, beginning to stand. Then a thought struck her and she sank back onto the bed again. "Oh, no. It's you, isn't it? *You're* my father."

"No," Wert said.

"I should have known," she said. "No wonder you were always following my mother around, saying *Damona* this and *Damona* that and looking at her like—"

"I am not your father," he said.

After a moment, Diasa said: "Oh."

"But I know who your father is."

Her heart began to beat faster, the way it did just before a fight or a training exercise. "Who? Who is it?"

He shook his head. "I can't tell you."

"*What?*"

"It's a secret."

"I know it's a secret, damn you! My mother spent twenty-five years keeping it from me! And now you say you know who it is but *you can't tell me?*" She stood up and grabbed him by the shirt. "You had better change your mind, little man."

Suddenly Ilfiss appeared in the hallway, with the little girl, Prehn, in tow. He cocked his head at the sight of Diasa half-lifting Wert off the ground. "Am I interrupting something?"

"Yes," Diasa said severely.

"Let him go, Diasa."

"He knows who my father is and he won't tell me."

"Diasa. You know you aren't going to beat it out of him. He'll tell you when he's ready, assuming he even really knows."

She held Wert's shirt a moment more, then sighed and half-tossed him away. He maintained his balance surprisingly well, and gave her a sad look. "You'll understand soon," he said.

She took a menacing step toward him; he turned and fled up the corridor, disappearing down the stairs. Ilfiss watched him go, then entered the room. "Here she is, fed and sleepy," he said, presenting Prehn to Diasa as if she were a debutante. "How are you feeling? Did you rest well?"

"Not particularly."

"I'm sorry. Dreams?"

She nodded.

"Anything you would care to talk about?"

"No."

"As you wish." Looking at the floor, he said: "I'll be leaving soon. One of the students wants me to go back to his father's estate and continue his instruction there."

"And you agreed, of course."

"Of course. I'm not much of an oracle, really, but I'm an excellent teacher."

"Which student?"

"Radovar."

"Oh." Diasa nodded. "The vintner's boy."

"Yes."

"Radovar's father has no idea what he's getting into."

"Indeed he does not. I will make sure my contract includes a generous allowance of wine and spirits." Ilfiss smiled. "You could come with me, you know. Radovar's father might have a position for you."

"I doubt a vintner has much need for the likes of me," she said. "Besides, Yttribia is no place for a woman with a profession. I'd be married off inside of a month, and Radovar's father would collect the dowry."

He laughed and said, "As if you would let that happen." Then, looking uncomfortable: "Radovar has used his father's good name and credit to hire a skiff. We'll be leaving as soon as it's ready. A few hours, I'm told."

"So soon?"

"The boy doesn't want to stay in Achengate a moment longer than he must. I can't say that I blame him." He put his hand on her shoulder. "You will be all right on your own?"

"Of course. I can take care of myself. I was the captain of the guard in Flaurent, as you recall."

"Is *that* why you were always carrying weapons around? And here I thought you were just unusually violent." Ilfiss grinned, but it faded quickly. He began looking around the room, as if searching for something more to say.

"You needn't feel guilty about taking this position, Ilfiss. You must eat and put clothes on your back."

He nodded, turned, and went to the door; but he stopped there, taking up most of the frame. "I know what you're planning to do," he said, not looking at her. "I don't need to be a very good oracle to see that. You must be careful. Setting yourself against a king is a deadly proposition."

"Dunshandrin is not a king."

"Close enough. I'll return for Prehn before I leave."

Diasa looked at the little girl, curled up on her bed, apparently asleep. If her dream were to be believed, the child's father was waiting for her somewhere in Astilan, and they were fated to meet. "I'll keep her," she said.

Ilfiss did look at her then, surprise on his face. "That isn't what you said earlier. You told me that a child had no place in your future."

"I know what I said." Diasa tugged at one of her curls, twisting the dark hair around her finger. "I have rethought my position."

"And if you are killed? What will happen to her then? Would you see her in an orphanage?"

"I saw her father in a dream, while I slept," Diasa said. "I promised to look after her."

"This is the dream you did not want to discuss?"

"Yes. A dream, a vision. I don't know what you would call it. Do you remember a student named Tolaria?"

"Of course. She was brilliant, and so your mother sent her to the Crosswaters. What about her?"

"She orchestrated the vision. Or maybe Wert did it; he knew the vision would come if I fell asleep. There were five of us there, and one was Prehn's father."

Ilfiss stroked his chin. "Still ... would it not be better to send the girl with me, and tell her father—if indeed you ever meet him—where she can be found?"

"I don't know." She looked at Prehn again. "I think I must keep my promise, and watch over her."

"But—"

From the room below, a voice called out: "Professor Ilfiss! The wagon has come to take us to the harbor!"

"His master's voice," Ilfiss murmured. He looked at the stairway, then at Diasa, then at the child. "You *will* keep her out of harm's way, I hope."

"As well as I keep myself."

"That," Ilfiss said, "is perhaps not as reassuring as you might think."

14

Tolaria stood at the prow of the *Pride* as it approached the docks of Achengate. A strong wind had kicked up out of the east, speeding their passage across the grey lake; they had arrived at the harbor considerably earlier than Talbrett had estimated. From her vantage point it didn't look like the city had changed much since the last time she'd passed through. Still dirty, still ramshackle. The dilapidated buildings along the harbor stood on rime-encrusted poles rising from the salty waters. She supposed some might find the town quaint and charming, but to her eyes it was merely dreary.

Far beyond Achengate she could see clouds of sand and dust towering over the Salt Flats. The same wind that had sped Talbrett's ship toward the city would be making life hellish out in the wastes, where she was going. Flaurent's high walls helped keep the salt out, but on a day like this grit would fall from the sky like hail.

She went to her tiny cabin below deck to gather what little she had —Talbrett had somehow scrounged a change of clothes for her—and also to get out of the way while the crew moored the ship. She tied the unworn clothes into a little wad of fabric, tucked it under her arm, and waited for the motion of the ship to stop before going back above. When she did, the boat had drawn adjacent to one of the piers, secured by long, drooping ropes and complicated knots. She found Talbrett at the railing, idly fingering the knuckle-like growths at the base of his skull. He didn't hear her approach; he was intent on staring into the city, as if trying to imprint it on his mind and take its memory with him from this world to the next. He glanced at her as she came to the railing next to him. "Here we are. Achengate."

She said nothing.

"Last time I'll see this place," he said, sounding wistful, though she knew the emotion was not directed at run-down Achengate but at the world in general. "I'll miss it."

"Thank you for helping me," she said. "I can't begin to repay you."

He shrugged. "I didn't do that much."

"You did more than many other men would have, and you didn't even claim the service that I promised you."

He smiled wanly. "Well, what does it really matter, in the end, who fathered the boy? I raised him, and that makes him mine." He pointed at the gangplank, which his crew had just finished securing. "Shall we disembark?"

"Certainly," she said.

He linked arms with her and escorted her down the walkway. After spending so much time on the water, the dock felt odd under her feet, solidly immobile. They walked up it, stopping at one of the flat-bottomed boats that navigated the network of shallow rivers out in the Salt Flats. "This one's mine," Talbrett said. "We'll transfer the cargo to it and head out into the wasteland. You're welcome to come if you want. We're not going to Flaurent, but we can take you part of the way."

"Thank you," she said. "Perhaps I will, if you think—"

Suddenly something flashed in the air, catching the oblique rays of the sun. Talbrett shouted and jumped in front of her, pushing her to the side, causing her to cry out in surprise. He grunted and reeled backwards, his pudgy hands clutching the wobbling black hilt of a dagger that had caught him neatly in his left eye. The little merchant crumpled to the dock, twitched a few times, fell still. She knelt beside him, her body trembling all over. Blood oozed from around the blade. She touched his fleshy throat, looking for the heartbeat. Nothing. It seemed the knuckles would not squeeze his life away after all.

Someone came out of the cabin of Talbrett's flatboat, a big, dangerous-looking man. He swaggered up the gangplank to the dock, and drew a long, gleaming sword as he approached.

Tolaria stood and faced him. "You killed Talbrett," she said.

The man shrugged. "I was *trying* to kill you. The fat fool spoiled a perfectly aimed throw."

"Dunshandrin sent you."

He shrugged.

"How did you find me?"

"Once we realized that you must have slipped away by boat, it wasn't hard to figure out which one you were on. I've been following you all the way up the river." He frowned. "I thought you would get off at the Crosswaters, but you didn't, so I flew ahead to intercept you here. Get back, all of you!" he shouted suddenly, pointing his sword at something behind her. She turned and saw that Talbrett's crew had begun to gather around. Would they risk their own lives to protect her from this man?

"Murderer!" Rennald cried. With Talbrett dead, Tolaria knew, the others would look to him as their leader. He stood ahead of the rest, his fists raised, as if bare hands would do any good against the killer's sharp blade.

"My business is with the lady," the assassin said, "but I will cut down any who interfere. The merchant chose his own death. Would you now choose yours as well?"

Rennald hesitated; the men behind him exchanged glances, waiting to see what he would do.

"I warn you," the man said. "Return to unloading your vessel, and you will be allowed to go about your business. Meddle in this affair, and you will—"

"*Gelt!*"

The killer turned; so did Tolaria. A woman sprinted toward them, her own blade upraised and gleaming in the sun.

"Well, look who's here," Gelt said. "Hello again, Diasa. Are you coming to finish our dance?"

"Diasa," Tolaria whispered, remembering her dream. Then, with no conscious thought, she jumped back a pace, feeling a breeze as Gelt's sword whipped through the air in front of her. The tip of it just nicked her belly.

He had tried to disembowel her while her head was turned.

The swordswoman reached them and swung her weapon. Coming out of his strike at Tolaria, Gelt parried it easily, the two blades clanging against each other, holding for a few seconds as the two of them gazed at each other; then Diasa's eyes shifted just a hair, to look at Tolaria instead.

"You're early," she said.

Laquin invited Pyodor Ponn to accompany him to the top of one of the ruined towers, where the young man perched on the crumbling wall and gazed over his city, looking toward the northeast. Ponn guessed that the room had once been some sort of library or retreat; remnants of shelves still clung to the curving wall, books and scrolls lay scattered among the rubble and fallen beams. The floor seemed sturdy enough, but Ponn felt uncomfortable being up so high.

"You see our fortifications," Laquin said, pointing to the ramparts along the ridge. "We have sufficient strength to man the walls, but that may well be irrelevant. They are meant to stop invaders on foot or horseback, not those who fly through the air."

"They can't take the city merely by bombarding it," Ponn said. "They'll have to come in on foot eventually."

"But if they use their sorcery to destroy the ramparts and the men who guard them? What then? Is their objective to occupy Astilan, or to destroy it?"

A voice from behind them said: "I would imagine, sire, that their objective is to capture *you*." Ponn glanced at the stairs as Lebbeck limped toward them. "And here you are, presenting them with a fine, inviting target."

Laquin looked at the castellan. His face was pale and he looked very much like the boy he was. "My people need me here. Would you have me flee to the interior?"

"Yes, I would." Lebbeck turned to Ponn, exasperation written across his face. "He seems to listen to you. Tell him he must retreat."

Laquin made an impatient noise and turned away, gazing once more toward the battlements. "Pyodor Ponn is not my adviser."

Lebbeck frowned and shook his head. Ponn went to him and murmured: "The king mentioned a royal seer of some sort. Could this person help us to locate T'Sian?"

"The seer? No, I do not think she will be assisting us. Perhaps my lord king neglected to tell you that this was once her apartment?"

"Yes," Ponn said, "he did neglect to mention that. That must be why he suggested we come to the tower. I thought he merely wanted to see the view."

"Perhaps he did. But perhaps he also hoped to find the seer here, weeping over the remains of her library."

"You needn't whisper," Laquin said, looking at them over his shoulder. "I can hear you both."

"Ah, youth, with its exceptional ears," Lebbeck said.

"Something is happening," Laquin said. "Come and look. Our men are abandoning the ramparts."

"What? Your fine soldiers would never do such a thing!"

"I tell you, they are doing it as we speak." He turned back to his view. "This troubles me greatly. There are no eagles in sight. Dunshandrin is up to some new mischief."

"Sire, you must evacuate," Lebbeck said.

Laquin did not turn. "No."

"Sire, we cannot hold the city!"

"No."

"If you are killed, who will lead us?"

Laquin looked over his shoulder at them, then glanced at Ponn. "How about him?" he said.

"*What?*" Ponn cried.

Further discourse was interrupted by a rumbling sound that came rolling from the ridge. Ponn recognized the noise of an earthquake or landslide and hurried to the edge of the tower. He watched as the central portion of the rampart collapsed, the cliff cracking asunder and falling into the plains below. A great cloud of dust arose, obscuring the scene; but Ponn thought he saw the churning earth moving, reforming itself, transforming the bluff into a wide, steep ramp.

"What is happening?" Lebbeck cried. "Someone tell an old man whose eyes are weak!"

"Dunshandrin turns the earth against us," Laquin said. "They are building themselves a road to bring them up the ridge and over the ramparts."

"What? Impossible!" Lebbeck joined them at the edge of the tower, squinting at the dust cloud, his mouth agape. He seized Laquin's arm. "You must get out of here," he said. "Now." The young king resisted for a moment, but then his resolve seemed to drain out of him and he allowed himself to be pulled away from the wall.

Ponn said: "Sire?"

"The castellan is right," Laquin said, looking at the floor. "We cannot hold the city, not when Dunshandrin has witched the very ground beneath us."

"But sire, your people … your city! Lebbeck, what did you tell me last night about not speaking of hopelessness?"

The old man gave him a sad look. "There are no common folk here. Flee while you can, Pyodor Ponn. Go where you will, with the king's honor and regard."

Lebbeck led Laquin away, down the rubble-strewn steps into the castle. Ponn watched them go, and then pulled himself up onto the perch that Laquin had abandoned. The sun, moving into the north, hung behind Dunshandrin's soldiers as they swarmed up the bluff and into the city; any defenders who remained would look into its glare as they attempted to strike with spears or arrows. Dunshandrin would probably extend his deviltry to the sun, if he could, and force it to face his enemies no matter where they stood.

Ponn realized that the tower had begun to vibrate. Bits of stonework and masonry shook loose, scratching and clattering as they bounced down to the ground. He clung to the wall as the shaking increased, but then a chunk of it pulled loose and fell away, forcing him to leap off. He landed hard on the floor, lost his balance, and fell in a cloud of dust. He scrambled toward the steps, only to find that the way down was blocked; part of the remaining wall had collapsed and buried the stairway with rubble and debris. He returned to the wall, wondering if he could climb down. The stone was certainly rough enough to provide handholds, but the shaking would make it difficult to maintain a grip. It would be like trying to shimmy down a tree while it whipped in a hurricane.

Through the blowing dust, he saw Dunshandrin's men moving toward the city. Earthen ramparts raised themselves around the soldiers as they advanced, protecting them from archers or footmen who might strike from the sides. Ponn had no idea what manner of wizardry could accomplish such a feat; certainly he had never seen the like. The churning of the ground to create fortifications must be the cause of the tremor.

The enemy column entered the town. Now the buildings themselves betrayed Astilan; the roiling ground caught them up and took them and made them part of the walls that protected

Dunshandrin's men. Wood, stone, earth, and masonry knit a crazy patchwork barrier, as if some gargantuan farmer were tilling the city into his field, carving a path straight through to the castle. Any structures in the way were sundered and leveled, shattered like a rowboat struck by the prow of a ship.

Blinking away tears—the dust and smoke had begun to sting his eyes—Ponn watched as the soldiers advanced through the city along their newly-built highway. They would soon reach the keep, and without encountering a shred of resistance from Laquin's forces. This could hardly be termed a battle; it wasn't even a rout. Astilan's defenders might as well have stayed in their homes.

Suddenly, something stirred near the head of the column, as it plowed aside a splintered heap of debris that had once been a building. Instead of quietly folding into the earth, this wreckage seemed to explode, sending beams and rubble flying in every direction as a massive shape shot into the sky.

Ponn had never seen the dragon in flight before except from below, clutched in one of her talons; she was beautiful, magnificent, and terrifying. The slanting light danced across her deep indigo scales, through the translucent, volcanic red of the mane that ran from the top of her head down the back of her neck. Enormous, powerful wings beat the air, carrying her high above the city. She wheeled around, hovered motionless a moment; he saw her smoky eyes look searchingly over the city, and felt a shiver go through him as her gaze alighted on him.

She would destroy the ranks of Dunshandrin's men. She would save them all.

As he cried out her name, the tower broke beneath him.

He fell, along with the fragments of the tower, twisting around to face the sky. T'Sian darted toward him, faster than an arrow in flight. She plowed through the tumbling debris and snatched him up in her claw, then carried him away, leaving the battlefield spinning below.

She did not turn to face the soldiers.

Instead, she kept going, up and up, carrying him away to the northwest, until Astilan had become a blackened smudge in the distance.

Gelt took a step away from the girl, Tolaria, keeping his blade pressed against Diasa's. A group of men, sailors from the look of them, gathered around the oracle and the dead man, forming a protective circle. Without weapons, though, they stood no chance against the swordsman. If Diasa failed and they refused to yield, they would die.

"Well," Gelt said. "I didn't expect to see *you* again."

"Surprise," Diasa said.

"I suppose this time I'll have to make sure you're dead." He stepped back. His sword slid along hers with a metallic scrape.

"Are you sure you can handle me without your pet wizard?"

"Perhaps I have him here with me."

"Perhaps he's far away in the west, helping Dunshandrin's pups overrun Astilan."

Gelt frowned at her, as if she were repeating unkind rumors. "One shouldn't go around accusing their betters of such things," he said. He held up his weapon, turned it sideways; the blade was longer than hers, but marred by nicks and dents and scratches.

They slowly circled each other. "Do you use that to chop firewood?" Diasa said. A crowd had begun to gather around them, toughs and rowdies drawn by the promise of swordplay. None of them seemed inclined to intervene, although the dead merchant's men—who had by now ventured to drag the man's corpse out of the way—continued to stare daggers at his killer. "Doesn't look like it would be good for anything else."

Gelt snorted. "And that little knife of yours? Is it for peeling fruit? Where's that big axe you used to haul around?"

"I seem to have left it in Flaurent," she said. "Along with the bodies of my mother and a number of my friends."

"Don't worry, you'll see them again soon."

"Then let's not keep them waiting," she said.

"Yes, let's not." The big man advanced; Diasa gave some ground, moving to her left. Gelt lunged experimentally, going for a stabbing wound to the gut. Diasa knocked the blade aside. Gelt grinned and struck again, aiming more to the right. She deflected the thrust again but he turned it into a slash, nearly cutting her across the thigh. She danced away and kicked him in the stomach, hoping to knock him off balance, but it was like kicking a boulder. He grabbed her foot and threw her backwards, sending her sprawling on the dock. She rolled over and was back on her feet before he could press his advantage.

They started circling each other again. She had his measure now; he was much stronger than she was, but not as fast. She had to rely on speed to win this fight. The dock had become jammed with people, the spectators forming the walls on an arena. Some town guards had joined the crowd, probably intending to get their entertainment from the fight and then arrest the winner, and she was sure she heard someone taking bets on the outcome.

Gelt made a sloppy lunge. She blocked it easily, but then felt a sting across her belly and leapt back. She felt the cold air bite against her stomach; he had cut her, slicing through her tunic, but not with his sword. She noted a tiny dagger in his left hand, the weapon so small she could scarcely see it in his beefy grip. He'd pulled the miniature blade from somewhere and nearly slit her open with it.

"Oh!" Gelt said. "Where did *this* come from?"

"Cheap theatrics," Diasa said.

"I fight to win, not for the thrill of combat." He held the tiny blade sideways, exactly the way he'd earlier held the sword. A single, glistening drop of blood slid off it and fell to the dock. Gelt smiled and tossed the dagger aside, then came at her again, bellowing and swinging the sword over his head. She parried the blow, and the next, and the next. He pressed the attack, forcing her to retreat. The crowd parted as he drove her back, not giving her time to launch her own strikes. She felt unaccountably slow and tired; her sword was an anchor, her arms weak as a feverish little girl's. Why couldn't she counterattack? Suddenly her legs gave out and she stumbled to her knees, then to her side. A hazy glow filled her vision; the cut in her belly throbbed, a thin line of fire, and she finally realized that the dagger must have been poisoned.

Gelt stepped up to her. She lifted her sword; the tip wavered in the air and he knocked it aside easily. He raised his weapon over his head, ready to strike her down.

Four dark shapes broke from the ranks of the spectators, came forward, closed around Gelt. Her darkening eyes could not make out any details, but she thought they carried pole arms, long-handled and heavy-bladed, axe heads black as burnt-out ashes. The Withered Ones. They fell on Gelt, attacking in a frenzy. She heard him grunting, heard his breath coming fast and heavy. His sword rang against their weapons. The shapes formed a tightening circle around him, keeping him at bay in the center of their formation.

She picked up her sword, hauled herself to her feet, and staggered to join her allies. They parted just as she reached them and she struck, ramming her blade into Gelt's stomach just above his groin. She twisted it and yanked it out. Ropy, slimy stuff came with it. Gelt, a look of astonishment on his face, pawed at the wound as if he thought he could hold his innards in, as if he would be all right if only he could get everything stuffed back inside. One of the Withered Ones struck him in the face with its weapon and he fell off the dock. Diasa swayed on her feet in front of the bloody splotch where he'd been standing; the sword fell out of her hands, clattering to the wooden surface.

Then she, too, toppled over, and the water came rushing up to meet her, cold and dark as death itself.

15

As soon as T'Sian landed—somewhere in the plains to the northeast of Astilan, out of sight of even the highest-flying eagle, well away from the fighting—Ponn stumbled out of her grip, turned, and gasped: "You flew away!"

She sat on her haunches and began shrinking into human form, not answering the implicit charge of cowardice. If they were looking for her, she would be much harder to spot as a woman. She lost sight of Ponn during the change, when her senses fled; after they returned, she saw him pacing around the vicinity, looking very agitated. Realizing she had come back to herself, he stopped and said: "What happened? You were supposed to save Astilan, not leave it in Dunshandrin's hands!"

"I am not *supposed* to do anything. In any case, there is little left of Astilan to save." Then, pointedly: "I was barely able to save *you*, Pyodor Ponn, and the only reason I could was because you told me where you were, in that dream."

He sighed. "Yes, I thank you for that, but I don't understand what happened. Who will repel Dunshandrin's men? They will take the castle easily. They've probably captured or killed the king by now. We cannot let them succeed."

"In the air, I met a man who spoke powerful words. He commanded a creature that controlled the earth. They took me by surprise and I … I could not defeat them."

"Words? You mean a wizard?"

"Is that what they are called?"

"Yes, but even a wizard will burn."

"Not this one. He had protected himself, and my flames would not touch him. And then he took hold of me somehow, and drained my fire away."

"What?"

"He emptied me. I have no fire left."

"But … you will make more, won't you?"

"The crystals make the fire, Ponn," she said. "In here." She touched her fingers to her chest. "I swallow the two kinds of stones, and together they burn. When I use them up, I must swallow more. I should have had enough fire to last for months, perhaps years, but the man took it all away. Until I find more crystals, I will have no fire."

"Should we return to the islands and get more stones?"

She shook her head. "Without the blue crystals, the red will not make fire. Neither suffices without the other. And as I told you, the blue crystals are far to the north, buried in the ice. I hoarded both kinds in my lair, but Dunshandrin's men killed my babies and took my stones, all of them."

"Well, if you kept crystals, then other dragons would as well. Perhaps you could borrow—"

"There is no *borrowing*," she said. "A dragon fends for itself. The nearest dragon that I know of is four days' flight from here, on an island far to the south. Even if I made the journey, I would have to kill him to take his stones." She thought for a moment. "It will not work. He is large and ancient and has his fire. He would kill me."

"Perhaps you could persuade this other dragon to help us."

"Dragons have no interest in the doings of men. If he had not slain my hatchlings, I would let this Dunshandrin swarm across the continent."

"What do you propose we do, then?" Ponn said. "If we cannot fight because you have no fire, and you will not go into the north to get more crystals, then what is our next move?"

"We will go to the place called Achengate," T'Sian said. "The others are there, are they not? The oracle and the woman who has your daughter?"

"Yes," Ponn said, brightening. "My daughter."

"Perhaps you can take her and make your way back to Enshenneah," the dragon said. "Then you would be out of this."

"Are you saying you would let me go?"

"I no longer have need of you," she said. "I know who my enemy is. I know where to find him."

Ponn looked thoughtful. "Enshenneah," he said. "Home." Then he shook his head. "No, I can't go home. Not yet."

"Your goal has always been to save your daughter. Once you have her back, why continue to risk your life? And hers?"

"Hers? No, I will not risk hers. She must stay safe."

"Then return with her to Enshenneah."

"But Dunshandrin and his sons must pay for their crimes. Their men may have murdered my son. They left me to die on that island. They killed the man who rescued my daughter."

"They will pay," T'Sian said, "but you are an innkeeper, a merchant, a smuggler. Our success or failure does not rest on your shoulders."

"Are you saying I have nothing to contribute?"

"I only mean that you must consider the likelihood that you will be killed, and weigh it against the benefits that your presence brings," she said. "Do not think yourself invulnerable. You are not a dragon."

Ponn began pacing back and forth and said nothing for a little while. Perhaps she had offended him, but she only spoke the truth. She moved some distance away and assumed her true form once more; when her senses returned, he was standing in front of her. "I've thought about what you said, and I will consider it. But for now I make no decision."

"Very well," she said. "Then let us go. The others wait for us in Achengate."

Diasa awoke, not in the water, but in a bed. She felt weak and exhausted, as if she had just crawled mewling from her mother's womb. She blinked, and blinked again, which seemed to make the room look a little less fuzzy; so she blinked a few more times, bringing her surroundings into some semblance of focus. She realized then that she lay in her tiny garret room at the inn.

Had it been a dream? Gelt, Tolaria, the guards from Flaurent appearing, like apparitions, to save her? She slid her hand down to where the short blade had cut her stomach, felt a bandage across her abdomen. The cloth was damp. Blood? She sniffed her fingertips, smelled alcohol and herbs.

"You're awake."

She looked to her left, where Tolaria sat in a small chair in front of the window. She looked young and frightened, like a runaway caught on the street. "Much to my surprise," Diasa said. "What happened?"

"Talbrett's sailors pulled you out of the water. We brought you back here. You were feverish from the poison."

So the blade *was* envenomed. "Why am I still alive?"

"Wert told me what ingredients I needed for an antidote."

"*Wert* told you?" Then: "And you *listened* to him?"

"I cannot say how he knew, but he told me exactly which herbs would draw out the venom and help you recover. And here you are, alive and speaking."

"Wert has become a spigot of unexpected information," Diasa said. She closed her eyes again. "Are they still here?"

"Who?"

"The Withered Ones."

"The what?"

"You were at Flaurent. Don't you remember the guards?"

"Yes, of course. I was thoroughly frightened of them."

"They came here to save my life."

"No they didn't. Talbrett's men saved you."

There was that name again. Diasa opened her eyes and tilted her head to regard Tolaria. "Who is Talbrett?"

"The merchant who took the knife meant for me. When you fell, his men attacked Gelt with boards, oars, anything at hand. Two of them were hurt and one was killed. I think Gelt would have killed all of them if you hadn't gotten up again."

"I saw … I mean, I thought I saw … the Withered Ones."

"It must have been the poison, making you hallucinate."

"I'm sure it was my guards," Diasa murmured. Tolaria looked at the floor and said nothing. "What of your friends, then? Those who were killed?"

"Gargan is being taken downriver by boat, to be returned to his family. We're going to take Talbrett out onto the lake tonight and sink him."

"A sort of burial at sea, eh?"

"As close as one can come to it in Achengate, at any rate," Tolaria said. "Why don't you get some more rest? I'll check on you later and make sure that you're all right."

Diasa nodded, lay back, closed her eyes. She was hungry, but tiredness won out; she decided to eat the next time she woke up, whenever that was.

She heard Tolaria get up and leave the room. The door clicked shut behind her.

"It *was* the Withered Ones," Diasa whispered. "I saw them."

Tolaria went down to the common room, where Wert and Ilfiss sat at a corner table with the girl, Prehn. Ilfiss appeared to be getting ready to make his farewells, because he stood as Tolaria approached. "How is Diasa?" he asked.

"Tired, but I think she'll be fine."

"Good." Ilfiss spread his arms. "I wish I could stay to see her get well, but my wagon is waiting for me. Radovar is already upset that our departure was delayed. I must go."

Tolaria nodded. "I'm sure Diasa will understand."

Ilfiss still looked anxious, as if he were afraid Diasa would send him angry letters for the rest of her life, accusing him of abandonment. He nodded and bowed to Tolaria, then returned to the table, said a few words to Wert, snatched up a tiny valise, and hurried out the door.

Tolaria sat at the table, across from Wert. He stared at her with pop-eyed fascination. "Tolaria," he said. "So good to see you again."

She hadn't realized that her presence at Flaurent had ever registered on the little old man. "Yes, it's good to see you too," she said, hoping she sounded sincere. Looking at him made her think about what she might become, as the months went by and the lingering effect of the vapors became clearer.

"Diasa is well, and yet you seem sad."

"Well, it's a bit much, isn't it?" She lowered her voice so no one would hear. "My friends murdered, Flaurent and the Crosswaters destroyed, Astilan overrun, Diasa nearly killed."

Wert nodded. "Yes, Dunshandrin has much to answer for." Then: "You'll all go together."

"Go? Where?"

"The castle," he said. "You'll all go together."

"What castle? Who are you talking about? Diasa and me?"

"Diasa and you, and the others. To the castle." Wert leaned forward, his eyes growing even larger. "*His* castle."

He meant Dunshandrin, of course. "And what then?"

"I don't know," he said, sounding rather annoyed that this information was denied him. "I can't see past what's coming."

"What's coming?"

"My death."

"Oh. I'm, ah, I'm sorry to hear that."

"Don't be," he said. "It's already beyond my time to go."

"You're sure about this? You've seen it?"

He shook his head. "I've *planned* it."

"Oh." Tolaria couldn't think of anything else to say. She looked over at Prehn. The top of her head barely reached the tabletop; all that showed was a mop of black hair, a crescent of bronze forehead, and two huge brown eyes that regarded Tolaria with grave suspicion. "So Diasa and I will be going to the castle … and who else?"

"The dragon. The savage."

"The savage?"

"Enshennean."

"They're in Astilan," she said.

"Not anymore."

"How do you see all these things?" she said. "Do they just come into your head?"

"Not mine," Wert said. "Yours. You just don't know it."

"*What?*"

"Whispers." The old man tugged his ear. "Whispers. I heard you whispering, after they gave you the vapors. I heard it when you escaped, when you drew the good merchant to yourself, when you brought everyone together in your dreams."

"Did *I* do that, or was it you?"

"You. Me." Wert shrugged, as if to suggest there was little difference between the two. Then he pointed into the air and hissed: "I can hear *him*, too, sometimes."

Trying not to sound exasperated, she said: "Who?"

Wert leaned forward. His eyes, unblinking, reminded her of a frog's. "The wizard."

"Orioke?"

Wert nodded, looking smug. "When he opened his mind to yours, it formed a connection, never properly closed, because he doesn't know it's there. I can hear him through you."

"If you're listening to him," Tolaria said, "how do you know he's not listening to you?"

"Oh, he is. But he only hears what I want him to hear, only sees what I want him to see."

"Are you sure?"

Wert frowned. "No. But what else can I do? I must know what he's up to. The wizard is the most unpredictable piece on the board."

"You can control this … gift of yours? You can stop listening if you want to?"

"I don't know."

"Try. Before he realizes you're there."

But Wert just gave her another of his infuriating grins. He tapped the side of his head, perhaps to indicate that he was smarter than Orioke, perhaps just that he was mad. He closed his eyes. After a moment he began to speak, his voice scarcely above a whisper. "We are in complete control of Astilan now; there is no organized resistance left. Varmot is dead, Laquin is in our custody, and his soldiers cannot surrender fast enough. But we have not yet found the dragon. Some of the men claim to have seen it during the march to the castle, but I am not convinced. If they saw it, where did it go?" He opened his eyes again; for a moment they seemed unfocused, as if looking at something invisible or far away. Then he said: "I touch his mind, but he does not know it. I misguide his senses, but he believes what I tell him."

"You must stop doing this, Wert," Tolaria said. "You are meddling with a dangerous and powerful sorcerer."

The old man shrugged. "What have I got to lose?" he said.

T'Sian landed in the dry, barren plains southeast of Achengate, raising a huge cloud of dust that hung in the still air, motionless as fog. She set Ponn down, then reared up and flapped her wings, driving the cloud away, toward the city.

"Salty," Ponn said.

She swiveled her head to look down at him. "*What?*"

"The dust you kicked up," he said. "It tastes salty."

"*We are near the Salt Flats*," she said. "*The earth is contaminated. That is why so little grows here.*"

"The Salt Flats." Ponn gazed off into the darkness of the wasteland to the south and west. "I've heard of this place. I never thought to be here myself."

"*I avoid it. The dust works into my scales, and itches.*"

He favored her with a sidelong glance. "Really? I thought your hide was impenetrable."

"*My scales will turn aside the sharpest weaponry, but the grit is so fine that it finds its way through.*"

"So we see how the smallest thing may vex the mightiest," a voice said from behind her. T'Sian snapped her head around, looking for the speaker. There he was, not far away, a small figure barely warmer than the surrounding night. She leaned forward, to see him more clearly, talons ready to rip him to shreds if need be. It was a man, shrunken and ancient; his hair was long and white, his skin a loose collection of wrinkles. The heat of life burned low in this one; he smelled of age and impending death.

"T'Sian, who's there?" Ponn said.

"*A little old man,*" she said.

The intruder giggled, as if she had said something amusing. "A little old man, that's me."

"*Who are you?*" she hissed. "*Tell me quickly, before I swallow you whole.*"

"You may call me Wert the Wart," he said. "I knew you were coming. I foresaw it. I will bring you to the others."

"What others?" Ponn said.

"You know who," Wert said, with a touch of petulance, as if Ponn were wasting his time. "Diasa and Tolaria."

"And Prehn," Ponn breathed. "You know where Prehn is?"

"Of course."

T'Sian backed off. Whoever this was, he did not seem to present any immediate danger. "*Watch him, Pyodor Ponn*," she said. "*I must change, and I will not be able to see him when I do.*"

"Yes, Pyodor Ponn," Wert said. "Watch me. I may perform tricks."

Ponn moved to stand near the old man, though he did not appear to be quite sure what he would do if Wert turned into a snarling beast or produced a weapon. T'Sian moved away, hiding herself in the darkness. She would have preferred to find shelter behind a hill or a copse of trees, so as not to be observed by the stranger as she transformed herself, but there was no such cover to be had in this flat, dry terrain. When she rejoined them, having returned to her guise as a human, Wert looked at her and said, "Are you ready to go now?"

"Yes."

"Where are you taking us?" Ponn asked.

"To a place by the water," Wert said.

"An inn?"

"Yes."

"And what then?" Pyodor Ponn said.

"Sit, eat, talk, learn," Wert said. "Plan."

"Plan?" T'Sian said.

"Can't go on without a plan," Wert said. "The wizard's got one. Do you?"

Rather than concede that she did not, T'Sian said, "My plans are no concern of yours. Take us to this inn." Wert chuckled as if he found her transparent and laughable, and, turning, began to walk away, moving more quickly than she would have expected given his age and apparent infirmity. They followed him to a nearby river, then along the bank to an old stone footbridge with wooden planking. The city hugged it closely on the other side. T'Sian watched Ponn, noted his eagerness, his excitement. He was going to be reunited with his child. Her hatchlings had been butchered, all of them, hacked to pieces and dismembered; his daughter had been kidnapped, but kept safe. He would have the warmth of a reunion. All she would have was the icy satisfaction of revenge.

After the bridge, they followed Wert through a bewildering array of back alleys and side streets. More than once T'Sian thought they had gotten lost, but Wert never hesitated; he marched on through as if he had built the entire city himself and had committed its layout to memory. Ponn seemed nervous about the route they took, sticking close to her side, knowing that she would protect him. They were accosted twice, first by a group of young ruffians, then by a single man with a long sword. Both times, she enjoyed making the villains regret it.

At length they emerged from a reeking alleyway onto the shore of the vast, dark lake. Wert turned left and they went along a wooden sidewalk, stopping at a narrow two-story building with a sharply peaked roof. The old man hopped up the front step and went inside; Ponn and T'Sian followed, entering a dim room pungent with woodsmoke and the smell of unwashed men. Wert had already started up a stairway on the other side of the room; they found him waiting in the hallway at the top. He went to a door at the very end, knocked, and said: "Diasa?"

No answer.

"Sleeping," he said. "She was wounded by an assassin this morning." He produced a tarnished key, inserted it into the lock, and swung the door inward. Ponn pushed past him, into the room. T'Sian stopped in the doorway. It was an extremely small chamber, with a peaked ceiling and walls that seemed about to squeeze like a fist, crushing everything inside. There was scarcely room for a bed and a rickety chair. Stretched out on the pallet was a sleeping woman, pale as fresh snow, black curls cascading around her shoulders. A small, copper-skinned girl lay curled up next to her.

Ponn went straight to the child, knelt, and touched her thin shoulder. "Prehn," he said.

She opened her eyes, looked at him without comprehension. Then she brightened, and reached up with chubby hands, and cried: "Da!" Ponn swept her off the bed and enfolded her in his arms.

T'Sian turned away.

"I will be downstairs," she said, and left.

Tolaria went out on the lake with Talbrett's remaining crew, to watch them sink the merchant's body in the cold, dark water. They took his flatboat, which would not be bearing the *Pride*'s cargo to its intended destination; the men, angry over the murder of their companions, had decided to sell it off to the highest bidder rather than shipping it to Dunshandrin's mines. Rennald had already arranged and executed a surreptitious auction of the goods, leaving everyone somewhat richer than they had been before the voyage began; he had even pressed a few coins into Tolaria's hand, ignoring her protests.

Talbrett's body lay in the shallow hold, wrapped in a watertight shroud and weighted with heavy stones so that he would sink. The men poled away from the dock, then rowed out onto the lake. Silence hung in the air, thick as the fog that issued from the cold water. A torch, set into the prow of the vessel, lit their way, making Tolaria think of Talbrett's spirit traveling to the netherworld. Her gaze kept straying to his body, wrapped like a caterpillar in its cocoon, although no moth or butterfly would emerge from this chrysalis.

They traveled a long way out, into the deeps, until the city had become little more than a collection of lights on the horizon. Then Rennald stood—a bit unsteadily, having spent a good portion of his auction money in a tavern with the others, getting drunker and angrier by the hour—and announced, with the utter seriousness of the inebriated, that this was the spot where Talbrett would be laid to rest. The rowers laid down their oars, and the boat slowly coasted to a drift.

"Men," Rennald said, "we're here tonight to say goodbye to Talbrett, our friend and captain, who was murdered—"

"Most foully!"

"Aye, most foully, struck down from cover by a cowardly assassin! But he died to save our lovely companion, Tolaria, and wherever he is, he is happy, knowing she is safe."

"Aye!" the others shouted.

"Lovely Tolaria," someone said, groping at her in the darkness. Whoever it was, she had to swat his hands away three times before he gave up.

"Now we prepare to commit Talbrett's body to the lake he plied for so many years," Rennald said, "but before we do, I would like to hear a few words from each of you, who knew him so long and so well—"

Before Rennald could finish his request for eulogies, the men began shouting praise and comments and bawdy asides. Tolaria could hardly pick out any coherent words from the babble, but she heard enough to gather that Talbrett had been free with both his money and his affections. He may have been concerned about the paternity of his son, but it sounded like he had hardly been a model of monogamy himself. Was that why he had helped her? Because she was young, because she was attractive? If she had been a man or a crone, would Talbrett have taken her aboard so readily? Tolaria looked at the sky, feeling small and ungrateful for even entertaining the thought, after Talbrett had died to save her life; still, she had known since adolescence that men would do things for a pretty face.

Perhaps that was why the treatment she'd received at the Crosswaters had shocked her so.

She realized suddenly that the sailors had fallen silent, and were now looking at her. Did they expect her to say something? Her gaze sought out Rennald; he met her eyes and gave a little nod. Evidently it was her turn to speak. She stood, nearly losing her balance in the gently rocking boat; several hands steadied her to keep her from falling overboard. "I didn't know Talbrett for very long," she said. "I only met him on the docks in Dunshandrin Town. I told him I was in trouble, and he helped me, and because of that he died. I'm sorry that—"

She broke off because they had started shouting again, protesting that she had nothing to apologize for, lauding Talbrett's heroism; one was so inebriated that he couldn't form actual words and settled for grunts and squeals. Rennald quieted them all with some cursing and a few well-placed cuffs, then turned to Tolaria and said: "Talbrett helped you because he wanted to. He took that dagger because he wanted to. You were under his protection; he couldn't let that bastard harm you."

She hung her head. "If he knew how things would turn out, he would have left me there on Dunshandrin's dock."

"Perhaps," Rennald said. "And perhaps he would have done everything exactly the same way. There are some things even an oracle cannot know, eh, Tolaria?"

After a moment, she said: "Yes. Yes, there are."

"So no more talk of being sorry," Rennald said. "You're alive, so be glad! Talbrett is dead, but he died nobly and courageously instead of twitching in his bed, so be glad!"

The others voiced their approval and she smiled a little. She thought she might speak more, but suddenly the torches went out and all the voices were stilled and she was alone on the lake, standing on the still, dark water as if it were solid earth. A wind rushed over her; the cold pinprick stars overhead disappeared as a massive shape passed above her, heading toward the town.

A moment later she was lying on her back with a number of concerned faces looking down at her.

"Are you all right?" Rennald said. "You swooned again."

"I'm all right," she said. "Just … faint. That's all."

"You haven't eaten enough today," Rennald said.

"She hasn't drunk enough!" someone cried. The men laughed, but Rennald silenced them with a look.

"We'll head back to shore, so you can rest," he said.

"No, I'm fine," she said. "Don't hurry back on my account. Stay here, and say a proper goodbye to Talbrett."

"Are you sure?"

"Yes."

"All right then. Who'd like to speak next?"

And, of course, they all started talking at once.

Pyodor Ponn sat on the chair in the tiny garret room, Prehn on his lap, as his daughter told him what had happened after Gelt had invited her to come and see his eagles. "We went to the waterfall," Prehn said. "He had a big pretty bird there. It had brown wings and a yellow head and—"

"Prehn, you were very naughty to go with that man," Ponn interrupted. "You know that, don't you?"

"I know."

"And you'll never do anything like that again, will you?"

"No, Da. I won't."

"All right. And what happened next?"

She continued with her story. Someone had grabbed her from behind, putting a sack over her head. She'd stayed in the sack a long time before being let out in the mountains, where the air was cold and thin. She told him about being kept in a net of rough rope that hurt her skin, then about being rescued.

A tired voice said: "The child talks."

Ponn looked toward the bed. The woman, Diasa, was awake and watching them. Her voice sounded dry, husky, totally unrested. "Of course she talks," Ponn said. "She's nearly five."

"Well," Diasa said, "she wouldn't talk to *me*."

"Don't talk to strangers," Prehn said.

Diasa laughed, then sagged back against the pillows and closed her eyes. "Don't talk to strangers," she murmured, shaking her head. "Too bad she didn't apply that to Gelt."

"He would have taken her by force, then," Ponn said.

Diasa grunted.

"Where's Adwan?" Prehn said.

"Adwan?"

"She means the footpad," Diasa said.

"Oh. He's … not here, Prehn. He's gone."

"Gone where?"

"He had to go away."

"But where?"

"Don't lie to the child," Diasa said. "Tell her the truth. Dunshandrin's miserable whelps killed him."

"Oh," Prehn said. "Killed dead?"

"Most likely," Diasa said.

"Oh." Then: "What's a whelp?"

"You are," Diasa said.

Ponn gave her a frosty look. "Kindly do not refer to my daughter as a *whelp*."

"Sorry. I meant no offense."

"I might find that easier to believe had you not just used the term to refer to Dunshandrin's children."

"You are not here to quarrel with each other," Wert said. "You were brought together to talk, to plan. We must take this battle to Dunshandrin's door now, or it will be too late."

They both looked at the old man, who stood, forgotten, in the doorway. "You know when we're coming, you know when we're going," Diasa said. "You know when I need to be at the dock to meet Tolaria, you know what potion Tolaria needs to save me from Gelt's poison. Now you know that we must go to Dunshandrin's castle. How do you know all these things?"

Wert drew himself to his full height, which made him scarcely taller than Pord, and said: "I am an oracle, and you would do well to remember it."

"For as long as I've known you, you've been a madman."

"Gelt is here?" Ponn said.

"He was. Now he's floating in the lake. Food for the fish, if any would eat the likes of him."

"You killed him?"

"I did."

"The old man told me you had been injured by an assassin. I didn't know he meant Gelt. Were you badly hurt?"

"The wound was barely a scratch, but the blade was poisoned," she said. "I think it's working its way out of me. I'm feeling stronger now."

"Good," Ponn said. "What about Gelt's mount? He must have ridden an eagle here."

"Most likely. I don't know where it might be; there hasn't been much opportunity to search for it, as you can imagine."

"He came alone?"

"Yes. He was sent here to kill Tolaria."

"Tolaria," Ponn said. "Where is she? Is she downstairs?"

"No," Diasa said. "She's at a funeral." Then, seeing the look on his face: "She'll be safe enough. She's surrounded by angry, drunken sailors."

"Well, that hardly sounds safe at all," Ponn said.

16

TALBRETT'S MEN SPENT A LONG time drinking toasts and liberally spiking the lake with cheap wine; after an hour or more of shivering on Lake Achenar, they finally rowed back to the dock, mooring the skiff near the now-empty *Pride*. With its cargo unloaded, the ship rode high in the water. As he helped Tolaria out of the boat, Rennald invited her to come to the saloon at the sailors' hostel; she demurred and instead he escorted her back to the inn where Diasa was staying, seeing her safely to the door before leaving. She entered and scanned the place, hoping to find the dragon in its human form; she spotted the creature immediately, sitting at a table in the back corner, watching the other patrons, her face devoid of expression. Tolaria went to her and said: "T'Sian?"

The woman looked at her. "Who are you?"

"Tolaria."

"How much can you pay?"

"What?"

"I charge extra for women."

"I'm sorry, I don't understand."

The woman sighed, as if Tolaria were being deliberately obtuse. "Don't give me a hard time," she said. "A lot of others wouldn't even take the likes of you."

Just then Tolaria felt a tug on her sleeve and, turning, saw Wert at her side. "Not her," he whispered. "She's a harlot." He pointed across the room, to a figure standing alone at the fireplace, staring into the flames. "You want to talk to *her*."

"Oh," Tolaria said, feeling herself flush. Then, to the prostitute:

"My mistake. I thought you were someone else."

The woman looked at T'Sian, then back at Tolaria. "Whoever that is, I'm better. And prettier."

"Sorry. Sorry." Tolaria fumbled a few coins out of her pocket and gave them to the woman. She felt the slattern's gaze on her back as Wert led her away.

"You didn't have to give her your money," Wert said.

"I know. I was embarrassed."

The dragon glanced at them as they approached; and now that Tolaria had actually seen T'Sian for herself, up close, she knew she would never mistake a human for a dragon again. T'Sian's face looked wrong, askew; her eyes were too far apart, her mouth too wide, her skin too tight, her gaze too intense. The whore had been right; despite her thick paint and hard eyes, she was by far the prettier of the two, if only because she was conventional.

Wert shoved Tolaria right in front of the dragon, presenting her for inspection. "T'Sian, this is Tolaria. Tolaria, T'Sian."

"Hello," Tolaria said.

T'Sian didn't answer.

Tolaria thought for a moment. "I know you have journeyed far, and you must have many questions. Why don't we—"

"Why does *he* get *his* child back?" T'Sian said.

"I'm sorry?"

"You are the oracle? The wise one? Tell me, why does Pyodor Ponn get his child back, while I get nothing?"

"I—" Tolaria broke off as T'Sian stormed away, moving off to the far corner, looking ready to burn the inn down.

"Go and talk to her," Wert said, giving Tolaria a firm push. She reluctantly went to where the dragon stood.

"Do you know how long it took me to have babies?" T'Sian said, as soon as Tolaria was near enough to hear her over the babble of the guests. "It is not easy for my kind, you know. We are few, and infertile. Not like you. You creatures produce children as easily as you draw breath. Pop, pop, pop!"

She had hardly expected her first conversation with the dragon to be like this. "Try to think about the babies you'll have in the future," she said. "After this is all over, and you have gone back to your home —"

T'Sian interrupted her with a fierce snort. Tolaria almost expected to see fire shoot out from between her ruby lips. "You know nothing about dragons," she said.

"How could I know anything?" Tolaria said. "What is written that I could read? Who knows that I could talk to? Certainly one hears of a dragon destroying a town or village now and then, but nothing about their ... reproduction."

"I told you we were not fertile. After one breeding, we are finished. Having those hatchlings nearly killed me. I spent years raising them. You would have been but an infant, if even that, when my babies were born."

"Oh."

"No doubt that is why they chose my lair," she said. "They knew I would have extra crystals, because of the hatchlings. I know of no other dragon who has had babies in decades, and now mine are dead. Wicked, wicked men."

"I'm sorry," Tolaria said. "I didn't know about ... that you couldn't ..."

"Dunshandrin must suffer my vengeance. Men cannot believe that they may trifle with the future of my kind."

They stood there a moment, looking at each other; and then Wert appeared between them, as if he had sprung out of the floorboards. "The savage has come down. We must talk."

The old man took them to a table near the stairs. Prehn was there, sitting on a man's lap; the resemblance, beyond even the color of the skin, eyes, and hair, was unmistakable. "You must be Pyodor Ponn," Tolaria said, confident that, for once this night, she would be correct.

"Yes. You are Tolaria?"

"I am."

"We need Diasa," Wert said. "Where is she?"

"When I left her, she was cleaning and oiling her weapon," Ponn said. "Apparently it had gotten wet."

Wert frowned. "She should be here."

"She said she would come down when she was finished."

The little man chewed his lip, then apparently decided that there was nothing to be done about it and sat back in his chair, eyeing the crowd. Tolaria watched him for a moment, then said: "Wert, are you looking for someone?"

"The wizard is coming," Wert said.

"Orioke?" Tolaria said. "Orioke is coming here?"

Wert looked at T'Sian. "He knows you are here."

"I cannot face him yet," T'Sian said. "I have no fire. He took it away from me."

Wert considered this; then his expression changed. He leaned forward and spoke, his voice low and serious and remarkably coherent. "This is what you must do. Take Diasa, and the five of you go back to Dunshandrin, to the castle. T'Sian will find—"

Ponn interrupted him. "Crystals. T'Sian will find crystals, to replenish her fire."

"Yes."

"Won't they be guarded?" Tolaria said.

"Not well. Most of Dunshandrin's men are in Barbareth."

"Do you propose I attack his stronghold without my greatest weapon?" T'Sian said. "I have seen how you men build your stone fortresses. I may damage it with my claws and tail, but to properly destroy it, I need my fire."

"Perhaps you can infiltrate, instead of attack," Ponn said.

"I have no skill at infiltration."

"Are you mad?" Ponn said. "You're doing it right now. You are sitting here in a room full of humans, and none are the wiser. You did the same thing when we were in Astilan."

"And Tolaria approached a human strumpet, thinking she was you," Wert said. Tolaria felt herself blush again.

"Even if I presented myself as a human, why would they let me in? They have started a war. They will not want strangers in their fortress."

"If you approached Qalor as a woman, you might persuade him to bring you into the castle," Tolaria said. "He is a very lonely man, I think, and would welcome any companionship. And he does not see well; his eyes are clouded, like Wert's."

"Yes, yes, these are good plans," Wert said. "But you must go quickly, before the wizard arrives. I will stay here and face him."

"You will not!" Diasa came out of the stairwell and stood beside the table, one hand braced on the back of the old man's chair. "Wert, you're an oracle, not a magician, and you are also quite mad. Orioke will go through you like a knife through bread."

"The wizard will find that it takes rather more than one stroke of his sword to bring me down," Wert said. He looked at the door, as if Orioke might be coming through it at any moment. "You must leave now. He will be here tomorrow, and I will not be able to hold him for long. A day, perhaps two."

"A day?" T'Sian exclaimed. "Two days? That is nonsense."

"They took Astilan in less than a day," Ponn said, "and that was defended by walls and soldiers."

"Ah, but Orioke comes here alone," Wert said. "He brings no army, nor does he bring Deliban."

"We cannot rely on this old man to delay the wizard," T'Sian said, looking at the others. No one spoke. "We cannot!"

"T'Sian is right," Diasa said. "Orioke broke our control over Deliban, and that spell was ancient. He will force you to tell him everything you know. You will betray us."

"I have taken precautions," Wert said. "I will not tell him anything he does not already know or cannot already guess."

Diasa said: "What precautions?"

"There are things an oracle can do."

"Such as?"

"I have no time to explain myself to you, child!" Wert exclaimed. "You must listen to me, and leave before Orioke draws any nearer. If he lays hands on the dragon, all is lost!"

No one moved.

"Go!" Wert cried, his eyes bulging.

"I will not go to the castle under these conditions," T'Sian said. "We will be caught."

"You must!" Wert said.

"No."

Wert scowled up at the dragon, then leaned back and folded his arms. "You're afraid," he said. "I understand."

"Fear has nothing to do with it."

"The wizard bested you, stole your fire. You said so yourself. Of course you fear him."

T'Sian's eyes narrowed. "I should pick you up and squeeze the life out of you right now," she hissed.

Tolaria bit her lip, watched the dragon's face. If T'Sian did try to kill Wert, could any of them stop her? What were the creature's capabilities in human form?

"Your crystals wait for you in Dunshandrin's castle," Wert said. "Forget your fear. Turn your anger that way instead."

T'Sian raised a hand, balled it into a fist, held it a moment, then relaxed it again. "Very well," she said. "If the old man wishes to be killed, let him. If he wishes to be tortured for information, let him. The rest of us will go to the castle, and he will remain here to become the wizard's plaything."

"We don't even know if Orioke is really coming," Ponn said.

"Oh, he is," Wert said. "But when he gets here, he will find something he never expected to see again."

After returning to her room to gather up her things—which amounted to a change of clothes, a few coins, and, of course, her weapon—Diasa went back to the common room. The others had gathered near the front door, looking glum and grave, except for T'Sian; she was tight-faced and angry, as if she would like to have burned the inn down and was frustrated that she couldn't.

Diasa paused at the table to say goodbye to Wert; he stared moodily into the fire and didn't answer, merely waved a hand in dismissal. Diasa shrugged and turned away, but then stopped, realizing that she had seen that gesture many times, but never from Wert. She hesitated, glanced at him from the corner of her eye, a vague and bizarre idea that had been fluttering around her mind suddenly becoming clear.

"Just go, child," Wert said. "There is nothing more you can do for either of us now."

Shaken, she left him—them—there and moved toward the others. They saw her coming and filed out of the inn; she joined them in the chill darkness outside. "We've decided to leave the city on foot, so as not to attract undue attention," Ponn said, "and then T'Sian will meet us in the plains and take us onward to Dunshandrin."

"Take us?" Diasa said. "You mean fly?"

"Yes."

"Through the air?"

"That's normally how one flies," Ponn said. "Do you know of a faster way to get there?"

Diasa closed her eyes and imagined soaring through the air with the dragon, and realized that she didn't even know what a dragon really looked like. She'd had seen drawings, sketches in books at Flaurent, but those were surely pallid imitations of the real thing. "If we must," she said.

"The old oracle believes that we are very short on time," T'Sian said, "so yes, we must." Then something like a smile split her face nearly in two. "Do not worry. I have not dropped Pyodor Ponn yet."

After a moment, Ponn said: "Was that a joke?"

"All right, then," Diasa said. "From here, the fastest way out of town would be by boat, not on foot. Perhaps we can find someone trustworthy to take us down the lake and then put us ashore."

"I know some people who can help us with that," Tolaria said. "Follow me." She led them along the street to a noisy, ramshackle tavern that stood on an old wharf, supported by brine-encrusted stilts that looked as if they might collapse at any moment. A variety of odd decorations hung from the dark underside of the building: Dead water birds trussed up by their feet, tattered women's clothing, the bones of fish large and small. Tolaria eyed the building, then looked at Pyodor Ponn until the Enshennean offered to accompany her inside. The oracle gratefully accepted; Ponn set his daughter down on the ground and asked Diasa and T'Sian to watch the child, and then the two of them disappeared into the building.

Prehn made to go after her father, but Diasa caught her arm and hoisted her up onto her own shoulders, wincing a bit as the movement brought a twinge of pain from her wound. T'Sian came up close and peered at the little girl. "You look like your father," she said.

"No I don't. I look like Mommy."

"I had babies once," T'Sian said. "They would have been about your age, if they had been little men."

"Where are they now?" Prehn said.

For a long time, the dragon didn't answer; then she said: "They died."

"Oh," Prehn said. "That's too bad."

"Yes," T'Sian said, after another lengthy silence. "Too bad."

She said nothing more, and eventually Tolaria and Ponn emerged from the inn with a sailor in tow. "This is Rennald," Tolaria said. "He's agreed to take us down the shore in his skiff."

"What is a skiff?" T'Sian said.

"It is a small, light boat, fast and quiet," Rennald said loudly. "Just the thing for stealthy water travel!" Then, looking confused as Tolaria and Ponn shushed him: "What?"

"A small, light boat will not support my weight," T'Sian said, "and I do not look forward to a dip in the lake."

The sailor belched loudly. "It holds ten men with ease. I think it can carry you lot."

"I weigh more than you think," T'Sian said. "Tell me where you are taking them and I will meet you there."

Rennald shrugged. "As you wish. East brings us out of town fastest, and the current—such as it is—will be with us. So we will go east." He pointed off into the darkness.

"That's west," Diasa said acidly.

"Oh, aye." Rennald dropped his arm and pointed in the other direction. "East."

T'Sian turned and stalked away, vanishing into the darkness toward shore. Rennald threw one arm around Tolaria and the other around Ponn, as if they were all old friends; or maybe it was to hold himself up. Diasa wondered if the man could be trusted to find his way safely to his skiff, let alone take them out on the lake and then return to Achengate in the darkness.

"So, Tolaria, why sneak away in the night?" Rennald said as they walked along the wharf. Once again, Ponn had to remind him to keep his voice down. "Is it because of the assassin Dunshandrin sent?" he continued, in an exaggerated whisper.

"No," Tolaria said, "there's a wiz—"

"Yes, there are more men coming," Diasa said, speaking nearly as loudly as the drunkard had, interrupting the oracle before she could say anything about the wizard. Tolaria kept talking, of course; she had told Diasa about her compulsion to answer direct questions truthfully. Still, the less Rennald knew about their situation, the better off all of them would be.

Fortunately, the sailor was so inebriated that he couldn't follow both answers at once, and so he went with the louder. "Don't run away!" he exclaimed. "Stay and fight! We'll help you! We haven't evened things up with those curs yet. We'll make them sorry they ever looked at you twice!"

"No, we must go," Tolaria said. "I've put you in too much danger already."

"Danger." Obviously Rennald scoffed at physical jeopardy. "I can have two dozen sailors jump them at once. We'll see how much good their poisonous tricks are against honest men and their swords."

"You're very brave," Tolaria said, "but no. Just do this one thing for us. Take us out of the city."

"Of course, of course. Here we are." They had reached a small flatboat, like the ones that plied the shallow rivers of the Salt Flats. Rennald helped Tolaria aboard, then Ponn. He tried to help Diasa, but she jumped down to it without assistance. The landing sent a small jolt of pain through her ribs, and the cut on her belly twinged like a cord drawn too tight, biting into her skin.

From behind her, she heard a splash. She glanced into the water, sighed, and said to the others: "Our deliverer needs to be pulled out of the lake before he drowns."

T'Sian made her way through the streets of Achengate, ignoring the other pedestrians as much as possible; apparently a woman walking alone in this part of town was taken to be looking for some sort of work, because men kept coming up to her and asking her how much she wanted. She never bothered to find out what they were talking about; she just pushed them aside and kept going. This often resulted in invective; once one of them went so far as to grab her and try to drag her into an alley. Without breaking stride, she flung that fool across the street and into the side of a building. She hoped she had hurt him badly.

At length she came to a vacant lot; the pallid moonlight illuminated an open space, surrounded by a low wooden fence, overgrown with weeds and tangled grass. The remains of a burnt-out building poked through the vegetation, empty and overgrown, like an ancient stump whose middle had long since rotted out. She kicked down a section of the fence and moved into the lot. She tasted the air; traces of the fire still lingered, a comforting scent not unlike the aroma of her lair, making her feel homesick. She had been away far too long, chasing the shadows of the wicked men who had wronged her. She hoped it would be over soon.

She took cover near the building, and began the change to her true self, shedding her human flesh to reveal the great beast beneath. Everything went dark and silent as her senses were extinguished and her massive serpentine body exploded outward. The scales that clung to her like a dress grew, stretched, locked into place, encasing her in a shell harder than iron. Her hands and feet elongated into talons, digging into the earth; her mane of hair lengthened and flowed along her neck and around her chin, the sensitive tendrils trembling in the light evening breeze. Her back split open, allowing her wings to unfold, gossamer-thin at first, then thickening like leather, becoming broad and strong. Her skull twisted and expanded, moving away from her body as her neck extended, snakelike, from her shoulders. Her teeth lowered into spikes larger than a human thumb. Her senses came back one by one, sight and smell and hearing, so much keener than they were in human form, as if she had emerged from a filthy, smothering cocoon.

She lifted her head up, swiveled it around. Her tongue flicked out, tasting the air. The lingering scent of ashes was very strong, especially since her growth had knocked over one of the remaining walls. She spread her wings, tensed her muscles, and leapt into the air. The earth spiraled away beneath her as she climbed the sky; then she banked around in a wide circle, flying out over the lake. She spotted the others, a blob of warmth on the cold, black water. They were heading east, as promised, but very slowly.

She circled overhead, waiting for them to come ashore.

Pyodor Ponn had agreed to help Rennald row the boat, but he seemed to be doing most of the work himself as the drunken sailor— whose ducking in the icy water didn't seem to have sobered him up at all—attempted to make time with a devastatingly uninterested Diasa. The man would pull once on the oars, then ask Diasa a question, then wait for the answer, if there was one; then he would think about the answer, and then, perhaps, pull the oars once more. Meanwhile, Ponn kept them moving eastward along the shore, leaving Achengate behind in the darkness.

"So you must be very grateful that I saved your life, eh?" Rennald asked. This was at least the third time he had brought up the incident on the docks; Ponn had lost count.

"Yes," Diasa said, not sounding grateful at all anymore.

"How grateful?"

"Just row the boat," Diasa suggested.

Rennald grinned and gave the oars a pull, then said: "So why didn't your friend want to come in the boat? Afraid of the water, is she?"

Ponn fielded that one. "She doesn't like water very much," he said. "She can't swim."

"Can't swim!" He found this absurd. "I could teach her."

"I don't think she's interested in learning."

"How's she going to know where to meet you?"

"She'll manage."

Rennald watched Ponn row for a little while, and then said: "Why didn't you lot go with her, then?"

"Why do you ask so many questions?" Diasa said.

"I'm a curious sort of fellow," Rennald said. "You know, seeing as I lost two friends and saved you and pretty Tolaria yesterday, you could be nicer to me."

"Sorry, Rennald," Tolaria said. "Diasa has had a rough time of it. Her mother was murdered and her home destroyed."

Diasa shot Tolaria a warning look.

"A terrible thing!" Rennald cried. "Dunshandrin again? All the more reason to fight!"

"We'll fight on our terms, not theirs," Diasa said. "Our strategy will not be decided by a drunken bosun."

Looking wounded, Rennald gave a half-hearted pull on the oars, moving the skiff right and forcing Ponn to compensate to keep them from running aground. Then, realizing that they had cleared the town and left most of the buildings behind, he decided this was as good a spot as any to put ashore. If nothing else, it would get them away from Rennald before Diasa truly lost what seemed likely to be a ferocious temper, or Tolaria volunteered any more information that didn't need to be shared. Using one oar as a pole, he pushed the boat alongside the crumbling, chalky bank, stopping it near a clump of rough grass that hung out over the water.

Rennald didn't seem to have noticed that they were ashore. "I never knew my mother," he said with drunken wistfulness. "I grew up on the docks."

"Now there's a shock," Diasa muttered as they clambered out of the skiff, leaving Rennald sitting alone, clutching the oars, a little tear glistening on his cheek. The fate of Diasa's mother had made him go all maudlin. Holding one hand over his heart, he reached beneath his seat with the other and pulled out a large, dark bottle, stopped up with a filthy-looking rag. He pulled the cloth out, cleaned the neck of the bottle with it, and took a deep pull of whatever was inside.

"Rennald, maybe you should stay here until morning," Tolaria said. "I don't want you to fall overboard and drown."

"What?" Rennald roared. "Drown? I've sailed drunker than this before! Don't you worry about me, love." He lifted the oars and gave them a tug, but the boat was firmly grounded and didn't move. Rennald tried again; again the boat didn't move. He looked up at them, shrugged, and set down the oars. "Perhaps you're right," he said. "The boat seems to be broken, anyway." He produced a blanket out from under his seat, wrapped himself up in it, and settled in to stare out across the dark waters of the lake.

Their little group moved away from the water, out into the dark grassland. Before long, a great rush of wind announced the dragon's approach. She landed not far away from them, raising a cloud of stinging dust, then dispersing it with the rapid beating of her wings.

"*Come,*" she said. "*You may sit along my neck and back. Use my hair and scales to hold yourselves in place.*"

Diasa said: "You're not going to carry us?"

"*You are too many, and the journey is too long. I do not want to accidentally harm one of you.*"

She must be thinking of Parillon. Ponn supposed it was an improvement that she was considering their safety at all; Diasa, however, didn't seem to see it that way. "But we might fall," she protested. "There's nothing to hold us in place."

"*I will fly carefully.*"

"If we can find Gelt's eagle—"

"*I do not relish playing the steed any more than you like the idea of being astride me, but this is the way we must do it.*" The dragon flattened herself against the ground. "*Climb on, or be left behind.*"

They mounted her enormous bulk one at a time, using the thick, rope-like strands of her hair to pull themselves up. The fleshy tendrils felt smooth and rubbery, warm as fresh bread. Tolaria and Diasa moved down to the wider part of her back, while Ponn straddled her neck at its base, positioning Prehn directly in front of him. He enfolded her in his cloak and tied the belt around her to keep her warm and secure. He squeezed T'Sian's neck with his knees and took hold of a length of her hair, twisting it around his wrist.

"*Are you ready?*" T'Sian hissed.

"I think I am," Tolaria said.

"No," Diasa said.

Ponn glanced back at her; she lay on her stomach on the dragon's broad back, clutching at the shorter trailers of flesh that grew there. Tolaria sat next to her, on the ridge of T'Sian's spine, looking similarly secured. "We're ready," Ponn said. "Go. And no aerobatics, if you please."

The dragon gave a snort that may have been a chuckle; then Ponn felt her muscles tense beneath him, and she sprang upward. Her powerful hind legs launched them into the sky like a gigantic locust; then her wings beat the air and caught it, pulling them higher. He had never been in this position before and the whirls of air felt strange, like the buffeting of a minor cyclone. Prehn looked at the ground as it fell away and screeched, a delighted expression on her face.

Ah, to be young and fearless.

Ponn closed his eyes and pretended he was on a horse.

17

ADARAN WOKE UP, AND IMMEDIATELY wished he hadn't. His extremities throbbed as if on fire; his skull felt like someone had cut a hole in the top and stuffed the cavity with hot peppers.

"So this is the man."

"Yes."

"He doesn't look like much, does he?"

"No."

The two voices came from either side of him, but they sounded the same. Adaran knew what that must mean. He raised his head, opened his eyes. They were gummy with something, tears, maybe blood. He was back in Dunshandrin's dungeon, possibly even in the same cell, with the same wall against his back and the same manacles around his wrists and ankles. He doubted they would pop open for him this time.

Two men with identical faces stood in front of him, watching him. "Look, Torrant," the one on the left said. "He's awake."

"So he is," said the other.

"I trust you remember us, thief."

"I remember you. You're Lord Dunshandrin's sons."

"Yes. And you killed our father."

"Thanks to you, we are orphans."

Adaran said nothing.

"You were clever with your hands, weren't you, thief? But no longer. Our men pierced them with hot blades."

"And you were swift on your feet, but no longer. Our—"

"Your men pierced them with hot blades." He looked at his right hand, but it was heavily swaddled in dirty-looking cloth and he couldn't see the damage they had done to it. "Why not just chop them off?"

"We wanted to, but our physician advised us that you might bleed to death," Tomari said, "and we wished to speak with you before you passed from this realm of misery."

"Our physician is quite competent, but he is not a worker of miracles," Torrant added. "He did a fine job removing the crossbow bolts from your legs, by the way."

"Remind me to thank him some time."

"You may not be so grateful by the time we're done with you," Tomari said, giggling a little.

Torrant said: "You see, we were thinking how odd it was that we sent Orioke to kill you, and yet you turned up here, sticking your dagger where it didn't belong."

"It wasn't my dagger."

"It was *a* dagger," Torrant said, "and you wielded it."

"Yes. You wielded it. And you were supposed to be dead." Tomari inspected his fingernails. "We're not sure that father's pet wizard can be trusted."

"Of course he can't. You need *me* to tell you that?"

"And yet he is a valuable asset," Torrant said, "and not to be cast aside lightly. You see our predicament."

"Not really, no."

Torrant sighed. "You will tell us, in detail, how you came to be here, and how you found your way into our father's chambers without being discovered. Then we will decide what to do about the situation."

Adaran opened his mouth to answer, but then he realized that he couldn't remember exactly what had happened; the events of the previous evening seemed to have faded from his mind, like the color from a cloth left out in the sun. He recalled being in the dungeon, and he recalled standing over Dunshandrin's bed after stabbing the man with a ceremonial dagger; but how had he gotten from the first place to the second?

"We are waiting," Torrant said.

"First I was here," Adaran said slowly. "In the dungeon."

"Yes?"

"And then I … I wasn't."

Torrant and Tomari exchanged a glance. Evidently this testimony did not impress them. "Obviously you weren't in the dungeon when you killed our father," Tomari said. "How did you move through the castle undetected?"

"I don't remember. I suppose I just did it."

"No one is *that* stealthy," Tomari said. "I see Orioke's hand in this, as well as in that other incident. What was he doing in the oracle's room, that Wyst would find him stripped and bound and hidden under her bed?"

"He claims he went there to evoke further visions."

"I know what he *claims*."

"We must be sure before we act against him."

Tomari made an exasperated noise. "Why? Let us have him killed, and be done with it."

"That would be over-hasty. The mage is still of use to us; if nothing else, he controls the earth elemental." Torrant went to the cell door and gave it three quick raps; it opened and a guard entered. Torrant whispered something to the man, who then came up to Adaran and delivered a vicious punch to his stomach. If he hadn't been fastened to the wall, he would have doubled over from the force of the blow. Instead he simply tried to vomit, but his stomach was empty and had nothing to heave out.

The guard glanced at the twins. Torrant shook his head and the man stepped away. The princes eyed Adaran as he gasped for breath. Finally, Torrant said: "Once again. Tell us how you made your way through the castle undetected. Tell us how you found our father's chambers and unlocked the doors."

"I told you, I don't remember. It's hidden in a fog."

"Dear me," Torrant said. "If that's the case, then this is going to be quite a lengthy interrogation."

Just before dawn, as T'Sian began to descend from the high, cold heavens, banking downward toward the night-shrouded earth, Tolaria could make out a few flickering lights in a village some distance to the north, and above that, the watch-fires of a keep: Dunshandrin Town, and the castle of its Lord. She had never expected to return to this place, certainly not in this fashion; and yet, here she was.

They landed hard, T'Sian's wings kicking up a furious wind as she checked her downward momentum. The tall, dead grass of Dunshandrin's plains waved and fluttered beneath them as they set down. Tolaria half-climbed, half-fell off the dragon's back, sliding down the smooth scales to land ungracefully on the ground. Her body felt stiff after hours of clinging to the great beast; even though the flight had been smooth and level, fear of falling had kept her muscles tense, and the warmth of the dragon's body hadn't quite been enough to overcome the chill of the wind. She tried to stand, but a cramp in her leg felled her; Ponn came by, Prehn slung over his shoulders, and helped her to her feet.

Once they were all off her back, the dragon slunk off, moving some distance away until she was invisible in the darkness; soon, odd sounds emanated from that direction. Diasa cocked her head, listening, and then said: "Why does she go off like that?"

"I think that she doesn't like to change shape in front of others," Ponn said.

"Why not?"

He shrugged. "Perhaps it would be like you or I changing clothes while everyone watched."

"A dragon with a sense of modesty?" Diasa shook her head and continued to look in the direction T'Sian had gone, although nothing was visible under the overcast sky. "Are you sure that's why? What happens when she changes? Perhaps she becomes vulnerable and doesn't want us to see."

Ponn said: "Do you think she doesn't trust us?"

"Do *you* trust *her*?"

He took some time before answering, and when he did, he seemed surprised at himself. "Yes, I suppose I do."

"Well, I'm glad that you've found yourself a friend," Diasa said, "but as for myself, I will be keeping a close eye on her."

Ponn shrugged. "Do as your nature dictates." He yawned hugely; he looked as if he were about to fall over under the burden of his sleeping child. His eyes were red as if from a night of heavy drinking, though of course it was irritation from wind and dust. Tolaria's eyes felt gritty as well and probably looked no better than his. "We must get some rest," he said. "I have not had a proper night's sleep in days."

"Sleep," Tolaria said. "I remember sleep. It's something you do when you have no lecherous princelings trying to bed you or assassins trying to kill you."

"Once the dragon comes back, we'll go into town and find lodging, so we can hide Tolaria away from anyone who might recognize her or, worse, ask her a question," Diasa said.

"What's wrong with asking her a question?" Ponn said.

Diasa gave a thin smile. "Tolaria, why would we want to avoid your being asked a question?"

"Because I am compelled to answer truthfully any question that is directed to me," Tolaria said; then she threw a scowl Diasa's way, annoyed at being made to perform like a sideshow attraction. Diasa ignored it, if she even noticed at all.

"So you see, were some young rake to ask Tolaria what she was doing in town, she would cheerfully tell him that she was here to help infiltrate the castle and, if possible, destroy it," Diasa said. "Therefore, she must be kept out of sight."

Tolaria sighed, not relishing the thought of becoming a prisoner once again. "Yes, I suppose I must."

"Of course you must," Diasa said. "It was bad enough that you were lounging around the common room of the inn at Achengate. Here, there is no choice; you must stay hidden."

As Diasa spoke, T'Sian emerged from the darkness nearby, disguised once again as a human female. In the dim light, she could perhaps pass for a woman, albeit an unusually sturdy one. Qalor's poor vision might allow her to fool him, at least for a little while.

"Welcome back," Diasa said. "That's a fascinating skill."

T'Sian gave her a frosty look. "What skill?"

"Taking the shape of a human. Why that, of all creatures?"

"Would you prefer something else?" T'Sian said. "Perhaps you would like me to turn into a dog, so that I could whine and lick your hand?"

Diasa said: "Can you?"

The dragon cast a long, withering glare Diasa's way; then she turned and stalked off toward the city.

"It would seem that she can't," Diasa said.

* * *

Just before first light, Ponn and the others reached the town square. The space was paved with worn, cracked flagstones and had a dry fountain at its center; shuttered booths and closed-up tents surrounded it. Evidently this was a sort of bazaar during the day. Already vendors were opening some of the booths; smoke drifted from a few of them, carrying the promise of breakfast and reminding Ponn that he hadn't eaten recently. Hunger played a brief tug-of-war with fatigue, and lost.

"There," Tolaria said, pointing at a lopsided two-story structure at the northwestern corner of the square. A sign swayed in the breeze with the faint sound of hinges in need of oiling. From this angle Ponn couldn't read the sign; as they approached he saw that it contained no writing, just a picture of a chair with a large, rusty nail on it, upon which a hefty man's posterior was about to descend.

Diasa eyed the building with evident suspicion. "Are you sure this is an inn?"

"Yes," Tolaria said. "I heard Talbrett's men talking about having rooms here. The owner is supposed to be discreet."

"This is a sailors' flophouse?" Diasa grimaced and peered around the narrow front porch, as if she had misplaced something.

"What are you looking for?" Tolaria said.

"Whores."

Ponn tried the door. Barred. As he gave it a few strong raps, he said: "Just because sailors stay here doesn't mean it's infested with whores, Diasa."

"I'm sure they're here somewhere."

"Do you suppose they're hiding under the floorboards?"

She shrugged. "Perhaps it's too early for them to be up."

Ponn shook his head, then turned his attention back to the door as he heard noises from the other side. A panel opened several inches above his head, revealing a pair of red-rimmed eyes. A gruff voice said: "What do you want at this hour?"

"Rooms," Ponn said.

A grunt. "Show me your money."

Tolaria stepped up, opened her pouch, and shook a few coins into her palm, then held them up for the eyes to see. After another grunt, the little panel snapped closed.

"Charming fellow," Diasa murmured.

"Would you hush?" Ponn said, as he heard the bar being withdrawn. "I'm sure we awakened him." A moment later the door swung inward to admit them to the dark interior of the inn. As they entered, the innkeeper—who was, in fact, at least a head shorter than Ponn—was walking away, carrying a three-legged stool.

"I'll see about the rooms," Tolaria said.

"You most certainly will not." Diasa took the oracle's money pouch and went to talk to the proprietor.

T'Sian said, too loudly for comfort, "Why can we not use the money I took from the guards?"

"Because that's coin from Barbareth," Ponn whispered. "The money Rennald gave Tolaria is from Dunshandrin."

"What difference does it make? It's all metal."

"We don't want to use foreign currency now, especially not *that* foreign currency. Trust me. Come, let's sit down."

Ponn went to a nearby bench and fell onto it. If he stretched out on the cold, hard wood, he thought, he would be asleep within minutes. He lay Prehn in his lap; she curled up, murmured something inaudible, and kept sleeping. T'Sian stayed near the door as if on guard duty, but Tolaria joined him after a moment. "I keep forgetting about my … problem."

"Perhaps it will wear off soon," Ponn said.

"I had hoped so, but now I think it is likely to be permanent. The same thing happened to Wert, and he never recovered."

"But Wert was mad," Ponn said. "You are not mad."

"Was he? He didn't seem mad at the end. Perhaps it took so much effort to keep himself lucid that he could only do it for short periods. Perhaps eventually I'll find it too much effort to stay sane, too."

"Well, you seem perfectly all right to me," he said. "And if you cannot lie, well, the world is already full of liars. Someone who always speaks the truth would be a welcome change."

Tolaria smiled a little then, but he knew she was not reassured. Why should she be? The words of an innkeeper could hardly make a difference to the fate of an oracle.

Fate. Oracle. He could ask her about Pord, he suddenly realized, his heart quickening. A simple question, and the uncertainty that had worried at him these past days would be resolved. She might say Pord was home, safe, tending to his chores around the inn. But what if she told him his son was dead? What if she launched into a description of his last moments, perhaps spent in the hold of the ship, screaming in terror as the dragon ripped it apart?

In the end he couldn't find the words or the nerve to ask the question; and soon Diasa came back, returning Tolaria's pouch. "He had two rooms available so I took them both. One for Tolaria and myself, the other for Ponn and Prehn."

"What about T'Sian?"

Diasa glanced at the door, where the dragon stood, scowling at nothing in particular. "I don't imagine she'll fancy sleeping in a human bed, but if she does, she'll no doubt want to stay with you."

"You're probably right." Ponn stood and lifted Prehn, slinging her over his shoulder like a bundle of clothes for washing. Tolaria stood as well, yawning immensely. T'Sian watched them, hesitated, and then came to stand with them. "It is arranged?" she said.

"Yes," Ponn said.

"Good. I will sleep in Pyodor Ponn's room."

"Of course you will," Diasa said.

T'Sian awoke to sunlight filtering through the shutters of the room she shared with Ponn and his child. She had elected to sleep on the floor; it seemed less humiliating, somehow, to stretch out there rather than on a bed that stank of men and their night-sweats. The shoddily-constructed human furniture was likely to collapse under her weight anyway.

She sat up. The floor groaned beneath her, but the beams in the room below were heavy and thick and she thought they would hold. She stood. Ponn and his daughter still slept; the sunbeam that had awakened her didn't yet touch the pallet that they shared. She looked down at them for a little while. Their thin blanket had slipped down a bit. Ponn lay on his side, Prehn curled up against him, the top of her head beneath his chin; he had a protective arm laid across her. She thought of her hatchlings. When they were very small, they had all fit under her wings, and she would cover them during the cold mountain nights to keep them warm.

The dragon reached down and pulled the blanket up to Ponn's shoulders; then she turned away, left the room, moved along the hallway to the stairs and down to the common room. A few patrons, all men, were finishing the remains of their morning meal, while a stout woman cleared dirty wooden bowls and platters. T'Sian noticed Diasa sitting by the fire, using her fingers to scrape the last bits of gruel from a tureen, and went to join her.

Without looking at her, Diasa said: "You're up early."

"Not as early as you," T'Sian said.

"I only slept for a few hours. I had … bad dreams." Then, after a few moments of silence: "Are you going to stand there all morning? Sit down."

T'Sian lowered herself into one of the chairs, ready to spring to her feet if her mass crushed it. Diasa didn't appear to be paying much attention, but then she said: "How much do you weigh, exactly?"

"I do not know. How much do *you* weigh?"

"Less than you, I'd wager. But you can't possibly weigh as much in that form as you do in your other. Where does the rest of you go?" T'Sian only grunted; such an impertinent question hardly rated an answer. "I gather you don't know that, either." Then, after setting her bowl aside: "Are you interested in breakfast?"

"No."

"You remind me of a snake. It eats, and then can go for weeks without another meal."

"Do I look like a snake to you?"

"Last night you did, a little bit."

"I am not a common reptile."

"I don't suggest that you are. I just wondered if you fed like one, that's all."

"How I feed is no concern of yours."

"I like how your scales turn into clothing. Are they still as hard now as they are in your true form?"

"Yes. Almost."

"May I touch them?"

"No. Why do you ask so many questions?"

"I never met a dragon before. I don't want to squander the opportunity to learn a little bit about you."

"I am not here for you to study," T'Sian said. "I am here for vengeance. When are we going to find this alchemist the oracle spoke of?"

"Soon. However, I'd suggest you not refer to her that way when we're in public." Diasa stood. "Let's see if she's awake."

"Very well." T'Sian followed Diasa up the stairs to the room that the warrior woman shared with Tolaria. They found the oracle asleep in her bed, lying on her back, breathing slowly.

"Wake her," T'Sian said. "I am tired of waiting."

"I've a better idea," Diasa said. She kneeled next to the bed. Leaning in close, she whispered, "Tolaria?"

"Why are you talking to her? She is asleep."

"Hush. This used to work on my mother sometimes, so it might work on her." Then, softly, her lips nearly touching Tolaria's ear: "Tolaria? Can you hear me?"

"Yes," the oracle murmured.

"Where can we find Qalor, the alchemist?"

"I don't know."

"Yes you do," Diasa said. "Where is Qalor?"

For a moment, Tolaria said nothing; then she whispered, "Across the square."

Diasa glanced over her shoulder at T'Sian. "There are many buildings across the square," she said. "Which one is Qalor in, Tolaria?"

"The tavern."

"What is the name of the tavern, Tolaria?"

Suddenly the oracle opened her eyes. Her head lolled to the side and she looked at Diasa, then across the room at T'Sian, then back to Diasa. "What are you doing?" she said.

"You were telling us where to find Qalor," T'Sian said.

The oracle looked confused. "I don't know where he is. He's probably in the castle."

"No," T'Sian said. "You told us he was nearby, in a tavern, somewhere on the square." She looked at Diasa. "Make her tell us the name of the building, so that we can find him."

Tolaria's gaze also moved to Diasa, and her eyes narrowed; T'Sian had been around men long enough now to realize that this meant she was angry. Pushing herself to a sitting position, she said: "You were asking me questions while I slept."

"Yes, I was." If Diasa was embarrassed at having been caught, she didn't show it. In some ways, T'Sian thought, the woman was more like herself than any other human she had met so far. "You needn't look so surprised. Your trances are not so different from sleep; I learned that much from my mother."

"You will not do this again without my permission," Tolaria said. "If you would have me answer questions in my sleep, you will tell me ahead of time."

Diasa shrugged. "If you insist."

"I do insist." Tolaria shook her head. "You are little better than the princes you so despise. They also sought to use me against my will and without my consent."

"That's absurd," Diasa said. "You hate Dunshandrin as much as the rest of us. You would have readily consented to use your skills to thwart him."

"All the more reason you should have asked me first."

"Oh, very well. I'm sorry if I have offended your delicate sensibilities." She stood, turned to T'Sian. "In any event, now we have the information we need to find Qalor. We'll just have to visit all the taverns until we come to the right one."

"How many taverns do you suppose that will be?" T'Sian asked.

"Probably quite a few," Diasa said. "In a town such as this, there usually isn't much to do besides drink."

By the time the torturer put away the switch, the various pointed implements, and the barbed hooks he'd been using in an attempt to extract information, Adaran felt like he'd been rolling around in a barrel full of stinging nettles, nails, and broken glass. He'd tried not to scream, but eventually he had, his voice going hoarse from the cries ripped from his throat.

"He's telling the truth," the torturer told his masters, as he finished cleaning and packing up his tools. The princes sat on royally carved chairs that they'd had brought into the cell so they could observe in comfort as their man did his work. Adaran wasn't sure, but through the haze of pain, he thought he had seen them eating a meal at one point. "He really can't remember. If he did, he would have told us."

"Unfortunate," Tomari said.

"Someone has meddled with the fool's memory," Torrant said. "We'll need something to restore it. Once he remembers, I'm sure he'll be happy to tell us what we want to know. Won't you, footpad?"

Adaran said nothing.

"Oh, yes," the torturer said. "He'll tell us."

"Qalor will be able to brew something," Torrant said. "A restorative potion to put his head back on straight and force him to speak the truth."

Why hadn't they thought of that *before* they'd tortured him? They probably had, Adaran thought, but torture was more enjoyable to watch.

"Where *is* Qalor?" Tomari said.

"Probably at that tavern he bought," Torrant said.

Tomari snorted. "Qalor, a tavern-keeper. Can you imagine? Who would drink his wine? Who would eat his food? I would be afraid he had mixed a potion into the ale that would make me grow ten feet tall or turn my skin purple."

"If Qalor wants to squander his pennies, let him." Torrant turned to the torturer. "Tell the stable-master to send a rider into the village to fetch Qalor and bring him here at once. We must get at the truth before the wizard returns."

"As my lords command," the torturer said, bowing and backing out the door.

When the man had gone, the twins got up and stood side by side, regarding Adaran as if he were an unusual sort of small animal that they had run down with their carriage and were now attempting to identify. At length, Torrant asked: "Have you nothing to say, footpad?"

Adaran coughed. His throat felt dry and cracked like old leather. "Water," he croaked.

"I think we'll let you stay thirsty until Qalor comes with a potion," Torrant said. "You'll be more inclined to drink it."

"Why don't you torture the wizard instead of me?"

Tomari stepped toward him, fist raised. He had delivered a few punches himself during the interrogation, apparently just for the joy of it. "You will not question your betters, oaf—"

Torrant put a hand on his brother's shoulder, forestalling him. "A perfectly reasonable question," he said, pulling Tomari back. "Orioke is not here. He is in the field, ostensibly serving our purposes. Unlike you, he is of use to us. And, also unlike you, he is dangerous."

"Yes," Tomari said. "Dangerous. I should not like to be the one to try to chain him to a wall and extract information."

"I'm dangerous too," Adaran whispered.

Tomari laughed; Torrant cocked his head and gave Adaran a look of condescension mixed with a modicum of pity. "Of course you are," he said, the way one might speak to a small child who was spouting nonsense. "You are very dangerous, and we are both quite afraid of you."

Tomari guffawed and clapped Adaran on the shoulder, as if they were old acquaintances who had run across each other in some distant port; in Adaran's present condition, this hearty show of fellowship was quite painful. "Yes, we are terrified!" Tomari cried. "We beg you not to harm us!"

Torrant pressed his lips together, the corners turning up slightly in a mirthless smile. "There is little danger of that," he said. Then he turned to his brother and said: "I grow weary of the dungeon. Let us return when Qalor arrives and there is something to learn from being here."

"Very well." Tomari looked at Adaran, then slapped him hard across the cheek. Laughing, the prince exited, followed by Torrant, who pulled the door shut behind him. Their footsteps echoed up the corridor outside and were gone.

Adaran coughed blood onto the floor. Tomari's parting blow had knocked one of his teeth loose; he held it in his mouth, rolling it on his tongue.

Perhaps he could spit it at them when they came back, and put out one of their eyes.

The sign over the door of the tavern depicted a large grey eagle, similar to the ones that had been used in the attack on Astilan. The creature's beak was open, evidently in a screech, and it clutched a small man in one of its talons as it spread its wings and soared over a distant landscape. T'Sian eyed the sign with distaste, remembering the involvement of such creatures in her earlier humiliation, and then went inside. The door resisted when she opened it and she realized that it had been bolted; evidently this establishment wasn't accepting patrons at the moment. Perhaps that was why the place was empty of the sort of dissolute-looking men who had haunted most of the other bars, even at this early hour; here, the only occupant stood near the back, scrubbing vigorously at some old brass-work along the edge of a counter. Turned the other way, head bent down over his work, he had not noticed her yet.

The place had a clean, sharp, unnatural odor quite unlike anything T'Sian had encountered before. Even humans would be able to smell it, she thought; it would probably put them off their eating and drinking. She took a few steps forward, stopping when the floorboards groaned and creaked beneath her. Still, the man didn't seem to notice that he had a visitor. T'Sian had never seen anyone so intent on cleaning.

She turned and slammed the door behind her.

The man paused in his work, shoulders tensing. He tossed his scrub-brush at a nearby bucket, missing it; then he turned, giving her a look at his face. This could only be Qalor. Tolaria had described him well: Tall and gaunt, sparse hair on his head, open sores on his face, eyes touched by the milk of cataracts. He wore a stained apron and breeches beneath, but no shirt or tunic, revealing a sunken, hairless, pockmarked chest. Thick, wet gloves covered his arms to his elbows. "Who's there?" Qalor said, squinting in T'Sian's direction. "We're closed. Go away."

"I thought this was a tavern," she said.

"It is, but I'm still cleaning it. It's not open yet. The door should have been locked. How did you get in?"

"The door opened for me," she said. T'Sian looked around, seeing the tidiest place she had ever been in. Every surface that could gleam, did; the woodwork shone with lacquer and polish; the floors were devoid of dust and grit, even between the boards. "How much cleaner do you expect to make it?"

"Everything must shine," Qalor said.

"From what I have seen, whether or not the interior of a tavern shines is of little consequence to those who go there. Just this morning I have been in several that were filthier than the foulest animal lair."

"I hope to attract a higher class of customer, people of more refined tastes. Artisans, philosophers, thinkers. Perhaps even members of the court, if they can be persuaded to leave the castle."

"Are there a large number of artisans and philosophers and

thinkers here who are lacking places to go?"

"I don't know. I haven't spent much time in town yet." He gave the bucket a nudge, pushing it against the wall; foamy water splashed over the side, making a small puddle on the floor, but Qalor did not appear to notice. "Forgive my earlier rudeness. Who are you? Not one of the common folk, I see."

"Only a traveler, looking for a clean place to eat, drink, and rest a while."

"I do have a small stock of food and drink on hand, and some recipes of my own creation that I haven't tried yet. If you would care to sample my cooking or my beverages—"

Qalor broke off as the tavern door burst open and several men entered. T'Sian turned and eyed them as they trooped in. Not customers; these men wore uniforms and carried weapons. Guards in Dunshandrin's service, she thought. Without sparing a glance in her direction, one of them said: "Qalor, you are urgently needed in the castle."

"But I have a guest," Qalor said. "I promised her a meal."

The soldier pursed his lips. "Perhaps I was not clear. The twins want you now. Your guest will have to go hungry."

"What is so important that it cannot ..." Qalor sighed and shook his head, leaving his complaint unfinished. "As my lords command, so must it be." He snapped off his long gloves, tossing them to the floor beside the bucket, then gave T'Sian a little bow and headed for the door. He paused there, turned to her, and said: "If you would care to wait here a little while, I will be happy to cook for you when I return."

She gave a little nod and then watched him leave, unable to think of a way to accompany him without arousing suspicion; the soldiers followed him out, except for the one who had spoken. He waited at the door, regarding her with curiosity. "Qalor seemed even unhappier than usual," he said, once the others were gone. "What were you two doing?"

"Talking."

"Talking, eh?" The man stepped away from the door and closed it behind him. "Well, perhaps you would like to talk to me instead."

Diasa and Pyodor Ponn had been shadowing T'Sian as she searched for Qalor. Ponn was sure they must make a suspicious pair—a tall, pale, armed woman and a short, dark, obviously foreign man—but they attracted little attention; people went about their business as if the two of them didn't exist. Perhaps Diasa's demeanor frightened them off. She conveyed the impression that she would cheerfully impale anyone who looked at her the wrong way. Especially now, as they waited for the guards to come out of the Screaming Eagle tavern; she had one hand on the hilt of her sword, fingers opening and closing, as if she were eager to draw the weapon and start hacking away.

A tall, misshapen man came out of the building, along with three of the four soldiers who had gone in not long before. "That can only be Qalor," Diasa whispered.

"What's going on?" Ponn said.

"I would guess the alchemist has been summoned to the castle. Perhaps one of Dunshandrin's whelps has need of an aphrodisiac, or a tonic to loosen his bowels."

Qalor mounted a spare horse and the four men rode off in a great clatter of hoof-beats; the remaining soldier's horse stamped its feet and snorted, unhappy at being left alone.

"One guard stayed behind," Ponn said.

"He's probably interrogating T'Sian," Diasa said.

"Oh," Ponn said. Then: "*That* isn't going to end well. Should we go in and—"

"No. Let's see how she handles herself."

"She'll most likely get angry and do something ostentatious and violent," Ponn said.

"You think so? Like what?"

Suddenly the guard came flying out through the tavern window, smashing through the shutters and rolling some distance into the square. Diasa immediately broke cover and raced for the fallen man. "Like that," Ponn muttered, hurrying after her. Crashing noises had begun to emanate from within the building, as if T'Sian were tearing the place to pieces.

Passers-by eyed the guard, but none went to his aid or acknowledged the ruckus from within the building; they kept their heads down and hurried on their way, willfully ignorant. Only two dirty, unshod urchins stopped at his side. For a moment Ponn thought they might try to help the man, but by the time Diasa arrived, one of them had stolen his purse while the other kicked him repeatedly in the head. She shooed them away, then grasped him under the shoulders began dragging him back to the tavern door. Ponn lifted his ankles and they carried him into the building.

The dragon had indeed wrecked the place. The remains of smashed tables and chairs littered the room; she had ripped sections of the bar out of the floor and dashed them to pieces. She was not in sight, but sounds of destruction continued to echo from the kitchen.

"T'Sian!" Ponn cried as they dropped the guard. "Stop!"

The sounds halted momentarily, and then she barreled through the kitchen door, knocking it off its hinges and sending it clattering to the floor. "I weary of these games," she said. "I am so, so tired of passing among you men!"

"What happened?"

She gave the unconscious soldier a look that could have set him on fire. "He put his hands on me, so I threw him." She started toward the tavern door. "I will pull their castle apart stone by stone," she said. "I will roast them in their own fat and feast on their charred remains!"

"You'll do nothing of the sort without your fire," Diasa said, getting in front of her. "Without your fire, you are nothing but a very large, talking, winged lizard."

T'Sian looked at Diasa with narrowed eyes; Ponn put a hand on Diasa's shoulder. "Have a care," he whispered.

"I could kill you with one claw," T'Sian hissed. "I could flatten this building with a flick of my tail."

"Perhaps," Diasa said. "But your stones are in the castle. Would you demolish it and bury them forever?"

"I could fly to the north," she said. "Where the blue crystals grow among the icy wastes. I do not have to get them from the castle."

"But you said it would take a long time," Ponn said. "You said sometimes dragons froze to death on the journey. Without any fire to keep you warm, what would happen to you?"

She grunted, saying nothing.

"I have another idea," Diasa said.

"What would *you* suggest, Pyodor Ponn?"

Astonished, Ponn said: "Are you asking me for advice?"

"Yes."

"What about seeking aid from other dragons?" he said. "Have you reconsidered that?"

"They would not help me."

"Not even the one who fathered your hatchlings?"

"He is dead."

"Are you certain?"

She gave him a look that froze his marrow. "Quite."

"I'm sure Ponn has been a brave and loyal friend, but we cannot afford to let Dunshandrin's pups run rampant while you journey as a supplicant to some other dragon who may or may not be willing to help you or travel hundreds of miles in search of fuel for your fire. Even now they will be consolidating their hold on Barbareth. No, we must look to the castle."

T'Sian said, "What is *your* idea, then?"

The guard groaned. Diasa glanced down at him, then kicked him in the head, hard. He fell silent again. "I have always been of the opinion that you can tell much about a ruler by observing how the people treat those who wear his colors," she murmured. Then, to Ponn: "Help me get his clothes off."

"What?"

"We're going to undress him," she said.

"His clothes won't fit me," Ponn said.

"Of course they won't. *I'm* going to wear them."

They quickly removed the man's uniform, leaving him in his noisome undergarments; Ponn found himself wishing for a basin to wash his hands. When Diasa began to disrobe, Ponn went and stood by the door. He only stole a few glances at Diasa as she donned the man's garb, although he could see that T'Sian stared at her quite openly.

At length, Diasa said: "How do I look?"

Ponn inspected her subterfuge. She had rolled up the sleeves of the uniform, which were too long, while the breeches ended in the middle of her calves. Because she lacked the guard's rather large belly, she'd had to gather the tunic in around her stomach; oddly enough, it fit perfectly around her chest. She had tucked her black curls under a leather helmet that seemed more artifice than protection, and had declined to take the man's sword, cinching her own scabbard around her waist instead.

"You look like a woman dressed up as a man," T'Sian said. "Even I can see that."

"She's right," Ponn said. "You won't pass."

Diasa pulled on the guard's heavy black cloak, which helped to disguise the ill fit of the clothing. "Better?"

"No."

"Well, it will have to do," Diasa said. Then, to T'Sian: "Are you ready?"

"Ready for what?"

"To be escorted into the castle."

"What?" Ponn cried. "That's madness! They'll know you're not a guard. They'll arrest you at the gates."

"If they try to stop us, they'll regret it." She hefted the soldier's sword, swung it a few times, ran her thumb along the edge. "Especially if they're all armed with blunt knives like this."

"And what should Tolaria and I do while you two are playing the spies?"

"Stay out of sight. If a hue and cry goes up, flee."

"If a hue and cry goes up, go to the window and watch, because I will be pulling the castle apart," T'Sian said.

"Yes, of course," Diasa said. "But just in case that's *not* what is happening, it would be prudent for Ponn and Tolaria to assume the worst."

"What about him?" Ponn said, pointing at the guard. "He's going to wake up eventually."

Diasa glanced down at the unconscious man, then stabbed him through the heart with his own dull sword. Ponn gave a little cry and turned away.

"No he isn't," Diasa said.

18

Tolaria looked up as her door opened, but it was only Ponn. He looked shaken, and was carrying what appeared to be Diasa's cloak, wadded up in his hands. "What happened?"

Ponn didn't answer; he only cast the cloak aside. It settled onto Diasa's bed like a dark stain.

Tolaria sat up. "What's happened? Where's Diasa?"

"I'm not sure I should tell you," Ponn said. "Diasa said that the less you know, the safer we'll be."

"Pyodor Ponn, you cannot come in here with that expression on your face, alone, carrying Diasa's cloak, and then say you will not tell me what's going on!"

Ponn sighed and sat on the edge of Diasa's narrow, straw-stuffed bed. "Things did not go as planned." He put his hand on Prehn's head; she lay curled up under the blanket, still sleeping. The child whimpered at his touch, as if her dreams distressed her. "Some of Dunshandrin's men came and took Qalor away while T'Sian was talking to him. One stayed behind to find out what she was doing. T'Sian threw him out the window, and then Diasa killed him and dressed in his clothes. She and the dragon are on their way to the castle right now."

"Diasa is trying to masquerade as a guard?"

"Yes, but you needn't worry. She is only obviously a woman if you look at her."

"The disguise is poor?"

"It's hardly a disguise at all; I'll be astonished if it gets them through the front gate. Even if they do gain admittance, they'll still need to find Qalor's laboratory. Diasa assumes that is where the crystals will be kept."

"And they plan to roam the castle looking for it?"

"Evidently."

"Aren't they afraid they'll be caught?"

Ponn snorted. "They seem to welcome the prospect. Diasa is eager for a fight, and T'Sian would rather knock the castle down than infiltrate it."

"What are we to do while this is going on?"

"Diasa said to listen for a hue and cry. If we hear one, we flee the village."

"*Flee?* To where? The only reason I escaped was because I stumbled across a boat that was ready to leave, and Talbrett took pity on me." Tolaria put her head in her hands. "I dislike this plan immensely."

"Calling it a plan is overly generous."

"Did you try to talk them out of it?"

"Of course, but all it earned me was a pat on the head and instructions to run along back to the inn."

She shook her head. "They're both reckless and hotheaded, and they encourage each other."

"You're right." Ponn fussed with a strand of his daughter's hair, tucking it behind her ear, where it refused to stay. "I would like to have met the man who rescued you," he said to the sleeping girl. Then: "Tolaria, do you know what they did with Adaran?"

As he finished his question, she felt sharp pain in her hands and feet, more pain throughout her body, some dull and throbbing, others jagged like toothed knives. It felt like she had been beaten with sticks and fists. Shackles chafed at her wrists, her ankles. She swooned, slumping back against the wall, knowing even as she did that this was not a vision but another strange contact like the one where she'd first stitched all their minds together.

"Adaran," she murmured, sensing his awareness as it turned toward her.

A shrill cry startled her out of the shallow trance; she sat up, looking around, unsure for a moment where she was. Then she saw Ponn, comforting Prehn. "I'm sorry," he said as he tried to soothe her. "She had a nightmare and started to scream."

"It's all right." Tolaria rubbed her temples, feeling groggy, like she had been awakened after only a few hours of sleep.

"It seemed like you swooned. You said Adaran's name."

"I saw him, shackled in Dunshandrin's dungeon. I think they've been torturing him, but I did not have time to communicate with him, though."

The hand caressing Prehn stopped. "Adaran is alive?"

"So it seems."

Ponn's brow furrowed. "We must find a way to rescue him."

"How? He's in the dungeon, and we are out here."

"We *must*," Ponn said. "He saved my daughter."

"I know, Ponn, but—"

"I am a man who pays his debts," Ponn said. He stood, Prehn clinging to him, little arms around his neck. Ponn disentangled himself and put the girl on the bed beside Tolaria, then picked up Diasa's cloak. "I will go. You stay here and watch over Prehn."

"But, Ponn—"

"I may be able to catch T'Sian and Diasa before they reach the castle. If I can, I will tell them about Adaran and then return here."

"And if you can't?"

"Then I will find my own way in," Ponn said, and left.

As she and T'Sian trudged up the cobbled road that led to the castle, Diasa kept glancing at the town below. It stretched along the eastern edge of the small lake, a grey blot on the plains and forests of northern Dunshandrin. It existed mainly to serve and support the castle, she thought, and the castle existed because its location—a promontory surrounded on three sides by a broad, swift river—was easily defended. The way up was steep, all of it within view of the towers; just before reaching the castle, the track narrowed and crossed a stone bridge over the river. Iron gates at either end of the bridge could be closed in an emergency, but they looked rusted and little-used. Even without them, a small number of men could hold the bridge against an army for quite some time; others, stationed on the ledge around the outer wall, could rain down stones and arrows upon enemies who tried to scale the cliffs. Whoever had built the castle had designed it well. A pity his descendants didn't share his wisdom.

They walked unchallenged across the bridge, ignored by the guards stationed along its length. Once on the other side, it was a short walk to the castle gates, which stood open to allow townsfolk and merchants to come and go. That was good, but she had been hoping for more activity than she saw; the light traffic would give the guards an opportunity to inspect her and T'Sian more closely than they otherwise might. Tolaria had spoken of numerous carts and heavy foot traffic into and out of the castle, but Dunshandrin had been secretly preparing for war at that point, and had probably been stocking up on food and other perishables. Now that the war had begun, trade had dwindled.

"Remember," she whispered to the dragon, "let me answer their questions, if they ask any." T'Sian grunted a response. If the dragon still had a tail, Diasa thought, it probably would be twitching in irritation.

The guards eyed them as they approached; two ambled over to meet them. "Who's this, then?" the one on the left said, peering at T'Sian.

"A visitor to see Qalor."

"And who are *you* supposed to be?"

His companion, staring at her while chewing on a hunk of dried meat, said: "I've never seen a girl guard before."

"And you aren't seeing one now," Diasa said. "I'm no *girl*. I'm a woman, and more than a match for you two."

The guard with the meat guffawed; the other one said: "Are the twins running so low on men that they need to start hiring girls?"

"I told you, I'm no girl. Let us through. Qalor is waiting."

"Let him wait. Qalor doesn't decide who passes through these gates. What's your name?"

"Diasa."

"Not you, her."

"I am T'Sian."

"Tuh-syan? What kind of name is that?"

After a moment, the dragon said: "An old one."

"Where are you from?"

Another long pause. "The mountains. Why do you ask so many questions?"

The two men exchanged a glance. "Because we're *guards*," the first one said, "and you two look suspicious."

Diasa decided that she had to put a stop to this before T'Sian lost her temper and did something ostentatious, such as flinging the men over the castle wall. "Are you going to let us through or not?" she said. "You're wasting my time."

"Well, here's the thing," the one on the left said. "You're dressed like a guard, but we've never seen you before. You're escorting someone who isn't a servant or a merchant or a courtesan. And you're armed. You see our problem."

"If you send for Qalor, he'll tell you—"

"I guess you didn't hear me the first time. Qalor doesn't say who comes and goes." The man stroked the thin growth of beard along his chin, eyeing Diasa. Was he planning to proposition her, offering admission to the castle in exchange for a little private time behind the guardhouse? But then he surprised her by saying: "Show me your blade."

He must have noticed that the hilt of her weapon looked different from the corded pommels of the swords that the real guards carried. She drew it from its scabbard and held it sideways for inspection, ready to bring it around and use it if the need arose; but the men merely stared at her steel in unabashed envy. "That didn't come from the armory. Where did you get it?"

"It was my father's. He told me it was forged by dwarves in the Oronj Mountains, using metal from a fallen star."

The man licked his lips. "Tell you what. If you'll trade your sword for mine, I'll let you in the castle."

"Yours?" his companion cried. "Why not mine?"

"Because I have seniority."

"But my uncle's the castellan."

"I don't care who's senior or who has powerful relatives," Diasa said. "I've seen the butter knives that you call swords," she said, sheathing her weapon. "It's no loss to me if you refuse us entry; you'll have to answer to your superiors when they find out, that's all."

"All right, I'll trade you my dagger as well."

"A spoon to go with the butter knife? I think not." She took T'Sian's hand and started to lead her away. "Come on, T'Sian, back to the village with you."

A new voice said: "What's going on over here?"

Diasa turned back. Yet another guard had joined them; this one evidently outranked the other two, judging by the way they stepped aside to make room for him.

"This woman seeks admittance to the castle, Maelus."

Giving Diasa a cold look, the one called Maelus said: "That uniform doesn't fit you very well."

"The tailors don't know how to stitch for a woman."

"So you purport to be a member of the guard, then?"

"I do."

"Really. And who is your captain?"

"My captain?"

The man nodded slightly; the other two watched, amused expressions on their faces. T'Sian also stood by, waiting. Diasa wondered how much longer it would be before the dragon started swinging her fists.

"I am waiting for an answer," he said.

"I'm not sure you will know his name."

"I know the names of all the guards and mercenaries," he said, "but I don't know you."

"Well," she said, "the man I report to is called Gelt."

After a moment, Maelus said: "You ... work for Gelt?"

"Oh, yes," she said. She put on a sardonic smile. "I was with him on several of his missions. I could not accompany him on his most recent journey, although he wanted to send me on ahead of him, as I had pressing business here."

Glancing back at the other guards, Maelus said: "You two are dismissed. I'll handle this." As the two returned to their positions near the gate, Maelus said softly, "You cannot discuss Gelt in front of the common men!"

"I didn't want to," Diasa said. "You forced me into it."

"And the ... woman? She is part of whatever you're doing?"

Narrowing her eyes, Diasa said: "Haven't you and your men meddled quite enough already in Gelt's affairs? When I report this incident to him, how angry do you suppose he will be?"

Maelus blanched slightly. "You may pass, of course," he said, stepping aside. "Please give your master my regards."

Not answering, Diasa took T'Sian's arm and guided her through the gates. The two guards Maelus had sent away gave them surreptitious looks as they passed, perhaps wondering who Gelt was and why his name had granted them entrance to the keep.

After they had gone through the gates, T'Sian said, "How did you know they would let us through if you said you worked for Gelt?"

"I didn't. It was the only name I had to offer."

"Oh." T'Sian was silent a moment, then said: "Was your father's sword really made by dwarves using metal from a fallen star?"

"No, of course not."

"Why *of course not?*"

Sometimes talking to the dragon was like talking to a child. "For one thing, it's not my father's sword, it's mine; I don't know who my father is. Besides, dwarves do not exist."

T'Sian chuckled.

"What?"

"I have lived in the mountains for many, many years, Diasa," the dragon said. "There are dwarves deep beneath the high peaks; a band of them once accidentally tunneled into the lower part of my lair."

"Really?"

"Yes," T'Sian said. "They tasted terrible."

Pyodor Ponn had just reached the bridge on the castle road when he saw T'Sian and Diasa talking with the guards at the gate. He paused there, tightening Diasa's cloak around his waist, and waited. He could hardly run up to them now; the two of them were spectacle enough without having himself scurry up to join them. He watched as Diasa conversed with the guards for some time, first two, then three, then one; he thought the guards would turn them away, but in the end they were allowed to pass. Ponn waited until they were in the castle, then moved slowly up the road, keeping his face turned toward the ground, the hood of Diasa's cloak up over his head. The garment was overly long on him, the hem dragging through the mud, the sleeves drooping past his wrists; wearing it, he felt constricted and ungraceful, but it helped to conceal his features. To the eyes of others on the road, he probably looked like a hunched old woman wearing scrounged clothing, which was preferable to looking like a furtive Enshennean.

But it would not be enough to get him through the gates; the attention Diasa had received convinced him of that. So when, on the far side of the bridge, he noticed a small, faint trail leading off to the right, he paused, eyeing it. The path skirted the stony hill, descending along the side of the stone outcropping on which the castle stood, eventually reaching the level of the river. Intrigued, Ponn followed it. He quickly lost sight of the main road, having circled partway around the northern face of the cliff. The fast-moving river rushed by to his right, constrained within steep, rocky banks; mist from the rapids slicked the red rocks, making the footing treacherous and putting a chill into the air. He pulled Diasa's cloak a little tighter as he walked, keeping an eye on the cliff to his left, hoping to find a spot that looked scalable. Unfortunately the palisades tipped outward near the top, such that he would have to climb upside-down in order to gain the ledge; not impossible, but very difficult, especially considering that he would be trying to bring a wounded man out with him.

At length the path widened into a roughly circular area where the stone had been well-trod; it went no further, as if the entire purpose of the trail were to reach this point. He poked around among the rocks, finding some scraps of garbage but nothing of much interest. He studied the wall for a few minutes, taking its measure, noticing a shallow chute in the side of the hill. It pierced the overhang through a notch. Could he climb here? The walls were smoother than he would have liked, but it was narrow enough that he could brace himself against each side.

Ponn slipped out of Diasa's cloak and tied it around his waist, then took off his shoes and secured them between the cloak and his back; he would climb barefoot, so that he could feel the rock beneath his toes. It looked damp and crumbly, with patches of slick blue-black lichen, and he anticipated a difficult ascent. He stepped into the chute and was struck by a stale, sour odor emanating from the rock, like rotting offal. The fiery mountains of Enshenneah emitted a similar stench, but this was clearly not a volcanic formation; why should it stink?

Pondering the mystery of the malodorous stone, Ponn began to climb. He had not gotten more than five or six feet up when a small projection broke off under his fingers, sending him sliding back to the bottom. He would have to choose his handholds more carefully. He started again, and got about ten feet before the brittle stone betrayed him again; he checked his fall by jamming his arms and legs against the side of the chute. Wedged in that position, he probed for a new toehold, found one, and tested it with part of his weight. It held, but this difficulty didn't bode well for the rest of the climb; he was scarcely a third of the way to the top. Much higher, and a fall would likely be injurious, if not fatal.

He resumed climbing, slowly, not committing his weight to any fissure or protuberance until he had tested it for several seconds. The cliff face continued to crumble beneath his fingers and toes. At about twenty feet up, he found himself stranded with no handholds within reach; he shimmied up the sides of the chute, the stone digging into his toes and knuckles, until he found a shelf wide enough to grip and strong enough to bear his weight. As he neared the top, he heard the screech of grinding metal. He froze, clinging to the stone, wondering what had made the sound; then a rush of noisome fluid washed down the chute, carrying rotten vegetables, spoiled meat, small bones, and moist clumps of unidentifiable excrement. He held on as the effluence splashed over him, eyes and mouth shut tight, trying to hold his breath; by the time the flood ended he was thoroughly coated in filth and smelled like a cesspool.

Ponn started climbing again, but now the channel was freshly slicked and he had to travel even more slowly than before. An exhausting few minutes later, he hauled himself over the edge, finding himself on a lip of stone barely six feet wide. The castle wall loomed above him, higher than the cliff had been, made of fitted blocks taller than a man. In the side of this fortress he saw a rusty iron lift-gate, still raised, revealing a stinking black maw on the other side. A thin trickle of effluence dribbled from the opening, the last remnant of the sewage that had inundated him. As he moved to investigate, he heard voices approaching from below. He pressed himself flat against the ledge, then crawled forward to peer over the lip. A trio of figures approached along the path he had followed, sad, hunched villagers clad in tattered clothing, chattering about village gossip. Two carried old wooden buckets at their hips, while the third carried a basket. They stopped directly below him, where the chute spilled onto the jumbled rocks above the river. Some of the discharged waste had accumulated among the stones, and the villagers began picking through the filth, taking vegetables, bones, bits of bread, whatever might be edible. They were going to take this salvaged food away, he realized. Perhaps they would eat it, or sell it. That explained the path, and why it ended where it did. Occasionally one of their finds would prove too rotten and they would throw it into the river, but they kept a distressingly large proportion of what they took.

Ponn stayed very still as the scavengers picked the craggy stones clean, until he heard a whirring sound and the door began to descend, groaning in its track; then he quickly pulled back and ducked through the hole, into the warm, stinking tunnel on the other side. Dim light came from somewhere up ahead, giving him the hope of a way out.

He would hate to be among the refuse that slid down the chute the next time this door opened.

19

After passing through the castle gate, Diasa and T'Sian entered a wide, churned courtyard. The open space smelled of horses, straw, sweat, earth. T'Sian heard flies buzzing nearby and quickly spotted a heap of manure off to the left, shielded from the elements by a wooden cover. A large overturned wheelbarrow lay beside the pile, along with a few shovels; a small cultivated area nearby appeared to have been allowed to go fallow, perhaps in anticipation of winter. "So this is what the interior of a man-castle looks like," she said. "It is even more squalid than I had imagined."

"Not up to the standards of your cave, eh?"

"My lair is not a *cave*." T'Sian sniffed the air. "This place reeks of garbage and filth, and I am sure that I smell those accursed birds."

"Tolaria did mention an entire aviary full of them."

"Yes. And when my fire has been restored, I will find them and roast them."

"I'm sure that will improve the odor. Hush, now."

After a moment, T'Sian said: "Did you just tell me to hush?"

"Only until we're well away from the guards. Then you may complain all you want."

T'Sian eyed the keep. The gravel path on which they walked led to a wide opening in the stone wall, blocked by a partially lowered portcullis. Guards stood on each side of the entrance, beneath little roofs to protect them from the elements; these looked remarkably similar to the shelter over the manure pile. The men watched as Diasa and T'Sian passed by, but did not challenge them. A short corridor waited beyond the gate, leading to a large, wide, well-lit hall.

Drying, muddy straw littered the floor, while torches lined the walls; those near the doors and windows were unlit, while others, farther back in the depths of the castle, provided guttering illumination. A number of doorways and arches beckoned, while stone stairways led both up and down. "So many ways to go," T'Sian said. "Where would a creature such as Qalor have his laboratory?"

"Somewhere that fires and explosions wouldn't damage the rest of the castle. A separate wing, or perhaps underground," Diasa said. "We can't just wander the castle looking for it, though. We'll arouse suspicion."

A number of people populated the room: Servants about their business, pages in feathered caps, giggling ladies whispering behind raised hands as they bustled through. "Ask one of these fools," the dragon said. "Someone must know."

"No, not here. We can't just walk in the front door and start asking about Qalor. I work for Gelt, I'm supposed to know these things."

"What do you suggest, then?"

"The kitchen staff," Diasa said. "They'll know. More to the point, they'll tell; such servants are cheaply bought or easily threatened."

"Very well. And where is the kitchen?"

"You're the one whose nose tells her everything," Diasa said. "Let's follow it and see where it leads."

Tolaria was bored and worried, a bad combination; boredom left her mind at leisure to wander down different avenues of conjecture about what the others were doing, and worry ensured that all of those avenues ended in disaster. How long had they been gone? She wished she had some sort of timepiece, or that the castle bell were audible here, so she could know for sure how long it had been. The triangle of sun creeping across Diasa's bed served as a crude measure of time, but it was hardly specific, and in any event she had lost that when the building next door had begun to block the light.

How had it come about that all three of her companions were trying to break into Dunshandrin's castle, leaving her here alone? Madness. She almost wished she would slip into another of her involuntary trances and get a glimpse of the future; not that it would do her much good. She probably wouldn't remember it anyway.

If only she could be more like Ponn's daughter! The child, well rested now, had been amusing herself by pulling straws out of the mattress and bending them into animal shapes. She presented each one gravely to Tolaria, as if offering them for sacrifice, though without saying what sort of creatures they were supposed to be; Tolaria had accumulated quite a menagerie of mystery beasts. Perhaps they were denizens of the Enshennean jungle, things that the girl had seen creeping around outside her windows at night.

Frustrated, she lay down on her cot, staring at the cracks in the ceiling, a prisoner with nothing to do but wait. Before long, she felt a small finger poking her on the shoulder. She turned; Prehn was holding up another figurine, this one formed from several bits of straw twisted together to create what looked like a very large snake. Perhaps it was supposed to be the dragon. "Thank you, Prehn," Tolaria said, taking it and putting it with the others. She could almost imagine it opening its vast jaws and slurping down the other miniatures.

Then, because it was more enjoyable, she imagined it swallowing Torrant and Tomari instead.

The dragon had done it; she'd found her way through the cold, dim corridors, bringing them to the kitchen, where servants toiled at the thankless task of feeding their betters. Diasa could feel heat radiating from the wide, open archway, and for the last several minutes had been able to smell the odor of cooking food. T'Sian had obviously smelled it all along, though, and had been able to tell where it was coming from, despite near-constant complaining about how dull her senses were when in human form. Diasa wondered if it was really true, or if the dragon was being disingenuous.

T'Sian said: "Now what?"

"Now we go inside and have a chat with the staff."

"Will we threaten them?"

"Not at first," Diasa said. "They should cooperate, if we ask the proper questions in the proper tone." T'Sian seemed a bit too disappointed by this response, so Diasa added: "Let me do the talking."

"Fine. You talk. If that does not work, then I will threaten."

"Fair enough."

They entered the kitchen. Diasa felt moisture break out across her face as the heat of the room closed around her like sweaty fingers. She counted four ovens of varying sizes, lining the wall opposite the entrance; huge fireplaces stood to the left and right, while a large central fire pit burned directly ahead of them. Cauldrons hung on hooks over the pit, while long-handled pots and massive frying pans simmered in the hearths. Soups, vegetables, meats, stews; the riot of odors rendered any individual food undetectable, except for the dominant smell of baking bread. Kitchen staff bustled about, ignoring their visitors. This did not surprise Diasa; their chief interest would be in making themselves invisible, lest they should be called upon to perform some particularly unpleasant or arduous task or singled out for blame because someone had disliked his afternoon meal. Diasa grabbed one of them by the wrist as she passed by. It was a slip of a girl, wearing a smudged tunic that looked like it may once have been a feedbag. She stared at Diasa with huge, hunted eyes. "Yes, my lord?" she said; then, realizing her mistake: "I mean, my lady?"

Before Diasa could speak, T'Sian said: "We're looking for the alchemist." Diasa shot the dragon a look of exasperation, but T'Sian merely smirked, her unnaturally wide mouth curling up at one edge.

The girl looked puzzled. "Qalor? He's not allowed in here, not since he put a potion in the soup. Everyone knows that."

Intrigued, Diasa almost asked what kind of potion it was; instead, she pulled the girl aside, near one of the fireplaces, so that the roaring of the flames would help drown out their words. T'Sian followed slowly, throwing fearsome glances at any who looked her way; she was rewarded with cringes and quick aversions. How had Ponn managed to develop a rapport with this creature? But of course, T'Sian considered everyone in the castle to be her enemy, and doubtless held each of them personally responsible for the slaughter of her hatchlings; she couldn't, or didn't choose to, appreciate the distinction between people like these kitchen workers, who were little better than slaves, and the lords who dwelt in finery above.

The servant girl had begun trying to pull away, pointing vaguely at the fires and whining protestations about her work. "Be quiet," Diasa said. "We know Qalor is not here. We were on our way to his laboratory and got turned around in these accursed corridors. How do we get there from here?"

"I don't know."

"She lies," T'Sian said.

"I'm not lying!"

T'Sian elaborately inspected her long, pointed, gleaming fingernails. "I think you are."

"You've never brought food to him?" Diasa said. "He's never asked for a special platter in the middle of the night?"

"We're not permitted in the laboratory," the girl said, eyeing T'Sian the way one might watch a man who was waving a sword and muttering to himself. "There's a dumbwaiter."

"A waiter who cannot speak? Can he lead us there?"

Now she graced Diasa with the same stare she'd given the dragon; obviously she thought they were both mad. "It's not a person, it's a little box. We put the food in it and lower it down. He puts the dirty plates back and raises it up."

"What nonsense is this?" T'Sian said. "A little moving box?"

"Show us this dumbwaiter, then," Diasa said.

The girl pointed at a small, square door in the wall, which Diasa had originally taken for a lesser oven. "That's it, right there."

Diasa and T'Sian stood before the dumbwaiter, which the kitchen maid had opened, revealing a boxlike cavity. It was large enough to accommodate a human such as Diasa, T'Sian thought, or even herself, although her own mass would likely overwhelm whatever wizardry allowed it to move up and down between the floors. "How does it work?" she said.

"It's something to do with water, that's all I know. You turn the knob and it moves. Left is for down, right is for up."

From behind them, someone said: "Qalor built it a few years ago, after they blocked up the main entrance to his suite. He said it worked by *hydraulics*, whatever that means." T'Sian turned to regard this new speaker, a fat man in a dirty smock who had apparently decided to wander into the conversation. He shooed the girl away, then took her place between Diasa and T'Sian. "What are you two doing here, then?" He looked at Diasa. "I don't believe that you're a guard." Then he turned to T'Sian. "And I don't know *what* you're supposed to be."

"Pray you do not find out," T'Sian said. Diasa made a noise that she took to be a warning, but she ignored her companion's displeasure. "This has gone on long enough," she said. "Diasa, secure the entrance to the kitchen."

"What?"

"Keep anyone from leaving." T'Sian grabbed the fat man by the shirt and hauled him close. His eyes widened in shock; the nearby kitchen staff stopped what they were doing and turned to stare at this marvel. Cursing, Diasa ran for the doorway, drawing her sword. T'Sian was not sure if she got there in time to keep everyone in the kitchen; nor did she care. "Listen, man," she hissed to the wide-eyed cook, "we are here to see Qalor. We want to go to the place where he performs his work. You say this so-called dumbwaiter goes there?"

"Yes," the man said, his once haughty voice reduced to a most satisfying squeak.

"T'Sian!" Diasa cried. "There's more than one door!"

She was right; the kitchen workers had begun to flee, pushing and shoving each other as they escaped through a narrow opening half-hidden behind a stack of casks. They would no doubt alert the soldiers, who would then come with weapons and armor and try to kill the intruders. T'Sian did not fear much for her own safety, although it was possible they would harm Diasa with their puny blades.

Did she care if that happened? She wasn't sure.

She turned back to the fat man and said: "These places where you make your fires. They have chimneys?"

"Yes, of course."

"Does Qalor's laboratory share them?"

"I ... I think so."

Diasa returned to T'Sian's side, sword sheathed; evidently she had decided it was pointless to guard the front exit when everyone had left through a different one. "You're completely mad," Diasa said. "Did you know that?"

"I am not mad," T'Sian said. "I am a dragon, and I will act like one." She tossed the pudgy man aside; he crashed into a table, fell to the floor, and scurried away on all fours like a beaten animal. "Diasa. Into the dumbwaiter."

"*What?*"

T'Sian picked Diasa up, shoved her into the boxlike space, and wrenched the knob to the left. The dumbwaiter dropped out of sight, taking its startled-looking passenger with it. That taken care of, T'Sian turned to the largest hearth, which—if these men had any sense—would have the widest chimney. She marched straight into the fire, feeling its warmth tickling her skin. Another opening gaped at its back, beyond a waist-high barrier of stone; T'Sian leaned over the half-wall, peering downward. The chimney looked more than large enough to accommodate her body; the alchemist's nefarious experiments no doubt required copious ventilation.

He would certainly not be expecting an invasion from this avenue.

Climbing over the barrier, she let herself slide down along the hot, rough bricks, into the darkness below.

Pyodor Ponn moved along the low, foul tunnel that he'd found on the other side of the vertical gate. The walls were of rough stone, the floor lined with smooth bricks; the passageway sloped sharply upward. Bent nearly double, he slipped and stumbled his way to the top, falling once when his foot turned on something soft and slick. He was grateful that he couldn't see what it was. Soon he hauled himself into a cylindrical basin with a slanted floor, perhaps five feet deep and of similar diameter. He spotted a corroded ladder, which he used to climb out of the cesspool, narrowly avoiding being splattered by the noisome discharge from one of perhaps a dozen dark, crusted openings in the ceiling.

The ladder led to a ledge that ran around the basin. He took a quick look around. The flickering light came from a single lantern, hung on a hook beside a heavy-looking door. A can of lamp oil sat on the floor beneath it, right next to a thin, ragged girl who was staring at him in frank astonishment. Startled, Ponn said: "Please don't be afraid. I won't hurt you."

"You came out of the pit."

"Yes. I climbed up the cliff." Ponn moved closer to her. He had been doused in sewage, he had crawled through the drainage chute of a cesspool, but still, he imagined he must be cleaner than this apparition. Her clothes were stained and torn, her skin sallow and filthy; she was skeleton-thin and her hair, which looked as if it had once been pale blonde, was caked with grime and sludge equal to the dirtiest chamberpot a guest had ever left at Ponn's inn.

"Nobody can climb the cliff," she said. "Are you a spirit?"

"No. I'm here looking for a friend."

"A friend?"

"Yes."

"You won't find any friends here," she said in a vague sort of way, leaving it unclear if she meant the room, the castle, or perhaps the world in general.

"Who are you?" he said.

"No one." The girl looked away as a splash of something unmentionable drooled out of the ceiling and into the basin.

"You must have a name."

"Wyst," the girl said, so softly he could hardly hear.

"Why are you here, Wyst?"

"I watch the pit," she said. "When it gets too full or smells too bad, I raise the gate so it drains."

"You opened the gate just now?"

She nodded.

"How does it work? Can you show me?"

Wyst shrugged and stood, moving toward an iron crank set into the wall not far from where she sat. She didn't have so much as a mat to lay on; she must sleep right on the cold, hard floor, like an ill-favored dog. Ponn noticed a manacle at her ankle, attached to a length of chain that ran to an iron ring in the floor near the lantern. "Wait. Are you a prisoner?"

The girl stopped, looked at him over her shoulder. Her eyes, shadowy in the torchlight, showed no emotion. "I live down here. I used to live upstairs, but I'm being punished."

"For what?"

She bit her lip, turned away. "This is how it works," she said. "You turn the crank this way, and the gate goes up."

"Wyst—"

"You slide this latch over and the crank can't turn, so the gate stays open. You slide it back and then you can close the gate. It's so simple that even I can do it."

"Wyst, do they bring you food?"

"A little. Sometimes food comes down the chutes. I eat that when I get hungry, if I can reach it."

"And water? What do you drink?"

She didn't answer, didn't look at him. It was as if she were trying to pretend he didn't exist; or maybe it was the other way around, and she was trying to will *herself* out of existence. "What about this?" he said, indicating the door. "Is it locked? Are there guards on the other side?"

"I don't know if it's locked," she said. "I don't think there are guards. There's nothing here that needs guarding."

"Have you tried to open it?"

The girl shook her head, went back to her spot. The chain dragged along behind her, whispering across the rough surface. "I can't leave," she said. "I'm being punished."

"You can't live like this for very long," Ponn said. "Look at you. You're starving. How long have you been here?"

She didn't answer.

"I can help you escape."

"That would only make things worse."

Ponn wondered how Wyst thought her situation might possibly get worse. Perhaps she was afraid they would shorten her chain. She settled back down onto the floor and looked away; it seemed that, as far as she was concerned, he was already gone, or had never been there in the first place. He put his hand on the door, tried the handle. It turned reluctantly, as if it didn't get much use, but it wasn't locked. He opened the door a crack and peered out into another room, poorly lit by another lantern. The ceiling hid behind a tangle of clay pipes, running into the chamber where Wyst sat; a number of them leaked at the joints, spattering the floor with unpleasant fluids.

Ponn glanced back at Wyst. She sat staring straight ahead, waiting for the cesspool to fill up again with effluent from the upper corridors whence she had been banished. He didn't know what she was being punished for, and it occurred to him that she might seek to mitigate her sentence by reporting that a man had entered the castle via the sewer; but even if she wanted to tell someone, how would she? She was alone down here, chained to the floor. Until her minders came to check on her, a most evidently rare occurrence, she would have no one to talk to. Besides, from their brief conversation, he really couldn't see her raising a hue and cry for the guards. She'd likely sit there and say nothing as they left her a piece of moldy bread and a cup of scummy water.

If he came back this way, Ponn thought, he was going to rescue that girl, whether she wanted him to or not.

As the dumbwaiter descended rapidly, accompanied by a wheezing noise and an unnerving shudder, Diasa cast dark thoughts toward her T'Sian. If the dragon kept up this sort of behavior, it was likely to get at least one of them killed, and Diasa was quite sure she knew which of them that would be.

Before long her downward motion slowed, as if the box had been caught by a gently yielding hand; shortly it hissed to a stop behind a closed door with a small, round, dirty window. Through it, she could discern a cramped chamber that looked like a crude dining room. It contained a square wooden table and a single chair, but no other furnishings or adornments. Evidently Qalor dined alone.

She couldn't figure out how to open the door—there was no handle on this side, and she couldn't achieve any sort of grip on it—so she gave it one hard, double-legged kick, then another. The entire thing popped off, clattering to the floor. She slipped out after it and pulled her sword, but no one came to investigate. Judging by the din emanating from a door to her left, no one would have heard it falling anyway.

Diasa went to the noisy door, listening to the sounds from beyond: Roaring fires, hissing steam, clanking machinery. What was going on in there? She opened the door a crack and peered inside, but saw only a sitting room containing a high-backed wooden bench and a low table covered with sheets of parchment. The noises seemed to come from a door in the sitting room, ajar, to the left of the one she had opened. To her right, a larger door looked like it might lead out of Qalor's rooms; another, smaller portal stood opposite her, perhaps leading into a bedchamber. If his other furniture signified, Qalor probably slept on a board, using a stone as a pillow.

She entered the sitting room, slipping quickly past the open door, stopping before the larger one. It had slots for a bar; assuming the kitchen staff would tell the soldiers what she and T'Sian had been after, they could expect unwelcome visitors to be arriving shortly. She quickly located the bar underneath the settle and shoved it into place, turning the latch to lock it down. That would delay the guards for a while.

That done, she went to the table and began sifting through the heap of scrolls. Most were drawings, diagrams of strange machinery and devices, as well as anatomical sketches of various sorts of animals. She found one that bore a schematic of a boxlike device, with two chambers containing crudely colored red and blue crystals and a third chamber underneath those two that appeared to contain some sort of liquid. Interesting. She dropped that one and moved on to others beneath it, finding drawings of giant eagles and a pattern for saddles to fit them, a map of Barbareth, what looked like a design of the castle's drainage system.

Now she came to a layer of older documents, the vellum brittle and discolored. She frowned, fingering the broken wax seal on one of them. Much of it was missing, but unless she was quite mistaken, this scroll belonged to the library at Flaurent. She glanced at the noisy door, then quickly flipped through the remaining scrolls, finding many more that had come from the college, most written in a runic language that she didn't understand. Some were illustrated, including an extremely detailed drawing of a dragon not unlike T'Sian in her true form, and beneath it a a stout man, with arrows connecting the two, measurements, copious notes in spidery, unreadable script. She found herself wishing she had shown a bit more interest when her mother had tried to teach her ancient languages.

How had Flaurent's scrolls gotten into Qalor's possession? She didn't think they had raided the library during their attack on Flaurent, so it must have been stolen earlier. Why hadn't anyone noticed the theft and reported it? Or perhaps they had, and for some reason, Damona had chosen not to pursue the matter. Well, nothing could be done about it now; she was hardly in a position to take the papers, and even if she did, there was no college to return them to. She would just have to add this to Dunshandrin's hefty list of crimes. Leaving the parchments, she drew her sword and then kicked open the door to the laboratory. T'Sian was already inside, Qalor lying prone at her feet, up on one elbow, his other arm raised defensively in front of his face. Behind him, a table lay on its side, smashed glassware and steaming liquid spread across the floor. Diasa hoped those rising vapors weren't poisonous; she knew what sort of chemicals alchemists used.

Seeing her in the doorway, weapon drawn, Qalor looked momentarily hopeful. "Save me!" he cried. "She came out of the fireplace! She's mad!"

T'Sian looked at her, her head swiveling on her neck, just like a reptile's. "There you are," she said. "I had begun to wonder where the dumbwaiter had taken you."

"I was doing some reconnaissance," Diasa said.

"Well, Qalor and I were just having a chat." Then, to the alchemist: "This is not one of your guards. She is with me."

"I thought *you* were with *me*," Diasa said.

"Well," the dragon said, "now you know better."

Diasa moved into the room and gave the cavernous laboratory a cursory examination. The place was crammed with tables and shelves, which were in turn full of jugs and bottles and decanters, boxes and bags, loose stones, dried plants, pickled animal parts floating in jars of yellow fluid. She saw evaporative bins, wooden vats and barrels, copper tubing, glass tanks. By comparison, Flaurent's small alchemical shop was little more than a country kitchen. Turning to the dragon, she said: "Have you secured the room?"

T'Sian gave her a blank look. Of course she hadn't bothered to look for other entrances, to anticipate the direction from which Dunshandrin's guards might attack; her strategy was to charge in and destroy everything in sight. Diasa moved into the room, inspecting it, memorizing the layout. "Qalor, how many doors are there?" she said.

"Just one."

"The one in the sitting room?"

"Yes."

"Where does it go?"

"Stairs. To the cesspool."

"You come and go through the cesspool?"

"I often have … things to dispose of. And after the fire, wise Lord Dunshandrin decreed that my laboratory be separated from the rest of the castle. They bricked up the main entrance, there." He pointed toward a large archway, sealed by massive blocks of stone that were a different color from those that constituted the walls. "Now the stairs are the only way in."

"You nearly burned down the castle?" T'Sian said. "A pity you did not succeed."

"Yes, yes," Qalor said, a whining, eager dog. "A pity."

Diasa returned to the dragon and her captive. "He seems to be telling the truth. If there's another way in, I don't see it."

"Of course. I would not lie to you."

"I like this man," T'Sian said, looking pleased. "He is easily intimidated."

The room beyond the cesspool had two doors, one on the left, the other on the right. Ponn hesitated, then went left and listened at the portal. Silence. He went to the door on the right and listened at that one as well. He heard faint noises, banging and clattering, like an army of small blacksmiths hammering away at cheap armor. He opened the door a crack, revealing a dark, damp, narrow flight of stairs leading upward. He went back and took the oil lamp, then returned to the staircase and made the short climb to the top, where he found a landing and another door. The sounds were louder up here. He gently pushed the door but it hardly moved. Barred on the other side, he thought. Rather than try to force it, which would be noisy and futile, he returned to the pipe room and opened the other door. This revealed an intermediate landing in yet another flight of stairs, from which he could go either up or down. Ponn thought for a moment. What could possibly be below the level of the cesspool?

The dungeon, of course.

Ponn turned the lamp flame low and descended slowly, keeping his back to the wall, making his footsteps light on the old stone. It seemed too much to hope that the dungeon itself would be unguarded. He hadn't quite worked out what he was going to do when faced with actual soldiers; he could not fight them like Diasa, nor pick them up and throw them like T'Sian, nor charm them like Tolaria. He hoped that when the moment arrived and enemies confronted him, he would manifest some undiscovered skill at persuasion or self-defense.

The stairs terminated in a small guard-post. Two rough cots stood against one wall, partially hidden behind a screen. A wooden table stood near them, flanked by benches. A pair of large, battered tankards stood on the table, surrounded by the scattered pieces of a board game, like conquering titans standing over the bodies of a vanquished army. Two barred doors stood in the opposite wall; he imagined these must lead to the actual cells.

Ponn stayed where he was, listening. The room was silent, evidently unoccupied. He crept into it, not making a sound. No one challenged him. Setting the lantern down on the table, he went and peered behind the screen. The cots, unmade, stood unoccupied. He returned to the table, sniffed the contents of a cup. It smelled like the sort of rotgut demanded by a certain kind of rough customer; he didn't stock such poison, but a tavern near his inn did, and he could send for it when necessary. He noticed a fire-pit in a corner, with a crude smoke-hole above it. The ashes still smoldered, the fire very recently doused by someone who'd found better things to do than drink and game. Engaging Diasa and T'Sian, perhaps.

Well, whatever trouble those two had gotten into, he could not help them; even if he were able to locate them, they would likely find him an encumbrance. Instead, he tried the doors. The one on the left was open, but the one on the right was locked; that must mean there were prisoners were behind it. He searched the room, starting with the table, and quickly found an iron ring sporting several heavy keys hidden beneath an overturned bowl. He snatched it up, returned to the door, and tried keys until he found one that turned in the lock. He threw off the bar and pulled the door open on protesting hinges, revealing a dark, narrow corridor beyond.

Abandoning caution, Ponn called: "Adaran?"

He heard a cough from somewhere in the darkness, and then a hoarse voice said: "No one here but us rats."

For all he knew this was some thug or murderer. "Adaran, is that you? This is Pyodor Ponn. Do you know who I am?"

After a moment the same voice came back, tiny, like a lost child found wandering in the woods. "Prehn's father?"

That must be the man he sought. Ponn retrieved the lantern, then crept into the corridor. The dim light showed walls carved through stone, glistening with moisture; the rank air smelled of mildew and rancid straw. "Where are you?"

"In a cell."

Accurate, but useless. "Which one?"

"I don't know."

"Keep talking, then," Ponn said. "I'll find you."

"Are you alone?"

"Yes."

"The guards—"

"The guards are gone." Ponn stopped in front of the last cell on the left. It was held shut by a complicated system of bars and latches, which looked much newer than the door to which it was attached; it took Ponn several seconds just to find the keyhole. It was easy, though, to find the correct key; it looked nothing like the others, being a long cylinder with several leaf-like blades near the end. Finally he got the latches open and pulled back the bars; the door swung out into the hallway, revealing a tiny cell that stank of excrement and blood and the sour whiff of infection. The majority of the stink emanated from the apparition chained to the wall to his left.

Ponn said: "Adaran?"

The prisoner smiled, blood oozing from his split lower lip.

"Forgive me if I don't shake your hand," Adaran said.

20

ADARAN WATCHED AS PYODOR PONN put his lantern down and set to work on the manacles that held him to the wall. He had no idea how the little Enshennean had managed to penetrate the dungeon, and for a while entertained the notion that he was in fact imagining this entire episode. As part of this lovely delusion, Ponn had somehow gotten hold of a set of keys, and fumbled through them until he found one that worked on the shackles around Adaran's feet. He wasn't quite tall enough to reach the ones around Adaran's wrists, which were fairly high up on the wall. Fortunately, the twins had not bothered to retrieve their thrones; Ponn didn't ask why the chairs were there, he just dragged one over, stood on it, and unlocked the manacles that held Adaran's hands, allowing him to drop to the floor. The landing sent spears of pain up his legs and he started to collapse, but Ponn was there to catch him and lower him to the ground.

Adaran looked at his rescuer and murmured, "You don't feel like a dream."

"I'm not a dream."

"You don't smell like a dream either."

"I came in through the cesspool. Can you stand?"

"I'm not sure."

Ponn got on his knees, examining Adaran's injuries, his face mostly impassive; but Adaran could see small muscles working around his jaws and eyes as he surveyed the damage that the torturer had inflicted. "Most of these wounds are superficial, but you'll need a healer for your feet and hands."

"Did you bring one?"

"No, but I'm told that Tolaria has some skill in that area. She may be able to help you, if I can bring you to her."

"I can stand. Just give me a moment more."

"We have no moments to spare. After you stand, you may need to climb. Can you climb?"

"Climb what?"

"Stairs."

"Yes," Adaran said. "I think I can climb stairs."

"Good. And after that, a cliff."

"Not the cliff that goes down to the river?"

"Yes, that one."

"No," Adaran said. "Definitely not."

"Perhaps I can lower you on a rope."

"Sorry," Adaran said. "Fresh out of rope."

"We'll think of something," Ponn said. "But you must get on your feet now." Ponn pulled him upright, forcing him to stand. His feet felt as if invisible dwarves were pounding invisible spikes through them, attaching them to the floor. Ponn caught his left arm and slid underneath it to help support his weight, gripping him around the wrist. This put pressure on Adaran's mutilated hand; he gave a small cry that, to his own ears, sounded distressingly like the bleat of an injured lamb. Ponn shifted his grip farther up Adaran's arm. "Better?"

Adaran nodded.

"Then let's be out of here before the guards return."

Leaning heavily on his savior, Adaran limped out of the cell and into the hallway.

"So tell me, man," T'Sian said, looming over the cringing alchemist, "where are my crystals?"

Qalor squinted up at her. "*Your* crystals?"

"The stones you took from my lair," she said. "The stones you took from the volcano. I want them."

"Your lair?" Qalor's eyes grew wide. "You are the dragon from the northern mountains?"

"Yes. You thought you could be the dragon, but you were wrong. *I* am the dragon, and I have come to reclaim what you stole. Give my crystals back to me, before I lose my patience and tear you to pieces."

"They are in the vats near the wall," Qalor said, gesturing with a quivering hand. "Behind the divider. There, there!"

"I'll watch Qalor while you fetch your stones," Diasa said. "Be quick about it. I don't know how long that bar will keep the guards out."

"Those men do not concern me."

"Well, they concern *me*."

"If they attack us, I will annihilate them." To illustrate her contempt for the soldiers and their puny weapons, she moved unhurriedly in the direction Qalor had indicated. Her gaze wandered over the bizarre equipment, the tables piled high with glass spheres and copper tubes and silver coils. Small flames burned beneath many containers, heating strange-smelling concoctions that bubbled or steamed or swirled or sparkled. The room swirled with fumes and stenches, none of them wholesome; perhaps they were responsible for the alchemist's strange appearance and physical deformities.

She stopped at the screen, which consisted of thick metal plates held together with wooden posts and leather straps. She studied it for a moment, then tore it down and cast it aside. Two large vats stood behind it, made of foggy glass festooned with gleaming pipes and tubes. Now she felt the energy coming from the crystals, like barbed-footed insects walking on her skin. The one on the left had a copper bottom; it was full of bubbling fluid and contained a jagged formation of reddish-orange crystals. They appeared to be growing along the bottom and up the sides of the container. Beneath it, a jet of fire hissed from a burner in the floor, blackening the copper. She put her hand on the vat and felt the heat beneath her palm; any human who touched it would no doubt be badly burned.

The second vat stood five or six feet from the first, separated from it by a wall of metal sandwiched between layers of brick. It was of a similar design to the other, but frosted coils wrapped around the bottom, ultimately running into a whirring, wheezing apparatus that stood nearby. A large pipe came out of the floor and entered the noisy machine on the left; another exited from the right side, curving down and returning to the floor.

A metal scaffold surrounded the vats, supporting them, the catwalk along the top accessible by climbing an iron ladder. She noted several leathery sacks lined up along the platform's edge, along with some sort of tool with tines and a toothed metal blade. The sacks resembled the organ where her kind held the stones within their bodies. The dragon shot a black look at Qalor. "What is all this?" she said.

"The blue crystals must be kept cool, to control their growth," Qalor said. "I spent years perfecting that machine you see there. It runs on steam, and chills river water almost to freezing."

"That's nonsense," Diasa said. "Steam is hot. You can't use it to make something colder."

"With the right combination of chemicals, it is possible to draw out the heat from the water, and—"

"I stored crystals for years without requiring such devices," T'Sian said. "Tell me how to get them out before I smash your vats like eggs."

"No, you mustn't do that!" Qalor cried. "There are hatches on top of the vats. Turn the valves to open them and you will have access to the crystals. Use the tool to remove what you need."

T'Sian eyed the ladder. "I cannot climb this," she said. "It will break."

"It's quite sturdy," Qalor said, sounding offended.

"Is it? You think it will hold me? Let us find out, then." She climbed the ladder to the platform. It wobbled and groaned, but did not fall; not immediately, anyway. She saw the hatches Qalor had mentioned, hinged domes with horizontal wheels sticking out of them; these must be the valves.

Diasa said: "T'Sian, hurry!"

T'Sian went first to the cold vat. She put her hands on the valve and gave it a twist. At first it refused to turn; she applied more force and it snapped off in her hands. She held up the wheel and examined it, thinking it unlikely that this was the proper mode of operation.

"What was that sound?" Qalor said.

"The wheel came off."

"You broke it?"

"Evidently," she said. "How do I get the crystals out now?"

"I will have to repair the valve."

"We don't have time for that," Diasa said.

"Then you will not get your crystals."

T'Sian glared down at him.

Then she put her hands on the vat, and pushed.

When T'Sian started to tip over the enormous tank, Diasa grabbed Qalor by the shoulders and hauled him away. Despite his size, he weighed almost nothing, as if he, too, were just another empty device, animated by steam and deviltry. As the apparatus pulled free of the pipes connecting it to the wall, frigid water sprayed into the laboratory, knocking over glassware, dousing the fire beneath the heated canister. Torn loose from its moorings, the container toppled over, hit the stone floor, and shattered, spreading slush and broken glass and chunks of luminous crystal across the floor. The spewing water washed away the slush, but the blue crystals remained where they had fallen, glowing softly, like pieces of the moon.

Diasa hauled Qalor to his feet. "Shut off the water," she told him.

"But the crystals—"

"Shut it off!"

Muttering, Qalor headed for a valve set into the wall near the now-sputtering apparatus, making a wide circle to avoid the spraying water and the crystals. T'Sian still crouched on the platform, watching Qalor move toward the machine. "Are you coming down?" Diasa called.

"Not until the water stops. Cold does not agree with me."

"You might have thought of that before you destroyed my cooling system," Qalor muttered.

The dragon shot him a murderous look, then turned back to Diasa. "Here, catch." T'Sian tossed her the strange tool for retrieving the crystals; she caught it by the shaft with both hands, managing to avoid the blade and claw-like prongs. "Cut off some of the blue crystal for me."

The dragon didn't hesitate to hurl what amounted to a pole arm at her; it probably didn't even occur to T'Sian that the tool could have killed her. Diasa bit back an angry comment and instead examined the device. It had a handle for working the saw back and forth, and a sliding lever in its midsection; she moved this back and forth and watched the tines extend and retract. Clever. You could cut the crystal with the blade, then pick it up with the metal fingers, never having to get within five feet of the mineral. Judging by Qalor's actions and movements, not to mention his appearance, there might be some benefit to avoiding close contact with those glowing facets.

She glanced at the alchemist. He was still trying to turn the valve; perhaps it was stuck, or rusted in place. T'Sian would have to stay on her perch a little longer. Moving into the ankle-deep water, she tried to pick up a shard of blue crystal, but it seemed to be stuck to the floor and would not be dislodged. She moved to another, tried again. It, too, refused to move.

How odd.

She approached one of the larger chunks and started sawing. The blade cut easily through the crystal; luminous chips fell into the gushing water and were swept away. Then a chunk came loose and she manipulated the lever, catching it in the tines as it fell.

Suddenly T'Sian cried: "He's running away!"

Diasa whirled, just in time to see Qalor disappear through the door to his quarters.

She cast the tool aside and sprinted after him.

T'Sian crouched on the platform and stared at the crystals, tantalizingly out of reach; the pipe continued to spew water, and even from here she could feel how cold it was. If she ventured into it, the low temperatures could harm her, make her sluggish and unable to defend herself, especially in her more vulnerable human shape. The laboratory was more than large enough to contain her true form; she could change, gobble up both the red and blue crystals, and then return to her human guise in order to escape the castle. Or perhaps she could escape up the chimney. It was quite large; she could probably force her way through it, just like she used to slither along the narrow throat of her lair in the mountains. Bones could shift; wings could retract. At worst, she would be forced to return to human form, drop back down to the laboratory, and fight her way out; but at best, she would emerge from the top of her enemies' castle and begin laying waste to everything they held dear.

Yes. Yes. Yes.

It was high time Dunshandrin's ilk tasted the vengeance they had earned.

* * *

Adaran did all right limping up the dungeon corridor and into the abandoned guard post; he even managed to stumble over to the table, snatch up the mugs of evil-smelling drink, and drain them both. But when they came to the stairs, he looked up at them, sighed, and said: "I forgot there were so many."

"You can make it," Ponn said. "I'll help you."

They ascended more slowly than Ponn would have liked; Adaran treated each step as if it were a pool of unknown depth and questionable temperature, testing it with one foot before committing to it. Ponn supported as much of the man's weight as he could, but he was heavier than he looked; there must be wiry muscle beneath his thin frame. He would never make it down the cliff, but what other path was available? They could hardly wander through the hallways looking for an exit. His filth and injuries clearly identified him as either a prisoner or a beggar, and a beggar was unlikely to be roaming about the castle accompanied by a dirty little foreigner who smelled like a forgotten chamberpot.

At last they reached the middle landing. Ponn steadied Adaran against the wall, then reached for the door to the cesspool, just as it burst open and someone came charging through, crashing into him. They went down in a tangle of limbs. Instinctively, Ponn kicked out with his legs, feeling them strike something; he heard a cry as the other person tumbled down the dungeon stairs like a bouncing ball made of arms and legs. Ponn jumped to his feet, grabbed the shocked-looking Adaran, and dragged him through the door. He was surprised to find the floor wet; icy water poured down the staircase across the room, swirling around their feet, flowing into the next room. He imagined Wyst standing there, watching the water flow into the cesspool, scooping it up and drinking it, or perhaps considering it some fresh punishment and letting it break over her as if she were a rock.

Splashing footsteps came fast down the stairs, but it was too late to hide. He pushed Adaran to the side and raised his fists just as Diasa entered the room, sword drawn. They stared at each other for a moment, and then Diasa said: "What are you doing here? Are you planning to hit me with those little fists?"

Ponn felt himself flush. He lowered his hands.

Her gaze moved over his shoulder to Adaran, back to Ponn, then to Adaran again. A frown creased her face. "Oh," she said. "It's you."

"Yes, it's me."

"I thought you were dead."

"Not yet. Sorry."

Ponn said: "Diasa, where is T'Sian?"

"In the laboratory. That way." She indicated the stairs down which she had come. "I'm after Qalor. He fled this way. Did you see him?"

That must be the man who'd crashed into him. "I think so. He fell down the dungeon stairs." Ponn pointed at the door behind him.

"Is he alive?"

"I don't know. Did you get the crystals?"

"Yes. Almost. There's a pipe spraying cold water, and T'Sian won't come down until it's shut off. You need to turn the valve in the wall to stop the water."

"I do?"

"Yes."

"What about you?"

"I'm going after Qalor."

"But—" He broke off because Diasa wasn't listening; she sprinted across the room and banged through the door to the landing, her footsteps fading rapidly. "Fine," he told the door. "Don't listen to me. After all, I give poor advice."

"Who are you talking to?" Adaran said.

"No one." Ponn turned to him. "I'm going to go check on T'Sian. Wait for me here."

"Do you suppose I might run away?" Adaran said.

Tolaria blinked a few times, as the ceiling gradually came into focus. She lay on the floor looking up at it, a sour, metallic taste in her mouth. After a moment she realized she had bitten her tongue, no doubt in the throes of a vision, and was tasting the blood.

She sat up, reaching out to steady herself against the bed. The room seemed to be slowing from a wild spin, like a top coming to rest, tipping onto its side. She tried to remember what she had seen, but could not; and there was no one here to tell her what she might have said, except for the little girl.

Tolaria attempted to speak, but it turned into a fit of coughing. When the attack passed, she tried again. "Prehn?"

No answer.

The oracle hauled herself onto the bed, sat on the edge. She didn't see Prehn. She got to her feet, felt unbalanced, sat down again. She needed to lie down for a little while, but for some reason felt she could not spare the time.

"Prehn?"

Still no answer. Where had the child gone? Was she hiding, perhaps frightened by Tolaria's behavior? No, the door to their room was ajar. Tolaria had latched it after Ponn left; Prehn must have opened it and gone out. She went to it and peeked out. The hallway was empty; the common room below seemed quiet, the noise barely rising to the level of a murmur. Lunch was long since ended, and dinner had not yet arrived. Had Prehn gone down there? Could she risk going to look for the girl? She was supposed to stay in the room, lest someone should recognize her or, worse, ask her a question; but she had told Ponn she would watch over his daughter, a simple task, at which she had failed.

Why had the others left her alone, putting her in such a predicament? The twins had crippled her with their meddling. She needed someone to watch over her at least as much as Prehn did. It was all in her mind, wasn't it? If she concentrated hard enough, could she not overcome it, say what needed to be said instead of the truth, ugly and unpainted? Probably not. When she answered questions, she did so automatically, below the level of thought. By the time she thought of a lie, she would have already answered with the truth.

Still, she had to go and find Prehn. She had promised.

As Tolaria stepped out into the hallway, Prehn came into view, tottering up the stairs, using both small hands to carry a wooden cup. Greatly relieved, Tolaria returned to the room, settling onto her bed. The straw crackled and shifted beneath her. Prehn entered momentarily; she closed the door and then wordlessly brought the cup over, proffering it to Tolaria. She took it, sniffed the contents, took a sip. Water.

"What's this for?" she said.

The little girl shrugged and climbed onto Diasa's bed, keeping a watchful gaze on Tolaria. The oracle thought for a moment, then said: "Did I ask for water?"

The child nodded.

So. Her vision must have involved water, but what about it? There was no shortage of it here; the lake was full, the river high. Perhaps the vision had been about a ship? A flood? It may have been completely unrelated to their current situation; after all, nothing required that everything she foretold must involve Dunshandrin.

"Did I say anything else?"

No answer. Prehn might be talkative with her father, but not with anyone else.

Tolaria was quite sure that she hadn't had a vision of herself being thirsty, but whatever the actual premonition had been, it was locked away inside her head, inaccessible. She rolled onto her back, feeling drained and useless, spouting predictions that no one heard, a town crier without a town.

The little girl was still watching her, perhaps waiting for her to drink the water. She took a sip. "Good water," she said. Prehn giggled and pushed her face into the straw-stuffed pillow as if trying to climb inside.

Well, at least she had made a child happy today. That put her ahead of many others, didn't it?

Diasa paused a moment on the landing, listening. She heard nothing, no footsteps rushing down to meet her, no tramping feet as the guards took up positions above or below. The utter lack of opposition had begun to worry her. At first she had attributed it to a shortage of manpower or to general incompetence—these were, after all, the same people who had let Tolaria simply walk out of their castle—but this negligence was too gross to be unintentional. No, she had to assume that someone somewhere in the chain of command, perhaps even the twins themselves, had realized what they were facing. The response, when it came, would be proportional to the threat; fortunately the wizard and Deliban were elsewhere, and if Ponn was correct, the alchemist was at the bottom of the steps.

She descended quickly, taking the stairs at a reckless pace. They ended in an abandoned guardroom. She noticed a thin trail of blood, and followed it to a cot against the wall, partially hidden behind a screen. Qalor lay on it, his face contorted. He looked at her and groaned. "Not you again. Haven't you tormented me enough?"

"Hardly," she said. Although his body had already been warped and twisted from his work, she thought that the tumble might have dislocated his right shoulder. He had other worries, though; his right leg was badly broken, the bone protruding from the skin. That was the source of the bleeding. She had hoped to take him as a hostage and a source of information, but in this condition that would be impossible. She would have to carry him up the stairs and out of the castle, and she could hardly do that. "Tell me why I shouldn't kill you right now for all that you've done."

"You would murder a man in this condition?"

"A man such as you?" Diasa said. "A man who was party to the destruction of my home? Who breeds monsters and crafts terrible weapons? I would, and I will."

"I was only doing as my liege commanded."

"Spoken like a true scoundrel."

He closed his eyes. "Get on with it, then."

She just stood there, and after a moment Qalor opened his eyes again. He said: "Well?"

"Tell me where you got those scrolls," she said.

After a careful climb, Ponn reached the top of the flooded steps. The door that earlier had been barred now stood open. He splashed across a shabby, barren room and entered a cavernous chamber that could only be Qalor's laboratory.

Suddenly a massive talon snatched him up, holding him roughly, the way a bully might hold a doll he had grabbed from a smaller child, just before dashing it against a rock. "T'Sian!" he cried.

"*Pyodor Ponn.*" The claw brought him up to the massive head, where one of T'Sian's smoldering eyes examined him. "*What are* you *doing here?*"

"Diasa asked me the same thing," Ponn said, "and I didn't have a satisfactory answer for her either."

The dragon set him down. Frigid water coursed over his feet and ankles, spurting from twisted pipes nearby. An iron wheel jutted from the wall nearby; that must be the water shut-off that Diasa had mentioned. It looked similar to the one that Wyst used to open the cesspool door, so it perhaps operated the same way. *"Has Diasa caught the alchemist yet?"*

"Probably," Ponn said. "She sent me here to make the water stop." He went to the wheel turned it, first one way and then, when it refused to move, the other. After a few rotations the flow of water diminished; after a few more it stopped, except for a slow, steady trickle from one of the pipes.

When he turned away, the dragon's head was right behind him, startling him. *"I've taken some of each crystal,"* she said. *"Even now they burn inside me."*

"You have your fire back?"

"Yes."

"Time to go, then?"

"Yes. You and the others must leave."

"What about you?"

"I will depart the same way I entered," she said. *"But my business here is not quite finished."*

"What are you going to do?"

Her glittery eyes narrowed; she moved her head even closer to him. Her face was as big as his body.

"I am going to see how an alchemist's shop burns," she said.

Her head full of information hastily related by Qalor, Diasa rushed up the stairs to the room where she had met Pyodor Ponn. He was not there, but the footpad was, sitting against the wall looking bedraggled and exhausted. He glanced at her as she entered, then looked away.

"Ponn hasn't come back yet?" she asked.

"No."

"Nor T'Sian?"

"No one has been here."

She crossed to the other side, but had only climbed a few steps before Ponn burst through the door and came racing toward her. He wasn't looking where he was going and nearly crashed into her, but she caught him and pushed him back. "Has the dragon taken the crystals?" she demanded.

"Yes."

"Hellfire. Where is she?"

"Gone up the chimney."

"Did you shut off the water?" Diasa said.

"Yes."

"Double hellfire. You must turn it back on."

"What? Why?"

"Qalor claims he did something to change the nature of the blue crystals. He says that if they're not kept cold, they'll become unstable."

"What does that mean?"

"I don't know, but he insisted the water be kept flowing, or something bad would happen."

"You can't possibly trust him."

"Of course I don't, but in this, I will take him at his word."

"If that's the case," Ponn said, "then we have a problem."

"Why?" Then, realizing something: "Do I smell smoke?"

The chimney proved to be a tighter squeeze than T'Sian had anticipated; the rough stone scratched at her diamond-hard scales, plucked at her folded wings. It was not like the vertical shaft that led to her lair after all; that was a sturdy passage through solid rock. Here, her talons kept dislodging bricks and masonry as she climbed, making the going treacherous.

Men and their works. Always imitating nature, and never succeeding.

She passed the kitchen, feeling the warmth of the fire that burned in the great hearth. Once she passed it, the chimney widened; the heat and pressure that had been building beneath her eased as the vapor from Qalor's burning laboratory found escape through the large fireplace. The kitchen would quickly fill with smoke now, and from there it would spread through the castle. She imagined the inhabitants gasping and choking as they tried to breathe the toxic air.

Good. Very, very good.

She hoped Pyodor Ponn had found a way to escape.

The dragon continued to draw herself upward, toward the spot of light at the top of the shaft. She had more than enough fire now to destroy this castle, and the town below it, and the surrounding countryside, and anything else in Dunshandrin's realm that could burn.   They would all pay for what they had done to her and her babies, oh, yes.

As she neared the top of the chimney she saw that there was some sort of cap over it, to keep out rain or snow or nesting birds. She spat at it, blowing it wide open; the shaft brightened as sunlight poured in like golden honey. She wondered if anyone had seen the flames shoot out of the chimney, if they understood what was about to befall them. The dragon reached upward, grasped the edges of the huge chimney with her front talons. Crumbling stone cascaded down the shaft, bounced off her face and head, clattered into the depths. With a final pull she drew herself forth, rising from the aperture like a dark, sinuous curl of smoke. She perched there for a moment, still as a gargoyle, surveying her surroundings.

Shapes surrounded the chimney, fluttering up to meet her: Men, mounted on eagles, just as she had faced in Astilan. But this time the wizard was not with them; this time they would not dare use their exploding devices, not above their own castle.

Eager to meet them, to demonstrate her mastery of the air, T'Sian spread her wings and leapt into the welcoming sky.

Ponn and Diasa returned to the room where Adaran waited, lying on the floor, like a drunkard who had been assaulted in an alley, robbed, and left for dead.   He looked at them as they entered.   "Are we leaving now?"

"Yes," Diasa said. "As fast as we can." The two of them hauled Adaran to his feet; he put an arm over each of their shoulders and they proceeded into the room that housed the cesspool. Wyst glanced at them and then turned away, evidently uninterested in their comings and goings; if she wondered about the smoke, she said nothing.

"*This* is your escape route?" Diasa said.

"Yes, unless you think we can get out through the castle," Ponn said. Leaving her to hold up Adaran, Ponn went to the wheel and turned it as Wyst had demonstrated, locking it in the open position. Wyst watched him, her face impassive. Ponn hesitated, then knelt next to her, checking the chain that tethered the girl to the floor. It was attached to the ring by a padlock; would one of the keys he had found open it? He began fumbling through them. "Ponn!" Diasa cried. "There's no time for that! We have to go. There's no telling what will happen when the fire reaches Qalor's chemicals!"

"We can't leave her here," Ponn said. He returned to the lock, trying one key after another, while Diasa made strangled noises of alarm. Smoke continued to drift into the room, thickening, the acrid tang beginning to overpower even the stench of filth and garbage. Finally one of the keys worked; the padlock popped open, allowing him to pull the chain free of the iron ring.

Wyst didn't move.

He went to the ladder that led into the pit. Diasa had already climbed down and was waiting at the bottom, eyeing the maw of the chute with considerable distaste. Ignoring the girl for the moment, Ponn helped Adaran down; the injured man made the climb gingerly, one rung at a time. When he was near the bottom, Diasa simply plucked him off the ladder and deposited him on the filth-ridden floor.

Wyst still hadn't moved.

"Are you mad?" Ponn cried. "Come with us! If you stay here, you'll choke!"

The girl shook her head, almost imperceptibly. "I have to stay," she said. "I'm being punished."

"Ponn, just leave her!" Diasa shouted.

He hesitated. Wyst obviously had no intention of coming willingly, and with the burden of Adaran he was in no position to drag her along. If there was time, perhaps he could come back for her. Muttering an apology to the girl's spirit, just in case, he swung himself around and slid down the ladder, taking the lead in the low, narrow chute. Going down proved more treacherous than going up; he had to sit, brace himself against the walls, and slide a few feet at a time. Adaran came next, his feet against Ponn's back; if Ponn slipped and began to slide, both of them would shoot out through the lift gate and over the precipice. He hoped Diasa had hold of Adaran's arms or shoulders, but doubted it; she was probably fully occupied with keeping herself in position.

At last they reached the bottom, emerging onto the narrow ledge between castle and cliff. He heard a commotion from above, alarm bells and shouting. He didn't know if it was because of the fire or because T'Sian had put in an appearance. Either way, attention was unlikely to focus on three bedraggled potholers.

Adaran crawled to the edge and eyed the drop to the river. "I can't climb this," he said. "Not now."

Diasa said: "This is how you got into the castle?"

"I'm a good climber," Ponn said.

"Well, I'm not," Diasa said. "Is there an easier way?"

"No."

"This may be the most poorly planned rescue attempt I've ever witnessed," she muttered.

"I didn't bring you out of the castle to leave you trapped here." Ponn stood; something semi-liquid sucked loose from the back of his cloak, splattering his ankles when it hit the rock. He ignored it. "I will get you down."

"Where's your pet dragon when we need her?" Diasa asked.

"Don't let T'Sian hear you call her my pet," Ponn said. "In any case, she's probably getting ready to destroy the castle. She won't concern herself with rescuing us right now." He began to lower himself over the edge of the cliff, swinging his legs over the brink and then turning to face them, his arms braced against the sides of the chute.

"Where are you going?" Diasa said.

"We have no choice. I will go back to the village and see if I can find a rope."

"And what are we supposed to do while we're waiting?"

After a moment, Ponn said: "Try to remain inconspicuous."

Adaran watched Ponn disappear over the edge of the cliff, feeling an odd mix of gratitude and resentment. Not long ago, Adaran had run through the castle, scaled the walls, jumped into the river, unstoppable as the wind; now he was reduced to an invalid, watching Ponn climb to freedom down a bluff that Adaran ought to have been able to descend as easily as walking down a street.

Diasa gave Adaran an unfriendly look. "All this trouble, just to rescue a footpad."

"A footpad is a common robber, a highwayman," Adaran said. "I'm a professional burglar. People pay me to penetrate secure places and retrieve things for them."

"Retrieve things." The distinction didn't appear to impress her.

"Whether you waylay travelers along a path or break into someone's palace, you're still a thief. You take what doesn't belong to you, or to the person who hired you."

"Like Pyodor Ponn's daughter, for instance."

After a moment, she said: "One good deed doesn't absolve all your sins."

He turned away. "I'm not going to argue with you."

"You've got no grounds for arguing."

Suddenly the wall to his back began to vibrate, the ground to shake. A roaring sound came from the mouth of the cesspool, like the rumble of a distant, massive cataract. Moments later, a section of castle wall ten or fifteen feet above the ledge not far to the south of them erupted outward in a burst of smoke and fire, sending stone and bricks and mortar cascading into the river. The roar became much louder, as if the waterfall were coming down right on their heads; then it faded, echoing off the surrounding hills. Black smoke continued to belch from the opening, thick and bilious, and *sinking* rather than floating away as proper smoke did.

"What was *that*?" Adaran said. His hearing felt deadened, as if he had jammed his fingers in his ears and forgotten to remove them.

"T'Sian set fire to Qalor's lab," Diasa said. "The chemicals must have exploded. I was afraid that might happen." Then: "If the wind changes, we should move away from the smoke. It won't be healthy to breathe."

Adaran thought of the Enshennean, clinging to the cliff wall. It had looked like a tricky climb before the explosion. He crawled to the edge, ignoring the pain in his hands and feet, and looked down the chute. Pyodor Ponn's filthy cloak lay among the rocks at the bottom, stuck on a jagged edge, one end of it trailing in the water like the branch of a fallen tree.

As he watched, it came loose and floated away.

Tolaria's shirt felt cold and wet and her left side hurt. She blinked a few times, then realized that she was on the floor again. The wooden cup Prehn had brought her lay at her side, overturned and empty. She pushed herself to a sitting position, leaned against the foot of the bed. Her head felt stuffed with dead leaves, dry and prickly. Another vision had overwhelmed her; was she becoming like Wert, a helpless victim of what had once been her gift?

"Prehn?" Her voice came out a croak; or maybe it didn't come out at all, and she only thought she had spoken. After a moment, though, the wide-eyed child peeked around the corner of Diasa's bed.

"Prehn, you must tell me … what did I say?"

At first she thought the girl would not answer, but then she did, in the barest whisper: "Thunder."

"I said something about thunder?"

Prehn nodded.

"Did I say anything—" She broke off as a rumble rattled the shutters on the window, making the floor quiver and the straw menagerie dance across the tabletop. Tolaria felt the vibration deep in her gut. She stumbled to the window, yanked the shutters open, poked her head out into the alley. Over the rooftops, she saw a large plume of smoke rising above the castle, curling, bulbous on top like a spreading fungus. Within the roiling cloud, tiny crystalline flecks glittered blue and red in the slanting rays of the sun.

What was it? Was it the dragon?

Behind her, Prehn said: "Boom."

21

QALOR'S LABORATORY HAD EXPLODED; HIS noxious deviltry and T'Sian's fire had proven a destructive mix, the blast leveling the southern quarter of the keep. The shockwave hit her as she swooped toward the men and their flying mounts. The dragon pulled up sharply, folding her wings inward to protect them, hanging motionless for a heartbeat. Heat rippled upward, pushing smoke and fire into a gigantic bloom. The eagles squawked and screeched as their riders fought for control; one of the men, improperly secured no doubt, fell from his seat and plummeted to the rocks below. The bird turned and flew back toward its aviary like a riderless horse returning to the stable.

Many of the defenders had been killed or stunned by the blast, but others had begun hauling devices onto the ramparts. These were clearly projectile weapons, enormous versions of the crossbows that they carried; they looked powerful enough to actually harm her should their aim be true. T'Sian spread her wings to catch the hot, rising air. She could see slivers of crystal floating amid the smoke and cinders, glimmering, dropping back into the castle as the updraft weakened. She gave a few beats, lifting herself higher, then wheeled around, dove, and laid a blanket of fire across the castle walls, setting man and machine ablaze. She heard small explosions from the area as she glided away.

She began a sharp vertical climb, knowing as earthbound men did not that altitude was an advantage in an aerial battle. The remaining riders had regrouped, and pursued her as she rose higher above the castle. Did they think they could harm her with their puny arrows?

Did they think she would allow them to drop their little bombs on her head? Foolish amateurs.

T'Sian pierced the low-hanging shroud of mist that hung over the castle, passing quickly through the cold, clinging vapor into a layer of crisp, clear air above. She stopped there, holding herself steady, waiting for her pursuers to appear so that she could burn them.

But before that happened, something collapsed over her back and hindquarters, fouling her wings. Startled, she began to fall, thrashing, trying to get free, but her struggles only tangled her more deeply. She twisted her long neck this way and that, spotting a rapidly retreating formation of eagle-riders. They had dropped a huge, weighted net on her, snaring her, turning her from a glider into a stone.

She lost sight of them as she plunged into the wispy clouds; but she heard them cheering, thinking she would be dashed to death against the jagged rocks below.

Foolish, foolish men.

After the explosion, Tolaria couldn't stay inside any longer. Hoping there would be too much commotion for anyone to pay attention to her, she took Prehn's hand and headed downstairs. As she expected, the common room had emptied into the street. She led Prehn out to the square, where villagers had gathered in small groups, staring at the roiling plume over the keep. They pointed, they whispered, they gasped and exclaimed when the sound of minor explosions reached their ears; overall, they seemed to find it a grand entertainment.

Tolaria headed north toward the castle, thinking she might get a better view from the main street. Along the way she passed a tavern whose sign depicted an eagle, its claws outstretched, its hooked beak open in a screech. One of the windows had a broken shutter. This must be where they had found Qalor. Diasa had killed a guard here, hadn't she? He had been helpless, unconscious, and she had stabbed him. Was he still inside?

Tolaria kept going. There was no reason for her to go look; she could do nothing to help a dead man. Besides, she had Prehn with her, and Prehn didn't need to see something like that. She stopped near the fountain, not far from the avenue that led out of town, up the the hillside, and across the stone bridge to the castle gate. She'd passed this way when riding in Dunshandrin's carriage, and again, on foot, when she had fled the castle in disguise. She noticed a nearby vendor, a purveyor of cloth and hats, who seemed to be closing up his booth. A few others were doing the same, but most seemed to take the milling crowd as an opportunity to hawk their wares even more loudly than usual. She went to the milliner's tent and asked, "What's going on?"

The man didn't look up; he was busily stuffing bolts of blue and red and orange fabric into a large sack behind the counter, perhaps getting ready to flee with his most expensive stock. "There was a fire at the castle, and then a dragon," he said.

"A dragon?" T'Sian had come out in her true form, then; and if she had fired the castle, she must have found the crystals. Tolaria searched the sky, but did not see the great beast. "Where did she go?"

"I'm not mad!" he cried, evidently thinking she doubted him. "It burned the castle, then flew up into the clouds!" He stood, hefting the sack over his shoulder like a runaway who had been unable to decide what to take and what to leave. "If you're wise, you'll flee, instead of staying here and watching like these other fools."

She mumbled thanks and led Prehn away from the man's booth, moving a short distance toward the castle. It loomed on its promontory, belching smoke from the side and along the battlements. Eagles flitted nervously about the towers. They reminded her of flies around a rotten piece of meat.

Where was T'Sian?

Suddenly a gasp went up from the people assembled in the square. What had they seen? It had to be the dragon, but where? She turned in a circle, scanning the sky, looking for T'Sian, but Prehn spotted her first. She raised her arm, pointed with a chubby finger. "Falling," she said.

"Oh, no," Tolaria whispered, as T'Sian, hopelessly entangled in a massive net, plunged toward rocky spires near the castle.

Diasa looked up as a shadow passed overhead, hoping the dragon was returning; but no, it was just one of the monstrous eagles, vanishing over the castle wall. Was it fleeing the battle, or moving to attack the dragon from a different direction? Or perhaps it was looking for other intruders.

She nudged Adaran. "We can't stay here," she said. "The twins have eagles in the air. We'll be spotted soon, if we haven't been already."

Adaran sighed. "Maybe I can steal one and fly away."

"That may have worked once, but I doubt you'll be so lucky a second time." She looked at the sky as shouts went up from the castle, wondering what the rampaging dragon had done now. "We're too exposed."

"What are you planning to do?"

"Go back into the cesspool."

"You want to go back inside? Are you mad?"

"No, but neither do I want to sit here waiting to be shot."

"Go if you want to," Adaran said. "I'll stay here, if it's all the same to you."

"Fine. Stay there. But don't expect me to rush to your aid when an eagle is feasting on your liver."

"I'll expect nothing from you whatsoever."

Diasa grunted and crawled back into the chute. A strong, acrid, smoky odor lay over the smell of human waste, as if someone had set fire to a field of manure and then tried to douse it with sulfur. She soon emerged into the cesspool, finding that chunks of wood and masonry and broken pipe now littered the basin. Most of the debris had come from the ceiling, which must have cracked in the blast; she also found pieces of the door and the battered remains of the lantern, still feebly burning.

She paused, listening, but the chamber was silent now. Most of the smoke had cleared, escaped through cracks and the massive hole blown in the castle; if anything, the air was somewhat less noisome than it had been the first time she had come through. A cool blue glow suffused the chamber, neither torch nor gas light; indeed, it was like no illumination she had ever seen before. Diasa didn't know what this meant, but it could hardly be anything good.

She picked her way through the rubble to the ladder and climbed out of the pit. There was the girl Ponn had tried to save; her body lay on the far side of the basin, wedged up against the wall. The explosion must have flung her there. Her ragged clothes had been burned off her back, exposing skin, once pale but now scorched by the flames; her long hair had burned to the roots, leaving her head charred and naked.

Diasa turned away, feeling a pang of guilt that she couldn't quite suppress. Perhaps if she had not hurried him so, Ponn could have convinced her to escape with them. She shook her head, reminded herself that the foolish girl had insisted on staying behind. She had been doomed by her own inaction; she hadn't *wanted* to be rescued. And if they had stayed much longer trying to persuade her, the blast would have caught them as well.

All true. But still, a girl who seemed blameless was dead, while Diasa had helped a common criminal get to safety. Unexpectedly troubled by this, she moved to the open doorway, where she stopped, staring into the antechamber. Here was the source of the blue glow: A mass of crystals had grown down the stairs from the laboratory, like a jagged, spiny glacier crawling along a mountain valley. The stuff had already spread halfway across the room, covering most of the side wall and encroaching on the ceiling and floor. Her ears detected a faint, glassy crackle, as if the walls whispered in shocked dismay; she realized that the sound came from the dragon stones as they crept across the surface, as the facets jousted with each other to see which could grow tallest.

If this was what Qalor had meant when he'd said the crystals would become unstable if not kept cool, then he'd been right. Spectacularly.

She backed away from the door, not liking the feeling the crystals engendered on her skin, a sensation of prickly heat like the beginning of a sunburn. The crystals shed energy the way a ditch-digger shed sweat in the summertime, and Qalor had told her that too much exposure could be dangerous. How much was too much? A minute? An hour?

In any case, she couldn't get through here. The ceiling had partially collapsed, blocking the door to the dungeon stairs; and she wasn't about to crawl over the blue crystals in an attempt to get to the dead-end laboratory. She returned to the cesspool instead, climbed back down the ladder, and made her way back to the ledge. Adaran was still there, lying in the shadow of the wall like a laborer who had decided to take a break. Seeing her, he said: "What happened? I thought you were going to sneak into the castle and conquer it from within."

"Something else is doing that already," she said.

* * *

T'Sian quickly examined the net: Thick rope, weighted at the corners, studded with metal barbs to dig in and keep it in place. The hooks did not even scratch her armor plating, but some had found purchase at her joints, against her wings, in the grooves between her scales. Her initial surprised thrashing had only entangled her more, let the hooks dig deeper; and the material was remarkably tough, as if it had been impregnated with the very essence of the stone on which the castle stood. More of the alchemist's work, no doubt.

But this net had not really been meant to hold the likes of her; it was made of rope and leather, and it would burn. She let loose a spray of fire over her back and wings, enough to ignite a small stand of trees; to her astonishment, this proved insufficient. The rope, blackened and smoldering, remained tight across her body; the metal hooks glowed dull red but kept their shape and their bite.

Unnerved now, T'Sian opened her mouth and drenched herself with fire, holding nothing back this time. She felt the heat of the stones inside her, a raging burn like nothing she had ever experienced before; the fire ate at her skin, so intense that it was actually *painful*. But it worked: The net loosened, then disintegrated; bits of molten metal dropped away, red-hot and steaming, falling to the ground like burning rain. Her wings broke free; she spread them wide, felt them catch the air. The great muscles across her back pulled taut against her spine and ribs, threatening to tear free of the bone; she was pulling too hard, she was going to injure herself. She banked downward, toward the village and the lake, then angled up, moving toward level instead of trying to reverse course. The surface of the water skimmed by beneath her, gleaming in the waning sunlight. The air felt icy on her wounded skin and her breast felt as if she had swallowed the sun; Qalor's altered stones burned so hot and so bright, not even *she* was proof against them.

No time to worry about that now, not while her enemies thought they ruled the sky. She tilted her wings upward and rose away from the lake, sweeping in a great arc back toward the castle. Eagles flitted among the towers, but they carried nothing like the net that had humiliated her and nearly brought her down. Four riders moved forward to engage her as she swept by the castle. She veered to meet them as they started firing their little weapons at her. She scarcely felt the arrows as they bounced off her scales; one or two pierced her wings, mild pinpricks, nothing more. One rider broke formation, retreating behind the castle. She let him go for now, concentrating on the others. Now that she was closer, they had loaded different ammunition, perhaps something with a shorter range. She sensed the power of her crystals in the new projectiles. They still hoped to defeat her with the alchemist's devices; they still thought that having the dragon stones could make them the dragons.

Perhaps they were right; she had considered these men to be less than nothing without the wizard at their backs, but she would not underestimate them again.

T'Sian closed the gap and bathed them in fire before they had a chance to discharge their weapons. The men screamed for a moment, their mounts screeched in pain and terror; then they exploded like overheated stones, popping one by one. Burning chunks of meat and saddlery flew into the castle like tiny shooting stars.

Banking to the right, the dragon went in pursuit of the rider who had fled. None would escape her wrath.

Not today.

Adaran watched as the dragon set herself on fire, escaped from the net, and swept up the hillside toward the castle. She was not merely a larger version of the hatchlings that he and the others had fought and killed; she was something an order of magnitude greater, like the difference between a summer storm and a hurricane. The great beast didn't notice them, didn't even look their way, before she disappeared over the castle wall to engage her enemies once more.

"Now we'll see something interesting," Diasa murmured. But they didn't see anything, interesting or otherwise; whatever action the dragon took, it was out of their view. They heard things, though: Men screaming, eagles shrieking, another round of small explosions. Suddenly a low-flying eagle came around the corner of the keep, evidently fleeing from the carnage. The rider spotted them and veered closer, crossbow leveled. Diasa stood and faced him, sword at the ready, though he was well out of range of her blade.

"Identify yourselves!" the man cried.

"Fly on, before the dragon roasts you!" Diasa countered.

Discomfited, the rider glanced back the way he had come, as if expecting to see the monster bearing down on him. He looked at Diasa, then lowered his weapon and urged his mount onward, flying off to the north, staying low before vanishing among the hills. Diasa, watching him go, sighed and put her sword away, as if she were disappointed that the man hadn't landed so that they could fight.

Suddenly a vast shadow swept by and a rush of wind buffeted them. The dragon had come looking for the rider, just as Diasa had threatened, swooping down from over the castle wall. It seemed as if she would pass without seeing them, but Diasa shouted: "T'Sian!"

The dragon pulled up short, holding herself steady on enormous wings that spanned wider than the river. Her head swiveled on her sinuous neck, luminous eyes regarding them for a moment before she flew toward them, landing on the bluff. Her cruel, curved talons dug into the stone as if it were mere earthwork. "*What are you doing here, Diasa?*" she said, her voice like lightning. Adaran, astonished, tried not to gawk; he had never imagined he might hear a dragon speak. The hatchlings hadn't, neither threats nor pleas for mercy, as he and the others had killed them.

"We can't get down. Will you carry us back to the village?"

"*There will not be a village for much longer.*"

"You can't destroy it while Tolaria is there."

"*I have my fire back. I will do as I please.*"

"If not for Tolaria, you would have as much fire as a toad. Is this how you would reward those who have aided you?"

The dragon regarded them with glittering, alien eyes; Adaran lowered his gaze and waited to be incinerated for Diasa's effrontery. What fool would expect gratitude from a creature such as this?

Then Diasa said: "Ponn would be very disappointed in you."

"*Very well,*" the beast said. "*I will take you to Tolaria.*"

"Thank you," Diasa said.

"*The castle is already burning and its defenders are in disarray, so this is a small thing, and of no consequence.*"

"Of course," Diasa said. "It means nothing."

"*Yes. Nothing.*" Adaran felt the monster's gaze on him, and raised his gaze to see it regarding him coldly. "*Who is this pitiful creature?*"

"This is Adaran," Diasa said. "He was a prisoner in the castle; he has been tortured and beaten. This is the man Ponn came to rescue."

"And where is Pyodor Ponn, Diasa? Why is he not with you?"
After a moment, Diasa said: "I'll tell you on the way."
"*Tell me now*," the dragon said.

Tolaria had stood by as the market square steadily emptied after the dragon freed herself from the net and returned to the castle to battle Dunshandrin's fliers; the exodus had increased dramatically once it became obvious that T'Sian would win the aerial battle. By the time she came at the town, flying low over the square, there were few people left to scream and flee. Those who did, though, were most dramatic about it, running into alleys or hiding under carts or simply lying with their faces against the dirty cobbles as if already dead.

She turned in a circle, watching T'Sian glide past, then bank left and return to the square. She had wondered if this might be an attack, if T'Sian would begin to rain fire down on the homes and shops; but instead she landed in the square, crushing a number of stalls, one massive claw smashing the poor, sad fountain into rubble. The beating of her wings tipped over nearby wagons and sent tents and awnings cartwheeling across the flagstones.

She opened her front talons, releasing two people. One was Diasa; the other was a man she had never seen before, thin, dirty, shabby, and very clearly injured. This must be Adaran, she realized.

Two people. Someone was missing.

Tolaria began walking toward them. Prehn started trying to pull free; Tolaria let go of her and she ran to the startled-looking Adaran, wrapping her arms around his leg. "Adwan!" she cried. Then, wrinkling her nose: "You smell bad."

"We just crawled through a sewer," Diasa said.

Tolaria said: "What?"

"Ponn's escape route led through the cesspool."

"Where is Ponn?" Tolaria said.

For a moment, T'Sian regarded Tolaria with gemstone eyes; then she spread her wings and launched herself into the air, winging back toward the castle. She found herself shivering, unnerved by the dragon's alien gaze.

"Adaran needs assistance," Diasa said.

Still staring after the dragon, Tolaria moved toward the injured man. "What's happened?" she said. "Where's Ponn?"

Diasa gave Prehn a sidelong glance, then moved closer to Tolaria. "Ponn's gone," she said quietly. "He fell into the river and was swept away."

"What? We must find him!"

"We can do him little good now. All we would do is present enticing targets for Dunshandrin's archers, should any remain." Diasa shook her head. "If he drowned, he is already beyond our help; if he did not, he is more likely to find his way to safety if not encumbered by escaped prisoners and known invaders of the castle."

"But what if he's injured?"

"He would want us to keep his daughter safe." Then, seeing the look on her face: "What would you have me do, Tolaria? It is down to the two of us. Should I watch over Prehn and Adaran while you search the river, or should I leave you my sword and go myself?"

Tolaria could hardly argue in favor of either option. "All right," she said. "But later, when it is safe, we will search for him."

"Of course." She glanced at Prehn. "I will say nothing to the girl until we know for sure what happened. If she asks you where her father is, try to say that you don't know. After all, it is the truth."

"I won't know what my answer will be until the question is asked," Tolaria said. She moved past Diasa, to where Adaran sat on the dusty cobbles. He stank of excrement, the odor woven through with red threads of infection; but his wounds were so filthy and numerous, it was hard for her to tell which might be inflamed. "I can make a poultice to help you heal," she told him. She looked at Diasa. "I'll need hot water and herbs that they may have in the kitchen at the inn."

"We can go to the inn to look for your herbs, but we can't stay there," Diasa said. "T'Sian agreed to spare the village only long enough for us to escape. She'll return soon, and she will be ... indiscriminate."

"But there are *people* here!"

"Of course there are. If there were no people here, she would hardly bother to destroy the town, would she?"

"These are peasants and fishermen. They aren't responsible for what Dunshandrin has done. They don't deserve to have their homes burned to the ground."

"If you think you can persuade the dragon of that," Diasa said, "feel free to stand atop the tallest building you can find, and shout at her when she goes by."

With Diasa supporting one of his arms and Tolaria supporting the other—and, of course, Prehn sitting on his shoulders—Adaran managed the short, painful walk to the inn. The dining hall was quiet, the fire doused; three other guests remained, standing near the hearth, speaking in low, urgent tones. It looked as if they, like others of good sense, were preparing to leave town before the dragon returned.

Tolaria went into the kitchen, while Diasa went upstairs to collect their few belongings. Adaran sagged onto a bench near the door and waited for them to return. That seemed his lot these days: Sitting, waiting, unable to do much for himself. He looked down at Prehn, sitting next to him, and said, "I'm not the same man I was when I rescued you, am I?"

She shook her head.

"Do you think I'll be better someday?"

Prehn shrugged. She was only a little girl; how could she know what his fate would be?

Tolaria came back, carrying a few small pouches. "Most everything is locked away, but I found some old flour to make paste, and a few dried herbs."

"Thank you," he said. Then: "So you're the oracle."

"I'm *an* oracle. There are others."

Redshen had occasionally consulted oracles before they took on exceptionally questionable capers; most of them had been female, and all of them had been old. Tolaria, on the other hand, was practically a child; if she'd passed her twentieth summer, it had probably been the one that had just ended. "I didn't expect you to be so young," Adaran said. Tolaria flushed. "Now I've embarrassed you."

"No, it's all right. More than one petitioner told me the same thing while I was at the Crosswaters. So did the other oracles, when I first arrived." She looked at the floor. "They're all dead now, anyway. Dunshandrin destroyed the complex, burned it to the ground, to test his new weapons."

Feeling foolish, Adaran mumbled an apology. Tolaria didn't

respond.   He thought again of Redshen.   She hadn't gone to the oracle when Dunshandrin's man had come with his offer; the summons had been urgent, there had been no time for such things.

If she *had* gone, what would the oracle have told her?

Diasa came clanking down the stairs, carrying some rolled-up blankets and a sack.   The men near the fire stopped whispering and watched as she went by.   "Ready?" she said.

Tolaria stood.   "Yes."

Diasa glanced over her shoulder as the smallest of the three men approached.   He looked like a merchant, Adaran thought, albeit a rather shabby one; if he saw the man on the street, he would have deemed the risk of cutting his purse not worth the potential reward. The other two had a thuggish look about them; mercenaries, most likely, hired by the merchant for protection from the likes of Adaran.

When it became obvious that the man was coming to talk to her, Diasa turned and put her hand on her sword; the merchant stopped and said: "What news from the castle?"

"The castle?" Diasa said. "The dragon is destroying it."

"What of the trading post? Is it intact?"

"If it is, it won't be by the time she's finished."

The merchant glanced nervously at his bodyguards.   "Will Lord Dunshandrin compensate me for the loss of my goods?"

"You must not know Dunshandrin very well, if you are even entertaining that possibility."

"This is my first visit here," the fellow murmured.

"Well, if you don't want it to be your last, you will forget about your merchandise and flee. The dragon will not be satisfied with the castle; she will be coming here next."

The man bowed and thanked Diasa and went back to his henchmen; a whispered argument ensued. Adaran gathered that the mercenaries expected to be paid regardless of the merchant's misfortune, but he had nothing with which to pay them.   Being a mercenary himself, Adaran was interested in how the argument would turn out; but then Diasa pulled him to his feet, and Tolaria took his other arm, and the three of them left the inn.

Outside, the street thronged with citizens and villagers fleeing the town. Some were empty-handed, perhaps because they had nothing worth saving, or they expected to be returning to intact homes; others carried their belongings on their backs, or hauled them in carts, or pushed them in wheelbarrows. Families walked together, mothers and fathers with children trailing along behind them like strings. Dogs wove in and out among the dozens of pairs of legs, yapping as they tried to keep up with their owners; goats, pigs, chickens, and other sorts of animals moved with the crowd, under their own power or as baggage. Adaran had never seen such an exodus before.

The two mercenaries passed them, shouldering their way through the crowd. Adaran glanced at Diasa; she had noticed them, too, watching them with narrowed eyes. She shook her head, then turned her gaze elsewhere. He could imagine what had happened; they had collected their pay in the form of the merchant's life and any valuables he might have had with him. At another time, Adaran might have scurried back to the inn and searched the man's body and room, looking for anything the killers had missed. He supposed that Diasa might have confronted the two thugs and held them to account, while Tolaria might have hurried to the merchant's side to see if she could keep him alive.

At another time, perhaps.

But today, they just kept walking.

Limited by Adaran's injuries, they made slow progress; it seemed as if even the smallest child and oldest grandmother walked faster than he did. Finally Diasa spotted an abandoned wheelbarrow overturned in an alley, and had the idea of dumping the footpad into it like a load of manure. Prehn, of course, insisted on climbing into the wheelbarrow with him. Evidently she had adopted him as a sort of surrogate father until Pyodor Ponn rejoined them. Diasa knew little enough about children, but she supposed that eventually the girl would realize that something had happened, that Ponn would not be coming back. Then there would be tears and wailing.

She would let Tolaria handle that.

Traffic became heavier as they moved toward the edge of town. There was a single main road out of the village; the other streets and avenues converged here, funneling everyone into the same spot. Nervous horses plowed furrows through the pedestrians; Diasa saw more than one commoner lying dead or injured, bleeding from wagon wheels or the blow of a driver's cudgel.

She cast a glance back at the castle, visible even from here atop its steep-sided perch. T'Sian flitted among the towers, destroying the keep at her leisure. All serious resistance had been eliminated; no eagles fluttered in the sky, no siege engines fired projectiles. The dragon could have reduced the entire castle to rubble by now, but it seemed that she tarried. Savoring the moment? No, she was looking for something, Diasa thought; the lords of the realm, perhaps, those who had orchestrated the slaughter of her hatchlings. If that was what the dragon sought, Diasa doubted she would find satisfaction. They surely had a bolt-hole or secret passage to ensure their escape in the event of an emergency or an attack, and would have used it at the first sign of serious trouble.

They traveled some distance along the road, moving with the flow of refugees just like wreckage of the castle floated in the river to the left. On the right, a denuded hillside rose gently to scrubby forest. The trees on the slope looked like they had been recently cut; the stumps were fresh, still bleeding sap, the wood not yet weathered. Diasa stopped, set down the wheelbarrow; people broke around them like water over a rock. "This is far enough," she said. "We'll stop here for now."

Adaran eyed the field of cut trees. "Here? This doesn't look like a good place to camp."

"Better than the dungeon, isn't it?" Diasa gave the wheelbarrow a kick, earning her a baleful look from Prehn. "On your feet."

He reached up. "Some assistance?"

She and Tolaria helped Adaran up, each taking an arm over her shoulder, abandoning the wheelbarrow by the riverside. Almost immediately, a passing family began piling their meager belongings into it; a better use than hauling a thief around, Diasa thought. They moved up onto the slope, taking care on the uneven ground, but hadn't gone far before Adaran began to complain, whining and muttering about his feet. Disgusted, Diasa shrugged his arm off her shoulder; Tolaria caught him before he fell and lowered him to the ground. "We're stopping here, then?" Tolaria said, her voice brittle.

"It's as good a place as any," Diasa said. She sat down on a stump, using the last of the daylight to watch T'Sian's antics. The dragon had perched partway up the north tower now, clinging to the bricks in the manner of a desert lizard sunning itself on the side of a rock;

but she clutched a crumbling stone column in her tail, and was using it as a club to smash the roof of the eastern keep. That was a trick no gecko could match. At length she cast aside the pillar and moved to the ruined wall of the keep, staring down into the interior, reminding Diasa of a cat that had spotted a vole and was waiting for it to reappear.

"We need a fire," Tolaria said. "There's a chill, and I must boil water to prepare a poultice."

"Fine," Diasa said, not looking at her. "They left behind plenty of branches when they cut down the trees. I'm sure you can find sufficient kindling to start an inferno."

After a moment, Tolaria said: "Yes, I suppose I can." Diasa heard her move off to gather wood. The oracle didn't like her much, Diasa supposed; she had probably been accustomed to being coddled for her talents and her looks, before the twins had taken her. In Tolaria's world, Diasa would be gathering the branches and laying them at her feet, lighting the fire, fetching her slippers.

This was *Diasa's* world, though.

And in Diasa's world, the woman with the sword did not gather the wood.

22

THE STONES WERE GROWING.

From her perch on the rampart, T'Sian could see the mass of blue crystals within the castle. She had cracked the keep open like a tasty bone, laying bare its marrow of hallways and stairs and chambers. The explosion of Qalor's laboratory had seeded the place with crystals, scattering bits of them across the structure. The red ones had merely fallen to the ground, but the blue ones had taken hold where they touched a surface, affixing themselves, spreading.

T'Sian was not sure what to make of this. She had never seen the crystals behave this way. They grew, but only at the source, where they were pushed up from the depths of the earth. Once removed, they did not continue to spread; they sat quietly in the back of her lair, where she could go and consume them when her fires burned low. If they *did* grow in the lair, then there would be no need to travel to the icy wastes north of Yttribia, to plumb the depths of the glacial caverns. Sometimes dragons died there, old ones mostly, overcome by the cold. She had seen the massive corpses, brittle and frozen, claws outstretched as if they were still trying to drag themselves along the frigid stone.

Clearly, Qalor had done this; the clever man had altered the crystals to make them grow for him, so that he would not have to go in search of them in the future. He wanted to raise them himself and have an endless supply. Why just the blue stones, though? Why not the red ones as well?

The damaged wall suddenly gave way beneath her, crumbling in a shower of rubble. She let go and gave her great wings a few beats, lifting her into the air, blowing dust, smoke, and cinders into whorls and eddies, covering the glowing stones in a thin layer of grit. Bemused, she left the castle, heading for the village. She circled it a few times, frightening the few humans who remained. She watched as they ran for the cover of their homes or businesses. She had just sacked their leader's fortress, and yet they thought thin walls of wood and plaster would protect them? Foolish men.

She had told Diasa not to remain in the village. Assuming they would have stopped not far from town, the dragon flew in a high spiral, soon spotting them gathered around a small fire on a hillside. She noted a rocky clearing in the woods, not far from where they had camped. She knew that the others preferred to deal with her when she wore a human shape; she could land in the clearing, transform, and approach them in the guise of a woman. She would be less likely to draw an attack that way, but also less able to defend herself.

No. She would stay in her true shape. Their sensitivities were of no concern anymore. They could face her as she was, not as they wished her to be.

She was finished accommodating the prejudices of men.

When Pyodor Ponn awoke, he found himself wedged among the debris that had accumulated against the bridge that led to the castle, like a storm-tossed log or a piece of driftwood. The sky was growing purple, streaked with dusk; he must have been in the water for quite some time. He thought for a moment, trying to remember how he had gotten here. He had been climbing down the cliff when there had been an explosion, like the ones Dunshandrin's forces had set off during the raid on Astilan. He'd lost his tenuous grip on the bluff and slid down the chute like a piece of garbage, bouncing off the jagged rocks at the bottom, striking his head. That was the last thing he remembered before waking up here. He reached up and felt his skull, finding a huge lump, but the cold had numbed him and there was no pain.

When the current had washed him up against the bridge, he had become entangled in the denuded branches of a tree; its half-rotted limbs cradled him like the arms of a rescuer, but they could just have easily have pinned him below the water and drowned him. In life, this must have been a beneficent tree. He gave brief thanks to its departed spirit for saving his life. Now he had to get out of the water; if he stayed much longer in the icy river, the cold would succeed in killing him where the water had failed. Taking hold of the branches with trembling hands, he hauled himself onto the unstable mat of reeds and leaves and yellowed grasses. He crawled along this small island, feeling it shift beneath his weight. His right hand suddenly broke through the thin crust of dry vegetation, plunging into a cold, wet, sticky layer of sand and muck and refuse from the cesspool. He freed himself with effort; the clammy mud didn't want to give up its prize, clinging to his wrist as he struggled to work it loose. When he finally pulled free, he nearly toppled over backwards, but the dead tree intervened again, catching him with its branches and keeping him from falling into the river.

After regaining his balance, Ponn rested a moment, then moved forward again. He soon reached the base of the bridge, where the pile rested on a foundation of stone. Holding the rock, he pulled himself to his feet; his legs were numb and weak, it felt very much like standing on a poorly constructed raft. Shivering, he peered under the bridge. The column rose from a small island of red rock that jutted up from the river; the arch curved overhead, an unbroken expanse of stone. This was a natural bridge, he realized; they had reinforced it with bricks and masonry, providing extra support, but the span itself had been carved by the natural action of water and time.

He looked up at the castle. Tendrils of smoke rose from a number of places, twining around each other like vines, eventually forming a massive, soft-looking column that drifted off to the north. While he'd been unconscious, T'Sian had reduced the place to a ruin; he was sorry to have missed the show.

He thought of Adaran and Diasa. They had been on the ledge beneath the wall when it exploded. Had they survived the blast? The destruction of the castle? Had he rescued Adaran from the dungeon only to leave him buried beneath tons of rubble? He would never find out unless he got off the river; he needed to find warmth and shelter, and quickly. His shivering worsened as his garment slowly dried in the chill night air, sucking warmth out of his body and giving it to the greedy wind. Could he swim or wade to shore? He felt too weak to brave the current as it rushed through the narrow gaps to either side of the stone column. It would surely sweep him away.

Perhaps there was another way out of here. The castle must have maintenance staff that periodically cleared the debris; otherwise it would become completely blocked and the river would flood. They would need a way to get down, unless they were lowered by a rope. Ponn stood and felt around the support, not finding any obvious handholds. He moved to the left, looking under the bridge, where a crumbling ledge of brick and masonry led along the abutment. He stepped down to it, first with his splayed toes, testing it with a few firm pushes. It seemed sturdy, so he followed with his other foot, standing on the narrow surface. Keeping his back against the rock, he sidled along the walkway. The water rushed by in front of him, black and foamy.

He soon emerged on the other side of the bridge. The platform was a larger here, giving him room to stand without fear of a misstep plunging him into the river. He spotted a crude ladder, as he had hoped, iron rungs leading up the piling to the top of the bridge. He had just grasped the first one when he heard a roar from the castle, reminding him of the sound when Laquin's tower had fallen beneath him, back in Astilan; some large piece of the keep must have just collapsed. He began to climb, taking the rungs as fast as he could in his condition. Halfway up, he felt a familiar rush of wind, the downdraft from enormous wings. T'Sian. He turned his head, evoking a stab of pain from the no longer numb knot on his skull. He saw the dragon gliding away from him, toward the village. He shouted to her, but the river's voice was louder than his and she did not hear.

Would she destroy the village now? Prehn was still there, and Tolaria. He climbed the rest of the way, gaining the top of the bridge while the dragon stalked above the town, a roving shadow against the indigo sky. She had not yet unleashed her fire; she seemed to be searching for something, flying in widening circles until finally she folded her wings to descend, vanishing from his sight. She had landed south of town. If he hurried, perhaps he could catch her before she took off again; he could find out what had happened to Prehn and Tolaria, Adaran and Diasa.

He took a last glance at the ruined, smoldering castle. She had finished with the keep; the town would be next.

Ponn pivoted, and started running.

Once she'd gotten the fire going, Tolaria produced a small, battered pot. She filled it with water from a skin, then put it into the fire to bring it to a boil. Then she took out a long, thin knife. Eyeing it warily, Adaran said: "What's that for?"

She turned it over, examining the blade. "Removing the bones from fowl and small animals," she said. "I'm going to use it to cut your wounds open."

"Why would you need to do that?"

"If they're infected, they must be drained."

"Oh. Will that hurt?"

"Yes."

"I'll do it," Diasa said.

The oracle gave her a half-lidded glare. "I'm not looking for volunteers." She began unwrapping Adaran's stained, stinking bandages, using quick, darting motions, like a bird pecking at an elusive worm. "Whoever dressed these did a poor job."

Diasa snorted. "He's lucky they bothered binding his wounds at all, after he killed Lord Dunshandrin."

"They said they didn't want me to die before they had a chance to question me."

One by one, Tolaria tossed the rags into the fire. "How did you get so filthy in a dungeon?"

"Have you ever *been* in a dungeon?"

"I told you," Diasa said, "Ponn took us out through the cesspool. I'm sure neither of us smells sweet at the moment."

"A cesspool." Tolaria shook her head. "That was the last place you should have been. Look at these injuries."

Adaran did, and wished he hadn't. On his feet, red, raw flesh puckered around the ragged wounds, which had gone dark and blackish in the middle. His hands were in similar condition. Tolaria inspected his palms, frowning. "Wiggle your fingers," she said.

He tried. The digits of his left hand moved as expected, but his right was unresponsive. Alarmed, he cried: "It doesn't work!"

Diasa said: "You're lucky the twins didn't cut them off."

Tolaria looked closely at the wound, as if trying to see through the flesh to the muscles and tendons beneath. "The blade must have severed something inside."

"Can you … can you fix it?"

"No. All I can do is help your body to heal itself. This injury is too severe." She let go of his hand; it fell into his lap, useless, like something broken he had found lying in the road. "I must deal with your left foot; the wound needs lancing." She reached toward the pot of water, which was now at a churning boil, and pulled out the knife. Wisps of steam rose from the blade, as if it were enchanted. "Remember, this is going to hurt."

He closed his eyes. "All right. Go ahead."

"Would you like something to bite down on?"

"Dunshandrin's hand."

"Failing that?"

"Just do—" He broke off with a gasp as a surge of blinding agony stabbed up from his foot. At first he was afraid he might black out; then he was afraid he might not. But the pain subsided quickly, and he opened his eyes to see blood and yellowish fluid mingling as they flowed from his wounded foot.

"The infection must drain for a little while before I apply the poultice," Tolaria said.

Suddenly another portion of the castle erupted in a flash of light, sending dust and debris. A moment later the rumble, like thunder after lightning, rolled across the hillside. "There goes another bit of Qalor's arsenal," Diasa said.

"When Dunshandrin ordered Qalor to make weapons out of the dragon stones, he never expected them to help destroy his own keep," Tolaria said. "It's justice of a sort, I suppose."

Adaran said: "Weapons?"

"Yes," Diasa said. "Qalor used the crystals to make devices that explode and burn, and bred giant eagles to carry them. Ponn said that Dunshandrin used them to destroy Astilan. I'm told they laid waste to entire blocks without having to put a single soldier on the ground."

"That's madness," Adaran said. "If we had known—"

Diasa gave him a sharp look. "If you had known what?"

"Nothing. Never mind."

"Well, if you will not say, then allow me to guess," Diasa said. "If you had known what Dunshandrin was planning, you would never have agreed to work for him." He said nothing; Diasa continued. "I'm not a fool, footpad, even if I do live by my sword. What else would you have been doing in the mountains? How else would you have gotten hold of one of their birds? You went to the dragon's lair. You helped kill T'Sian's hatchlings."

Tolaria looked at Adaran as if he had just reached over and slit Prehn's throat as she slept on the ground beside him. "Is this true?" she said.

He knew Diasa despised him, but he didn't want the oracle to hate him as well. "It was … just a job," he said. "People like Dunshandrin hire people like me all the time. We do things their soldiers can't."

"What did you do?" she asked. "What did you do that his soldiers couldn't?"

"Diasa already—"

"No. *You* tell me. I would hear it from *your* lips."

Resigned, he said: "Dunshandrin sent a group of us to retrieve the dragon stones. After we did the job, his men betrayed us. They killed my partner and a fighter named Jenune, but failed to kill me and the sorcerer, Orioke. I got away, rescued Prehn, stole an eagle, and made my way to Flaurent."

Diasa snorted. "Most likely you left your partner behind in order to escape."

"I did not! They murdered her right in front of my eyes!"

"Her?" Diasa raised an eyebrow. "A partner in more than crime, then?"

Adaran felt himself flush. "She was my best friend," he said. "Nothing more, nothing less."

"Perhaps her death will teach you to be more careful when choosing an employer."

He raised his right hand, limp and useless. "I don't think my services will be much in demand in the future."

Tolaria shook her head, looked off into the night, toward the castle. "You had best pray T'Sian does not learn of your role in this," she said.

"Oh, I don't know," Diasa said. "I think I might like to watch him try to explain that killing her hatchlings was *just a job*."

"You won't tell her, will you?" Adaran asked.

"No," Diasa said, "but only for Ponn's sake. He risked and

probably lost his life to get you out of the castle."

He turned to the oracle. "What about you, Tolaria?"

"I won't tell unless someone asks me."

"What?"

"Our lovely Tolaria is compelled to answer all questions truthfully," Diasa said. "It's a side effect of something the twins did while they held her prisoner. For example: Tolaria, what do you think of Adaran, now that you know what he did?"

"He disgusts me," she said, glaring at him, then at Diasa.

"You see?" Diasa said. "Honesty can be such an ugly thing."

Tolaria excused herself and left to gather wood for the fire, more to avoid having to deal with Diasa and Adaran than because the flames had begun to burn low. She could scarcely believe what she had learned; Ponn had sacrificed himself to rescue Adaran, and he turned out to be one of Dunshandrin's cast-off lackeys. If they hadn't tried to kill him, he would have collected his gold and gone on to perform some other mission for them. It might have been him rather than Gelt on the dock at Achengate, lying in wait to murder her. She'd sensed Diasa's hostility toward the man ever since the dragon brought them back; now she understood it. How long ago had Diasa guessed the truth?

Diasa … the woman alternated between treating her like a crippled, somewhat stupid child and a party favor, her own personal truth-telling device. She almost preferred Klem's outright hostility. At least she knew what to expect from him.

A rush of wind announced the arrival of the dragon. Tolaria quickly spotted her, a huge dark blot against the stars, and followed her approach as she settled down near the campsite. Her scales whisked over the cut stumps, the sound like a giant snake slithering through tall grass. Soon she came into the firelight, looming over it, a monster emerging from nightmare into waking. The flames made her scales glitter, cast mask-like shadows across her face. Diasa stepped up to the giant head; she scarcely reached the level of T'Sian's eyes. The two of them began to talk. Tolaria couldn't make out their words, but she could feel the dragon's deep voice rumbling in her abdomen. Perhaps they were discussing T'Sian's next move. No, not *discussing*; with Ponn gone, Tolaria doubted that the dragon would *discuss* her plans with anyone. Most likely, T'Sian was merely telling Diasa what she was going to do next.

Adaran sat very still near the fire, probably hoping to avoid being noticed. Prehn was back in his lap. The child, innocent that she was, trusted him; she knew nothing of what he had done, only that he had saved her from whatever fate had been waiting for her in the mountains.

The dragon moved away from the fire now, coming across the hill toward Tolaria. She stood there waiting as T'Sian approached, holding an armful of sticks, wondering what the beast might want with her. Soon she arrived; they stood face to face. The smell of burning iron filled Diasa's nostrils. Such an odor had always followed the dragon, but Tolaria had never smelled it this strongly before.

"Diasa says I should ask you a question," T'Sian said.

Dunshandrin Town appeared to be completely deserted; it was eerie, passing through empty streets that had so recently been full of people. The abandoned city reminded Ponn of a fishing village on an island off the Enshennean coast, halfway to the border with Barbareth. He used to anchor his ship there while moving cargo north, to pick up supplies and to let the crew spend some time ashore; but one day they had sailed into the lagoon and found the village deserted. Everything was intact, but the people were gone, as if something had come and snatched them away. The volcano near the center of the island had erupted recently; he could only assume the islanders had fled, but never learned where they had gone or why they hadn't returned. The superstitious among his crew reckoned they had angered the spirit of the mountain, and that it had taken them in retribution.

The analogy was apt, he thought; T'Sian, like that volcano, was very much a force of nature. Still, he could not carry the similarity too far. That had been an island village; this was a small city. There were almost certainly still people here, hiding in their homes, guarding their businesses. Most would be harmless, but some would seek to capitalize on the town's sudden abandonment. Looters, thugs, robbers; a lone traveler such as himself would attract the attention of such types. He carried nothing worth stealing, but that wouldn't prevent him from being waylaid and searched.

He stopped by the inn where they had been staying. This building looked as deserted as the rest; the others were not here. Most likely they were outside the city, where T'Sian had landed. He hurried down the avenue, making furtive haste through the town. The streets were unfamiliar, and he began to worry about getting lost. He had been so tired the night of their arrival that the details of their route were fuzzy in his mind. Most of the street lanterns had been snuffed or stolen, and the resulting darkness didn't make it any easier to find his way. It did make it easier to hide from others, though, as when he encountered a man, tattered, armed, and obviously drunk, staggering along the middle of the road, cursing and muttering to himself. Ponn stayed very still, keeping to the shadows until the fellow passed by.

He began walking again, and soon the lake came into view, black water reflecting glimmers of moonlight. Now he knew where he was. He continued on this route, keeping the lake in sight, until he came to the next major intersection. He took the road that led to the west. It curved gently to the left and then straightened as it neared the shore. A wharf ran alongside it, too small for commerce, but suitable for tying up fishing skiffs and personal craft. Shops built into the wharf sold bait and tackle, supplies for boats, netting, and the like; shanties and taverns dotted the other side of the street.

Here he spotted more people, a group of young toughs who were obviously plundering the mean homes, taking advantage of the poor construction to bash down the doors and ransack the contents. Ponn couldn't imagine what sorts of valuables they might be finding. Fishing poles? Burlap sacks? Bottles of strong drink? Or perhaps they were merely doing it for the pleasure of breaking and entering. In any event, he certainly didn't want to be noticed by *this* crowd. He waited until they were involved with prying open a particularly resistant door, then darted across the street, cutting through a narrow alley between a fish market and a chandlery, coming out on the wooden planks of the quay. He stole along it as quietly as he could; the timbers creaked beneath his feet, but the sound was indistinguishable from the other groans and sighs that the structure made as the water rose and fell beneath it.

At length the wharf detached from the shoreline, which had become rocky and unstable; now there was a gap to his right, four or five feet of black water. Too far to jump, but a gangplank lay ahead of him, leading to shore where the boardwalk ended. He was near the edge of town now, could see empty land ahead, barren riverbank dotted with boulders, tufts of saw-grass, leaning trees that trailed long branches like maidenhair in the river. It might have been such a tree that had saved him when he should have drowned.

He reached the gangplank, started across it, heading for the shore; but before he reached it, he heard a voice from beneath the bridge hiss: "You there! Foreigner! Hold!"

Ponn froze, looking down at the riverside. Two pairs of suspicious eyes looked back, belonging to men dressed in the uniform of Dunshandrin's town guard. They had spread bedrolls among the rocks beneath the shelter of the footbridge, evidently deciding it would be a good place to camp. Neither of them appeared to be armed, and it would be a rough scramble up the bank to pursue him. Hoping they would not think it worth the trouble to give chase, Ponn bolted for shore, ignoring a shouted order to stop.

He heard a crossbow discharge, the twang scarcely audible. He dodged, but the bolt struck him in the left shoulder, spun him around, sent him sprawling in the mud. Agony. He reached around, felt for the shaft. It had struck just to the outside of his shoulder-blade. He couldn't get a grip on it; his fingertips barely brushed it, but even that slight touch sent ripples of burning pain spreading across his back.

He looked back, saw three dark shapes climbing up to the road. Three, not two. He had missed one of them, and that one had been armed with a crossbow.

Why bother shooting at him? Why bother chasing him? Did they know he was with the dragon? Or were they just looking for someone they could kill?

Hoping he wouldn't find out, he stumbled to his feet, and ran.

23

T'Sian peered down at Tolaria. The oracle seemed nervous in her presence; perhaps the dragon form frightened her, especially now that she had witnessed the destruction T'Sian had wrought at the castle.

Good. A frightened human was a compliant one.

"What … what do you want to know?" Tolaria said.

"*I want you to tell me*—" She broke off at a shout from the river, followed by the sound of a crossbow firing. That could only mean Dunshandrin's soldiers.

Tolaria said: "What's wrong?"

She turned back to the oracle. "*Return to the fire. Stay with Diasa. Warn her that there are men about, and they are armed.*"

Tolaria, open-mouthed, nodded, dropped the sticks she had gathered, and hurried away. T'Sian headed for the river, sliding across the ground, keeping her body low and her wings folded. Her vision showed her three warm shapes gathered around a fourth, who lay in the road. The men, occupied with kicking the fallen one, did not notice her approach until she was very near; then two of them screamed and fled, while the other foolishly raised his crossbow and fired it at her. The bolt bounced harmlessly off her nose. Annoyed, she lashed her tail forward and snapped it like a whip across his midsection; he died at once, a look of astonishment on his face, as the top half of his body fell one way and the bottom fell another.

That done, T'Sian examined the man on the ground; anyone drawing the ire of Dunshandrin's men was worthy of attention. But she was surprised to find that she knew him.

"You were supposed to have been drowned, not shot and beaten," T'Sian said.

Pyodor Ponn looked up at her. He must be in considerable pain, she thought, but still, a faint smile flickered across his blood-smeared lips. "Drowning was less painful than this," he said. "You ran them off?"

"Two of them. One stayed to fight, so I killed him."

"Thank you. What about the others? Are they safe?"

He must mean Prehn and the rest. Typical Ponn, always concerned about himself last. *"They are here. I will bring you to them."* But then something occurred to her. *"You are injured. If I move you, will you die?"*

"I don't think I'm hurt that badly. Just be careful."

She delicately picked him up in one of her massive claws, mindful of what had happened to the other man—Ponn's friend, whose name she had forgotten—when she had been too rough with him. Holding him as gently as she could, she returned to the campsite. Tolaria was tending to the injured prisoner; Diasa had her weapon drawn and watched guardedly as T'Sian approached. When she reached them, Diasa said: "What's going on? Tolaria said there are armed men around?"

"No longer." T'Sian laid her burden on the ground. *"I found Pyodor Ponn. He is hurt."*

"Ponn?" Diasa crouched down beside him, examining him. "First you fall in the river, and then you get yourself shot. Are you always this unlucky?"

"I'm not *that* unlucky," he said. "I'm still alive."

"So you are," Diasa said.

"He will live, will he not?" T'Sian said.

"Yes, if we can remove the arrow and stanch the bleeding," Tolaria said. "The wound itself doesn't look too serious. Diasa, what do you think?"

"I agree."

"Pull it out, then," Ponn said. "I'm ready."

"Absolutely not," Diasa said. "We have to push it all the way through to the other side and then cut the head off."

Ponn looked horrified. "What? Why?"

"Dunshandrin uses arrows with barbed heads. Pulling it safely would require tools that we don't have. If we just yank it out, it will

tear your flesh and you could bleed to death." She looked thoughtful.
"Does your arm still work?"

"Yes."

"We must be careful not to do more damage when we remove it,
then. Otherwise you could end up like Adaran."

"*You men are so fragile*," T'Sian said.

Ponn closed his eyes. "Don't start that again," he said.

Tolaria had stuffed her pockets with the rags she'd been able to find
in the inn's kitchen. They had not been particularly clean, so she'd
boiled them for a while before using them to bind Adaran's wounds;
now she needed a few more for Ponn. She stirred up the small pot,
swirling the scraps of fabric around with a stick to make sure they
sank in the roiling water.

"Why are you doing that?"

Startled, she jumped and nearly tipped over the pot, even as she
answered automatically, "I'm going to use them to bandage Ponn's
shoulder."

T'Sian, shrunken down to human form again, had silently come up
behind her; Tolaria hadn't even realized that the dragon had slunk
off to make her transformation. For such an enormous creature, she
could move with remarkable stealth.

The dragon peered into the water. "Why do you have to cook
them first?"

"I'm not cooking them, I'm boiling them because they aren't clean.
There could be things living in the cloth that would make Pyodor
Ponn sick; the hot water will kill them."

"Things living in the cloth?" T'Sian looked dubious. "Like
insects?"

"No, smaller. Have you ever had food poisoning?"

"What is that?"

"It's when you eat something spoiled and it makes you sick."

"I eat whatever I want. It never harms me."

Of course it didn't. "Well, sometimes people get sick from what
they eat." Tolaria poked and stirred the rags. "You can't see the
things in the food that are bad for you, but they're still there. It's the
same with these rags. They were probably used to wipe off counters
or dry dishes. If they touch Ponn's open wound, the things that live

in them might get into his body and make him ill."

T'Sian appeared to consider this. Tolaria wondered if she was going to have to launch into a full-blown explanation of sanitation and disease. At Flaurent, it had taken months for many of the students to accept that invisible creatures lived on many surfaces, and that some of them could make people very sick. Such concepts were largely unknown to the general public; even some oracles left Flaurent unconvinced. Certainly a dragon, not subject to the ailments common to humans, would be completely unaware of the subject.

Finally, T'Sian shook her head and said: "You men. Always making up stories to explain away your frailties."

"Yes," Tolaria said, "we are an imaginative bunch, aren't we?" She lifted one of the rags, examined it. "Are you sure it's wise to be back in human form when there are soldiers about?"

"They cannot hurt me."

"They can hurt the rest of us."

"None will be foolish enough to approach."

"Why not? Those other men tried to kill Ponn."

"They attacked Ponn because he is small, and he was alone and unarmed. They have no spirit left for a true fight."

Tolaria remained unconvinced, but decided to drop the matter; Ponn and Diasa might be willing to debate the dragon, but not her. "You're probably right."

"Certainly. I *am* concerned about something, though."

"What?"

"Qalor's crystals. Something is wrong with them."

"Wrong?"

"They will not stop growing. Look at the castle, and tell me what you see."

Tolaria looked. Against the evening sky, it glowed orange, lit up by the small fires that still burned within the structure. "It's on fire," she said.

"Look closer. Can you see the blue glow?"

She squinted, but couldn't see what T'Sian described. "No."

"Then trust me. The blue crystals are there, and they are spreading quickly."

"All right."

"I never asked you my question, before."

So they were back to that. Tolaria glanced at Adaran. Diasa had taken over bandaging him; now he lay on the dirt, staring up at the night sky. She hoped the question would not be about him. Ponn sat nearby, his face gleaming. She didn't know if he was sweating from the pain, fear of Diasa's prescribed treatment, or both. Nearby, Prehn lay asleep, the only one of their group who was getting any rest.

Tolaria turned back to look at the dragon. "What is your question?"

"I already swallowed some of Qalor's crystals." T'Sian put her hand over her chest. "I feel them inside me; they burn much hotter than the natural variety. I am … afraid that they will harm me in some way, or that they already have."

"I'm not an alchemist," Tolaria said. "I can't answer that."

"You are an oracle. You tell the future. Is that not why Dunshandrin took you in the first place?"

"Yes."

"Then tell me if the crystals will harm me or not."

Tolaria looked at the dragon, feeling nothing, no oncoming trance. T'Sian watched her expectantly, evidently believing she could spout prophecy on demand.

"I don't know," Tolaria said.

Diasa approached. "You must ask her a question," she said. "You've just been making statements. But we may not need to ask the oracle; I've been thinking about what Qalor told me."

"Yes?" T'Sian said.

"Qalor altered the crystals. He knew it would be difficult to obtain more, so he experimented with them, exposing them to his potions and chemicals until they began to grow on their own. Then he found he couldn't control the growth of the blue ones, except by keeping them very cold, so he connected them to that device that funneled river water into their vat."

"What does that have to do with me?"

"The crystals are almost certainly growing inside you now, but if you keep breathing fire and consume them faster than they can spread, eventually they will be used up. Then you can go wherever it is you go, and get more of the normal crystals."

"But when I use them to their full power, they … they burn me," the dragon said. She seemed to have difficulty even discussing this; to her it must be like admitting some horrible weakness, Tolaria thought, the equivalent, perhaps, of a man revealing that he was impotent, or a woman that she was barren.

"Can you just disgorge them?" Diasa said.

"No. Food, yes, but not the crystals."

"You can't use them up and you can't spit them out?"

"So it would seem," T'Sian said.

"A blue stone spreads across the land like ice," Adaran said.

They all turned to him. Tolaria said: "What?"

"When I was at Flaurent, the headmistress had a vision of a blue stone in a tank. She said the stone spread across the land like ice, covering everything. We … I thought the stone was Dunshandrin spreading his influence, but maybe it was literally a stone."

"The crystals," Ponn said.

"Qalor was very upset when the dragon destroyed his cooling system," Diasa said. "The crystals had already begun to spread by the time we escaped; now T'Sian says they have grown all throughout the castle. What's to stop them from coming down the hill and covering the town? The entire region? Who knows what the limit of their growth might be? They could go all the way to the sea. They could go across Barbareth."

"You think it's possible that the crystals will spread so far?" Tolaria said. "What sort of madman would create such a thing? Didn't they realize what could happen?"

"Perhaps they did," Diasa said, "but they didn't care. They wanted the power the crystals could bring."

"Yes," T'Sian said. "They wanted to be the dragons."

"Can we stop the stones from spreading?" Tolaria asked.

"The mass is already too large to be contained within the castle walls," T'Sian said. "In any case, first we must tend to Pyodor Ponn. Are your rags finished cooking yet?"

Tolaria lifted a limp piece of cloth out of the pot; a cloud of steam formed around it in the chill air. "I think so."

"It's time, then?" Ponn said.

"Yes." Diasa knelt beside him, examined the arrow shaft again. She did not touch it. "This is going to hurt."

"It already hurts."

"This is going to hurt more."

"Then do it before Prehn wakes up and has to watch."

"All right. Tolaria, I want you to push the arrow forward until the head breaks through the skin. Then I'll cut it off, and you can pull it out again. Take it slowly."

Tolaria moved around behind Ponn. There was the arrow, sticking out of his shoulder, like a feather that someone had missed while plucking a chicken. She set the pot down on a nearby stump, then looked at Diasa and said: "Are you sure we can't just pull it out?"

"Positive."

Ponn gave her a nervous glance over his shoulder. "Have you ever done this before?" he asked.

"No. I've treated fevers, infections, broken bones." She glanced obliquely at Diasa. "Poisonings. I've never removed an arrow."

He turned to Diasa. "Have you?"

"Once."

"Once?" Ponn grimaced. "Did the person live?"

"Yes," Diasa said, "I did. Tolaria, start pushing. Be. Very. Careful."

Tolaria applied gentle pressure to the end of the bolt, taking care not to shift it in any direction; Diasa had told her to push it straight through or risk doing more damage. The muscles in Ponn's neck bulged as he clenched his jaws, grinding his teeth, trying not to cry out. More sweat broke out, beaded on his coppery skin, trickled down his neck. T'Sian wandered over, watching with interest, but Adaran had turned away. He seemed to be keeping an eye on the sleeping Prehn, perhaps making sure she did not wake up unexpectedly and run to her father. Tolaria was only half-aware of these things, though; most of her concentration was on the task at hand, on pushing the arrow. When would this be over?

Diasa said: "Stop."

Tolaria pulled her hand away. She had pushed the bolt so far that the three small rows of fletching nearly touched Ponn's skin.

"Now what?" T'Sian said.

"I take off the head." Diasa gripped the shaft with one hand and, with the other, worked her dagger into the binding that held the cruel tip in place. Ponn grunted and winced at the movement, balled his hands into fists, punched the earth. Then the barbed, bloody point came loose and fell to the ground.

"All right," Diasa said. "I'll push, you pull. It's almost over, Ponn." The Enshennean, breathing raggedly, only nodded.

Tolaria gently tugged on the arrow. It moved more easily this time, no longer being forced through intact flesh. Diasa pushed with her finger until Ponn's skin swallowed the shaft; then she snatched up one of the hot rags and pressed it up against his shoulder, pushing hard to stanch the flow of blood. Tolaria continued to pull on the projectile until it finally popped free. She tossed it aside, simultaneously bringing up a piece of cloth and shoving it against the wound. It became soaked with blood almost immediately, and she pressed another on top of it.

Ponn twisted his neck to look at her. "Done?"

"Done."

"Good," Ponn said, and passed out.

Diasa stood watch while the others slept. T'Sian had flown off on some unspecified business; Diasa thought she might be looking for something to eat, as there was little left to be destroyed at the castle and she had given no indication that she intended to burn the town yet. The dragon had promised not to be gone too long; Diasa looked forward to her return, because it meant she could get some rest herself. It had been a taxing day.

Ponn stirred. He'd remained unconscious since they had finished extracting the arrow from his body; at first he'd fainted from the pain, but Diasa thought it had turned into ordinary sleep at some point. He must be as exhausted as the rest of them. She crept over and crouched down beside him. He was awake, looking at the sky over the castle. She checked his bandages, making sure they were still tight. Blood had soaked through to the surface, forming large crimson splotches on the grey cloth. The dressing should be changed, she thought, but they had nothing to change them for.

He was looking at her now, his dark eyes gleaming in the low firelight. "I didn't properly thank you, before."

"No thanks are required," she said. "How do you feel?"

"Sore. Both the wound and where those men kicked me."

"Your arm still works?"

He lifted it, moved it a little, lowered it again.

"A yes or no would've sufficed," Diasa said. "You shouldn't move your arm; you might start bleeding again."

"Perhaps, but I didn't know the answer myself." Using his other arm, Ponn pointed at the sky over the castle. "Is that blue light coming from the dragon stones?"

The illumination from the crystals had been strengthening throughout the night, and was now clearly visible over the the glow of the fires that still burned here and there. T'Sian hadn't left anyone alive in the keep to put the flames out, and the townsfolk certainly weren't going climb the hill to do it.

"Yes," Diasa said. "It appears they are still growing."

"You said Qalor was using river water to cool them."

"He had constructed some sort of device that used river water and chemicals to chill the stones until they were nearly frozen. It was colder than river water alone."

"But the river is still very cold. If we could put the stones in the river, it would at least slow the growth, wouldn't it?"

"Perhaps, but it's too late for that now. They've spread too far. Not only that, but they seem to attach themselves to the earth where they touch it; we cannot move them. We may have to hope they eventually stop on their own."

"And the vision that Adaran spoke about? What of that?"

"He's hardly qualified to interpret such things. In any case, oracles aren't always right."

"Not even the headmistress?"

"Not even the headmistress."

"Well, I know little enough of oracles," Ponn said, "but I have come to know T'Sian well enough. She is very worried about these crystals."

"You think so? I can't imagine that she'd care if the entire kingdom were swallowed up."

"She doesn't. Something else concerns her."

"What?"

"I don't know," Ponn said. "And if I asked, she probably wouldn't tell me. She largely keeps her own counsel."

Diasa laughed. "You have a gift for understatement."

* * *

T'Sian perched on a hillside north of the castle, looking down on it from high above. The blue stones had filled the ruined shell of the keep, spilling out into the courtyard, bulging from doorways and open windows, like water overflowing a basin. She had never seen anything quite like it.

As she had told the others, the blue crystals normally grew far to the north, past the icy wastes of northern Yttribia and Madroval, deep in a network of caves that riddled the mountains along the rim of the world. The journey to get them was long and arduous, nothing like the easy flight to the southern islands; and the bitter cold of the northern lands was inimical to her kind.

She could not permit that.

Ponn and the others worried that the crystals would spread across the land, overrunning the green plants, driving out the humans. As far as T'Sian was concerned, the entire realm could become entombed beneath a sheet of glassy stone, and she would not mourn. But eventually, other dragons would learn that the blue crystals had become available somewhere less hostile than Yttribia. They would come to Dunshandrin to gather the stones, not knowing that they were tainted by Qalor's mischief. Some would consume them and be harmed, as she was being harmed.

Perhaps they would die.

Spreading her wings, she took to the air, swooping down over the ruined keep. She circled it a few times, looking at it from different angles. She had thoroughly destroyed the place; there was no trace of movement, no sign of life. The aviary, once full of monstrous, squawking eagles, now gaped like a broken rib cage. The crystals had not yet reached this part of the castle. She landed nearby, stuck her head inside. It stank of its former occupants, but the creatures themselves were gone. She had incinerated most of them, but some had escaped; maybe they would become wild and, in time, men would tell of stories about monstrous birds that descended on their villages, carrying off their livestock and their children. The same sort of stories were, she knew, told about dragons.

She crawled away from the aviary, moving into the grounds between the outer wall and the keep. She had passed through here earlier, wearing human flesh, plodding along the muddy ground under the leering gaze of stupid men who could not perceive the beast beneath her skin. The courtyard had looked much bigger then, viewed through human-sized eyes; now it seemed like a minor alcove of a minor room of her distant lair. The scent of men—their perfumes, their food, their bodily functions—lingered beneath the odor of destruction that she had brought to them. In time their smells would fade, and all that would remain would be blackened stone and ashes, frozen forever beneath a layer of crystals, blue and translucent like glacial ice.

T'Sian sat up on her hind legs, claws digging into the castle wall. No one was here; no one had ventured back, no one had come to loot the questionable treasures of this place. Perhaps they had feared that she would return; perhaps they feared the vengeance of their lords. Diasa had said the rulers had probably escaped, fled through some secret means, going to ground in an unknown redoubt.

No matter.

She would find them, wherever they had gone.

They sat in silence for a while, until Prehn started whimpering in her sleep. Ponn asked Diasa to bring her over, which she did, setting her gently in his lap. He stroked her hair until she settled down again, sighing, a smile on her little face.

After watching this for a little while, Diasa said: "You took a tremendous risk, sneaking into the castle. You came very close to not returning to your daughter."

"We talked about this already," Ponn said. "Adaran saved her; I had to save him."

"I know you feel indebted to him, but he's no hero."

"I know what he is."

"I don't think you do. He's a thief and a scoundrel, not to be trusted."

"He's in no condition to harm us. We have nothing for him to steal. He certainly won't betray us to Dunshandrin's forces, if that's what concerns you."

"It's not," Diasa said.

"Then what?"

She shook her head. "You're better off not knowing. How does your shoulder feel?"

"Like there's a hole in it from side to side."

"The arrow didn't harm anything vital. The pain will pass in time, and you'll have is a nice scar to show your children."

A scar to show his children. Such an injury would have fascinated Pord. Ponn stroked his daughter's hair and thought about his son; he still didn't know what had happened to the boy. Had he merely gone off in a sulk? Had he stowed away on the boat, which now lay in wreckage at the bottom of that distant lagoon? What must Plenn and the other children think, now that he and Prehn had been away for so many days? Would Plenn be painting her face with the chalky white mud of mourning?

"What's the matter?" Diasa said.

"Just thinking about my family," Ponn said. "I've been away too long. They must wonder what has become of me."

"You'll return to them soon," Diasa said.

"Will I?" Ponn sighed. "I wonder."

"You've survived being marooned on an island, the fall of Astilan, breaking into a castle, an alchemical explosion, falling into a river, and being shot with a crossbow. You may not think you're lucky, but *I* do."

"Have a care," he said. "You tempt my fate."

"We make our own fates."

"Tolaria might disagree with you."

"No. She would tell you that nothing is graven in stone, and even the most explicit prophecy may not come to pass."

"Like your mother's prophecy about the stones?"

"That wasn't a prophecy," Diasa said. "That was a vision."

"What's the difference?"

After a moment, she answered: "It's the difference between what you see, and what you dream."

Ponn wasn't sure what to make of that, and said so.

Diasa shrugged. "It's something my mother used to say. It never made much sense to me either. I suppose that a vision is a glimpse of events occurring elsewhere, and a prophecy is a glimpse into events that are more likely to happen than not."

"Then what Adaran described was a prophecy, wasn't it? The events hadn't come to pass yet when the headmistress told him about it."

"Perhaps so." Diasa poked the remnants of the fire with a stick, stirring up a few cinders but little flame. "I never could comprehend much of what she tried to tell me. I'm sure I was a disappointment to her; she probably would rather have had a daughter like Tolaria."

"You had to follow your own trail," Ponn said. "I'm sure she understood that."

Diasa only grunted.

"Where will you go when this is over?"

She shrugged. "I don't know. Flaurent is probably half-buried under salt and dust by now. It's coming into the windy season; the Withered Ones always had to spend extra time clearing dunes from the walls this time of year." She shook her head. "You at least have a home and a family to return to. The rest of us have nothing."

"You're certainly feeling melancholy," Ponn said. "If I didn't know better, I would say you'd been drinking."

"Perhaps I should start," she said.

A sudden rush of wind caused the bonfire to dance and shimmy, kicking up a swirl of shriveled leaves, small twigs, grit and pebbles. That must be T'Sian, returning from her evening hunt, or wherever it was that she had gone. After a little while she came within range of the firelight, once again wearing her human disguise.

"Welcome back," Diasa said.

The dragon acknowledged her greeting with a nod, then stepped over to Ponn. "You are awake," she said.

"Yes."

"You are supposed to sleep and heal."

"I've slept enough. Diasa says I'll be fine."

"Why not ask the oracle?"

"Ponn's wound is not life-threatening," Diasa said. "I think Tolaria wearies of being made to do parlor tricks."

T'Sian cocked her head. "What is a parlor trick?"

Suddenly the night lit up around them, the moonlight overwhelmed, all the colors bleached to pale by a harsh white flare hovering high above the ground. The brilliant flame burned silently, steadily, like a cold sun lowered to the earth. Prehn stirred in Ponn's arms, opened her eyes, began to cry.

Diasa was already on her feet, sword drawn. "*This* is a parlor trick," she said.

A hoarse whisper: "It's Orioke."

Ponn looked to his left. Adaran and Tolaria had awakened; the oracle sat up, squinting in the glare. Adaran stayed on his side, shading his eyes with his good hand. "The wizard is here?" Ponn asked.

"I've seen this magic before."

"So have I," Diasa said. "I knew Wert couldn't delay him for long."

"*Greetings, my friends.*"

The voice, like reeds scratching on paper, seemed to come from the light itself. T'Sian moved to stand beneath it, staring directly into it, eyes unblinking. "Show yourself, wizard, so that I may kill you."

"*A tempting request, but one I must decline.*"

"Where is Deliban?" Diasa said. "Have you misplaced it so soon after stealing it from us?"

"*The earth creature is busy elsewhere,*" Orioke said. "*You may as well stop waving your sword around. I did not come to fight, but to ask a question.*"

"What question?" Tolaria said.

"*It's not for you. It's for the dragon.*"

T'Sian said: "What question could you possibly ask that I would deign to answer?"

"*Merely this: You have been searching with such fury for the ones who killed your hatchlings, and yet when one of the killers is in your midst, you do nothing. So tell me, dragon: Why does Adaran still live?*"

And the light went out.

24

As THE NIGHT CAME RUSHING back in to fill the void left by the light's disappearance, T'Sian turned to the others. "Is this true?" she demanded. No one answered. Tolaria did not feel the compulsion to respond, because the question had not been explicitly directed at her. But she was sure the next one would be. And, indeed, the dragon stepped forward, closer to the light, and pointed a long finger at Tolaria. "You. Oracle, who cannot lie. Is it true, what the wizard said?"

"Yes."

The finger swiveled toward Adaran, who looked as if he would very much like to be somewhere, anywhere, else. "This one helped to kill my young?"

"Yes."

The dragon's other fingers unfurled one by one, forming hands that looked like the talons of a great bird. She advanced toward the footpad, until Ponn moved to stand in her way. She towered over him, and yet she stopped, staring down at him with incredulity. "Pyodor Ponn," she said, "step aside."

"T'Sian, wait," Ponn said. "Think. You are doing exactly what the wizard wants you to."

"I am doing what *I* want to do."

"You did not come here to fight a wounded, crippled man."

She gave Adaran a reptilian look of utter contempt. "It will hardly be a fight."

Tolaria shot a pleading look at Diasa, but the woman stood back, impassive, watching. She obviously had no intention of intervening,

389

and pretended not to notice Tolaria's gaze.

"T'Sian, please ... he saved my daughter."

"And you rescued him from the castle, at serious cost to yourself. You have more than settled your debt with him. Now I will settle mine."

Ponn took a deep breath. "I cannot let you do this."

"He's not worth it, Ponn," Diasa said quietly. "I told you he was a scoundrel."

T'Sian wheeled on her. "You knew this?" she demanded.

"Adaran let it slip a little while ago, before Ponn came back. I've had my suspicions, but—"

"And you, oracle?" T'Sian glared down at Tolaria. "You knew as well. When I asked you if it was true, you said yes. You did not need your so-called visions to tell you that."

"I found out when Diasa did."

"And you both planned to say nothing, to protect your fellow human. It fell to the *wizard*—my *enemy*—to speak the truth!"

"He only told you so that you would do this," Ponn said. "He is trying to make you turn on us."

"Turn on *you*? *You* are turning on *me*! Keeping secrets. Helping a man who killed my babies. What about you, Ponn? Did you know?"

"No."

"But you must have suspected. You are not a fool. How would he have been in the position to rescue your daughter but that he was already there, among those who had taken her?"

"I ... should have suspected, yes. But I was so happy to have Prehn back—"

"So happy to have her back. But I will not experience such a reunion, will I, Pyodor Ponn? *Because of him!*"

Ponn hesitated. Tolaria could imagine what he was thinking: He and T'Sian had been companions. She had saved his life. Her rage was completely justified. But Adaran had saved Ponn's daughter, and he could not let the dragon kill him.

"You know that I could *make* you move," T'Sian said.

"Yes," Ponn said.

"You know that if you were any of the others, I would have killed you already."

"Yes."

The two of them stood there, staring at each other, neither saying a word; then an unexpected voice broke the silence.

"Stand aside, Ponn, and let the dragon do what she must," Adaran said. "I've earned her vengeance."

Diasa said: "The footpad is right, for once."

"But we can't just—" Tolaria broke off, feeling something impinging on her, a presence nearby, poking at her mind. The last time she had felt something like this, the wizard had been about to force a prophecy out of her, making her a puppet, trying to impress the twins. It had to be him; but what was he doing now?

The others were still speaking but she could hardly hear them anymore. Orioke had gummed up her ears, as if he were standing behind her with his fingers in them. Now she understood why he had thrown that light up in their midst, why he had revealed Adaran's role in the slaughter of T'Sian's hatchlings. Eliminating the thief wasn't really his goal; he had stirred up this mischief as a distraction, so that he could move against *her*.

She tried to speak, to cry a warning; but it was too late, her voice was no longer her own. Orioke had taken it away.

Tolaria slumped sideways into the grass, as the night came down around her.

Adaran didn't know what Ponn thought he was doing. Did he believe he could reason with the dragon? Did he think she would say he was right, there had been enough death, she was going to try forgiveness instead? Hardly. She would kill him, cast his maimed body aside, and then come to Adaran and finish the job Dunshandrin's men had started. There would be no escape this time. He couldn't run, couldn't jump, couldn't hide. And so he spoke up, told Ponn to move, thinking that in some way this might make up for what he had done; and the astonished looks that his words drew told him what the others thought of him.

"It's all right," Adaran said, when Ponn hesitated. "You must stand aside."

Moving his gaze between Adaran and T'Sian, Ponn stepped out of the way, leaving the thief to face the dragon.

"Stand up, man," T'Sian said.

He picked up the branch Diasa had used as a poker and, holding it like a cane, began struggling to rise. Ponn moved to assist him, but T'Sian checked him with a raised arm and curt command: "No. He will do it on his own."

Adaran finally gained his feet. The dragon stepped forward, looking him up and down. Although they were about the same height, T'Sian was much more solidly built than he was. She could pick him up and break him over her knee if she wanted to, although he expected that his death would come a different way.

"Look at you," T'Sian said. She began pacing, walking in a slow circle around him. Adaran stood still; if she wanted to inspect him from every side, he would let her. "Such a little man. How could you kill my hatchlings?"

"It wasn't just me," Adaran said.

"I know that. How many?"

"Five."

"What skills have you, that Dunshandrin sought you out?"

"I get in and out of places. I rigged up the ropes and hooks that we used to lower ourselves into your lair."

"I saw no such devices."

"We removed them when we left."

"And what happened when you entered my home?"

"We attacked the little dragons. Orioke cast a spell to put them to sleep, but it only made them groggy."

"Of course. My hatchlings were not kittens, ready to nap at the whim of a sorcerer. Tell me how they fought."

Why did she want to know this? "They used claws, tails, a little bit of fire. They killed a man named Kryback, a mercenary from Madroval. I knew him; he was very good with weapons."

"Yes, I found him where you left him," T'Sian said. "He obviously meant a great deal to you."

Sarcasm? "I didn't know him well," he said. Diasa rolled her eyes.

"And what did *you* do during the battle?"

"I avoid melee; I stayed back and threw daggers."

"Daggers." T'Sian snorted. She was back in front of him now, but she kept moving, circling him again. The dragonets had done the same thing during the fight: Circling, attacking, circling again. Looking for weaknesses. "Pinpricks."

"Hand to hand combat isn't my strong point."

"No," T'Sian said.   "You are the sort who deals in trickery and subterfuge, are you not? Like the wizard. The sort who strikes at an exposed back, a turned head, a sleeping victim."

Adaran said nothing.

"You were once five, but now you are only two." She was behind him again.   "I found the one who was killed by my young. What happened to the others?"

This time he did turn to face her, leaning heavily on his makeshift cane.   "Dunshandrin's men tried to kill us. Only Orioke and I escaped."

"Ah," she said. "And so you learned that Dunshandrin valued your life as little as you valued the lives of my young."

"I suppose so."

T'Sian looked at him for a little while, then said: "You have told me what I wanted to know, and so your death will be quick. I cannot guarantee it will be painless."

Adaran closed his eyes, waiting for the blow, for the fire; but it did not come, and when he looked again, Diasa had come up to T'Sian and was speaking quietly to her, pointing off to the side. He followed the line of her finger, which led to the oracle. She lay on her side, eyes open but unfocused; if not for the rise and fall of her chest, Adaran would have thought her dead. Ponn knelt beside her, holding her hand by the wrist, pinching lightly.

Diasa was explaining that Tolaria could not be awakened. "Orioke must have done this," she said.   "He distracted us so he could strike her down without being noticed, and it worked."

"I can kill this cretin and then deal with the wizard."

"Yes, go ahead, kill Adaran," Ponn said, not looking up from Tolaria. "Show Orioke how well you play his fool. I'm sure he will be pleased."

The dragon hissed in anger and frustration, the sound like a pit of angry snakes. How could such a cacophony issue from a human-looking mouth? Adaran expected her to charge over and rend him to pieces, but instead she turned and vanished into the night. He stood there for a moment, staring after her; then his legs began to tremble and he used the stick to lower himself to the ground.

"Where do you suppose she's going?" Diasa asked.

"Most likely to change shape and look for the wizard," Ponn said.

"There will be more fire this night."

Adaran crawled over to join Ponn beside the oracle. She lay unresponsive, unblinking, her eyes reflecting moonlight. "I don't understand," he said. "If Orioke wanted to take away our oracle, why didn't he just kill her?"

"She's more of a burden this way," Diasa said. "He knows we won't abandon her, so not only do we lose her abilities, but we gain something fragile that we have to protect."

"Besides, the twins might still hope to get her back. She won't be of much use if she's dead." Ponn glanced at him. "You are most familiar with the wizard," he said, his tone suggesting that Adaran had gained this knowledge in the manner of one who learned the identity of a murderer by helping him commit his crimes. "Will T'Sian find him?"

"He'll have a glamour to keep himself from being seen," he said. "Orioke is an expert in illusions, tricks of the mind. I don't know how well it will work on a full-grown dragon, but it seemed to keep the young ones from finding him."

Diasa joined them. "What did he do to Tolaria?"

"I don't know. Some sort of false sleep, I suppose. Perhaps the same spell he tried to use on the baby dragons. It didn't work this well on them though."

"Yet another example of human inferiority," Diasa said.

Her transformation complete, T'Sian took to the sky. She swam up through the air with powerful strokes of her wings, the meadow and road and forest spinning away beneath her. She scanned the darkness, her heat-sensitive vision picking out the broad glow of the bonfire, the fading column of its heat rising into the sky. Her companions, arranged near the flames, were lost within the circle of its warmth.

The forest lay to the northwest of their sad little camp, the canopy of leaves concealing what lay beneath. Through gaps in the trees she saw a few small fires; these, she was sure, belonged to villagers who had fled the town during her attack on the castle. The man she sought would not have lit a fire for himself.

This so-called wizard knew tricks no man should know. Fouling the thoughts of her hatchlings so that lesser men could slay them; pulling the fire out of her belly like a gaudy ribbon; striking Tolaria down from hidden cover. He was probably down there right now, hiding behind his magic, looking into the sky and laughing at her.

She hovered hundreds of feet up, scanning the forest. How would this man have gotten here? The mad little oracle had said Orioke was coming to Achengate yesterday; today he was here. He must have flown in on an eagle. Where would such a creature have landed? Not out in the open, certainly, and not in the trees. So he most likely had put down in one of the many clearings that dotted the woodland. She could check them one by one, and see if his tricks could stop her fire this time.

Or she could just burn the entire forest and see what came out.

As the night turned orange, Diasa moved away from the others, heading down the slope toward the road, hoping for a better look at the dragon's activities. T'Sian, a black shape against the fiery glow, wove a curving pattern in the air as she vomited a stream of fire into the trees, igniting wide swaths of the forest. She had evidently decided to burn Orioke out rather than search for him.

Diasa quickly returned to the others. "We need to move," she said. "T'Sian is setting fire to the forest. We're too close to it for my peace of mind."

"She's frustrated," Ponn said.

"Her frustration could burn all of us to death." Diasa hefted Tolaria, slinging the limp oracle over her shoulders. Ponn lifted Prehn, while Adaran used the branch to lever himself to his feet. They slowly retreated from the forest, moving toward the road, joined and passed by villagers fleeing from the burning woodland. Diasa wondered how many fell among the trees, overcome by heat or flame or smoke, reduced to sizzling fat and blackened bones.

By the time they reached the riverbank, the entire forest seemed to be alight. Embers wafted into the sky, drifting eastward on a light breeze that carried them toward the village. If they didn't set it ablaze by nestling in thatched roofs or exposed haylofts, Diasa thought, T'Sian would surely be along shortly to take care of that job herself.

Suddenly she spotted a dark shape rising from the forest, winged like the dragon, but much smaller. An eagle. Was there a rider?

Diasa couldn't tell.   The thing fluttered madly, panicked and disoriented by the fire and smoke. As the great bird rose above the flames, T'Sian dove toward it, snatching it out of the sky with a massive talon; when it fell to earth a few moments later, it was a crushed wad of bones and feathers.

Diasa was still not sure if there had been a rider on the eagle. She suspected not; would Orioke be so rash as to take to the air while the dragon prowled above the forest? He had surprised her in Astilan, and, with Deliban's help, bested her there; he might have thought to do the same again. On the other hand, he might have sent his mount up as a diversion, if T'Sian had come close enough to him to force him to sacrifice his transportation.

But if the dragon killed him, what would happen to Tolaria?

Adaran stared at the huge clouds of choking smoke that the burning forest sent into the night sky. Bits of ash and glowing embers drifted along the hillside, falling into the grass and mud, most of them snuffed out as they touched the damp ground. Some reached the village, starting a few small fires here and there.

The dragon banked to her left, away from the woods, heading toward the town. She intended to burn it now, he realized. The villagers had done nothing to earn her wrath, but she was in a fury, and anything that belonged to Dunshandrin would suffer her vengeance.

When she was done, she would come back for him.

Did he really want to wait for her to come back and incinerate him as well? His moment of courage, when he had told Ponn to stand aside, was long past.   Ponn and Diasa had stopped paying any attention to him; they both stood, staring at the village, watching the spectacle as the dragon burned it down to its foundations. Even Prehn, awake now in her father's arms, stared raptly at the dancing flames. It was the perfect opportunity. After all, Diasa was right, wasn't she? He was a thief, he was a scoundrel. His specialty was slinking away from trouble.

He crawled away, toward the tall reeds, and the river.

Tolaria understood that her surroundings were not, could not be, real. Surely Orioke did not have the power to tear her away from

Dunshandrin and hurl her hundreds of miles, back to Yttribia, to the back alleys and seedy avenues of chill Torbinton, the city where she had grown up. No, he must have reached into her mind, thrust his greedy fingers deep into her memories, and conjured up images from her past. He had created a little world to keep her mind occupied, giving her winding streets to wander as if in a maze. But rather than spend her energies in fruitless exploration, she remained here, where she had awakened, and thought.

She knew little of wizards and their secrets, but it stood to reason that it took some small amount of effort for Orioke to keep her locked up this way. Some minor portion of his power had been allocated to her, in the same way that some went toward keeping Deliban leashed. If she pushed in the correct way, perhaps she could free herself. The headmistress had said that Tolaria was the most gifted oracle to come through Flaurent in a generation; surely that must count for something against the wizard's trickery.

She leaned back, feeling the cold brick wall, firm against her back. It didn't really exist, but it felt as solid as any other surface, as solid as the walls of her prison in Dunshandrin's castle. She closed her eyes, modulated her breathing to be slow and deep, the way she had been taught to do it when inhaling the vapors that induced a trance. She had no herbs, no powders, no potions; but as this place was imaginary, she could merely pretend that the things she needed were present: A cushion at her back, a bowl in her lap, fragrant mist rising into her nose.

After concentrating for a few minutes, she actually began to feel a stone crock resting on her legs, rough and heavy, just like the one she had left behind when she escaped from the castle. If she opened her eyes, would she see it there? Would she be surrounded by thin smoke, like incense? Perhaps; perhaps not. She felt no need to check, to see with her gaze. She knew the vapors were present, and that was what mattered.

But instead of seeking knowledge of the future, she bent her thoughts toward the present, and the wizard.

When the town was satisfactorily aflame, T'Sian landed in the square near the inn where they had spent the night. Fires burned all around her; under other circumstances she might have curled up here and slept for a while, letting the soothing heat soak into her body, breathing deep the pleasing smell of smoke and ashes. But now she could only pause for a little while; pause, and reflect, and give the burning pain in her chest some time to cool.

When she had spotted the eagle, her first thought had been that she would find the wizard on its back; but no, he had not been astride his mount. She'd realized at once that the giant bird's flight had been a diversion. The crafty man had perhaps cut partway through its tether and then fled, so that when the creature broke free it would attract her attention. That the ploy had worked made her even angrier than she had been before. Three times now, he had tricked and humiliated her.

She would kill him. She would burn his flesh to ashes; she would chew on his cracked and blackened bones.

But first she had to catch him.

She spread her wings and took to the air, rising on the thermals from the burning buildings. She tilted forward and, with several great beats, sped toward where she had left the others. The firelight formed a patchwork of light and shadow on the ground as it swept by beneath her.

She stopped outside of town, holding steady, looking for her companions. She spotted them near the river. They had withdrawn from the forest, driven back by the flames. She set down nearby and lumbered toward them. Diasa, of course, was the first to notice her approach. "Well, this is certainly an impressive forest fire that you've started," she said.

"*It will burn itself out,*" T'Sian said. "*The forest thins to the west and south.*"

"And you've made good on your threat to destroy the town."

"*I was provoked.*"

"As we all were," Diasa said. "And the wizard?"

T'Sian said nothing.

"He escaped?" Diasa did not seem surprised. "The eagle was a diversion?"

"*Yes.*" Galling, being forced to admit it. "*He escaped.*"

"He'll try to make his way back to the twins."

"You think they're still alive?" Ponn asked.

"Of course," Diasa said. "Unless I have completely misjudged them, they will have bolted at the first sign of a serious attack."

"*Where would they go?*" T'Sian said.

"Who knows? A secret cave, a camp in the woods, an outlying village. They'll have soldiers with them."

"Most of their soldiers are in Barbareth, or burned up and buried in the castle," Ponn said.

"I'm sure they kept a few in reserve."

"*A few. A hundred*," T'Sian said. "*Soldiers cannot protect them from my revenge.*" Then, recalling unfinished business, she raised her head, moved it from side to side, lifted it up high. She spotted Tolaria lying on the ground near the others, but Adaran was not there. She could see, faintly, a warm, man-sized depression in the grass; but if this was where Adaran had lain, he was no longer there.

She poked her head forward, arching her neck over Ponn and Diasa, sniffing the grass. Yes, this was where the sly one had been; she recognized his odor, a combination of infection and sewage and the herbs Tolaria had used to treat his wounds. He had crawled away, toward the river, slipping down the bank and into the water. She could see the route he had taken, the bent grass, the lingering traces of warmth. The current was lazy here, quite unlike the torrent that rushed through the rocks near the castle. Even with his injuries, the thief would likely be able to paddle a small distance.

She twisted her neck around, bringing her head up to Ponn and Diasa. "*You let him escape*," she hissed.

"What?" Ponn turned to look at the spot where Adaran had been. T'Sian had already moved back a few paces. She leaped into the air, catching herself with her great wings, hauling herself upward. Adaran might be in the river, but she could find him from the air.

And when she did, she would boil him alive.

The downdraft of the dragon's wings nearly knocked Ponn over, but Diasa caught him and set him back on his feet; she, of course, had braced herself and not been unbalanced by T'Sian's departure. Prehn locked her arms around Ponn's neck and held on tightly, as if afraid that the dragon might pluck her from his grasp and fly away with her.

Diasa watched the sky over the river as the dragon moved up and down it, searching for Adaran. "That's the angriest creature I've ever seen," she murmured. "She reminds me of my mother."

"You should have seen her when I first met her," Ponn said.

"Will she find him, do you think?"

"I don't know. He seems to be good at escaping."

Prehn kept trying to look where the dragon had gone; Ponn kept turning her so that she couldn't see. If T'Sian was going to kill Adaran, his daughter didn't need to watch.

Diasa went to the water's edge, ruddy in the reflected light of the forest fire. "We should find a way across the river before the fire gets any closer."

"It wants to burn uphill," Ponn said. "Besides, the wind is blowing it toward the village."

"Wind tends to change."

"We can hardly swim, not with Tolaria in this condition. We should stay here. We can move into the water if the fire comes closer. If we cover ourselves with mud it will help keep us cool."

"I suppose," Diasa said, studying the river as if hoping to find Dunshandrin's twins drifting by. "How far do you think Adaran will have gotten?"

"I suppose it depends on the current, and how well he can swim with his injuries. It's not easy to paddle when your hands and feet are wrapped up in cloth."

"What if he didn't really swim away at all?" Diasa said. She pulled out her sword. "What if he's hiding in the reeds, say, right about here?" She gently poked her blade into the cattails and rushes; Ponn heard a small exclamation from the tall weeds. Diasa lunged forward and hauled Adaran to his feet. He was covered in mud and duckweed, like some sort of swamp-dwelling apparition. She tossed him to the roadside, where he fell on his back in a splatter of muck and slime. Ponn, startled, took a step back as Adaran pushed himself to a sitting position. Diasa glared down at him. "Hiding in the brush," she said. "Just like a highwayman."

"I'm not a highwayman," Adaran said. "Why didn't you just leave me hidden? You don't want me in your group, and the dragon wants me dead."

"I'm sure she's at the end of a long, long list," Diasa said.

Prehn started to cry. "Hush," Ponn said, trying to soothe her. Plenn was better at calming the children than he was. He wished they were back at the inn, this odyssey nothing but a horrid memory, like a nightmare from long ago. Gradually her whimpers subsided, although she still stared at Adaran with wide eyes, her cheeks glistening with tears. "Really, Diasa, why not let him hide?"

"We can't have T'Sian spending all her time trying to find him," Diasa said. "We have more important things to worry about."

"You *want* her to kill me. You've hated me since Flaurent."

"You don't rate hatred, only contempt."

"I know you don't like Adaran, and I know you blame him for what happened at Flaurent," Ponn said. "That doesn't matter now. Put aside your personal feelings, and when this is over, walk away and never look at his face again."

"Put aside my personal feelings?" She sounded incredulous. "You can stand there and tell me that after you, because of *your* personal feelings, invaded the castle to rescue him?"

"I owed him a debt," Ponn said.

Diasa stared at him for a moment, then turned away, looking into the fire. "So do I."

"Your debt is vengeance," Ponn said. "Mine was gratitude."

"All of us owe a debt of vengeance."

"There's vengeance, and then there's justice," Ponn said. "You have the two confused."

She stood very still; then, in a single fluid motion, she drew a small blade, spun, and threw it at Adaran. The dagger stuck into the ground between his feet, eliciting a startled yelp.

By the time Ponn realized what Diasa had done, she had already returned to her earlier position by the fire. He knelt and picked up the weapon; it took more effort than he had expected, as it had gotten stuck in some roots. "This is not helping," he said.

"It made me feel a little better."

From behind him, Ponn heard T'Sian say: "Well, I remain unsatisfied."

25

THE DRAGON HAD RETURNED TO her human form; she stood a few yards away from Ponn, looking down at Adaran. "Look at this fool, Pyodor Ponn," she said. "He cannot swing a weapon; he can hardly stand upright. What possible use is he against our enemies?"

"No man alive is useless," Ponn said. "Not even him."

Adaran wondered if he should take that as an insult.

"The world will not mourn the loss of one mangled thief." Tiny wisps of smoke escaped from the dragon's mouth as she spoke; fire burned behind her lips, always ready to incinerate her enemies at will. Was it the fire that made her so quick to anger? If a man had the power to destroy something with a breath, what sort of creature would he become?

One not unlike Lord Dunshandrin, Adaran thought.

Prehn stirred in Ponn's arms, opening her eyes, looking around in confusion. She glanced at T'Sian, at Adaran, at Diasa; then she turned her gaze up at her father and said, in a clear, strong voice: "Deliban is coming."

For a moment, no one spoke; then Diasa said: "What?"

"It's me, Tolaria," Prehn said. "Orioke has summoned the earth elemental. It will be here soon. We must think of a way to deal with it before it arrives."

"Tolaria?" Ponn held up his daughter, looking into her face, as if he might see the oracle hiding there. "What ... how?"

"I haven't harmed her, I'm just borrowing her voice," she said. "The wizard has trapped me in some sort of hallucinatory prison. I'm conscious, but barred from animating my own body. The rest of

403

you are too alert for me to contact; Prehn was the only one I could reach."

"You're learning all sorts of new tricks," Diasa said.

"Of necessity."

"How do you know Orioke summoned Deliban?"

"He left a … a connection between us, so he can maintain the illusion. I followed it back and spied on him."

"That's just what Wert was doing," Diasa said.

T'Sian came up behind Ponn, peering at the child in his arms. "Do you know where the wizard is?"

"Yes."

She raised her hands, curled them into fists. "Where is he?"

"He's hiding nearby." Pause. "If you kill him now, I don't know what will happen to me."

"*Where* is he hiding?" the dragon demanded.

"On the hillside west of town, in the cleft of a large rock outcropping."

T'Sian turned and stomped off into the night.

Tolaria, seeing through Prehn's eyes, watched T'Sian walk away. This brought her gaze to Adaran, pale and shivering beneath a layer of muck, which then led to her own body, lying still and staring by the roadside.   Her mouth was slightly open, her eyes glazed, her breathing shallow; it was like witnessing her own slow death.

Ponn saw where she was looking. "Are you afraid that if T'Sian kills Orioke, you will die?"

"Yes."

"Or you could be freed, and wake up at once," Diasa said.

"That's possible too."

"What about Deliban?" Adaran said. "If the dragon kills Orioke, what happens to Deliban?"

"Deliban will be freed from Orioke's control," Diasa said. "For the first time in centuries, it will be completely unfettered. There's no telling what it will do; it might just go away."

"Or it might open the earth and bury us all," Adaran said.

Diasa looked thoughtful. "Tolaria, can you be more specific about where Orioke hides? What is the fastest way to find him?"

"The crack that looks like lightning will lead you to him."

Diasa turned and hurried off after the dragon, disappearing into the night. Tolaria watched her go. Clearly she intended to find the wizard before the dragon did, but what would she do then?

Suddenly she felt something shift inside her consciousness; her vision blurred and rapidly faded. At first this frightened her, but then she realized that Prehn had begun to wake up, reasserting control over her own body. Tolaria didn't resist, fearing she might inadvertently harm the little girl with this power she didn't really understand. After a few moments she found herself back in the illusion that Orioke had prepared for her. It had begun to snow there, the sky disgorging small, hard flakes that stung with tiny pricks of cold before melting quite realistically into tiny droplets of water.

Melting snow. That was what fed the icy current of the river that ran in a loop around the castle. Qalor had used it to help keep the dragon stones cool. T'Sian had destroyed the chilling device; now there was no way to bring the water up to the ruins of the keep. The cold, cold river could no longer keep the crystals in check.

But Deliban was coming, and it had vast power to move the earth. Ponn had told them how the creature had raised a ramp over the walls of the city, how it had created a road through town by simply demolishing everything that stood in its way. Properly directed, such power could hinder the growth of the crystals; it could crumble the butte, raise a levee, dam the river, drown the castle. But only its master could command it to do so.

And what were the chances of that?

T'Sian moved quickly through the tall grass. She knew the outcropping of which Tolaria had spoken; she had seen it from the air while circling above the village, a stubby thumb of red rock split with cracks and crevices. Some of them would admit a man, especially one as gaunt as the wizard. He may escaped her so far with his trickery, but that would not save him when she filled all his bolt-holes with smoke and fire.

Diasa caught up with her and fell into step to her right. T'Sian stopped walking; Diasa continued for a few paces before halting as well. She turned and stood there, waiting.

T'Sian said: "What are you doing here?"

"I'm coming with you."

"Why?"

"To help you kill Orioke."

"I do not need your help."

"Well, in that case, I'll just watch while you roast him in his own fat or whatever it is you like to do." Diasa grinned. "I'd hate to miss that, believe me."

"And the others? You have left them without a defender."

"So have you." Then, pointing in the direction of the outcropping, which loomed dark in the distance against the firelit sky: "We had best get this done soon, before Deliban arrives. The wizard alone will be troublesome enough."

T'Sian eyed Diasa, trying to decide if she intended to cause mischief. She could not fathom why Diasa would want to meddle while she killed the wizard; Diasa hated him for his part in the destruction of Flaurent, and had no reason to wish his miserable existence to continue. "Fine," she said. "Watch if you wish. But do not interfere; the wizard is mine."

"As you wish."

They began walking again, continuing a little while in silence, and then Diasa said: "Why are you in human form?"

"The wizard will not be expecting me to come for him like this," T'Sian said. "He will be looking for me in the sky, not on the ground."

"Perhaps," Diasa said, "but the wizard is formidable. Aren't you more vulnerable in this guise? What if you transform and take him from the air, while I take him from the ground? He'll be less able to defend himself from an attack on two fronts."

"He cannot defend himself from my fire."

"Really? My understanding was that he did defend himself, quite capably, when you encountered him in Astilan."

"He surprised me. That will not happen again."

"Of course it won't. But the wizard is a wily foe; he's been goading you, hoping you'll make a mistake, like trying to take him while in human form. He'll slip away through passages too narrow for you to enter, or trap you in a crevice where you'll be unable to transform." Pause. "You don't want him to escape again, do you?"

T'Sian considered. What Diasa said sounded reasonable; the wizard could trap her inside the stone, the way she had been trapped beneath the collapsed building in Astilan, unable to move, unable to change. If she accepted Diasa's strategy, it might be easier to corner the slippery magician.

"All right," the dragon said. "I will strike from above; you keep him from escaping through cracks in the stone. But take care. If you are too near him when I attack, I may burn you."

"I'll be careful," Diasa said.

They stopped when they reached the rubble-strewn hillside east of the city. Diasa could see the outcropping, not far away, jutting out of the ground like a stone finger admonishing the village beneath it. It resembled the much larger promontory on which the castle had stood, but older and more weathered; its crumbled sides were undoubtedly the source of the rocks and boulders that littered the hillside below.

Without a word, the dragon moved away, seeking her usual privacy when changing shape. Diasa waited a moment, then crept after her. She had been roughly timing these absences, trying to ascertain exactly how long it took for T'Sian to complete the transformation. She thought she had a good understanding of it at this point, but she needed to wait until the process actually began before making her move, lest the dragon should see what she was doing.

She spotted T'Sian behind a boulder the size of a large wagon. It was sufficient to conceal her human form, though of course when she assumed her true shape it would scarcely cover her head. Diasa crouched nearby, watching as the dragon began to quiver all over, her skin rippling and shifting. Then she exploded, her body bursting into a vaporous cloud of pink and red, green and blue. The swirling matter expanded, flowing across the ground, drifting through the air, beginning to resemble the giant beast it would become.

Putting aside her fascination, Diasa bolted, weaving through the boulders at top speed, heading for the massive rock. She had run through blinding storms of stinging salt dust and shifting dunes; threading the debris-ridden slope was simple in comparison. She quickly reached Orioke's hiding place, and spotted a broad, jagged split that came down almost vertically before forking near the bottom.

She glanced back at T'Sian. Her transformation was nearly complete; she seemed to be quite solid now, and would shortly be able to take wing. There was no time to see if some other crack looked more like lightning than this one. She chose the wider fork and slipped into the crevice, sidling along sideways until the passage widened into a sort of chimney. She paused in the open space, listening, sniffing the air. Nothing. She scanned the small area, examining the shape of the walls, the sparse grass that grew where dirt had accumulated in the cracks. She noticed a spot where the vegetation was bent flat, as if an invisible weight lay upon it. The stone curved gently behind it, forming a small nook. A weary fugitive, confident that he would not be found, might well seek refuge there, lean back, and close his eyes to rest. She hoped that, in his haste, he might have failed to lay wards about that would protect him from the likes of her.

Diasa unsheathed her dagger, knelt where she judged the wizard to be, and grabbed for his unseen throat. She felt flesh under her fingers; she had gotten him right below the jaw, a good spot to hold onto. As the invisible being awoke and began to struggle, she pressed the edge of her blade below her hand, pushing just hard enough to feel the resistance.

"The dragon will be here momentarily," she whispered. "If you don't want to be burnt to a crisp, do exactly as I say."

"Diasa." The wizard's voice. "What are you doing?"

"Saving your life. Now move. And not a word or a whisper from your lips, or I will kill you."

She pulled him to his feet, keeping the knife against his throat, ready to cut with a single motion. He didn't resist as she dragged him out of the shelter of the rock, but as they emerged onto the hillside, he said: "You're mad. The dragon will roast us both."

"Perhaps," Diasa said. "Better that than to be buried alive like my mother." He gave a low chuckle; she pressed the blade a little harder and the chuckling stopped. "Do I amuse you?"

"No. But Damona did not die in Flaurent; she traveled with you all the way to Achengate, hiding within the soul of another. You left her there to face me alone."

He meant Wert, of course. Diasa had suspected as much, at the very end, but there'd been no time to elicit the truth, or for a tearful farewell. "It was her choice. She thought she could delay you for a few days."

"You left her there to face me *alone*. She ensnared me in a false Achengate, an illusion of her own creation, and made me wander through it for hours, searching for her. But my time was not wasted; I extracted the skill from her before she died, and put it to good use against your oracle."

She tightened her grip on Orioke's throat. "Enough," she said, moving away from the stone, out into the open. She couldn't see T'Sian, but knew she was nearby; the great beast would certainly spot them momentarily. Indeed, within seconds the dragon dropped out of the night sky, landing in front of them, a mass of scales and smoke. The wind of her wings washed over them, laden with the stench of brimstone.

"*What are you doing, Diasa?*"

"I have someone here." Diasa nudged Orioke in the back with her knee. "Show yourself, wizard."

He muttered something, and the glamour of invisibility fell away, leaving him standing there, burned, bleeding, clothing filthy and torn. He must have only just escaped when T'Sian had set fire to the woods. The dragon's glimmering, unblinking eyes regarded him for a moment; then she shifted her gaze to Diasa and said: "*You are trying to take the wizard prisoner.*"

"Yes. We need him alive."

The dragon moved her head in close; Diasa could see each individual scale of her face, and in the ones that weren't too smudged or scorched, she could make out a dim reflection of herself and the wizard, grimy apparitions separated by a gleaming blade. "*What makes you think I will not burn you both?*" T'Sian said. "*I could. Not even ashes would remain to mark the place where you fell.*"

"You certainly could do that," Orioke said. "Your makers crafted you well."

T'Sian pulled her head back a bit. "*What did you say?*"

"I said that your makers crafted you well. Well, not *your* makers; the original dragons were brought to life eons ago, by ancient alchemists now long dead. But they created your race, so it could be said that they created *you*. Indirectly."

"*What nonsense is this?*"

"Qalor wasn't the first to make weapons using the crystals. Many centuries ago, other men tried something similar. They created a race of intelligent creatures, shapeshifters, that could consume the stones and produce fire in their bellies. These creatures could also go forth in stealth, disguised as humans; they could attack by surprise and burn their enemies to ash before they knew an attack was even underway. Do you know what these creatures were?"

Silence.

"Well? Do you?"

Thinking of the scrolls she'd found in Qalor's apartment, Diasa said: "Dragons."

"Very good, Diasa," Orioke said, sounding like one of the professors at Flaurent, derisively pleased that a student had answered an obvious question. "Dragons. But they proved too intelligent, too powerful, to be controlled. They turned on their creators and incinerated them, their cities, their forests, their fields. They boiled away the lakes and streams, scorched the topsoil, and left behind an eternal wasteland. Do you know what this wasteland is called now?"

Another obvious question. "The Salt Flats."

"Indeed. An entire region, rendered uninhabitable forever. The knowledge that had created the dragons was lost, except for a few scraps of research, scrolls and sketches that found their way into the library at Flaurent. Torrant obtained them, and brought them back to Dunshandrin, who passed them to Qalor, who showed them to me."

"If Flaurent had had such documents, I would have known," Diasa said, even though she had seen the scrolls sitting on Qalor's table with Flaurent's broken seal upon them.

"These were the most secret of papers, known only to the headmaster or mistress. They were kept hidden away, along with other scrolls describing mystical skills—telepathy, illusion, empathy, domination—that the rulers of the lands forbade oracles to exercise."

This was new information. "What lies are these that you tell?" Diasa said. "Oracles don't have such power."

The wizard snorted. "Are you so willfully blind that you can't see what is right before your eyes? Flaurent was not only a school where oracles were taught how to use their gifts; it was a place where their gifts were suppressed. Those who resisted, or seemed that they might become dangerous, would get lost in the desert, perhaps, or perhaps suffer an overdose of vapors and go mad."

Diasa imagined a professor mixing up powder for a young Wert, altering the ratios, knowing it would leave him a ranting fool; she imagined young oracles being taken from their beds, dragged out into the desert, left to die in the wastes. It couldn't possibly be true; her mother would never have harmed her own students. "What basis do you have for these claims?"

"Poor girl. Don't you understand? I was *at* Flaurent, first as a student, then as headmaster; I *participated* in the things I describe."

"Now I know you lie," Diasa said. "You are not on the roster of headmasters."

"My name was stricken from the rolls years ago, when I left to pursue magic, as well as for … other reasons." He smirked. "I knew Damona, when she was young, and looked like you."

Before Diasa could formulate a response to this startling comment, T'Sian brought her head down close, the acrid tang of her breath heating the chill air. *"You say Qalor showed you these scrolls, wizard? If you were once the master of this place, why did you not know about them already?"*

"I was not headmaster for long, and I was more interested in mentalism than alchemy; those were the scrolls I sought out during my tenure."

"But if Qalor really had such knowledge, he would have created his own dragons, not feeble imitations!"

"And repeat the mistake that had doomed the ancient alchemists? No, Qalor was too canny for that; he left control of the crystals firmly in the hands of men. But Dunshandrin, in his haste and greed, sent us to retrieve crystals from your lair, because he did not want to wait until spring to mount an expedition to Yttribia. He insisted on striking Barbareth this season, before the snows began, thinking he could consolidate his hold during the winter. It seems he underestimated your determination, and your desire for revenge."

"Enough! You are a liar! My race was not created by men!"

"Oh, but it was. Your ancestors were grown like homunculi in vats in the ancients' great laboratories. Dragons were never meant to be breeding stock; that is why you are slowly dying out. Most of you are infertile, and those that are not, such as yourself, will produce at most one batch of young. You live a long time, but you do not live forever; and one day, not so far in the future, there will be no more dragons."

For a long moment, T'Sian said no more; she just stared at Orioke with those luminous eyes. Diasa thought she might make good on her threat and incinerate them both; but at last, the dragon spoke. *"These papers from Flaurent could be used to restore the race of dragons?"*

"Certainly."

"And to remove the tainted stones that I swallowed?"

"Perhaps."

"But the castle is burnt and demolished," Diasa said. "The scrolls are destroyed."

"I have seen the documents; I read them, and discussed them with Qalor, and I remember them in perfect detail. Kill me, and the knowledge truly will be lost; but if we can come to an arrangement, then—"

Diasa pressed the blade firmly against Orioke's throat. "That," she said, "is most definitely enough talking."

T'Sian said: *"No. Let us bargain."*

"But—"

"This was your doing, Diasa. You kept the wizard alive. Now let me hear what ... arrangement he offers."

Damn the wizard! She should have left him for the dragon. Releasing him, she sheathed her small blade. "Fine," she said. "But when you find that you've become the wizard's plaything, don't place the blame with me."

Ponn was surprised to see Diasa return with a disheveled man in tow, and even more surprised when T'Sian landed nearby, her great wings stirring up the ashes that had settled in the grass. "Is this the legendary Orioke?" he said, eyeing the man.

"Indeed," the man said. "Who are you?"

"I thought you had gone to kill the wizard, not bring him back," he said, ignoring the question, looking from Diasa to T'Sian and back again.

T'Sian said nothing; Diasa just shrugged. "Plans change."

"Hello again, Adaran," Orioke said. "I don't suppose you'll accept my apology for all that's happened?"

The footpad fixed him with a murderous glare, then turned away.

"Ah," the wizard said. "I thought not."

"Enough small talk," Diasa said. "Fix Tolaria."

"I released the oracle some time ago. Now, she is merely sleeping.

See? She awakens already."

Tolaria stirred, then opened her eyes. She rolled onto her hands and knees, retched a little, then sat back on the grass and looked around a touch dazedly. Her gaze lingered on the wizard. "What's *he* doing here?"

"He's my prisoner," Diasa said.

Tolaria rubbed her temples, as if she had a bad headache; she probably did. "He doesn't *look* like a prisoner."

"You're very astute," Orioke said.

"Will someone tell me what happened?" Ponn asked. "Why did you bring him back here, after all he's done?"

"With Tolaria unconscious and Deliban coming, we couldn't afford to kill him. I caught him before T'Sian had a chance to burn him." She glowered at her putative captive. "Then he started talking."

"Some of us live by the strength of our arms," Orioke said. "Others live by stealth. I live by my wits and my words."

"Yes, you do," Diasa said. "That's why I would very much like you to be quiet."

"He'll turn on us the first chance he gets," Adaran said.

"Said the snake of the scorpion," Diasa murmured.

"Why should I turn on you?" Orioke said. "I am not some mad, cackling villain. I have come to an understanding with the dragon; the rest of you do not concern me."

"That's hardly reassuring," she said.

"*Enough. The wizard is no longer a threat. Leave him be.*"

"I disagree," Diasa said. "All he cares about is his deal with you. What's to stop him from betraying the rest of us?"

"*If you harm any of the others, wizard, then our agreement is at an end. Understood?*"

"Quite." Then, to Diasa: "Satisfied?"

"Not really."

"*Another thing*," T'Sian said. "*Your earth creature. I do not want it here. Send it back to where it came from.*"

"No!" Tolaria cried. "We need Deliban to stop the crystals!"

They all looked at her; Orioke said: "I don't understand."

"Deliban can collapse the hill and dam the river," she said. "It can drown the crystals in cold water and stop them from growing, or at least slow them. It's the only way to stop them from spreading across

Dunshandrin, maybe beyond."

"That actually might work," Diasa said after a moment.

Orioke glanced at the dragon, who gave a slight now.   "As you wish," the wizard said. "I will instruct Deliban to create this pond for you; then the dragon and I will take our leave of your little band. You will go back to your own business, and stop meddling in affairs that no longer concern you."

Ponn could scarcely believe what he was hearing. He looked at the dragon; she sat with her back to the fire, staring at the castle, the bony ridge along her spine shadowed like a mountain range at sunset. He wondered what had transpired, why she had spared the wizard. "T'Sian? You agree to this?"

"Do as the wizard says, Ponn.   All of you, hear me: Your part in this adventure has come to an end."

And before Ponn could say another word or ask another question, she spread her wings and launched herself into the fire-stained sky.

T'Sian spiraled away from the earth, rising on the thermals created by the fires she had set. The flames seemed to be dying out in the forest, which was damp from recent rains; but the town, with its wooden buildings and thatched roofs, still burned nicely. She rose higher, lifting herself with slow sweeps of her great wings. To the north, the ruins of the castle glowed with ghostly light, illuminated by the crystals that had grown over and through it like rot through a fallen log.

So. Qalor had been trying to duplicate the successes and avoid the failures of an earlier, greater breed of alchemist. She tried to imagine the dragons of old, the sky black with them as they laid waste to the region that had become the Salt Flats. What a sight it must have been, so much more majestic than puny men strapped onto the backs of overgrown chickens!

Over the years, she had encountered a few others of her kind at the archipelago, luxuriating in the heat of the volcanoes before returning across oceans and continents to their scattered lairs. How many?   A dozen, perhaps?   The older dragons were the most talkative; from them she had learned that it had once been common to see fifteen dragons in the skies above the islands. Then ten. Then five. She had at most seen two. Often she was there alone, as when she had met Pyodor Ponn. She felt the truth of Orioke's words; the dragons *were* fading, as even the greatest forest fire must eventually die out. And while the mighty dragons verged on extinction, men, short-lived but fecund, infested the world like insects in a carcass. How could such puny creatures have created the likes of herself? The wizard was willing to save her from Qalor's evil stones, to help maintain the line of dragons, but only because he sought control over her, and them. He dangled the survival of her species in front of her like bait before the noose.

She had never expected revenge to become so complicated.

T'Sian had by now drifted north of the village and the castle, rising ever higher; the earth stretched out beneath her, vast tracts of darkness interspersed with human settlements, smudges of heat formed by the collective glow of numerous fires. She remembered the eagle-rider who had fled when she burned the castle. It had headed in this direction, but she hadn't pursued. Diasa believed that the rulers of Dunshandrin would have escaped to a redoubt in the wilderness; perhaps the rider had intended to join them there. Between her rage and the confusion of the wizard's appearance, she had not thought to ask the oracle where Dunshandrin's cowardly children had gone, but perhaps she might find them on her own, as a dragon should, without help from men.

T'Sian continued along, scanning the ground for a likely human hideaway. Eventually she spied a large dwelling far below, nestled in a densely wooded valley north of the castle. It appeared to contain the heat of several hearths. Curious, she approached it, dropping lower to get a better look. She picked out a large stockade surrounding several wooden buildings, including a good-sized lodge. She circled it warily, skimming the treetops, tasting the air. Trees, woodsmoke, horses, men. She moved lower still, tongue flicking in and out, gathering more scents. Eagles. Not many, perhaps only one or two, and they had only been here a short while; it was not like the castle, which reeked of them. Still, their presence confirmed that this was the place she sought.

She landed on top of the lodge, her rear claws digging into the sturdy roof. She tore at the wooden shakes and the planking beneath, opening a hole big enough to admit her head; she shoved her face through, sending debris crashing into a large room below. The interior was dim, but she could make out the ghastly trappings of a hunter's den: Preserved animals glowered from niches; purloined skins and pelts, stretched and flattened, decorated the floor; mounted heads stared sightlessly from the walls, surveying the scene around them.

This place obviously belonged to the sort of men who would think little of slaughtering her hatchlings in order to get what they wanted.

She heard shouting, then running footsteps; the ants had realized that their nest was breached.   She exhaled a dribble of fire; the furniture, rugs, and rubble beneath her began to burn.   Then she withdrew from the hole, peering through it as a group of men came into the hall below. Most of them were clad in nightclothes, but a few wore uniforms like the one Diasa had taken from the guard she had killed.   They focused on the fire, not sparing a glance toward the ceiling; T'Sian watched as they smothered the flames with rugs dragged over from other parts of the room.   Once it had been extinguished, one of the men noticed the hole in the roof, pointing it out to the others. An argument ensued. They seemed to blame both hole and fire on a falling star, but no one wanted the task of awakening the princes and telling them about it.

So Dunshandrin's children *were* hiding here.

She thrust her head back into the hole and let loose a gout of flame, scouring the great hall with a roaring maelstrom. The screams from within ended almost as soon as they began; the night lit up as flames blew out the windows of the lodge, rushing air knocking the wooden shutters open, letting the inferno burst free.

T'Sian continued to exhale death into the lodge, Qalor's altered stones burning fiercely in her breast, the sound of the inferno like a cataract in her ears.   When she finally pulled her head out of the roof, orange-red tongues spurted through the opening like a volcano erupting.

She jumped into the air, caught the heat, rose above the burning lodge.   She turned and dove, sweeping over the compound, laying down a blanket of destruction across the outlying structures.   Once the entire complex was engulfed and burning brightly, she climbed again, circling above it, wings spread wide, drifting, watching for any signs of movement.   Soon someone stumbled out of the rear of the main building, staggering and choking as flames threatened from every side. She dove, snatched the man up in one of her rear claws, and climbed back into the sky. Hovering above the flames, she stretched out her neck, swiveled, looked him in the face. Barefoot and sooty, he wore a torn, smudged night-shirt of a dark color threaded with gold. The material looked kingly enough to belong to a prince. He goggled at her, his eyes wide, his skin pallid.

"*What is your name?*" she said.

His eyes rolled up and his head fell to the side. She gave him a little shake, to no avail; still, she thought he was not dead, but merely unconscious. She must have frightened him too much. She would hold onto him, and question him later, when he awakened.

T'Sian waited, watching to see who else might come out from the flames. One other person, his clothes and hair and flesh burning, emerged from the same door as her captive; he only went a step or two before collapsing in a sizzling heap. A group of men, guards by the look of them, escaped from the lodge, only to be trapped between buildings, with no way out. She watched as their strength gave out, the smoke overcame them, and they fell, becoming fuel for the blaze. She saw no others; she had taken them asleep and unaware, and most of them had probably burned or choked in their beds.

She looked again at the unconscious man she had taken. Perhaps he was only pretending. Diasa would be able to tell, and Tolaria could identify him as one of the twins or not. A pity that the other fellow had already been so badly charred; if he had looked exactly the same as her captive, then she would have known that she had the twins. Then again, sometimes it was difficult for her to tell humans apart anyway; they tended to look very much alike.

Leaving the inferno behind her, the dragon flew away, carrying her prize.

26

DAWN BROKE RED AND HAZY, the sunlight filtering through the haze of last night's fires. Ponn's eyes felt dry and gritty, perhaps from the smoke that lingered in the air, perhaps from an incipient cold; he had spent a long time in the icy river yesterday, and would hardly be surprised if he took sick.

He sat up.   Prehn was already awake, playing with a stick, scratching crude pictures in the dirt. He thought she might be trying to draw the dragon.   He gently patted her head, then stood and stretched and looked around. The others were still asleep, except for Diasa, who sat keeping a watchful eye on Orioke. Had she slept at all last night?   It wouldn't surprise him if she hadn't; she seemed as tireless as the dragon, and, sometimes, almost as alien.

He went to her, shaking the stiffness out of his legs. It would be so fine to be back in his own bed, back with Plenn, back at the inn! If T'Sian kept to her bargain with the wizard, he might be on his way home by the end of the day.   He wondered if they had enough money left to pay for passage on a ship, or if he would have to barter for it; somehow, he didn't see himself returning to Astilan to dig up what treasure the dragon had buried.

Diasa acknowledged him with a nod. "Were you up all night?" he asked.

"I'll sleep when the dragon comes back. I don't trust our slippery friend here."   She pointed at Orioke.   "The oracle told me he communicates with Deliban by speaking mind to mind. What's to stop him from secretly telling it to bury us all, then claiming we must have wandered off?"

419

"He made a bargain with T'Sian."

Diasa snorted. "If you believe he'll honor *that* agreement, then I have an orchard in the Salt Flats I'd like to sell you."

"I believed him, when he said he wouldn't harm us."

"Yes, he's quite a persuasive liar," she said, "but he's a liar nonetheless. And T'Sian isn't here, is she?"

Suddenly Tolaria's eyes snapped open; she didn't seem to be seeing anything, though. "The dragon returns," she said, her voice flat. "She carries a villain." Then she blinked a few times, coughed, and pushed herself upright. "Is it morning already?"

Diasa shrugged, poked the dying fire. "Some would say so."

Ponn, scanning the sky, spotted a dark shape to the northeast, growing rapidly larger as it approached. "Tolaria was right," he said. "Here comes T'Sian now."

"Oh … did I predict something?"

"Nothing of consequence," Diasa said.

The three of them watched as T'Sian circled the camp. Ponn could see that she clutched someone in one of her rear claws, and remembered when he had flown in a similar position. It was like being caged, long fingers strong as iron folded around him, black talons sharp and cold against his skin. She could easily gut a horse with those cruel daggers, which had made the experience particularly unnerving, at first.

T'Sian landed in the road just east of where they had camped. She opened her claw, letting her passenger spill out onto the grass. "*Tell me if this man is dead,*" she said.

Diasa went over, rolled the fellow onto his back, and gave him a quick examination. "No, he's not dead. He's just unconscious, or pretending to be." She looked up at the dragon. "Judging by his garment, he's rich, important, or both. Where did you find him?"

"*I took him when I burned some buildings in the woods east of the castle,*" T'Sian said. "*It was like the place you described, where you thought the princes would go. A stronghold, with high walls and guards and horses. And eagles.*"

"Eagles, eh?" Diasa turned to the oracle. "Tolaria, come here. We need you to perform an identification."

Tolaria slowly approached Diasa and the dragon. She could already tell from the man's nightshirt that he was one of Dunshandrin's sons;

the only question was which. She stood nearby, out of reach, looking down at him, his burned, torn finery, his smudged skin. Hugging herself around the elbows, she said: "It's one of the princes."

His eyes opened. "I know that voice."

"Faking," Diasa said. "I thought as much. You're lucky I didn't stick you with my dagger to see if you'd yelp."

The prince's cold gaze moved to Diasa. "If you had, I would have had you killed. I will anyway, to punish your insolence."

Diasa, unfazed, snorted at the threat. "Look around," she said. "Do you see any of your henchmen here? Who do you expect to carry out your orders?"

"*I burned his stronghold to the ground*," T'Sian said. "*I stayed and watched. None escaped.*"

"You are not in your castle now, Tomari," Tolaria said. "Your father is not here. Your brother is not here. You have no soldiers at your command. You have nothing." She turned away. "You *are* nothing."

"A stirring speech, Tolaria," he said. "But I am Torrant, not Tomari." Then: "You used to be able to tell us apart."

"You used to behave differently," she said after a moment. "I suppose I must have difficulty recognizing you when you are not trying to seduce me."

She noticed that Orioke was awake, and looking at her. He got to his feet and approached; she thought he might speak to her, but instead he went on by. She turned, watching as he stopped in front of Torrant and said, "Greetings, my liege."

"Wizard." One less genteel than Torrant might have spat at the sorcerer's feet, Tolaria thought. "I see that Tomari was right about you. I suppose you sent the dragon to destroy my father's hunting lodge."

"No, she found it on her own. But I have struck a bargain with her, and I'm afraid it supersedes the one I made with you."

"Did you hear that?" Tolaria said. "The wizard has betrayed you. Your schemes have cost you everything you cared about. Your servants, your castle, your kingdom. You took me prisoner because you wanted to know how your plans would turn out. Now I will tell you willingly. Ask me what your future holds."

"What?"

"Ask me what your future holds."

Torrant said: "No."

"Go ahead," Diasa said, nudging him with her foot. "Ask ."

"I will not."

Adaran said: "Tolaria, what does Torrant's future hold?"

Her mind opened up and the future rushed in like dark water, filling her thoughts, pouring out her mouth. When she came back to herself, still standing—she hadn't swooned this time—Torrant was staring at her, his earlier sneer vanished, his face gone ashen. His fate would not be bright, it seemed.

She turned her back on him and walked away, returning to where Ponn and Adaran sat. Prehn, in Adaran's lap, watched wide-eyed as she approached. She sat next to the thief and whispered, "What did I say?"

"You said the tides of war would be reversed, that the invaded would become the invader. You said the name of Dunshandrin would be scorned for decades as a synonym for greed and treachery, before being lost to the ages."

"And that's why he's looking at me that way?" She had expected to hear something worse; then again, to one such as Torrant, the extinction of his line might be the worst fate imaginable.

Adaran shook his head. "No, that's probably because you said the dragon was going to eat him." He looked past her, toward T'Sian. "It might already be coming true, I think."

She turned. T'Sian had lifted Torrant up into the air and now held him upside-down by one of his legs as the prince squirmed and screamed and made unconvincing threats. But, she noted, he did not beg. He had that much dignity, at least.

"*Do you believe in prophecies, man?*" T'Sian said. "*You must, or you would not have taken Tolaria to be your prisoner.*"

"Put me down!" Torrant screamed. "I rule this land!"

The dragon opened her mouth wide, then hesitated. The ground had begun to tremble beneath them, as if a minor earthquake were occurring nearby. Moments later the hillside split open, the dirt rising and twisting to form a manlike shape. This must be Deliban, finally answering Orioke's call. Hard to believe that this creature, which had dwelt in the earth beneath Flaurent for all those years, quietly maintaining underground irrigation channels, bringing salt to the surface for the college to sell, had been transformed into a weapon of war and destruction. Which was closer to its true nature? Did it even have one?

Deliban's muddy head swiveled this way and that, looking them over. It had stones for eyes, a stump for a nose, roots for lips. She wondered if it actually used them to see, to smell, to speak, or had merely constructed an imitation of a human face, perhaps in honor of its master, or in mockery.

"Deliban!" Torrant screamed. "Destroy them! Save me!"

"Deliban obeys *me*, not you," Orioke said. Then, turning to the earth creature: "There is a ruined castle just to the north, on a bluff overlooking a river. You will flatten the hill and raise an earthen wall around it to dam the river. The wall will be high enough so that a lake is created, completely submerging the castle and all its grounds. Do you understand?"

After a moment, the thing that was Deliban nodded.

"Then go, and carry out my command."

The earth trembled as Deliban withdrew once more into the ground. Tolaria watched as the dirt and rubble that formed its body spread across the hillside like wax from a melting candle, leaving tree roots sticking up into the air like the stiff legs of dead insects. The creature's face was the last thing to disappear, stretching, distorting, flattening; one of the rocks that had formed its eyes rolled down the hill, bouncing across the road to splash into the river beyond.

Torrant, still clutched in T'Sian's talon, cried: "You would have that creature drown my father's castle?"

Orioke shrugged. "The dragon already destroyed it. What difference does it make if the ruins are underwater?"

"We're trying to save the rest of your kingdom," Tolaria told him. "Qalor's crystals are growing unchecked. They will eventually spread and contaminate the entire realm."

"Without the Dunshandrian line, there *is* no realm!"

"*Good*," T'Sian said. She lifted him up, dangling him over her yawning jaws. Her long grey tongue, delicately forked at the end, flicked out, dancing across Torrant's face. He screamed and grabbed it, perhaps thinking he could tear it out. But the dragon's tongue turned out to be as clever as her tail; it twined around his wrists, effectively binding them, then drew him into her maw. The prince's screams became muffled as he entered T'Sian's throat head-first. The last things Tolaria saw before turning away were Torrant's wildly kicking legs, bared as his robe slid up toward his head, sticking out of T'Sian's mouth.

Despite everything Torrant had done, seeing him swallowed like an earthworm made her feel slightly ill.

"Let's go to the castle and make sure Deliban does what it's told," Ponn said.

"Yes," Diasa said, "let's."

After carrying the others over the charred village and depositing them on the road to the castle, T'Sian returned to the air, circling the site that had become the graveyard of Dunshandrin's ambitions. She could see that the earth creature was obeying the wizard's instructions; it had already transformed the butte into a crater, and had begun raising massive ramparts of earth and stone around it. The crystals had already spread well outside the walls of the keep, but not beyond the boundaries of the future lake. The river had already begun to form a churning, muddy pool behind the dam. The stone bridge, outside the walls, now stood over a muddy channel riddled with silvery pools and slick red rocks.

She felt the stones she had swallowed burning inside her, creating a fire hotter than was natural, renewing themselves every moment that she did not draw upon them. Despite all the fire she had produced this night and day, the crystals continued to spread inside her, a brittle, glassy irritant. She could not deny that Qalor had done his work well, however misguided it had been. His achievement was going to kill her.

Hovering high overhead, she watched the others cross the bridge. By the time they reached the top of the earthworks, Deliban's work was complete. The creature's power was perhaps greater even than her own; she wondered if it, too, were the product of the ancient alchemists, or if it were some other sort of entity, older still. She had destroyed the castle easily enough, but she could not transform the landscape at her whim. If Dunshandrin had known the wizard could harness such a force, would he have still sought the crystals, still built his devices? She thought he probably would have. Such a man was never satisfied with the power at his disposal, and always sought more.

The water level within the crater was rising quickly; soon it would begin flowing into the sunken courtyard.

She almost wished she had kept the haughty prince alive a little longer, just so he could have seen his castle vanish beneath the icy water.

Adaran gazed down at the ruined castle. When Deliban had crumbled the bluff, the stone walls and timbers had become churned together with natural earth and stone to create a jumble of charred wood, cracked masonry, burnt furnishings, scorched and crushed bodies. It was like looking down into a massive charnel pit.

Then there were the crystals. The red ones lay scattered across the crater floor, gleaming like frozen drops of blood catching the rays of the sun; the blue ones had formed a spreading mass with spires and towers and arches, like some fairytale palace. The whole thing glowed with internal energy and thrummed with the sound of a distant swarm of bees. The fairies in their palace had seen the approaching flood, and it made them angry.

"It will soon be over," Orioke murmured, "and the dragon will come away with me."

Adaran glanced at the wizard, who stood not far to his right, beside Deliban's hulking, rocky mass, which had arisen from the earth to join them. Orioke's eyes, hard and glittering as the crystals themselves, were fixed on the dragon stones; Adaran thought the mage must be wondering if he could find a way to use them himself. Perhaps he would return someday, Deliban in tow, to drain the new lake and claim the deadly treasure hidden beneath the surface.

Well, that would be T'Sian's problem, wouldn't it? She had told the rest of them that the situation was no longer their concern, and that was fine with him.

He felt a tug on his tattered sleeve. Prehn, wanting to be picked up. He shook his head, showed her his bandages. "I can't lift you," he said. The little girl took one of his hands and inspected it, sniffing the bandage and making a face at the smell. Letting go, she seized his tunic and scaled him, hand over hand, as if he were a wall or a tree. In short order she had settled onto his shoulders, her knees locked around his neck to hold herself in place.

Ponn, observing this, said, "She hasn't forgotten what you did for her." Then, after a moment: "Nor have I."

Steadying himself on the stick he had been using as a cane, Adaran said: "But you're here now. Why didn't she climb you?"

"She tried, but I told her no, because of my shoulder. Besides, you're taller. You provide a better view."

Chuckling, Adaran turned his gaze back to the castle. The river had begun to lap against the nearest edge of the crystal dome; wisps of vapor rose from the point of contact. As the water drowned the glowing stones, the vapor became bubbles, which became smaller and smaller as the pond grew deeper.

Suddenly he noticed the dragon plunging down from the heights, coming straight toward them.

It was over.

Dunshandrin was dead, his castle destroyed, his line eradicated. The river was dammed, and Qalor's tainted crystals would be lost beneath the icy water, unable to harm unwary dragons.

All that remained were two small items of deferred revenge.

She would only have once chance at this. She had to strike quickly, before the wizard realized what she was doing; otherwise he would loose his elemental, would bring powers to bear against her. She could not deal with both of them at once; events in Astilan had most clearly demonstrated that. Nor could she take Orioke but leave Deliban. Freed from any constraint, the creature might rampage and harm the others. Not that she cared for the fate of a few humans; but she had given her word that they would not be harmed, and she would not have it bruited about that a dragon's promise was a meaningless thing.

She drifted nearer to where they stood, all her attention focused on the wizard, waiting for the right moment, for him to be distracted. That moment came when the water began to reach the large mass of crystals; he leaned forward, peering into the crater, his crafty little mind probably racing ahead to his plans for her once they were away from the others. The fool had such confidence in his powers of persuasion that it never occurred to him that she might have plans of her own.

She dove at them, claws outstretched, plummeting from the sky like a massive tephra hurled through the air by a volcanic explosion. But at the last moment before striking, she realized that Pyodor Ponn's daughter sat upon the shoulders of the one called Adaran. She could not take him without taking the little girl as well.

For a fraction of an instant, T'Sian hesitated; then she drew that claw back, out of the way.

One last gift to Pyodor Ponn, then.

Her other talon closed around Orioke's body like the iron bars of a prison; at the same time she whipped her tail at Deliban, snaring the earth creature around the midsection. Pulling it away from the ground was like uprooting an ancient and massive tree, but she had tremendous momentum behind her; she tore the elemental off the dam, bringing it with her, a clot of dirt and rubble held together by roots and willpower.

Laden with this burden, she flew toward the deep, cold lake.

Tolaria stared at the dragon as she flew sharply upward, Orioke wriggling in one claw, Deliban clutched in her long tail. Mud and stones fell from the creature's body like dirt shaking loose from the roots of a plant.

"T'Sian!" Ponn cried. "What are you doing?"

Adaran, ashen, whispered: "She was going to take me."

"T'Sian!" Ponn broke into a run, racing down the dam toward the village, even though there was little chance that she could hear him, and none at all that he could catch her.

Adaran turned to Tolaria and Diasa. "She was going to take me," he said again. "She wanted to carry me off, too."

"Of course she did," Diasa said. "She hates you."

He turned, looking off toward the lake, and the receding form of the dragon. "Why did she change her mind?"

"If I must guess?" Diasa pointed at Prehn. "But you can't carry Ponn's daughter around forever."

"He won't need to," Tolaria said. "I don't think T'Sian is planning to come back."

T'Sian beat her wings harder, gathering speed and altitude. Climbing was difficult with the extra weight of the earth creature; the thick muscles across her back began to ache as she rose higher and higher above the black waters of the lake.

The wizard struggled feebly in her claw. She had squeezed him very tightly, just the way Ponn had told her not to, keeping him from drawing enough breath to use his words against her. She wanted him alive and conscious, until the final moment, so that he could see his fate coming to meet him; but she did not want him casting any spells.

When she had achieved a sufficient height, she released Deliban, flinging the mass of dirt away from herself. It lost shape as it plummeted, becoming a rain of earth and rock. She had no idea if the creature's spirit was still contained within it, or if it had been left back by the dam when she pulled its body off the ground. Either way, she had done all she could to keep the others safe. Pivoting now, she turned her face down, toward the lake, and pulled in her wings.

She began to fall through the chill morning air. She drew up her legs, making herself smooth to lessen the resistance. The water raced up to meet her; at this velocity, the impact would be like crashing into solid stone.

Here came the lake. Now she could see the individual waves; now she could see the ripples, and the reflection of the rising sun on each, a field of small fires, like the extinguished light in the eyes of her young. They waited for her on the other side of that dark surface.

Just before slamming into water, she thrust her arm forward, the one that held tight the wizard. His eyes were wide, his mouth open in a scream that was lost in the rushing wind. The dragon felt an instant of pain as her outstretched limb struck the lake, but it was worth it, to see the wizard smashed to jelly before her eyes.

Then came the water, and the cold, and the darkness.

T'Sian's impact threw up a tremendous splash, so high it seemed like a geyser erupting; Ponn could see it from the bridge north of the village. He stopped then, panting, hands on his knees. There was no reason to keep running now.

By the time Ponn rejoined the others on the dam, the spot where the dragon had slammed into the water was calm again, a large field of fizzing bubbles the only sign of her impact. Those would surely dissipate soon, as the stones inside T'Sian's body cooled and her fires went out forever.

He felt a hand on his shoulder. Diasa. "I'm sorry, Ponn."

"Sorry?" He looked at her. "There's no reason to be sorry. It's not as if she was my friend."

"No, of course not," Diasa said. "You went charging down the hill because you wanted a better view as she crashed into the lake; and the wetness about your eyes is merely spray from the splash."

Ponn said nothing.

"And obviously she cared nothing for you," Diasa said. "That she intended to take Adaran as well, but spared him because he had your little girl on his shoulders, signifies nothing."

Ponn looked at the footpad. "Really?"

"She had her claw out and ready," Adaran said; he still sounded shaken. "I saw it coming right at me, but at the last second she pulled it back."

"So you see, despite what you claim to believe, the dragon *was* your friend," Diasa said. "And you were hers. If you don't believe it, just ask the oracle."

"No, don't ask the oracle," Tolaria said. "For once, just be satisfied with the evidence of your own eyes."

The five of them returned to the ruined village, Ponn carrying Prehn, Tolaria and Diasa on either side of Adaran to help him walk. None of them spoke as they made their way along the scorched cobbles and cracked, dried mud, past buildings that still leached smoke into the air. T'Sian was gone, but the legacy of her final hours lay all around them.

This was the work of just *one* dragon. Diasa imagined the destruction of whatever kingdom had preceded the Salt Flats, the sky squirming with dragons, raining lethal fire over every square inch of land, laying waste to everything, every green plant, every creature that walked upon the earth or crawled beneath it. If Orioke had spoken the truth, that had happened many centuries ago, but even now nothing grew there, nothing dwelt in those ruined lands, except for ghosts, and a few stubborn miners, and, once upon a time, a school.

They eventually found their way to the lake. The structures along the waterfront had suffered major tsunami damage, the docks largely in splinters; there were a few boats left, though, bobbing in the gentle waves. A high water mark slowly dried in the weak autumn sun, showing the size of the wave that had come ashore after the dragon plunged into the lake. It had been easily as tall as a man, and looked to have smashed some of the smaller vessels and the shoddy lake-front shops. Even in her final moments, the dragon had been an impressive force for destruction.

They stood a while, looking out across the water that had become T'Sian's grave. Eventually, Diasa noticed people moving along the shore, not approaching the town just yet, but edging in that direction. Locals, probably, who hadn't fled as far as most, and had seen the dragon's plunge, and were working up the nerve to come home.

Home. Where was that, anyway?

Finally, Tolaria said: "So now what do we do? How do we get back to where we belong?"

Ponn gestured toward a small sailing vessel that floated nearby, attached to a crooked, ruined dock by a frayed length of rope. "A journey begins when you release your moorings," he said. "Are you ready?"

"*I* am," Diasa said. "Let's get out of this forsaken town."

First Epilogue

TOLARIA, DIASA IN TOW, CLIMBED the hill to the Crosswaters in a hard, cold rain, just like the storm on the day she had left. It seemed a lifetime since she had first made this trip, a novice seer unsure of what lay ahead, and another lifetime since she had been sent on a fool's errand to give advice and counsel to Lord Dunshandrin's sons.

As she approached the outer walls of the Crosswaters, she began to smell the odor of burned wood, intensified by the precipitation and the moisture. The main gates hung open, giving a view into the grounds and the ruins of the central temple

She glanced at Diasa. The woman had insisted on escorting her back to the temple; her job was to protect the students and oracles of Flaurent, she'd said, and Tolaria was the closest thing left to one of her charges. Also, Tolaria suspected, she had wanted to see the destruction for herself, as if she needed another reason to hate Dunshandrin.

They paused a while at the ruined entrance, where guards had once inquired after the business of those who sought entry to the Crosswaters. Beyond, the grounds showed signs of widespread conflagration; at least the walls had contained the flames, preventing them from spreading to the surrounding meadow or to the village at the base of the hill.

Tolaria moved into the compound, where the smell of old fire became stronger. She first went up the wide gravel track that led to the main sanctuary. It had been devastated, blown out from within and reduced to a jumble of blackened walls and beams. She wondered if the bodies of the other oracles were still inside; finding that out would be a task for another day.

"You were right. This wasn't just a fire," Diasa said. "It was a trial run. Dunshandrin tested out Qalor's devices here."

"Does that mean there will be crystals growing inside?"

"I doubt it. Qalor told me that as part of the reaction, the stones destroyed each other."

"But what if the destruction was incomplete, and there was a little bit left? What then?"

Diasa thought for a moment, then said: "Well, if you intend to stay here, perhaps you should check the ruins for crystals from time to time."

Not reassured by this, Tolaria proceeded along a narrow side path that eventually arrived at the small, mean hut to which Klem had banished her. It came into view as they circled the temple. Separate from the main building, it had somehow survived the fire that had obliterated the sanctuary; the southerly winds, common this time of year, would have helped to keep the flames at bay. Only a few spots on the roof showed scorch marks.

"This is where you lived?" Diasa said, eyeing the structure.

Tolaria nodded.

"My mother thought Klem would give you a place of honor, based on the recommendation in the letter she sent with you."

"I think the letter is what prompted him to put me here," she said. "It made him angry and envious. Anyway, it wasn't so bad. I planted a garden."

"I see nothing but weeds."

"Clearing it will help pass the time."

"Word will spread that an oracle has returned," Diasa said. "You'll soon be too busy to putter around with flowers."

Diasa was probably right, but Tolaria hadn't given much thought yet to how she would handle being the only oracle at the Crosswaters. "Petitioners will have to learn patience, I suppose," she said, as they moved along the path through the remains of the garden toward the front door of the hut.

"Perhaps you can start your own school here."

That hadn't occurred to her. Headmistress Tolaria. She supposed it was a possibility, although it might be difficult to be an administrator when you were compelled to answer all questions truthfully. "Well, first the sanctuary needs to be rebuilt. That alone will take years." Then: "You *will* stay and help, won't you?"

"I told you, I must return to Flaurent."

"But why? What's there for you?"

"There are still … beings living in the ruins," Diasa said. "One of them told me we would meet again."

"And that means you have to go back?"

Diasa shrugged. "I need to find out a few things."

By now they had reached the entrance of the hut. The door stood partly open. Tolaria gave it a push and it swung inward, revealing an interior in disarray: The spartan furniture had been upended, the rough cabinets emptied, the bedding strewn across the floor.

"Looters," Diasa said in disgust.

"I'm sure they left disappointed." Tolaria stepped inside. Windblown rain had caused water damage in the vicinity of the door, and it looked like an animal had nested in the hearth. "I suppose I'll have to get this cleaned up, too." She proceeded to her writing desk, against the left wall. It had been emptied, her papers spilled and then spread by the breezes. In the damp, some of them had stuck to the walls and even to the ceiling. She didn't remember having this many scrolls before she left. She picked up a few, looked them over. Mediation requests. Klem must have been piling up petitions for her to review upon her return.

Turning to Diasa, she said, "What do you think I should do with —" She broke off, realizing that her companion was no longer there. She hurried to the door, looking across the grounds, and spotted Diasa some distance away, moving toward the front entrance. Just before disappearing from view, Diasa paused, looked back, waved goodbye. Tolaria waved back uncertainly, then watched Diasa vanish through the gates.

She went back into the hut. Diasa had promised to see her safely back to the Crosswaters, and had done so; but still, she might have stayed a little longer; she might have said goodbye. Feeling abandoned, Tolaria shut the door, and went to clear the hearth for a fire. What wood she could find was damp, and burned smokily.

Not long after, a tentative knock on the door brought the first of many petitioners that day, coming to see the oracle.

Second Epilogue

After dropping off Tolaria and Diasa, Adaran and Pyodor Ponn took their stolen boat downriver to the port of Kilkarat, east of Astilan. The town was largely empty; it turned out that most of the able-bodied men had gone to join Laquin's forces, who were harrying the remnants of Dunshandrin's army as it tried to retreat from Barbareth. Laquin, it seemed, had recently been freed from captivity during a nighttime raid on the Dunshandrian general's encampment, and had rallied his troops to drive out the invaders.

With neither the wizard nor the earth elemental at their disposal, their supply lines destroyed, and unable to replenish their weapons with Qalor's alchemy, the Dunshandrians could not hold Astilan. Everyone they spoke to in Kilkarat agreed that surrender was imminent, that when the battles were over, Dunshandrin would be an unimportant province of Barbareth, presumably with a new name. Tolaria's final prophecy for Torrant had already started to come true, it seemed.

Through a deceased friend, Ponn had minor connections in Kilkarat—Adaran wasn't sure what sort of connections they were; Ponn referred to it as covert shipping, which obviously meant smuggling, much to Adaran's astonishment—and he managed to get them passage on one of the last trading ships of the season, heading southeast along the coast to Enshenneah. Adaran's work had never taken him on an ocean-going vessel before, and he quickly discovered that he had an unfortunate predisposition to seasickness.

The ship docked briefly in Astilan to unload supplies for use in rebuilding the city; it docked again in Dyvversant, taking on cargo.

Ponn vaguely remarked that it would be a good idea if they stayed aboard the ship and out of sight instead of going into either city.

After Dyvversant, they sailed around the mountainous outcroppings to the south, giving a wide berth to a region of smoldering volcanoes. Adaran had never seen such a thing before and, in between bouts of vomiting, scanned the peaks for signs of eruption. Unfortunately, he had to be satisfied with a few steaming vents in the distant black rock.

At length the mountains and palisades gave way to the jungles of Enshenneah. Now Ponn began to spend more time at the ship's rail as well, Prehn at his side or on his shoulders, watching the wild tangle slowly slide past. Sometimes, when he wasn't feeling particularly nauseated, Adaran joined them; when he thought he was likely to throw up, he stayed away.

The third day out from Dyvversant, when Adaran limped to where Ponn stood, the Enshennean glanced at him and said: "Nearly there."

Adaran said nothing. He had accepted Ponn's invitation to work at his inn for a while, but had no idea what his duties would be. He suspected that Ponn was planning to give him some sinecure, out of gratitude or pity or both. He thought he was unlikely to enjoy a stationary life in the steamy wilds of Enshenneah, but it was something to do while he recovered from his injuries; although he was able to walk unassisted now, his injured hand was still useless, as Tolaria had said it would be. He might not be good for burglary anymore, but he still needed to eat.

They reached Ponn's village the next morning. This proved to be a collection of small, round buildings nestled about a rocky lagoon. A tall wooden fence ran off into the lush green jungle that reared up behind the structures, verdant and shaggy; the stockade held it at bay, though it looked as if the surrounding creepers never stopped trying to reclaim the territory. The helmsman carefully steered the ship between jagged arms of black rock; Adaran braced himself, expecting the vessel to run aground at any moment. It had a shallow draft, though, and even though both sides of the hull scraped against the encircling shoals, they entered the broad, placid water of the harbor afloat and intact. The ship cut toward a series of docks made of lengths of round, hollow wood lashed together with fibrous vines.

The sophistication of the structure belied the impression of Enshenneah he'd gotten from the headmistress and others; this was hardly the work of savages.

After the ship tied up, Adaran followed Pyodor Ponn down the gangplank to the pier, then to the black sand beach. The Enshennean had grown quiet, overtaken by excitement and anxiety that were evident in his face; Prehn, on the other hand, jabbered endlessly about nothing, pointing at things and naming them, pointing at people and naming them, too. All the people here seemed to know Ponn, and he constantly had to stop to exchange greetings, explain his long absence, and introduce his strange-looking companion. He began to grow visibly impatient with all the questions and started to ignore them, hurrying through the winding village paths as fast as Adaran's injured feet allowed.

But he was still too slow; word of his return must have reached his wife before he did, because a woman appeared in front of them and Ponn stopped short. Prehn squealed and scrambled away from him, running up and leaping into the woman's arms.

"Plenn," Ponn said, taking a step forward.

She slapped him, pivoted on her heel, and stalked away, carrying Prehn with her.

Ponn stood there for a few seconds, apparently stunned; then he ran after her, leaving Adaran to hobble along after and hope he wouldn't get lost.

Third Epilogue

PONN CAUGHT UP WITH PLENN at the door to the inn and followed her inside. He waited as she set Prehn down and sent her into the back room, inducing squeals from the other children who waited there. He followed Plenn again when she went into the kitchen. Finally she turned, pointed at him, opened her mouth, closed it, started to cry, and crushed him with a hug.

At last she let go of him, stepped back, and said: "Pord?"

The boy hadn't returned, then. Ponn slumped back against a wooden table and shook his head.

"No," Plenn said. "No, no, no."

"He wanted to come with us to the islands; he must have been hiding on the ship when the dragon sank it." The homecoming tasted bitter suddenly, a loaf of bread that looked perfect but had been burned on the bottom. "He was always so stubborn."

"But with a good, strong heart," Plenn said. "He would have grown into a brave man." Then: "Did you say a *dragon* sank the ship?"

"Yes, in the islands, after we had moored in a lagoon. I did ask her if she had seen a child in the wreckage, and she said no, so I thought perhaps—"

"You *asked* her?"

"We became companions, of a sort, after she rescued me. Gelt had abandoned me on the volcano, and—"

"That's not what *I* heard," Plenn said, interrupting, her amber eyes narrow. "*I* heard you were in Dyvversant squiring some fancy lady about, and Apperand had you arrested and thrown in jail."

So that part of the tale had made its way back here; gossip was an illicit cargo that needed no smuggler. "The woman was T'Sian, the dragon," he said. "She could take on human form. And Apperand did have me arrested, but it had nothing to do with her. Gelt had reported us to the authorities; Apperand threw Parillon and me in jail to save his own skin. T'Sian freed us, but she accidentally killed Parillon after we escaped."

"This dragon sounds careless," Plenn said, "*accidentally* killing Pord, then Parillon. What was her interest in you?"

"Her hatchlings had been butchered by the same man who sent Gelt here. She thought I could help her find them." She looked dubious, so he quickly gave her the whole tale, from being carried off by T'Sian until his arrival back at the village earlier that morning. Plenn folded her arms and listened, her face betraying increasing skepticism as he spoke of the attack on Astilan, the flight to Achengate, the destruction of the castle. As he talked, he heard the door to the inn open, the clunk of a cane on the floor, and then Prehn's squeal and giggle. Adaran must have arrived. "Come into the common room with me," Ponn said, taking Plenn's arm. "There is someone you must meet."

Plenn made a token resistance, then allowed him to lead her to the kitchen door. He opened it a crack so that they could see Adaran sitting at a table near the door, Prehn in his lap, regaling the other children with her own version of their adventures. Plenn put her hand on Ponn's shoulder and touched a finger to her lips, telling him to wait. The two of them stood there, listening, as Prehn described being carried off by the eagle, being rescued by Adaran and then by Diasa, flying on the dragon's back. Ponn noticed that Plenn had begun crying. He closed the door and turned to her; she crashed into his arms, crushing him with a powerful hug.

"I'm sorry I doubted you," she whispered.

"It's all right. I would doubt a story like that too."

"I thought you were all dead, you and Pord and Prehn. I thought they had dumped your bodies in the sea. I tried not to show my fears, but the children kept asking—"

"Hush," Ponn said. "It's all right. We're home, we're safe."

Still sniffling a little, Plenn stepped back, holding him at arm's length, looking at him. Wiping her eyes, she said: "There'll be no more adventures now, will there, Ponn?   You'll stay here and be a simple innkeeper?"

"Of course," Ponn said. "At least, until I replace my ship. There is still one thing I must do."

"What?"

"Return to the islands, and see if I can find Pord," he said.

"But you nearly died there!"

"This time I will have my own crew," he said, "and a small boat that can better navigate the shoals."

"And if you meet another dragon?"

"Then I'll see if it knew T'Sian," he said, "and we can swap stories about her."

Fourth Epilogue

Diasa stood on what was left of the stone dock outside the ruined walls of Flaurent. The drifting, stinging sand had obscured most of the buildings, the wasteland reclaiming what had been carved out of it. In the distance the mountains loomed, tall, dark, indistinct behind veils of dust and salt.

"My lady, we can't stay here much longer. There's a storm coming; we must leave soon if we're to reach Achengate ahead of it."

She glanced over her shoulder at the flatboat that had brought her home. She'd had some difficulty and spent a great deal of money finding a pilot willing to take her this far into the Salt Flats; everyone knew Flaurent had been destroyed, and rumors had spread of curses and sorcery. Even without the approaching storm, the captain would have been in a hurry to be gone.

"You will leave without me," she said.

"What?"

"I'm staying here."

The captain shook his head. "But, my lady—"

"Please stop calling me that," Diasa said. "Do I look like someone who is accustomed to being addressed as *my lady*?"

"No, my lady, but regardless, you can't stay here. If the bandits and the phantoms don't get you, you'll be dead of thirst within a week."

"I didn't pay you to look after my well-being," Diasa said. She picked up her pack and headed for the compound, ignoring the man's half-hearted protests. By the time she had climbed the mounded sand that had piled up in front of the wall, the boat was already leaving, the relieved crew pushing it away from the dock with their poles.

It was an easy slide down the other side of the dune and through the gates, and then she was inside the college. She wandered a while through the wreckage. It no longer looked like the place where she had been born and raised. The trees stood withered and dead, their leaves dried up and blown away; the flowers and yards lay beneath a layer of fine powder, as if they had never been. The ruined buildings were nearly buried as well, reduced to mounds beneath the wasteland.

She stopped after making a circuit of the place, in front of the dark entrance to the guardhouse. It, at least, remained free of debris. This was where she had last seen Flaurent's sleepless guardians, unless she counted what had happened on the docks in Achengate. Tolaria had told her the Withered Ones weren't there, but that didn't mean she was right.

She had no idea what lay beyond the black opening; no one went through that doorway except the Withered Ones.

Something flickered at the edges of her vision; shadowy figures moved in the interior of the guardhouse, barely visible, watching her. She approached cautiously, a hand on her sword; as she passed into the shadow of the wall the remaining Withered Ones came out to meet her, four of them, moving single-file. Two carried swords; two carried axes.   They lined up before her as if presenting arms for inspection.

"Were you in Achengate?" she asked. "Did you save me?"

"We guard," it said, its voice sand blowing in the wind.

"So you *were* there," she said.

The Withered One didn't answer. Instead, it stretched out its arms, showing her what it held: A dusty, hooded robe, identical to the ones that the Withered Ones wore themselves.

"I don't understand," Diasa said, looking at it.

"We guard," it said. "You guard."

"You want me to join you?" It nodded. She imagined she could hear the dry flesh of its chin and neck creaking like old rope. "But I told you, there's nothing left here to guard."

"We guard secrets," it whispered. "Secrets below."

What was it talking about? More things she didn't know about

Flaurent, more things her mother hadn't told her?

"Come," it said. "Guard secrets."

Diasa unbuckled her sword belt, then took the robe from the Withered One's outstretched hands. She slipped it on; the fabric felt stiff and prickly against her skin, as if it were attaching itself to her with thousands of tiny, gripping claws. She put her scabbard back on. Already it seemed her waist and hips had shrunk. She looked at her hands, blackened and shriveled, like those of a body burned beyond recognition. Burned, perhaps, in the fires of a thousand dragons. Except for the prickling, though, she felt no different from before.

She lifted the hood up over her head. Her vision changed, the colors fading, replaced by a twilit view of dim shapes and striated temperatures. Was this how they saw the world, her mysterious, vigilant, silent brothers?

The Withered Ones turned away and shuffled back to the entrance of their guard house. She followed, seeing the doorway differently now. Strange letters were carved on the lintel, up and down the sides, glyphs that she had never seen before. They glowed in her new vision, a greeting perhaps, or a warning.

She passed through the opening, and into the darkness.

About the Author

James V. Viscosi is the author of several horror and fantasy novels. An expatriate New Yorker, he currently resides with his wife and various finned and furry animals in sunny Southern California, where he spends most of his time hiding beneath a very large hat. Visit him at www.jamesviscosi.com.